When a ruthl...
woman... S...
are...

Mag...

**Fantastic novels from favourite
bestselling author**

Lynne
GRAHAM

Lynne Graham Collection

February 2012

March 2012

April 2012

May 2012

Lynne GRAHAM

Magnates

MILLS & BOON

Mills & Boon, an imprint of Harlequin (UK) Limited, Eton House, 18-24 Paradise Road, Richmond, Surrey TW9 1SR

MAGNATES © Harlequin Enterprises II B.V./S.à.r.l. 2012

Desert Prince, Bride of Innocence © Lynne Graham 2009
Ruthless Magnate, Convenient Wife © Lynne Graham 2009
Greek Tycoon, Inexperienced Mistress © Lynne Graham 2010

ISBN: 978 0 263 89771 5

052-0512

Harlequin (UK) policy is to use papers that are natural, renewable and recyclable products and made from wood grown in sustainable forests. The logging and manufacturing processes conform to the legal environmental regulations of the country of origin.

Printed and bound in Spain
by Blackprint CPI, Barcelona

DESERT PRINCE, BRIDE OF INNOCENCE

Lynne Graham

Lynne Graham was born in Northern Ireland and has been a keen Mills & Boon® reader since her teens. She is very happily married, with an understanding husband who has learned to cook since she started to write! Her five children keep her on her toes. She has a very large dog, which knocks everything over, a very small terrier, which barks a lot, and two cats. When time allows, Lynne is a keen gardener.

Look out for Lynne Graham's latest exciting new trilogy, available from March to May in Mills & Boon® Modern™.

CHAPTER ONE

His royal highness, Prince Jasim bin Hamid al Rais, frowned when his aide told him that his brother's wife was waiting to see him. 'You should have told me that the Princess was here. My family always have first call on my time,' he admonished.

Jasim was renowned in financial circles for the astute speed and strategy he utilised in the pursuit of profit in the Rais international business empire, and his employees had a healthy respect for their chairman. He was a tough employer who set high standards and accepted nothing less than excellence. His natural survival skills were honed to a fine cutting edge by a challenging family and palace politics. He was a tall, powerfully built man in his early thirties and he was possessed of a degree of dark, devastating good looks and potent masculinity that women found irresistible.

His French-born sister-in-law, Yaminah, was a small, rather homely brunette with a strained set to her rounded face that warned him that she was struggling to control her emotions. Jasim greeted the older woman with warmth and concern. To see her he was keeping a government minister waiting, but his smooth sophistication was more than equal to the task of hiding that fact and he ordered refreshments and asked her to sit down as if time were of no object.

'Are you comfortable at Woodrow Court?' His elder brother, Crown Prince Murad, and his family were currently using Jasim's country house in Kent while they had a brand new English property built to order nearby.

'Oh, yes. It's a wonderful house and we are being very well looked after,' Yaminah rushed to assure him. 'But we never meant to put you out of your own home, Jasim. Won't you come down this weekend?'

'Of course, if you would like me to but, believe me, I am very comfortable in my town house. It is not a sacrifice to stay in the city,' Jasim responded. 'But that is not why you are here to see me, is it? I believe something may be troubling you?'

Yaminah compressed her lips, her anxious brown gaze suddenly flooding with tears. With an exclamation of embarrassment and a choked apology, she drew out a tissue and mopped at her overflowing eyes. 'I shouldn't be bothering you with this, Jasim—'

Jasim sat down in the sofa opposite her in an effort to make the older woman feel more at ease. 'You have never *bothered* me in your life,' he reproved her. 'Why are you worrying about such a thing?'

Yaminah breathed in slow and deep. 'It's…it's our nanny.'

His dark brows drew together in a satiric quirk that questioned her tragic tone of voice. 'If the nanny my staff engaged to take care of my niece is not to your liking, sack her.'

'If only it were so simple…' Yaminah sighed, shredding the tissue between her restless hands and staring down at it. 'She is an excellent nanny and Zahrah is very fond of her. I'm afraid that the problem is…Murad.'

Jasim immediately became very still. His self-discipline was absolute and his lean, strong face betrayed nothing of his exasperation. His brother had always been a womaniser and his lifestyle had got him into trouble more than once. Such a weakness was a dangerous flaw in the future ruler of a small oil-rich and very conservative country like Quaram. Even worse, if Murad was targeting a member of his household right beneath his loyal and loving wife's nose his behaviour had reached a new inexcusable low in his brother's opinion.

'I cannot sack the girl. It would infuriate Murad if I was to interfere. At present I believe it is only a flirtation but she is a *very* beautiful girl, Jasim,' his sister-in-law murmured shakily. 'If she leaves our employ it will only drive the affair out into the open and, you know, Murad really cannot afford to be involved in another scandal.'

'I agree. The King has no patience left with him.' His handsome mouth settling into a grim line, Jasim wondered in angry frustration if his parent's weak heart would even withstand the stress of another upsetting outbreak of bad publicity and scurrilous gossip about his firstborn's morals. Would his elder brother *ever* learn sense and restraint? Why could he never put the needs of his family first? The older man seemed unable to withstand temptation and, this time around, Jasim felt unnervingly responsible. After all, *his* people had hired the wretched nanny! Why hadn't it occurred to him to order an embargo on appointing a young and beautiful woman?

His brother's wife studied him anxiously. 'Will you help me, Jasim?'

Jasim dealt her a wry look. 'Murad will not accept advice from me.'

'He is too stubborn to take advice from anyone, but you *could* help me,' Yaminah told him urgently.

Jasim frowned, believing that she overestimated his influence with his brother. Murad had not been the heir to the throne of Quaram for over fifty years without acquiring a healthy sense of his own importance. While Jasim was very fond of the older man, he knew his brother was equally fond of getting his own way, even if doing so meant trampling on other people. 'In what way might I help?'

Yaminah worried at her lower lip with her teeth. 'If you were prepared to show an interest in her yourself, the problem would disappear,' she declared in a sudden burst of enthusiasm. 'You're young and single and Murad is middle-aged and married. There can be no comparison and the girl is certain to turn her attention to you instead—'

Distaste at such a suggestion slivering through his lean, well-built frame and cooling his eyes to the darkness of a wintry night, Jasim raised his hands in a gesture that urged restraint and calm. 'Yaminah, please be sensible—'

'I am being sensible. Furthermore, if Murad thought you had a fancy for the girl, I'm convinced that he would step back,' Yaminah asserted doggedly. 'He has often said how much he wishes you would meet a woman—'

'But not one on whom *he* has set his heart,' Jasim was moved to insert drily.

'No, you are wrong. Since that…er…unpleasant business with that Englishwoman you were with a few years ago, Murad has been sincerely troubled by the fact that you are still unmarried. He mentioned it only yesterday, and if he believed that *you* were interested in Elinor Tempest he would leave her alone!' the older woman forecast with a vehemence that betrayed how desperate she was to win him round to her state of thinking.

His lean, strong face clenching, Jasim was tense. Indeed his bronzed skin had paled across his hard cheekbones, for the episode in his life that she was referring to was one he preferred not to recall. When the tabloid press had exposed the sleazy past of the woman he had planned to marry three years earlier, Jasim had experienced a degree of rage and humiliation over his own lack of judgement that he was in no way eager to recall. Ever since he had remained resolutely single and he now chose women only to warm his bed and entertain him. Lower expectations had led to much greater satisfaction, he acknowledged inwardly.

Although he had immediately discounted Yaminah's dramatic request for his assistance, however, he remained troubled enough by her visit to want more information about the woman who was the cause of her distress. He instructed his aide to check out the nanny by questioning the staff who had hired her. The initial facts he received later that same morning were disturbing enough to fix his ebony brows into a brooding frown. He studied the small photo of Elinor Tempest: she had long hair that was a particularly vibrant shade of red, a creamy English rose complexion and exotic green eyes. Certainly, even though Jasim had never found that strange colour of hair attractive, his brother's nanny was at the very least unusual and strikingly pretty.

Worryingly, however, Elinor Tempest had not won an interview for her job by appearing on the select list of trusted nannies advanced by the employment agency engaged for the purpose. Indeed, it was unlikely that the girl would ever have made it on her own merits as she was only twenty years old and had had little work experience. Evidently, Murad had personally put forward the girl's name and insisted that she be interviewed. That startling fact put his brother's relationship with the young woman onto an altogether more questionable level. Jasim was taken aback and angered by what he was finding out. How could Murad set up such a situation beneath his own roof? And what sort of young woman accepted a position from a libidinous married man and encouraged his advances? Was Yaminah wrong? Was Murad already sexually involved with his daughter's nanny?

Repugnance engulfed Jasim. His strong principles revolted against such a sordid association in the vicinity of his innocent sister-in-law and niece. He had already learnt to his own cost that the royal status and oil wealth of the Rais family made both him and his brother targets for the most unscrupulous gold-diggers, eager to use their guile and their seductive bodies to enrich themselves. Murad had already suffered several blackmail attempts that had required police intervention. Yet, once again, his brother was recklessly running the risk of an explosive scandal, whose aftershocks would reverberate all the way home to Quaram and rock the very foundation of the monarchy.

There and then, Jasim reached a cool and snappy decision. When a crisis arose he liked to deal with it quickly. His firmly modelled lips compressed, he lifted his dark imperious head high. He would spend the weekend at Woodrow Court and size up the situation. One way or another, he would rid Yaminah's household of this calculating little slut who was threatening everything that he held dear...

'My word, what came over you?' As Louise took in Elinor's fashionable appearance her pale blue eyes rounded with surprise below her brown fringe. 'You usually dress like somebody's granny!'

Elinor winced at that blunt condemnation, her bright green eyes veiling. She supposed her lifelong reluctance to be bold in the fashion stakes dated back to her father's poisonous attacks on any garment that outlined her curves or showed her knees. A university professor and an unrepentant intellectual snob, Ernest Tempest had always been a ferociously critical parent to his only child. Only now that she was living away from home was Elinor able to spread her wings and relax, but she was the first to admit that, but for the encouragement of a shrewd and attentive saleswoman, she would not even have dared to try on the garment, never mind buy it.

Elinor strove to recall the mirror reflection that had reassured her earlier that evening. The dress's neat fit had seemed to emphasise her willowy curves but it did display a generous length of her shapely legs. Beneath her companion's critical gaze, Elinor raised an uncertain hand to its glittering beaded neckline. 'I just fell in love with it.'

Louise rolled her eyes and said drily, 'Well, you can certainly afford to lash out in the fashion stakes these days. How *is* life in the royal family of Quaram? You must be stacking up the cash in an offshore account by now.'

'You must be joking,' Elinor hastened to declare. 'And it isn't money for jam. I *do* work extremely long hours—'

'Nonsense! You've only the one kid to look after and she's at nursery school,' Louise protested as she thrust a tumbler full of liquid into Elinor's hand. 'Drink up! You're not allowed to be a party-pooper at your own twenty-first birthday bash!'

Elinor sipped at the sickly sweet concoction even though it wasn't to her taste. She didn't want to get off on the wrong foot with hot-tempered Louise, who was quick to see any form of alcoholic sobriety as a personal challenge. Both women had trained as nannies at the same college and remained friends afterwards, but Elinor was uneasily aware of the undertones in the atmosphere. It had taken months for Louise to find a decent job and she had very much resented Elinor's good fortune in the same field.

'How is work?' Louise prompted.

'The prince and his wife often go abroad or spend weekends in London and I'm left in full charge of Zahrah at Woodrow, so time off—or the lack of it—is a problem. In fact sometimes I feel more like her mother than her nanny,' Elinor confided ruefully. 'I attend everything on her behalf…even the events at her school.'

'There's got to be some drawback to all that lovely cash you're earning!' Louise commented tartly.

'Nothing's ever perfect.' Elinor shrugged with the easy tolerance of someone accustomed to an imperfect world. 'The rest of the staff are from Quaram and speak their own language, so it's quite a lonely household to live in as well. Shall we get going? Our transport awaits us.'

When Prince Murad had realised it was her birthday, he had presented Elinor with free vouchers for an upmarket London nightclub and had insisted that she make use of a

LYNNE GRAHAM   15

chauffeur-driven limousine to travel into London. The same vehicle would also waft her home at the end of the evening.

'A twenty-first birthday only comes once in a lifetime,' Zahrah's father had pointed out cheerfully. 'Make the most of being young. Time moves cruelly fast. On my twenty-first, my father took me hawking in the desert and instructed me on what I should never forget when I became King in his place.' A wry expression had crossed the older man's visage. 'It did not occur to me then that thirty years on I would still be waiting in the wings. Not that I would have it any other way, of course; my honoured father is a very wise ruler and any man would struggle to follow his example.'

Prince Murad was a benevolent man, Elinor acknowledged reflectively. She admired the older man's strong sense of the family values of love, trust and loyalty. After her mother's death when she was ten years old, Elinor's upbringing had conspicuously lacked such sterling qualities and she was still feeling the pain of that loss. If only her own father had had an ounce of the prince's warm and kindly nature!

While Louise squealed with delight at first sight of the luxurious limousine, Elinor was thinking instead about her father's lifelong lack of interest in her. No matter how hard she had studied, her exam grades had never been good enough to please him. He had often told her that he was ashamed of her stupidity and that she was a severe disappointment to him. Her decision to become a nanny had outraged him and he had called her 'A glorified nursemaid, nothing better than a servant!' The dark shadows of those unhappy years had for ever marked her and she often felt as if she had no family at all. After all, her father had remarried without inviting her to his wedding and seemed to prefer to act as if he were childless.

'I was reading an article about Prince Murad in a magazine,' Louise remarked. 'There were hints that he has quite an eye for the ladies and that he's had affairs on the side. Watch your step with the old boy!'

Elinor frowned. 'Oh, he's definitely *not* like that with me—he's more sort of fatherly—'

'Don't be so naïve. Ninety-nine per cent of middle-aged men are lechers with young attractive women,' Louise derided with a scornful smile. 'And if you remind him of your mother…'

'I don't think that's very likely,' Elinor interrupted in some amusement. 'Mum was small, blonde and blue-eyed and I don't look one bit like her.'

'Whatever.' Louise shrugged. 'But if you didn't remind him of your mother, why the heck did he offer you—a total stranger—the job of taking care of his precious daughter?'

'It wasn't quite as easy as you make it sound,' Elinor fielded uncomfortably. 'The prince put my name forward, but I went through the same recruitment process as everybody else that applied. He said he wanted to help me out because my mother once meant something to him. He also thought I'd be young enough to appeal to his daughter as a companion. And don't forget that his wife only speaks Arabic and French, so my fluent French comes in very useful. I agree that getting the job was an extraordinary piece of good luck for me but there was nothing more sinister to it.'

Louise was still staring stonily at the younger woman. 'But *would* you sleep with him—if he asked you?'

'No, of course I wouldn't! For goodness' sake, he's almost as old as my dad!' Elinor objected with a shiver of distaste.

'Now if it was his brother, Prince Jasim, you wouldn't be shivering,' Louise quipped. 'There was a picture of him in the same article. He's sex on legs: over six foot tall, single and movie-star handsome.'

'Is he? I haven't met him.' Elinor turned her head away to look out of the limo at the well-lit city streets. Louise's persistence and murky insinuations had annoyed her. Why were people always so willing to think the worst? Elinor would not have dreamt of working for Prince Murad and his wife if there had been anything questionable in the older man's attitude towards her. Anyway, an unfortunate incident during her months of previous work experience had made Elinor very wary of flirtatious male employers.

'A shame that the brother who's going to be King one day should be short, balding and portly,' Louise commented snidely. 'Although plenty of women wouldn't let that get in the way of their ambition.'

'The fact that he's married would be enough to deter me,' Elinor replied very drily.

'It's got to be a shaky marriage though, with only a little girl to show for all those years he's been with his wife,' Louise insisted. 'I'm surprised he hasn't divorced her when there's no male heir for the next generation—'

'But there *is* an heir—the prince's younger brother,' Elinor pointed out.

'He has to be the real catch in the family, then.' A calculating glint shone in Louise's gaze. 'But after three months you still haven't met him, even though you're living in *his* house with his relatives, so that's not too promising.'

Elinor didn't waste her breath pointing out that falling in love with an Arab prince hadn't done her late mother, Rose, any favours. Rose had met Murad at university and they had fallen head over heels in love. Elinor still had the engagement ring that Murad had given her mother. The young couple's happiness had proved short-lived, however, because Murad had been threatened with disinheritance and exile if he married a foreigner. He had eventually returned to Quaram to act the dutiful son and do as he was told, while Rose had ended up marrying Ernest Tempest on the rebound. The marriage of two such ill-matched people had proved deeply unhappy.

'You haven't got any foreign travel out of the job either,' Louise reminded her sourly. 'At least I got ten days out in Cyprus with my family.'

'I'm not that fussed about travelling,' Elinor heard herself lie, her irritation at her companion's snide remarks and put-downs strong enough to make her wonder why she had bothered to maintain such a one-sided friendship.

In the exclusive club they were treated to free drinks on the strength of Prince Murad's vouchers, which was just as well as they could never have afforded to pay the high bar prices. Elinor reminded herself that it *was* her birthday and tried to shake off the sense of disappointment that had dogged her all week.

Her job was a lonely one and she often craved adult company; she knew that she needed to make the most out of a rare night out. Although she had the use of a car, Woodrow Court was deep in the Kentish countryside and within easy reach of few attractions beyond a small town. Zahrah's parents travelled a great deal and preferred to leave their daughter at home rather than disrupt her schooling. As a result, Elinor had found her own freedom severely curtailed, as when her employers were absent they expected their nanny to be in constant attendance on their child. Elinor was travelling back to Woodrow Court in a limo later because leaving her charge in the care of the household staff overnight was not an option the prince was willing to allow. Even so, after being exposed to Louise's bitter comments, Elinor was no longer feeling deprived by the fact that she had been denied the chance of a girlie sleepover.

'You're already getting the eye,' Louise sighed enviously.

Elinor tensed and refused to look in the same direction. She found socialising with the opposite sex a challenging and often humiliating experience. She was unusually tall and made six feet even in modest heels. Guys happy to chat her up while she was sitting down wanted to run once she unfurled her giraffe-long legs and stood up to tower over them. Men, she had learnt from her awkward adolescent years when she was frequently a wallflower, preferred small dainty women at whom they could look down and feel tall beside. She knew she had an attractive face and a good figure, but neither counted for anything against her ungainly height. While men noticed her, they rarely approached her.

Some hours later she said goodbye to Louise, who had picked up an admirer. Elinor, on the other hand, had experienced a particularly painful evening when a young man had come up to her table to ask her to join him and then snarled, 'Forget it!' the instant she'd got up and he'd realised in horror that he barely reached her shoulder. He and his mates had heckled her and sniggered for what remained of the night as if she were a freak at a sideshow. As a result, she had had a little too much to drink to power the nonchalant expression she'd been forced to put on to conceal her misery.

She heaved a deep-felt sigh of relief when the limo turned down the long, winding, tree-lined drive to Woodrow Court. It passed between the towers of the imposing arched gatehouse entrance into a gravelled courtyard that stretched the length of the magnificent Tudor house. It struck her that there were more lights burning than usual. She climbed out and the cool evening air went to her head as much as the alcohol had earlier. She sucked in a sustaining breath in an effort to clear her swimming head and struggled to negotiate a straight path to the front door that was already opening for her.

Her steps weaved around a little as she crossed the echoing hall. A man was emerging from the library and her attention locked straight on to him. He was a stranger and so absolutely beautiful that one glance deprived her of oxygen and brain power. She came to a wobbly halt to stare. Black hair was swept back from his brow, bronzed skin stretched taut over his high slashing cheekbones, arrogant nose and aggressive jaw line. There was something uniquely compelling about his lean, arrestingly handsome features. He had gorgeous eyes, dark, deep set and bold, and when he stepped below the overhead chandelier they burned a pure hot gold. Her heart started to hammer as if she were sprinting.

Jasim was not in a good mood. He had not been amused when he'd arrived for the weekend only to discover that his brother and sister-in-law and even his quarry were all out and unavailable, making his presence as an interested onlooker somewhat superfluous. 'Miss Tempest?'

'Er…yes?' Elinor reached out a trembling hand to brace herself on the carved pedestal at the foot of the massive wooden staircase. He had a gorgeous face that inexplicably continued to draw her attention like a powerful magnet. She just wanted to stare and stare. 'Sorry, you…are?'

'Prince Murad's brother, Jasim,' he breathed, surveying her with forbidding cool, in spite of the powerfully masculine interest she fired in him.

He immediately wanted to know if she looked at his brother in the same awestruck way. Any man might be flattered by a woman looking at him with a wonder more worthy of a supernatural being. In the flesh, Elinor Tempest was, he already appreciated, a much more dangerous entity than he had ever imagined she might be. In a dress that hugged the sensual swell of her breasts and revealed her incredibly long legs, she was out-and-out stunning. Hair that had looked garishly bright in the photo was, in reality, a rich dark auburn and a crowning glory that hung in a luxuriant curling tangle halfway down her back. Only the finest emeralds could have equalled the amazing green of her eyes. With that spectacular hair, those wide eyes and a lush pink mouth set against flawless creamy skin, she was literally the stuff of male fantasy. It was a challenging instant before Jasim, universally renowned for his cool head, could concentrate his thoughts again.

'You appear to be drunk,' Jasim breathed icily, his stern intonation roughened by the disturbing hardening at his groin as his body reacted involuntarily to the sexually appealing vision she made.

Colour flared in Elinor's cheeks. 'P-possibly…er…a little bit,' she stammered in great discomfiture, dragging in a long deep breath that made the rounded mounds of her breasts shimmy beneath the fine fabric of her dress. 'I don't usually drink much but it was a special occasion.'

Jasim was finding it a challenge to keep his attention above her chin. 'If you worked for me, I would not tolerate you appearing in this state.'

'Luckily I'm not working for you,' Elinor flipped back, before she could think better of it. 'Nor am I working at this precise moment. I'm on my own time. I had the evening off—'

'Nevertheless, while you live beneath this roof I consider such conduct unacceptable.'

Elinor registered that he had drawn closer and that she actually had to tip back her head to take all of him in. He was very tall, she noted belatedly, at least six feet four inches, considerably taller than his older brother. In fact there was nothing about him that reminded her of Prince Murad, for Jasim was broad-shouldered and muscular in build. He carried not an ounce of excess weight on his lean, lithe physique. Of course, the two men were only half-brothers, she recalled, born to different mothers.

'What if Zahrah was to wake up and see you in such a condition?' Jasim demanded, meeting her intense gaze with his own and stiffening at the rampant response of his body to her encouragement. If that was how she looked at his brother, he totally understood how Murad could have been tempted off the straight and narrow. The ripe fullness of her soft pink mouth was a sensual invitation all on its own.

'The nurse who has been with Zahrah since she was

born sleeps next door to her. I think you're being very un-reasonable,' Elinor told him tightly.

Jasim was staggered by that disrespectful rejoinder and decided that she was utterly without shame. Nor had it escaped his notice that she apparently had a limousine at her private disposal. That was a flagrant display of his brother's special favour, which could only add weight to Yaminah's worst fears. 'Is this how you speak to my brother?'

'Your brother, who *is* my employer, is a great deal more pleasant and less critical. I don't work for you and I'm entitled to a social life,' Elinor declared, her chin at a defiant tilt even though she could feel a tension headache building like a painful band of steel round her temples. Her self-esteem, already battered by the treatment she had earlier withstood at the nightclub, refused to bear any more in saintly silence. 'And now, if you don't mind, I'd like to go to bed.'

Jasim only knew in that moment of red-hot outrage at her impertinence that he wanted to take her to that bed, spread her across it and make love to her until she begged him for more and ached from his passion. As he struggled to master the fierce desire threatening his usually rigid self-control he was shocked by the sheer novelty of a lust that powerful. No woman ever came between Jasim and his wits, not even the one he had once briefly planned to marry. But as he watched Elinor Tempest endeavour to mount the stairs without swaying and stumbling from the effects of the alcohol she had consumed, he knew that he would know no peace until he had bedded her and made her his.

Her foot, shod in a sandal with a thin slippery sole, slid off a step and she lurched back with a cry of alarm breaking from her lips as she clutched frantically at the solid balustrade for support.

'Safety is yet another reason why you shouldn't drink like this,' Jasim breathed hatefully close, a splayed hand like an iron bar bracing her spine to prevent her from falling backwards down the stairs.

'I don't need your help,' Elinor protested furiously, sliding off her shoes to ensure there were no further accidents and gathering them together in one impatient hand. 'I hate people who preach.... I bet you say, "I told you so", as well!'

The scent of her hair and her skin assailed Jasim in an evocative wave of sensuous appeal. She smelt like peaches and made him think of hot sunlight and even hotter sex. He was convinced that she would be a willing partner. Her style of dress and her behaviour had already persuaded him that she was far from being an innocent. Murad was much too trusting to be left at the mercy of his own lust and the manipulations of a rapacious youthful temptress. Elinor Tempest, Jasim decided, was a justifiable target for his calculating plan to bring about her downfall. Striving to keep the lid on his temper and his libido, he urged her upstairs.

'All right...I'll be fine now,' Elinor muttered as she reached her comfortable bedroom. The defiance was steadily seeping out of her, for she was exhausted and her spirits were low. 'You've been the perfect conclusion to a truly horrible birthday and now, *please*, I'd like to be left alone.'

Jasim subjected her to a measured assessment from the doorway. Alienating her was not a good idea. What had he been thinking of? Desire was pulsing through him and already as much entrenched there as the beat of the blood through his veins. He wanted her and once he took her to his bed Murad would turn his back on her. Taking her to bed would not be a sacrifice. Picturing her there with those flame-coloured curls loose and her eyes soft with longing offered him the prospect of a sweeter and more sensual pleasure than he had ever dreamt he might find in so pre-meditated an encounter.

Conservation needs had put the thrill of the hunt out of reach in Quaram and Jasim had long missed the excitement. He discovered that he could hardly wait for the satisfying conclusion of what promised to be a most enjoyable sexual game. It did not once occur to him that he might fail to get her into his bed—since he had never yet met with a refusal…

CHAPTER TWO

THE next morning, while Elinor showered, she turned clammy with horror when she recalled her dialogue with Prince Jasim. Alcohol had made an idiot of her! She should have been more careful about how much she'd drunk. But then it was six months since she had even tasted alcohol, she thought, biting anxiously at her lower lip. Furthermore she had been resentful about the fact that she couldn't just have a couple of days off when she asked for them and a taste of youthful freedom.

But not so resentful that she wanted to lose her very well-paid job, she reflected worriedly, a job, moreover, which would add solid-gold appeal to her CV when she went off in pursuit of her next position. No, the very last thing she needed now was to get sacked for being cheeky to a prince! She hadn't even called him 'sir' when she'd addressed him and she bit back a moan at the recollection. She was usually so sensible and polite. Why hadn't she kept her tongue between her teeth? The truth was that she had been in a bad mood and the unhappy combination of his undeniable good looks and fanciability, followed by his cutting criticism, had proved the proverbial last straw. She already knew from hearing Prince Murad erupt when the smallest thing annoyed him that royal egos were eggshell thin and super-sensitive and royal tempers quick to ignite. Prince Jasim would never forgive her for being rude to him and he was certain to complain to his brother.

It was a Saturday and Zahrah had a riding lesson. While her charge was being taught, Elinor usually went riding as well since she was an accomplished horsewoman and the stables contained an enviable selection of mounts. She pulled on her shabby navy breeches, a lemon T-shirt and finally her boots. She was about to leave her bedroom when a knock sounded on the door. She opened it and was startled when a big basket of beautifully arranged flowers was presented to her by one of the manservants.

At first Elinor couldn't believe the magnificent flowers were for her and she drank in the heady scent of the glorious pink roses with a blissful sigh before she detached the card envelope and opened it.

'Happy belated birthday wishes and my apologies, Jasim'

Elinor was stunned. *He* was apologising to *her*? He was even wishing her a happy birthday and giving her flowers? Her jaw was ready to crash to the floor in disbelief. She summoned up a misty image of him. As well as being more beautiful than any man had the right to be, Prince Jasim had impressed her as being arrogant, autocratic and very proud. He definitely hadn't struck her as being the apologising type. In fact she had seen him more as the sort of guy who always had the last word and a disparaging one at that.

But obviously first impressions had been kind to neither of them the night before. It was the first time a man had given Elinor flowers and she was hopelessly impressed and pleased by the gesture because she really had had a lousy, disappointing birthday. Zahrah raced into the room. Bubbling with life, the four-year-old was a pretty child with a mop of silky dark curls and sparkling brown eyes.

'Morning, Elinor!' Zahrah carolled, giving her an affectionate hug. 'Are you coming for breakfast now?'

They went downstairs and Elinor was about to head for the small dining room where she usually ate with the child when Ahmed, the major domo of the household, intercepted her. Zahrah acted as translator and informed Elinor that they were having breakfast with her Uncle Jasim today. They were ushered into the massive formal dining room.

Zahrah let out a yelp of excitement and bowled down the room to throw herself into Jasim's arms. It gave Elinor a minute to compose herself as Jasim, having thrown down his newspaper, rose from the table to greet their arrival. In the full light flooding through the tall windows, his bronzed aristocratic face was startlingly handsome and once again she discovered that she found it virtually impossible to look away from him. He dominated the room with his powerful presence and she was hooked afresh by a fevered compulsion to study those lean classic features, still driven to try and work out what it was about them that repeatedly drew her attention. Her heart was already pounding, making it hard for her to breathe levelly. Then he smiled down at the child in his arms and the high-voltage force of his charismatic attraction hit her like a rod of lightning striking the ground.

'Miss Tempest...' he murmured lazily as he swung out a chair beside his own. Clad in tailored riding gear, he looked outrageously elegant and sophisticated. 'Please join us.'

Elinor had to force herself to walk down the length of the table to join him in a seat a good deal closer than she would have chosen for herself. She was flustered. Butterflies were fluttering in her tummy and she didn't know what to do with her hands any more. She felt ridiculously like a schoolgirl, self-conscious and silly and awkward, all at the same time. 'Thank you for the flowers. You were very generous,' she muttered in a rush, keen to get the acknowledgement out of the way while Zahrah was busy chattering to Ahmed about her favourite cereal.

The brilliant ebony eyes screened by dense black lashes rested on her and she honestly thought her heart might stop beating altogether. 'It was nothing.'

'I owe you an apology…I was rude,' she framed.

'A novel experience for me,' the prince purred like a sleek panther being stroked.

For a split second Elinor wanted to slap him rather than stroke him for not giving a more gracious response to her attempt to make amends. 'Nobody ever answers you back? Or quarrels with you?' she heard herself query.

'Nobody,' Jasim confirmed as if that was a perfectly normal state of affairs. He watched her glance up at him from below her feathery lashes, a delicate flush of colour on her cheeks, and thought what a class act she was putting on for his benefit. He could hardly credit that it was the same woman, for no hint of the strident, argumentative redhead he had met the night before was on show. Everything about her this morning from her show of apparent unease to her soft tone of voice and her girlish reluctance to meet his eyes shouted the kind of shy uncertainty and sexual innocence that was most likely to ensnare an older man. No wonder his brother was upsetting his wife over the scheming little slut, he reflected grimly. The act didn't work quite so well on Jasim. But then he was rather more sophisticated than Murad and better attuned to the liberal sexual mores of Elinor Tempest's age group. As Yaminah had doubtless intended when she invited Jasim for a weekend while she and his brother were elsewhere, Jasim intended to make full and immediate use of the clear field she had given him.

'More coffee?' Jasim snapped long brown fingers with a natural assumption of command that seemed to come as instinctively as breathing to him. On immediate alert, a servant surged forward with alacrity to refresh the coffee cups. Zahrah had been inclined to treat Elinor the same way, until Elinor had taught the little girl otherwise. Even so, Elinor had daily exposure to the reality that members of the Quarami royal family were one step down from Divinity in the eyes of those who waited on them.

'Tell me why your birthday was horrible,' Jasim instructed silkily, studying her with those stunning dark eyes and relaxing back into his chair with the confident air of a male awaiting the commencement of the entertainment.

A pulse beating somewhere at the base of her throat and her nerves reacting like jumping beans, Elinor had grown very tense. 'That wouldn't be appropriate, sir.'

The dense black lashes lifted over frowning deep golden eyes. 'I decide what is appropriate,' he told her in immediate contradiction. *'Talk.'*

For an instant Elinor was astonished by that imperious command delivered with the absolute expectation of a male accustomed to instant obedience. It was a relief when Zahrah stole the moment with her nonsensical chatter.

'You can explain later.' Jasim delivered the reprieve over his niece's downbent head. 'I'm coming down to the stables with you and Zahrah.'

The prospect unnerved Elinor and she looked up at him again and froze at the hungry light in his measuring gaze before hurriedly glancing down at her coffee again. Shock decimated her appetite for her toast, while her tummy performed an enervating series of little somersaults. His close scrutiny might suggest that he found her attractive, but she could not believe that a prince could have developed a personal interest in her and scolded herself for letting her imagination take flight. Perhaps he was more like his kindly brother than she had appreciated and was simply keen to smooth over the unpleasantness of their first encounter.

Ahmed secured Zahrah in a child's seat in the back of a glossy black Range Rover. Elinor climbed into the passenger seat and watched Jasim stroll round the bonnet. Even with his black hair tousled by the breeze he was as strikingly sleek and beautiful as a bronzed angel. She met his eyes through the windscreen and suddenly she was wildly, hopelessly aware of her own body. Her full breasts felt constrained inside her bra and an odd little clenching sensation low in her pelvis made her shift uneasily in her seat. She was shocked, for she hadn't realised that being drawn to a man could be such a physical experience, that her body could feel as if it were all revved up for a race. Mortified colour mantled her cheeks. A lean brown long-fingered hand as wondrously well-proportioned as the rest of him depressed the handbrake and the engine fired.

'Are you fond of horses?' Jasim enquired.

'I've been mad about them since I was a kid,' Elinor confessed with a rueful laugh. 'I started riding lessons at the same age as Zahrah. A neighbour kept stables and I used to go there and help out after school.'

'Have you ever had a horse of your own?'

Elinor tensed and her face fell. 'Yes, from the age of nine to fourteen. My father sold her then. He thought the time I spent with Starlight was interfering with my studies—'

'You must've been upset.'

'I was devastated.' Elinor folded her lips, unable to find adequate words to explain just how shattering a blow that sudden loss had been to her. Her father had not even warned her of his intentions and she had not got the chance to say goodbye to the horse she'd loved. Starlight had also been her last link with her late mother and her only real friend, the one element in her wretchedly unhappy teen years that had kept her going through thick and thin. 'But she was still a young horse and I'm sure she went to some other girl to be absolutely adored all over again.'

'It sounds as though your father was very strict,' Jasim remarked, keen to extract more information from her. He was not at all surprised that the very first thing she should tell him should be a sob story guaranteed to paint her in a sympathetic light.

'*Too* strict. After that, I wasn't allowed any interests at all outside school. It was a relief to leave home,' Elinor admitted ruefully, thinking of the release of no longer having to live daily with constant wounding criticism and reproaches for her unacceptable exam results. Although greater maturity had enabled her to appreciate that she had simply been an average student rather than a completely stupid one, her father had made her feel like a hopeless failure at the tender age of sixteen years and her self-esteem had still to recover from his abrasive style of parenting.

Jasim's sculpted sensual mouth tightened as once again she confirmed his suspicions about her true nature. He recalled the widening invitation of her expressive and artful eyes as she met his gaze, the revealingly taut points of her nipples that were currently showing through her T-shirt. She was certainly very responsive and he found her inability to conceal her reaction to him very, very sexy.

A decent parent, however, would naturally have sought to impose restrictions on so free-spirited a daughter, he reasoned, expecting to feel disgusted at the mounting proof of her probable promiscuity. Instead he tensed at the heavy arousal stirring at his groin and cursed the ready sexual heat that afflicted him in Elinor Tempest's company. Only sexual satisfaction would take care of that problem and he had no intention of practising patience, nor even the suspicion that patience would prove necessary. Mindful of his niece's presence, he concentrated on *not* thinking about how thoroughly Elinor would be persuaded to ease the demands of his high-voltage sex drive.

'I'll give you a tour of the stud farm,' Jasim drawled.

As they were early for Zahrah's lesson, Elinor made no protest and indeed her interest quickened at the prospect of a special viewing in the owner's company, because although she often visited the stables to ride she had stayed away from the stud. It was a large impressive operation housed in immaculately maintained buildings, complete with all-weather gallops and paddocks, and it was heavily staffed. The manager hurried out of the office to greet Jasim. The resident vet and other senior staff soon joined them. Keen though she was on horses, the dialogue soon ranged beyond Elinor's knowledge with talk of racing prospects and recent wins on the turf. Some way through it, she left to check that Zahrah's horse was saddled up. The little girl's instructor arrived soon afterwards.

'Will you be taking Amaranth out?' the groom asked Elinor then.

'Yes, please.' A huge smile on her face, Elinor went to greet the big brown gelding impatiently shifting in his box as he recognised the sound of her voice. She petted him and led him out. It had taken a month of regular visits for the head groom to trust her with the more lively mounts. The freedom to ride pretty much whenever she liked and without cost was yet another good reason why she wanted to hang on to her job.

In the midst of trying to disengage from his staff, Jasim saw her ride out and his ebony brows shot up. 'You let the nanny ride Amaranth?' he demanded in a tone of censure.

'Elinor is well able to control him, Your Highness,' the head groom responded. 'She's a terrific rider.'

At that moment Jasim received the perfect opportunity to see that truth for himself as she spurred the spirited gelding towards a fence, soaring over it with a grace and ease that impressed even him.

Elinor heard the thump of pursuing hooves and turned her head. On the back of his powerful black stallion, Mercury, Jasim was catching up on her fast. Her chin came up and she urged Amaranth on in a flat-out race across the lush rolling acres of parkland that made Woodrow Court such a paradise for a horse lover.

Jasim was stunned that she had the nerve to challenge him, for he had expected her to come to a halt and wait for him. He rarely rode in female company because women tended to cling to him like superglue and chatter and flirt continually, behaviour that interfered with his relaxation. In comparison, Elinor gave him the opportunity to chase her and he appreciated that her control of her mount and her skill were worthy of his respect.

Amaranth ran out of steam by the lake and Elinor reined him in and dismounted below some trees. Jasim was talking on a cell phone as he rode up on Mercury. He slid down to the ground with effortless grace and watched her remove her riding cap, releasing the piled up mass of her hair in a silken tangle of luxuriance and stretching in a movement that delineated every curve and ensured that her generous little breasts strained beneath her T-shirt. Although he was convinced it was a deliberate move to attract his attention to her body, that cheap little trick still worked on him. Indeed desire knifed through him, making him hot and hard within seconds. Conscious of the reality that the breeches would conceal nothing, he peeled off his cap and strode over to the edge of the lake, willing the tumult of his rampant hormones back under control. He was furious and knocked off balance by a loss of self-discipline that he had not experienced since the years of adolescence.

Elinor looked across the lake and rejoiced in the early summer lushness and the natural beauty of her surroundings. Although she sometimes felt isolated at Woodrow, she had no desire to exchange the countryside and the sense of well-being it gave her for the noise and buzz of the city.

'You're an excellent rider,' Jasim murmured levelly.

Helpless amusement sparkled in her green eyes as she sensed that she had irritated him. 'You'd have beaten me hollow on Mercury if I hadn't had such a head start.'

His keen attention was welded to her. He wasn't used to being teased and he was so bone-deep competitive that he was accustomed to coming first in every field of his busy life. Even his best friend could not have called him a good loser. Yet confronted by the captivating mixture of mischief and artless innocence that momentarily shone in her smile, his exasperation vanished. He was seeing, he told himself harshly, what his brother had to see in her. Even though it was undoubtedly a fake front put on to attract, it was also indisputably effective when a guy as cynical as he was about women started questioning his view of her.

Her skin warming below the intensity of his stare, Elinor drank in the fresh air and decided that being alone with Jasim in such circumstances was likely to cause the kind of talk that would only damage her standing in an old-fashioned household. 'I'd better get back. Zahrah's lesson will be over soon.'

'Her nurse is coming down from the house to collect her. I've ordered refreshments for us…ah, there they are now.'

Her lower lip had fallen away from the upper as she turned to follow his gaze and saw an estate Land Rover trundling towards them across the grass. 'You ordered refreshments for us…to be served out here?'

His satiric sable brows pleated. 'Why not?'

His disregard of the obvious was superb and he managed to magnify her awareness of the huge inequality between them. She was also taken aback that he should reorganise her day by calling in her charge's nurse to take care of her when she herself could perfectly have done so. After all, looking after Zahrah was her job. But her surprise had been replaced by pure amazement at his casual announcement that refreshments were to be served in the middle of the park at his request. He saw nothing strange in the indulgence, she realised, for, like his royal brother, expecting immediate fulfilment of his every command was as normal to Jasim as disappointment and compromise were to her.

Staff emerged from the vehicle at the double and an array of hot and cold drinks, china, glasses and snacks were laid out while an exquisite wool rug was spread across the grass. Elinor, who had dimly expected a picnic-style metal mug to be thrust into her hand, was nonplussed once again. Jasim drank only water. She watched his sensationally attractive face hollow as he drank and swallowed, noticed how the sunlight glimmered across his hard bronzed cheekbones and reflected off black hair that the breeze had ruffled into faint curls. Her throat felt tight. Seated on the rug while he lounged back against the tree with the pure animal fluidity that distinguished his every move, she sipped awkwardly at her coffee in its elegant china cup.

'Now you can tell me why your birthday was a disappointment,' Jasim decreed.

'I hoped you would forget about that comment,' Elinor confided.

Jasim flashed her a mocking smile that tilted her heart on its axis and made her feel so warm that she was momentarily afraid that she might spontaneously combust. Unable to take her eyes off him, she explained about the nightclub tickets, while wondering why his handsome bone structure seemed to tighten when she praised his brother's kindness.

'Murad is a very generous employer.' Her admission was yet another nail in her coffin as far as Jasim was concerned, as he saw in it good reason for Yaminah's concern. He could not credit that such favouritism could be innocent, or that its recipient had not deliberately flirted and coaxed her way into his brother's notice and regard. He even understood why Murad had put a family limo at her disposal. His brother had naturally wished to ensure that she came back to Woodrow at the end of the evening.

'Yes, but I'm not that fussed about nightclubs,' Elinor admitted. 'I never meet anyone anyway, I'm far too tall for most men—'

'But exactly the right height for me,' Jasim inserted softly, his dark accented drawl roughening the vowel sounds in a way that sent a responsive quiver down her taut spinal cord.

Perturbed by that personal comment, Elinor reddened. 'Well, I find being this tall an embarrassment.'

Jasim stretched down a hand. 'Stand up. Let me see you.'

Setting down her cup with a noisy rattle that betrayed her confusion, Elinor clasped his hand and he levered her upright. For a long timeless moment eyes as dark as liquid oil, richly enhanced by inky, spiky lashes of inordinate length, inspected her hectically flushed face. She leant her hips back against the tree trunk for support because her knees felt wobbly.

'You have fabulous long legs,' Jasim murmured, lean fingers brushing curling strands of rich red hair back from her brow. 'Glorious hair and a mouth that is a temptation to any red-blooded man.' His attention dropped in emphasis to the generous swell of her lips and so caught up was she in the power of the moment that she trembled. 'From the first instant I saw you I wanted to kiss you—'

'You were furious with me,' she contradicted, even though she was locked to the allure of his gorgeous eyes.

'It didn't stop me wondering what you would taste like.' Jasim was so close that she could barely breathe until he finally lowered his proud dark head to satisfy his curiosity.

It was a good few months since Elinor had been kissed. But never, ever had she been kissed as Jasim bin Hamid al Rais kissed her. His sheer passion blew her away. His tongue delved and dipped between her readily parted lips with sensual skill and explicit eroticism. A slow, almost painfully sweet ache awakened between her slender thighs and a slight gasp escaped her. Her nipples pinched into taut tingling buds that pushed painfully against the scratchy lace cups of her bra. Her hands clutched his shoulders to keep her upright. He rocked against her and she felt the raw urgency of his arousal and exulted in his response to her with an earthiness that startled her. All of a sudden she was finding out what it was to really want a man, and the strength of that longing shook her back into an awareness of what she was doing.

Almost the instant she reclaimed her sanity, she pulled away from him, turning to hide her face, shaking hands flying up to rake her hair out of her eyes and brush her swollen tingling mouth as if she still could not credit what she had felt. 'Sorry, this isn't right,' she muttered unevenly.

Jasim went from surprise at the apparent rejection to bleak amusement at what he saw as a clever ploy by an experienced woman. There was nothing more tantalising to a man than a brief taste of forbidden fruit followed by a maidenly show of reluctance. He too preferred the thrill of the chase to an easy surrender, but the urgency of his arousal had almost persuaded him to forget the game of sexual entrapment he was engaged in playing.

'How is it wrong?'

'I work for your family…we're worlds apart. How many reasons do you need?' she retorted in a surge of grudging candour, for the last thing she wanted to do just then was make it easier for him to walk away from her.

Jasim decided to give her what he knew she must want— the encouragement to ditch her designs on his brother and concentrate on him instead. He went in for the kill with words that were the virtual antithesis of his usual cool, uncommitted approach to her sex. 'I find you incredibly attractive and I am not a snob. My great-great-grandfather was a poor but proud man when he took the throne of Quaram. I have known many women but I have never felt like this before. We *must* explore what is between us.'

Her troubled green eyes switched back to him and clung to his lean dark features. She craved that visual contact and wanted to trust in what he had said, but at the same time she was terrified of getting hurt as her mother had been in a fairy-tale romance that had swiftly crumbled and led to a lifetime of unhappy comparisons and regret.

'I don't think your brother would approve and I value my job,' Elinor framed uncertainly.

His shrewd dark-as-charcoal eyes glinted as he received what he deemed to be her most honest answer yet. Which brother was she to place her trust in? After all, she wouldn't want to fall between the proverbial two stools and end up with neither man in tow. He reached down and closed his hands firmly over hers. 'I promise you—you will come to no harm with me.'

And that heartening vow reverberated through Elinor while Jasim made easy conversation about horses on the ride back to the stables. Nothing but trouble could come from an ordinary person trifling with royalty, she told herself fiercely, but she could still taste him on her lips and she couldn't help reliving the heady excitement of that stolen embrace. Zahrah was already with her nurse when Elinor reappeared and she saw the older woman note in surprise that Jasim was with her and stare. She wondered if her mouth was as swollen as it felt and she flushed brick red with discomfiture. He insisted that she travel back to the house with him, another mark of conspicuous favour that embarrassed her.

That afternoon, Elinor clung to her usual schedule and took Zahrah out shopping and then on to a newly released children's film showing at the local cinema. As was usual on a Saturday, they ate a light supper in the nursery. She gave Zahrah her bath and tucked the little girl into bed afterwards with a fond hug. Too enervated to settle for an evening by the television, she put on her swimsuit, donned a towelling robe and headed downstairs to the indoor swimming pool. When Zahrah's parents were in residence she didn't like to use the facility unless she had Zahrah with her, but with the couple away she felt there was no harm in doing so. The pool complex was huge and spectacular, complete with a stunning waterfall and underwater jets, and a spa to one side of it.

Emerging from the lift, Jasim was impressed when he saw that Elinor was already waiting in the water for him. This was not a girl who let moss grow over an opportunity, or who was prepared to run the risk of a man losing interest from lack of exposure to her available charms. He watched her slide from the bubbling spa into the main pool, giving him a ravishing display of her slender but curvaceous body sheathed in tight purple stretchy fabric that left little to the imagination. The ripe swell of her firm little breasts and the heart-shaped femininity of her derriere were wonderfully visible and would have awakened any man's appreciation. But Jasim resented the powerful pull she exerted over him and thought that the look of surprise and self-consciousness she then assumed at first glimpse of him was an award-winning effort. What an actress she was! How many other men had she practised her wiles on? Nobody knew better than Jasim that once a woman got a man weak with lust, she could convince him of virtually anything. Bitterness assailed him as he recalled his own past.

Elinor didn't feel right staying in the pool when Jasim was in it as well. After all, it was his house and his pool and she couldn't help worrying that the other staff would think she was throwing herself at their prince if they saw her there, daring to share the same water as royalty. She climbed out and pulled on her towelling robe.

Jasim swam over to the side and heaved himself out. Water streaming in rivulets from the taut contours of his lean bronzed body, he approached her and lifted a towel. 'Why are you leaving?'

'I just think it's wiser,' Elinor mumbled tautly, trying not to let her attention linger anywhere it shouldn't while he towelled himself dry. She was grateful that he favoured loose shorts rather than body-hugging briefs.

Dark golden eyes smouldered over her and lingered on her pouting mouth. 'For whom? You want me too. Don't deny that this feeling is mutual.'

The very boldness of that statement struck hot colour into her face. She tied the sash on the robe with clumsy hands. He spoke with such terrifying confidence, and even though it scared her, his complete assurance drew her like a bonfire on an icy day. 'But it's not enough,' she protested, still trying to get a grip on a situation that felt as though it were flying fast out of her control.

Jasim closed his hands round her narrow wrists and drew her firmly to him. 'This is only the beginning…'

And she fell into the depths of the hot, hungry kiss that followed like a novice swimmer with a suicide wish as she sank deeper and deeper out of her depth. One feverish kiss led hotly into the next. He crushed her mouth with devastating urgency and her excitement rose and rose until she was shaking and shivering against him, her body on fire with her craving for more.

'This is not the place for this, but you are irresistible,' he breathed thickly against her reddened lips. Bending, he scooped her off her feet and carried her into the lift.

She had never been in the lift before, for it travelled only to the master bedroom to facilitate the early-morning swims that the owner of the house apparently enjoyed. He set her down beside the giant divan bed and pushed the loosened robe off her slim shoulders so that it fell in a heap round her bare feet. She looked up at him with sensually stunned eyes, the swollen contours of her strawberry-pink mouth like a magnet reeling him back down to her again.

'We can't do this!' she exclaimed, pushed to the edge of panic by the intimacy of the bedroom. She thought she had been very naïve in failing to appreciate that he might expect her to go to bed with him without further ado.

He tugged her hand down to the front of his wet shorts where the fabric was moulded to the massive width and length of his erection. '*Please*…I won't be able to sleep for wanting you.'

And Elinor could have withstood almost any other response but, even as he plunged her into agonies of self-conscious embarrassment, that roughened sensual appeal thrilled her to the core of her being and touched her to the heart. When had any man ever wanted her like that? When had she *ever* contrived to rouse such a storm of desire? Far more often than she cared to recall she had been made to feel freakishly tall and unfeminine. Meeting his smouldering dark golden eyes, she rejoiced in his need for her and suppressed the voice of reason urging caution and restraint at the back of her mind. Hadn't she always been sensible and controlled? Was there any real harm in taking a risk for once? Especially when she was falling for him like a ton of bricks: she affixed to that last thought, eager to be daring and worthy of such a passion as his. This might well be the *only* time in her life when a man called her 'irresistible'…

CHAPTER THREE

BEFORE Elinor could even register what Jasim was about, he had peeled down the top of her swimsuit so that the pale plump mounds of her breasts tumbled free. A low masculine growl of hunger escaped him when he saw the luscious and prominent protrusion of her rose-pink nipples. 'You have the most wonderful body.'

He kneaded those tender tips with expert fingers and she cried out in shaken acknowledgement of the arrow of sensation darting straight down to the balloon of burgeoning heat expanding low in her pelvis. That fast she was in uncharted territory and at the mercy of the hunger he had unleashed inside her. She craved more and he was not slow to answer that craving. He brought her down on the bed and closed his mouth fiercely to a straining pink crest, taking it between his teeth and toying with the tender tip until her fingers formed into claws that raked the sheet beneath her hands. A frantic sense of swollen heat between her splayed thighs was sending up her temperature and threatening what little remained of her control. He touched her there where she was most tender of all just once while he played with her lush breasts and her spine arched off the bed in a reaction so strong it almost frightened her.

'You're too tense,' he censured, wrenching her free of her swimsuit and rolling off the bed to remove his wet shorts.

Nerves and doubts immediately attacked Elinor again. Everything was going too fast for her and she was trying to work out how she could have allowed matters to go so far without seriously questioning what she was about to do. After all, sleeping with a man for the first time was a very big deal on her terms. Elinor stared at her first daunting view of a man unclothed. He seemed endowed out of all reasonable proportion to her untried body. The shameless burn at the heart of her felt as scary as it was exciting and she wondered feverishly if she was doing the right thing or simply letting passion and the joy of attracting so super-lative a male go to her head.

Jasim looked down at her with an amount of pleasure that took even him aback. She looked like a goddess, he decided in awe, the fiery abundance of her hair the perfect comple-ment to her full creamy curves. Never before had a woman made him ache with such ravenous hunger…no, not even Sophia had had that power. But he would never be vul-nerable with a woman again or allow desire to overwhelm his judgement, he told himself with fierce confidence.

'I want you now,' Jasim confessed, coming down on the bed beside her, his lean powerful body taut with sexual im-patience. Overwhelming desire made it an effort for him to recall that his primary motivation in taking her was to ensure she lost the power to lure his brother into an affair.

Just looking at his lean bronzed features, which were compellingly handsome and strikingly serious, Elinor felt her mouth run dry and her heart threatened to drum its way out of her chest. 'I've never felt this way before,' she whispered unevenly and held back the craven admission that feeling as she did just then was distinctly intimidating.

Immediately discarding that ingenuous assurance as a pre-planned sop voiced to stroke his male ego, Jasim bit back an appreciative sound of amusement and ravished her soft mouth afresh. Against her will, Elinor felt herself melt again. Her insecurities ebbed while every nerve ending leapt in helpless response to the scent and touch of him. He felt like living hair-roughened bronze next to her, hot and hard and strong. She had a delirious image of what it would feel like to have him inside her and was shattered at the leap of her body and the newly wanton direction of her thoughts.

Jasim rubbed the tiny bud below her mound and listened to her cry out her pleasure. She was swollen with arousal and as slippery as wet silk. With a forefinger he probed the delicate cleft and discovered that she was deliciously small and tight within. She gasped and winced and he marvelled at her theatrical ability. Of course, just like Sophia she most likely assumed that an Arab male would only properly value her if she pretended to be a virgin. Sophia had paid a small fortune to have her hymen surgically restored and he had been absolutely fooled by her masquerade, he remembered with deep bitterness.

'What's wrong?' Elinor exclaimed, glimpsing the dark shadowed look in his brilliant eyes at the breathless peak of a rippling wave of almost torturous pleasure. His lovemaking enthralled her, but now she wondered if he had finally registered her lack of experience. Was that a turn-off for him?

'Nothing could be wrong…'

'I've never slept with anyone else,' Elinor admitted awkwardly. 'Is that a problem?'

'How could it be, when you are about to honour me beyond all other men?' The sardonic light in his gaze hardened at her careful last-minute assurance of her sexual innocence. Afraid that he might not get the message, she was leaving nothing to chance. He was wild for the hot, tight satisfaction of her body under his, but he would have preferred the cool self-restraint to tell her that she was a liar and that her shoddy, foolish pretence didn't fool him for a moment.

He settled into the cradle of her thighs and he was so eager for her that little tremors were racking his lean, muscular frame. He pushed into her moist, warm entrance and revelled in the taut feel and softness of her silky inner passage. Driven by a ferocious sense of need, he thrust back her thighs to deepen his penetration and at the same instant that he ensured she stretched to accommodate all of him she vented a sharp cry of pain. He froze, not having expected her to go to town on the virgin act to this extent.

Elinor was mortified. 'I'm sorry, it just hurt a bit…it's all right,' she muttered, her mortification so great that she wanted the bed to open up and swallow her.

'It is for me to apologise. I should have been more gentle,' Jasim breathed, marvelling that he could match her masquerade, all the while inching his aching shaft into the velvet-smooth honeyed welcome at the heart of her.

As her discomfort receded the excitement came back in steady increments that were stoked by every skilled move he made. Elinor gasped and wrapped her arms round him and discovered he could once again be the giver of such energising sensation as she had never dared to dream existed. The pace quickened to a hypnotic tempo and she was swept away by the erotic excitement of his sensual rhythm. The sweet surges of pleasure ran closer and closer together, driving her to the very peak of an explosive climax and then tipping her off the edge into a blissful weightless fall and satiated indolence.

Jasim stared down at her in the aftermath, his dark eyes blazing gold with passionate appreciation. 'You took me to paradise and I have never been there with a woman before.'

As he held her to him, his heart pounding against hers, Elinor blinked back sudden tears, for she felt very emotional. She also felt incredibly tender towards him and strung a line of kisses across a broad brown shoulder. She fiercely fought off the sense of shame and awkwardness that she guiltily knew was waiting to pounce on her. He made her feel special and she was desperate to hold on to that reassuring sensation.

'I should go back to my own room,' she mumbled, however, a few minutes later.

Jasim's arms tightened like bars of steel round her. He had every intention of fully satisfying his desire for her. 'Tonight you are mine and you stay here with me,' he spelt out thickly.

And she *was* his now, he reflected in male triumph, his hungry body already quickening against hers again. One stolen night, however, was all he could dare to take beneath a roof that also housed his niece. Anything more would be an insult.

* * *

Elinor wakened in the early hours of the next morning when light was filtering with increasing strength through the curtains and illuminating the magnificent unfamiliar room. In that first instant of reason after a very eventful night, she knew only pure terror when she thought of the unknown that faced her.

What the heck had come over her? Complete insanity? It was barely thirty-six hours since they had met and she had spent the night in Prince Jasim's bed, letting him make love to her over and over again. In truth she wasn't sure she would be able to walk if she got out of bed, since he had proved a very demanding and seemingly tireless lover.

She lay watching him in the half-light, dreamily, tenderly admiring the strong classic bones of his profile and the way blue-black stubble enhanced his wide stubborn mouth. While her body might ache from his attentions, familiarity had not bred contempt. He was beautiful. He still took her breath away and that scared her, because she had never believed in love at first sight.

But what else was she to make of the powerful emotions assailing her? He had not been out of her mind for a second since they'd met and she felt remarkably comfortable with images and reflections of him fully occupying her every waking thought. On a horse and in bed he was her every dream come true. Yet she hardly knew him and surely he could only think less of her because of the ease with which she had fallen into his arms?

Content to be the full focus of her admiration, Jasim was wondering if he dared take her one more time. He couldn't get enough of the sweet, tight release of her warm, willing body. But the servants would be up and about soon, and a lifetime in a royal palace had taught him how fast scandal hit the household grapevine and went places one would prefer it did not reach. The deed was done, accomplished in record time too, he savoured with ruthless satisfaction. His brother would never look at her now. Too warm, he sat up and tossed back the duvet and saw the blood stain on the white linen sheet.

'Good morning,' she whispered, looking all shy and flushed and utterly adorable.

Unlike his unlamented Sophia, Elinor *had* been a virgin, Jasim registered in substantial shock. Yet he had taken her with all the finesse of a stallion covering a mare. A virgin: quite a statement for a young woman of twenty-one in a world where casual sex was commonplace. A twinge of rare guilt pierced Jasim; he would never have chosen to seduce a virgin. But even had he known beforehand, would he have left her untouched while he was aware that Murad would have found such purity a mouth-watering temptation? He had now contrived to smash the possibility of a relation-ship that could well have driven his brother into setting Yaminah aside and replacing her with Elinor as a second wife. For all his extra-marital affairs, Murad was a staunchly traditional man and Jasim was convinced that, had Elinor slept with Murad, his brother would have offered her marriage. Well, at least that disaster could not be enacted now.

Jasim reached for Elinor and pulled her into his arms. 'Good morning,' he husked, cupping her pouting breasts and gently teasing the swollen pink buds that crowned them.

Elinor was very tense. 'I need to go back to my room—'

'One of the servants will bring you clothes and pack for

you,' Jasim intoned, arranging her against the tumbled pillows and letting his tousled dark head swoop down to capture a straining nipple. One more time, he was thinking, just to get him through the day ahead.

Elinor went from being all soft and purring and quivering with response to sudden rigidity. '*Pack*…for me?'

Jasim wished he had taken more thorough advantage of her before he broke that news. He lifted his handsome dark head and met the anxious questions clouding her green eyes. 'You can no longer stay at Woodrow Court.'

'What are you talking about?' Elinor gasped in bewilderment, pulling away from him and yanking the duvet up over breasts that suddenly felt indecently bare.

Jasim released his breath on a slow hiss of impatience. 'Of course you can't stay here now that we have shared a bed. It would be most inappropriate for you to continue caring for my niece.'

Elinor was so shocked by that announcement that she felt the blood drain from her face and leave her pale. 'You mean that having sex with you is grounds for giving me the sack?'

'I wouldn't put it quite as crudely as that.'

Elinor hugged the duvet to her with furious defensive hands, her eyes prickling with stinging tears. She could not credit what he was telling her, or that he could say such offensive things in that smooth low-key style, as though he were merely making polite conversation. 'Then how would you put it?'

'Our relationship will enter another phase,' he drawled, smooth as polished glass and with a decided hint of warning ice in his tone.

Deaf to that loaded hint of icy withdrawal, Elinor stared

straight ahead and worried at her full lower lip with her teeth. 'What sort of a phase?'

'I want you to move to London so that we can see more of each other.'

Now horribly conscious of her nudity below the bedding, Elinor flung him as frozen a look as she could contrive. 'But I like working here. I love looking after Zahrah.'

'It's unfortunate but it can no longer continue. I cannot conduct an affair with you in the presence of my family.'

'Because you're ashamed of your association with me!' Elinor condemned, and she flung herself out of bed in a passion of self-loathing regret and snatched up the towelling robe.

'No, it would be indiscreet and unacceptable behaviour on my part. In London I can do as I like and what I would like is to see more of you,' Jasim declared, brilliant dark eyes welded to her angry bemused face as he willed her to accept the change in her status. 'We can't turn back the clock on our intimacy. You must trust me. Say your good-byes to Zahrah and I will have you out of here by lunch-time.'

Elinor snatched up her discarded swimsuit with a shaking hand. She was in shock and deeply confused. Throughout the night hours he had been the passionate lover of her dreams but, all of a sudden, he was laying down the law and making non-negotiable demands that threatened to tear apart her entire life. 'And if I was to say, no, I'm not going anywhere and let's forget we ever crossed the boundaries?'

'I believe you are too sensible to challenge me.'

This time around she felt the distinct chill in the air and

it raised goosebumps on her exposed skin. His dark gaze was black and cold. For the very first time, she sensed the steel of him, the fierce ruthless purpose that powered him beneath the charisma. The discovery of what lay at the core of him unnerved her. He was determined that she leave Woodrow Court and if that was how strongly he felt, she did not see how she could remain and live in constant fear of her wanton behaviour being exposed. 'I wish I had known what I was getting into,' she breathed starkly.

'You do now,' Jasim pointed out silkily.

Elinor wanted to shout, but she was too shaken by what had happened to let go of her temper until she knew exactly where she stood. In her own heart she was committed to him but she did not like the way he was treating her. What were the chances that a royal prince would treat her with respect? Or come to truly care for her as anything other than a sexual partner? She realised that she had thrown the dice in a game without knowing what she was really playing for and now it was too late to go back and argue about the rules. As long as she could get a reference she would soon get another job in London. Whatever, it seemed she had thoroughly burned her boats at Woodrow Court.

She managed to return to her room, mercifully without running into anyone. She stood in the shower with tears running down her taut cheeks, trying to overcome the suspicion that in sleeping with Jasim she might well have made the biggest mistake of her life. He was turning her life upside down but she wasn't ready yet to give up hope of a better future and walk away. As soon as she was dressed she sought out Zahrah and told the little girl that she had to leave to go and see her family. She hated telling a lie and Zahrah was quite tearful until her beloved nurse took her off for breakfast. Elinor knew her charge would be fine without her. Zahrah's main source of security was the elderly nurse who had always been with her.

She skipped breakfast and packed. A manservant came to the door for her luggage and Jasim called her on the house phone at noon. 'I'll see you in London,' he told her. 'I'm grateful that you're being sensible about this. I couldn't hide our relationship and I don't intend to.'

Strengthened by what felt like a far-reaching pledge of faith on her terms, Elinor got into the car waiting outside for her and it was only then that she marvelled at her failure to demand to know exactly where she was being taken. Mid-afternoon, she preceded her driver into a lift in a tall block of luxury flats. He had not a word of English so she couldn't question him and she wondered as she was shown into an apartment if it was where Jasim lived when he was in the city. Was he moving her in with him? Surely not? She reminded herself that she had a healthy bank account and was far from powerless when it came to looking out for her own best interests. But, even so, the sudden changes had cost her dear; she had a cautious personality and her strong attachment to him added entire layers of complexity that made her feel out of control.

An hour later, Jasim strode through the front door. He hauled her straight into his arms and kissed her as if he was set on reminding her of his power over her. Pink lit her cheeks and butterflies fluttered inside her. Everything, she promised herself as she gazed up into his breathtakingly handsome face, was going to be fine. She just had to give them both a little time and space.

But time, she soon learned, was at premium.

'This evening I'm flying to New York for two weeks,' Jasim imparted with a casualness that made her vulnerable heart sink like a stone. 'That's why I had you brought here. I own this apartment and you'll be comfortable here while I'm abroad.'

'I can afford my own accommodation, although I may not need it for long. Most nanny jobs are live-in and if you can sort out a reference for me, I'll have another job by the time you get back—'

Jasim studied her in wonderment. Unable to believe that she could possibly be serious in her desire to be self-sufficient, he released a slightly harsh laugh. 'There's no need for you to look for another position. Nannies must work hellish hours—how would I ever see you? Don't you understand what I'm offering you?'

Elinor stood there very still and straight-backed and increasingly pale. 'No, I must be incredibly thick because I haven't quite worked out yet what you're offering me…'

His charismatic smile slashed his lean dark visage and he took a measured step forward. 'Naturally, I want to take care of you…'

'No, thanks.' Elinor forced a smile that felt rigid on her tense mouth and mentally willed him not to demean her with some sordid proposition. 'The only man who will ever take *care* of me with my agreement will be my husband. I'm willing to wait for you to come back but I'm not willing to be kept by you. I'm a very independent woman and what I give, I give freely.'

Jasim frowned. 'You make it all sound so serious.'

'What happened between us last night drove a coach and

horses through my life and left pure chaos in its wake,' she reminded him gently, a slender hand resting on the lapel of his pinstripe suit jacket. 'Right now, I don't know whether I'm on my head or my heels. I'll stay for a while because I have nowhere else to go in the short term, but I need to fall back to Planet Earth again so maybe it's good that you'll be away for a while.'

Jasim pulled out his wallet to extract a card. 'My private number,' he told her, presenting her with it as though it was a precious gift—which indeed it was. Many women would have done just about anything to gain access to that direct hotline to him, but his staff guarded his privacy with scrupulous care.

Before he could close the wallet, his thumb brushed over the condom packet slotted into it and his blood ran cold in his veins in a deeply disturbing wake-up call. He realised that in his excitement the evening before he had neglected to use contraception with Elinor. Consternation rolled through him. How could he have made such a serious oversight? Although he was usually very careful, they had shared numerous encounters of unprotected sex during the night. What if he had got her pregnant? He reminded himself that, according to Murad, a woman didn't fall pregnant that easily. Certainly, Yaminah had been most unfortunate in that regard. He thought of all that he had read about 'morning-after pills', but he had too much respect for the gift of new life to persuade a woman into taking that option as a preventative measure. He decided that he could more easily live with hoping for the best. Yet, he knew that an unplanned pregnancy would engulf his life like an avalanche, crush his freedom and suffocate him. He barely stilled a shudder at the threat of such an outcome and thought how ironic it was that what his older brother had longed and prayed for to secure the line to the throne should strike Jasim as an absolute disaster.

Within twenty-four hours of Jasim's departure, Elinor quietly signed up with an agency as a relief nanny and found herself plunged straight back into regular, reasonably well-paid employment. Going from one family to the next and staying only a few days in each household was surprisingly enjoyable and kept her too busy to brood. She knew she wouldn't like dealing with a merry-go-round of change for ever but, just then, the freedom from having to forge new meaningful relationships felt like what she most needed. Every night she returned to the luxurious but anonymous comfort of the apartment and fell asleep within minutes of getting into bed.

Jasim phoned her almost every day. The conversations were curiously impersonal and unsatisfying and only made her feel more insecure. The only information he gave about himself was superficial. He never mentioned the future, or that he was missing her. Her period was due at the end of that first week and when it didn't arrive as expected she tried not to worry. She started to feel that she had been very foolish once she acknowledged that she had no memory of Jasim taking precautions that night at Woodrow Court. Had he falsely assumed that she was taking contraceptive pills as so many women did? How could she have been so dense? When her nerves could stand the waiting game no longer, she bought a pregnancy test. The test was guaranteed to give an accurate result within days of a malfunctioning menstrual cycle, so she made immediate use of it.

The positive result stunned Elinor. Somehow she hadn't really believed that she *could* have conceived; somehow such a development hadn't really seemed possible to her. Now she learned that she was very much mistaken. She was expecting a baby, a real, live little baby. In the space of one wildly reckless night Jasim had contrived to get her pregnant.

That same evening she received an unexpected visitor. The doorbell buzzed and when she addressed the caller through the intercom, it was Prince Murad's voice that answered her. Elinor was appalled by his arrival and would have done just about anything to avoid the humiliation of answering the door and actually having to deal with her former employer. Unfortunately there was no decent way of avoiding the issue.

'May I come in and speak with you?' the older man asked politely.

'Of course.' In the elegant living room, Elinor linked her hands tightly together. 'You must be wondering why I left Woodrow so suddenly—'

'Elinor…let me be frank. I know that this apartment block belongs to my brother,' the prince admitted, his expression grave and concerned. 'I am sorry that you have left my employment and I would rather that it had been for any other reason than this. I had a great affection for your mother and I feel responsible for you as her daughter. You have chosen to take a most ill-advised step.'

Her strained face flamed with colour. 'I know you mean well, but I'm an adult and I'm here of my own free will, Your Highness.'

'Jasim has had many women in his life, Elinor. He cherishes none of them, and he will not marry any woman who has already lived with him.'

Elinor's hands twisted. Confronted by such cruel candour, she felt as if her heart were being ripped out at the seams. 'I'm not looking for marriage—'

'But you deserve better than this tawdry arrangement,' Murad pronounced with an angry wave of dismissal that encompassed their surroundings. A small and portly but still dignified figure, he sighed. 'I loved and respected your mother. I would never have asked her to be my mistress. You must value yourself more. Surely this cannot be the future that you wanted?'

Although it was still only early evening, when Murad left Elinor went to bed and cried. Seeing how she had sunk in the older man's estimation had upset her. But, at the same time, she knew that there was no way that she was prepared to become Jasim's mistress! Apart from anything else, her pregnancy would alter everything, she reasoned wretchedly. When he had carted her off to bed in an excess of lusty passion, conceiving a child with her would have been the very last thing on his mind. How was he likely to react to such a shattering development?

Jasim had returned from New York a day early. Warned by his security team that his brother had visited Elinor, he arrived at the apartment a couple of hours later. Murad's seeking out of Elinor had confirmed his every suspicion about the nature of their relationship and he was angry and full of distrust. Never before had his older sibling sought to interfere in his private life! So what kind of a hold did Elinor have over Murad that he had felt the need to come up to London specifically to confront her?

'Jasim…' Elinor sat up in bed with a start as the over-head light went on. 'I had no idea you were coming back tonight!'

Sheathed in a charcoal grey business suit that was beau-tifully tailored to fit his lean, tautly muscled physique, he looked spectacular. Deprived of the sight of him for almost two weeks, she couldn't help staring and drinking in every tiny detail of his appearance.

In his turn, Jasim was studying the tumbled bed, ques-tioning why she was in it at barely past eight o'clock and asking himself if his own brother could have shared it with her earlier that evening. Her nose was pink and her eyelids reddened and swollen, making it clear that she had been upset and that she had cried. Fierce anger and disgust filled him. 'Evidently…'

'What's that supposed to mean?' she questioned in bewilderment.

'Did you entertain my brother in that bed as well?'

Her eyes widened in shock at that question. 'That's a horrible thing to ask me—'

'But an even more disgusting thing to have to suspect,' Jasim countered rawly, dark eyes glittering like golden diamonds of derision over her. He strode round to the side of the bed, closed a hand round her arm and tugged her upright to face him without ceremony. *'Answer me.'*

'Why? Do you and your brother make a habit of *sharing* women?' Elinor demanded shakily, her outrage threaten-ing to strangle her voice. 'I slept with you so, for that reason, you assume I'm just some slut who would be quite happy to sleep with your brother as well?'

The level of her incredulity cooled Jasim's temper and

sharpened his wits. He registered that he had come within an ace of revealing too much knowledge. He had given her no reason to suspect his motives in pursuing her and if Murad was still chasing after her, it would be unwise to either alienate her or turn her loose.

Deeply wounded by his lack of faith in her, Elinor stared at him in angry reproach. What had happened to the guy who had sworn he wanted to see more of her? He pushed a hand through the black hair on his brow and raked it back in a gesture of frustration. She noticed that his hand wasn't quite steady and registered that he was a great deal more disturbed than he was prepared to show. On the outside he seemed so cool and controlled, but inside he seethed with anger, outrage and passion. Suddenly she believed she understood what was wrong. Evidently, the reverse side of that passion was a jealous, suspicious streak a mile wide. On the balance side, however, when she had challenged him he had backed off, presumably appreciating that his suspicions were ridiculously irrational. She wondered if the behaviour of some other woman had taught him to distrust her sex.

'How did you know your brother came to see me?'

'My security team have been keeping an eye on this apartment.'

Wondering if she was supposed to be flattered that he should consider she required that protection, Elinor nodded and began to pull clean clothes out of the drawers in the cabinet by the bed. 'I'll get dressed. We have to talk.'

Jasim tensed. The idea of further discussion was the sort of womanly threat he avoided like the plague. He would much have preferred joining her in bed. Sex would have released his tension and buried the argument much more effectively than a verbal post-mortem.

Stiff and self-conscious now in his presence, Elinor went into the en-suite bathroom to dress, pulling on the jeans and the T-shirt she had chosen at speed. She wished she had had some warning that he would be returning early, for she would have liked the chance to dress up. Glancing in the mirror, she groaned, convinced that she looked horribly plain with her pink-rimmed eyes and weary pallor. When she re-entered the bedroom, Jasim was standing by the window in the living room. He still looked unrelentingly severe and he swung round, saying flatly, 'What did my brother want with you?'

An uneasy flush warmed her cheeks and she wished she could have been more frank with him about her late mother's relationship with Murad. But, on her first day of employment, the older man had made her promise never to divulge that connection to anyone, for he had feared that the truth would be misinterpreted and would cause them both embarrassment. Since her friend, Louise, had already made seedy insinuations about the same issue, Elinor had decided that Prince Murad had been more astute than she in foreseeing what others might make of the story and she had no intention of being equally frank with anyone else. 'The prince thought that I was making a mistake leaving my job and getting involved with you. He said that he felt responsible for me.'

Jasim's superb bone structure set hard as granite beneath his bronzed skin. Well, that was certainly telling him the lie of the land! Murad had been sufficiently angry to follow her to London and question her current circumstances. Jasim studied her exquisite face and the tumble of Titian curls that were so bright against her creamy skin. He wondered how he had ever deemed that hair unattractive. How had he also failed to appreciate the obvious fact that so beautiful a woman might also have the power to set brother against brother? He was stunned that he had contrived to overlook that obvious angle and it was now too late to redress the balance. Wasn't it? He was outraged that Murad had even dared to approach her, crossing boundaries that Jasim had assumed would be respected. She was *his* now.

Elinor sank down in a leather armchair and straightened her slight shoulders. 'I have something to tell you.' Having breathed in deep, she mustered the strength not to make a theatrical production out of her news. 'I'm pregnant.'

However, her quiet low-pitched admission had the same effect on Jasim as a sudden devastatingly loud clap of thunder. He went very still. His expressive eyes hooded over and his aggressive jaw line clenched hard. His sins, it seemed, had truly come home to roost and the minute she spoke he saw his well-organised life spinning out of control. 'It's my fault,' he acknowledged flatly. 'When we spent the night together I didn't use protection.'

A little less defensive once he assumed the lion's share of the blame for her condition, Elinor released her pent-up breath.

'I deserve to pay the price for this,' Jasim said heavily, his classic profile as grim as his tone of voice.

'The price? There is no price—'

'You're wrong. Either we pay the price, or our child will. If you give birth to a boy he will be an heir to the throne of Quaram, but he can only assume that status if we marry and he is born within wedlock. If he is not, my family will never recognise him.'

'An heir to the throne—would he be….honestly?' Elinor exclaimed in astonishment. *'Marry?'*

'I don't think that we have a choice. As soon as you've had your pregnancy confirmed by a doctor, I have to marry you. I refuse to embarrass my family with a scandal and it is imperative that our child is born legitimate.'

Elinor realised that his decisions were based on a different set of parameters from hers but she was impressed by his willingness to stand by their child and look into the future. 'I could have a little girl.'

'She, too, would be denied her inheritance if she is not born within marriage. The birth of an illegitimate child is still a very serious matter in my country.'

'You're prepared to marry me to stop that happening?' Elinor prompted, because she just couldn't accept that he was prepared to go to such lengths.

'I am. Isn't securing our child's future the most important issue at stake here?'

'But we hardly know each other.' Elinor dealt him a pained glance of shame as she forced out that admission. 'I'm only a nanny…you're a prince.'

'Our child won't care who or what we are as long as we love him…or her,' he responded wryly.

She was touched by that assurance and the thought that had gone into it. He was so responsible and he would make a good father; he was already worrying about what was best for their child. All right, she had eyes in her head and she could see that he wasn't exactly celebrating at the prospect of marrying her, but neither was he thinking of leaving her to deal alone with her pregnancy. 'Do you think we could make a marriage work?' she murmured half under her breath.

'I'm willing to make the effort.' His beautiful dark eyes wandered over her at a leisurely pace and lingered on her soft pink mouth and the ripe pout of her breasts until her face burned and she shifted in her chair. 'I find you very attractive. That's a healthy foundation.'

Elinor knew that, with the smallest encouragement, he would scoop her up and take her back to bed to sate the hunger he made no attempt to hide. Her nipples were tightening and the familiar hollow ache was awakening between her thighs. But she felt too vulnerable to give him that signal. She wanted to be more than the woman who satisfied his sexual needs. But even though she wanted more she knew that she was still prepared to marry him on the practical and unemotional basis that he had outlined. If he was ready to give her his full support, she was willing to do whatever it took to ensure a more secure and happy future for her baby.

'I'll marry you, then,' she told him gruffly.

Jasim almost laughed out loud at the idea that he might have required that confirmation. Of course she was going to marry him and snatch at the chance to live in luxury for the rest of her days! Not for one moment had he doubted that fact. 'I'll make the arrangements. Please don't share our plans with anyone for the moment. We need to keep this a secret if we want to keep the tabloid press out of the picture.'

Jasim retreated back to the doorway. Dark-driven anger was stirring out of the ashes of his shock. He had known that he was dealing with a devious and mercenary young woman, who was willing to encourage a married man's

pursuit to feather her nest. Yet, even armed with that awareness, he too had fallen for her wiles and straight into a
sexual honey-trap refined by the guilt-inducing gift of her
virginity. He had played into her scheming hands as easily
as a testosterone-driven teenager. Elinor Tempest had
simply traded her body to the highest and most available
bidder and the pay-off promised to be *huge* on her terms.
Marriage into the Rais ruling family would reward her
with immense wealth and status and that unhappy truth
galled him.

Her face full of uncertainty, Elinor hovered by the bed.
His beautiful golden gaze was cold as charity and she
flushed. 'Are you leaving?'

'I have work to do,' Jasim delivered curtly. 'I'll be in
touch.'

On the day of the wedding, Elinor was torn in two with indecision. She had barely laid eyes on Jasim since the day
she told him she was pregnant. He had personally accompanied her to the office of a gynaecologist in private
practice, who had confirmed her pregnancy. She rather suspected that Jasim had regretted doing so when a well-
dressed lady in the waiting room had recognised him and
begun chattering away to him. Since then, though she had
given up her temping work, he had not visited the apartment again or accompanied her anywhere and they had
communicated only by phone. In every way possible he had
distanced himself from her, retreating behind a smooth,
polite façade that she could not penetrate.

She had fallen crazily in love with a guy who didn't
return her feelings, Elinor conceded wretchedly. Would he

ever love her back? Or did the very fact that he felt he *had* to marry her for the sake of their child mean that she would never, ever inspire him to any warmer emotions? Those were the questions that Elinor struggled to find a fair answer to while she prepared all on her own for what she had once thought would be the happiest day of her life.

Too insecure to purchase the white wedding gown of her dreams and wear it, Elinor made do with a cream lace suit composed of a jacket and a slim skirt that came to just below her knees. None of the romantic frills that most women craved seemed appropriate. Jasim sent a car to collect her and she was ushered into the register office where the civil ceremony was to take place. A limp flower arrangement was the dusty room's only claim to glamour. But her attention zeroed straight in on Jasim, dramatically handsome in a dark suit teamed with a gold silk tie, his bronzed angel face grave and oddly forbidding.

Her tummy flipped with nerves rather than excitement because her bridegroom looked more as though he were attending a funeral. *Give him the option of walking away*, a little voice in her head urged her. 'Could I have a word with you in private?' Elinor enquired tautly.

Jasim detached himself from the company of the two aides flanking him and approached her. 'What is it? We haven't much time.'

'There is no obligation on you to do this. If you don't want to marry me, just walk away now. I won't hold it against you. I won't stop you seeing the baby either,' she whispered frantically. 'Just don't marry me because you feel you have to, because it'll cause us both nothing but unhappiness.'

Jasim dealt her a raw appraisal that warned her that he

was seething with emotion beneath the cool front. 'We have a future together with our child. I cannot walk away from either of you.'

'But I don't want a noble, self-sacrificing hero of a husband,' Elinor declared, even as he turned away from her.

Jasim closed a hand over hers and walked her back with him to where the registrar was standing. 'We haven't got time for this nonsense.'

The ceremony was brief and over with very quickly. A shiny new ring on her wedding finger, Elinor got into a limousine that wafted them back through the busy city streets to a hugely impressive Georgian town house set in a dignified square with a lush garden at its centre. Jasim spent the entire journey on his cell phone, which, Elinor acknowledged bitterly, at least saved him from the challenge of having to chat to her. She wondered how he would manage without it in bed, or even if he ever planned to make physical contact with her again. *I've made a mistake*, she thought fearfully. *I've made a terrible, terrible mistake marrying him and now it's too late to do anything about it!*

'We'll have lunch now,' Jasim murmured, guiding her up the steps of the town house and into a spacious hall hung with beautiful oil paintings. 'Why are you so quiet?'

Elinor almost lost her temper with him there and then, almost told him what a horrible wedding it had been and how she had given him the opportunity to back out and that, if he hadn't taken it, the least he could have done was make the effort to ensure that it was a pleasant occasion! But, conscious that his bodyguards and the housekeeper were hovering, she bit back her ire. 'I suppose I'm just tired.'

'You should lie down for an hour.' Jasim signalled the

housekeeper and she was escorted upstairs to a beautiful bedroom.

Angry tears in her eyes at the ease with which he had dismissed her from his presence, Elinor soon decided that she should go back downstairs and tell Jasim exactly what she thought of the wedding he had put her through. Maintaining a stiff upper lip was unlikely to improve the atmosphere between them, but maybe an argument would, she reasoned in desperation. After all, if he didn't know how she was feeling, how could he make things better? But what if he didn't care enough to even want to make things better? That was her biggest fear.

From the window she saw a limo draw up outside. She frowned when she saw Murad's wife, Yaminah, scrambling out, for it had not escaped her notice that no member of his family had attended their wedding. She left the bedroom and headed for the stairs.

The sound of a shrill, raised, female voice greeted Elinor even before she reached the hall. It was Yaminah and she was ranting in French.

'It's my fault you got involved with the girl...didn't I beg you to show an interest in her so that she would *lose* interest in my husband and pay him no heed?' the older woman cried feverishly. 'Now I've ruined your life! I can't believe what you've done. You didn't even get your father's permission to marry her!'

The deep steady tones of Jasim's rich drawl interposed, 'The King would never have given his permission—'

'Then it's not too late. The marriage can be invalidated,' Yaminah exclaimed. 'It doesn't matter that she's pregnant, that can be hushed up. Pay her off, do whatever you have to do, anything *other* than sacrifice your happiness with this mockery of a marriage!'

Listening to that uniquely revealing dialogue, Elinor felt much as if she were being eviscerated with a knife. Perspiration beading her upper lip, she hurried back to the bedroom and straight into the adjoining bathroom where she was horribly sick. All of a sudden, she was realising what a total idiot she had been not to question why a spectacularly handsome prince would start showing a pronounced interest in *her*. Yaminah had asked him to. Murad's wife had feared that her husband was at risk of being led astray by the nanny and had persuaded her brother-in-law to present himself as an alternative option. Goodness, had they really feared that she might have an affair with a married man as old as Murad? Jasim had been a dazzling success when it came to seduction and too virile for his own good, Elinor conceded painfully. No wonder the complication of a pregnancy had hit him hard! Jasim had never really wanted her at all and even less must he have wanted to marry her.

Elinor freshened up and pressed trembling hands to her damp cheeks. She would do Jasim one last favour: for the benefit of them both she would leave him. There was no true marriage to work at, no future to weave dreams around and clearly no togetherness or mutual passion to retrieve. Their whole relationship from start to finish had been a lie, a big fat fakery, to ensnare her and draw her in. She had been more than a little desperate to believe that he could find her irresistible—even though no other man ever had—and now all she was conscious of was a deeply painful sense of shame and humiliation. What a pushover and a patsy she had been!

She rooted through her luggage, which had been brought up, extracting jewellery, keepsakes, important documentation and a few necessities to keep her clothed until she had time to go shopping. She didn't care about abandoning the rest—indeed her entire being was bent on leaving the town house just as fast as she possibly could. She piled everything she was taking with her into a smaller bag and changed into a more practical outfit of jeans and a jacket.

She yanked off her wedding ring and left it on the dressing table. Instantly she felt better about herself. He was gorgeous, rich and royal, but he had taken her for a cruelly manipulative ride that she would never forget. How naïve and immature she had been to give her trust so easily! A woman needed a man like a fish needed a bicycle, she quoted to herself, because her heart felt as if it were being pounded into pieces inside her. She didn't need him when she had herself to depend on, a willingness to work and a comfortable savings account. She and her baby would get by just fine without him.

Even so, tears dampened her face as she crept through the hall and slid like an eel out the front door with barely a sound. She walked briskly down the street and she didn't once look back. She was already making plans to ensure that even though he looked for her he would find it very difficult to find her again.

CHAPTER FOUR

'ALL right, so he's not there right now,' Alissa conceded grudgingly, lodged at the front window and scanning the pavement opposite for the young man she had noticed earlier. 'But I swear he was out there looking up at this apartment most of the day.'

Lindy, a curvaceous brunette, groaned out loud and rolled her eyes at Elinor. 'We haven't got a boyfriend between us but we've attracted a stalker? We don't have a lot of luck, do we?'

Elinor didn't laugh. Anything out of the ordinary tended to make her tense. She was always a little on her guard. Eighteen months had passed since she had set out to make a new life and preserve her independence by cutting all ties with the old. Kneeling, she bent over Sami, slotting her baby son into a stretchy sleep-suit covered with pictures of toy racing cars. He thought it was a game and continually tried to roll away out of reach. She closed a hand round a chubby ankle to hold him steady.

'Sami…stay still,' she scolded, trying to be stern.

Enormous brown eyes surrounded by black lashes as

long as fly swats danced with mischief. He rolled again. At ten months old, Sami had buckets of charm and a huge amount of personality. He was a fearless extrovert to his fingertips. When life went his way he was all sunny smiles and chuckles, but when it went wrong he seethed with melodrama and sobbed up a heartbreaking storm.

'It's bedtime,' Elinor told the little boy, tenderly hugging him close, revelling in his squirming warmth and cuddliness and the sweet familiar scent of his skin.

She usually kept Sami up quite late in the evenings because he was cared for in a crèche during the day while she worked full time. Every morning when she left him there she felt guilty, and evenings, weekends and holidays revolved exclusively around ensuring that Sami had lots of fun and got all her attention.

'Night, Sami.' Lindy patted his little curly dark head fondly as she moved past Elinor to head into the kitchen. 'Fancy a cup of tea before bed?'

'I'd love one,' Elinor admitted wearily.

'Nighty-night,' Alissa said to Sami, tugging Elinor down onto the arm of the sofa so that she could kiss the little boy's cheek.

Elinor tucked her son into his cot beside her bed. His eyes sparkled and he kicked while she went through their usual bedtime ritual, winding up the music box to play its customary lullaby and tucking his toy lamb in beside him. She read his favourite story, showing him the pictures through the bars of the cot. Slowly Sami wound down, lowering his eyelids until his thick ebony lashes fringed his olive-toned baby cheeks. Content to watch him, Elinor got ready for bed and stayed until he was fast asleep.

'You've let the tea get cold,' Lindy sighed when she emerged.

'I'm used to cold tea.'

Alissa had already retired for the night. Lindy was frowning at Elinor. 'You looked really worried when Alissa mentioned that she thought that guy had been watching the apartment. Did you think it might be Sami's dad? Was he violent?'

Elinor froze and gave her flatmate a shocked look. 'My goodness, no, nothing like that!'

'I couldn't help wondering and I felt I had to ask just in case someone turns up asking for you.' Lindy watched Elinor pale at the idea. 'What *are* you scared of, then?'

If Elinor had not been so accustomed to sidestepping all such questions to conceal her past history she might have weakened and told all. Lindy and Alissa were more than just flatmates. They were true friends, who had stuck by her throughout her pregnancy and done their utmost to be supportive.

'Not violence but…maybe losing custody of Sami,' she confided, finally voicing her deepest fear.

'I don't know what you're worried about. Single mothers outrank single fathers in the custody stakes.'

Elinor shrugged, reluctant to admit that she had married her child's father, although she was pretty sure that the marriage would have since been dissolved. For what reason would Jasim have retained that bond with an unwanted wife, who had vanished on their wedding day? But she was always afraid that he might still be looking for them because she had kept his child from him. And she felt amazingly bad about that sometimes. However, she didn't feel she could trust a man who had done what Jasim had done to her. It was Jasim who had taught her how devious, cruel and cold-blooded he could be. He might have married her, but he hadn't cared about her or even respected her, so how likely was it that he would be happy to share Sami with her? Sami was far too precious to be put at risk.

The following morning, Elinor checked Sami into the workplace crèche that made her daily life so much simpler than it might otherwise have been. The crèche was brand new and state-of-the-art and it was the main reason why Elinor had been overjoyed when she got a job at Havertons. Having passed a year-long business course with flying colours after Sami's birth, she was now happily employed in a position with the company. Indeed there was only one cloud in Elinor's sky. At the start of the month, finding it difficult to negotiate the uncertainties of the financial markets, Havertons had changed hands, swallowed up by a much larger player in the insurance hierarchy. Ever since then office tensions had risen. Everyone was worried that jobs would be shed and Elinor was equally afraid that the new ownership would close the crèche as a cost-cutting measure.

When Elinor arrived at her desk, the buzz in the accounts department was unusually loud. 'What's all the racket about?' she asked her neighbour.

'The CEO of RS Industries is paying us a personal visit today. The big bosses are hyper at only getting a few hours' notice.'

Just over an hour later Elinor was summoned to her manager's office and she was only a little anxious as to the cause.

'Miss Leslie,' Daniel Harper greeted her with a frown, using the surname she had assumed when she'd left Jasim. 'You're to go up to the top floor immediately and present yourself at Executive Reception.'

Elinor looped a straying auburn curl back behind a delicate ear and murmured uncertainly, 'Am I allowed to ask why?'

Daniel sighed. 'You can ask but I can't answer you. Your presence has been requested upstairs and I'm afraid that's all I know about the matter.'

Made uneasy by his perplexity and concerned that somehow she had got into trouble, for she had never before been on the executive floor, Elinor headed for the lift. As she was whirred up several floors she reminded herself that her recent appraisal had rated her well for her diligence. She studied her reflection in the shiny stainless-steel wall, wondering if she should have taken a moment to tidy her hair, for her rebellious curls were always trying to escape confinement. Her calf-length grey skirt and white ruffled blouse were unexciting, but when she had begun putting together an office wardrobe she had found it easiest to ring the changes by sticking to plain base colours.

In the act of walking towards the reception area she centred her attention on the group of men already standing there. She recognised the MD of Havertons first, a tall toothy man with thinning hair and an anxious expression. Only as she drew closer did she recognise the bold classic profile of the even taller male to one side of the MD and her footsteps faltered. Shock washed over her like a drowning tidal wave. Her skin turned clammy and broke out in goose bumps. It was Jasim! Yet she fought the conviction, reasoning that such a coincidence was so unlikely that she *had* to be mistaken.

But when he turned his arrogant dark head in her direction there could no longer be any room for doubt. Her heart started to thump frighteningly fast, adrenalin pumping up her responses as apprehension threatened to overwhelm her. Sheathed in a faultlessly cut black business suit that was the last word in tailored sophistication, Jasim looked spectacularly handsome and stylish. For a split second, Elinor collided with deep-set dark golden eyes that glittered like fire in the impassive planes of his bronzed face. Her throat closed over. Yet, even on edge with stress and trepidation, she could not suppress the leap of her senses in response to his presence. Although she hated him she could not be impervious to his charisma or the simple fact that, from the crown of his proud dark head to the soles of his almost certainly handmade shoes, he was still indisputably the most gorgeous guy she had ever seen in human form.

'Miss Leslie?' The MD addressed her as affably as though they were friends instead of complete strangers. 'I believe you have a child in the crèche here. His Royal Highness, Prince Jasim, the CEO of our parent company, has requested a tour of the crèche facility in your company.'

So determined was Elinor not to betray her nervous tension that she automatically half extended a hand in polite greeting and then let it drop back to her side again as Jasim's stunning eyes smouldered like punitive flames over her. She sensed the anger restrained by his fierce self-discipline and, since she considered herself to be just as much an injured party as he evidently did, she lifted her head high and thrust up her chin in challenge.

Jasim was inflamed by that defiant look in her bright

green eyes. After what she had done, how dared she challenge him? How dared she masquerade under a name that was not hers and stroll up to him without so much as a womanly blush on her cheeks? What a performer she was! A woman without a drop of shame over her conduct, he reflected bitterly, repressing his bitter anger with difficulty, for she had run away with his son and kept him apart from him.

'Miss Leslie,' he breathed in gritty acknowledgement, his veiled gaze scanning her flawless features and lingering for several taut seconds before lowering to the cushioned swell of her full lower lip. His memory of the taste of her sent a current of electrifying erotic intent straight to his groin and he set his teeth together, infuriated by that unruly physical reaction.

An aide already had the lift waiting for them. Elinor stepped in again, her mind a hive of bemused activity. 'CEO of our parent company,' the managing director had said. *Jasim?* Did that mean that his was the visit that had got everyone in such a tizzy? And that he was the new owner of Havertons and also the CEO of RS Industries? And if it did, did that mean he had *accidentally* contrived to take over the company that employed her? Elinor did not believe in ridiculous coincidences. In her opinion if something looked suspicious, it probably was. The silence sizzled with undertones. Her tummy sank like a stone while the lift travelled downward. Sami was surely the only reason that would lead Jasim into professing an interest in seeing the crèche, she reasoned fearfully. He had to know that their son was there…he wanted to see Sami.

'I wasn't expecting our next meeting to happen in a public

place,' Elinor remarked, only recalling the two bulky body-guards occupying the lift with them after she had spoken.

'Be grateful for it,' Jasim breathed with roughened bite.

The raw anger in his hard gaze sent a spooky chill down her taut spinal cord. Even so, Elinor could not resist shrugging a slim shoulder in dismissal of that masculine warning. 'We have nothing to say to each other.'

'On the contrary,' Jasim contradicted icily. 'I have a great deal to say to you.'

Infuriated by his patronising tone of address, Elinor breathed in deep, because while she could easily have matched that assurance she was not looking forward to the inevitable confrontation. He was a rat, a dangerously clever, unfeeling and unscrupulous rat, who had brazenly played on her trust and naivety to get her into bed. Her face burned at the humiliating recollection of what an easy touch she had proved to be. At the same time, however, there was one subject that she felt she had to tackle.

'I was very sorry to hear of your brother's death,' she remarked stiffly, recollecting how shocked and upset she had been to read about Prince Murad's sudden death from a heart attack the previous year.

'We were all shocked. Murad had a health check every few months but nothing irregular was ever identified,' Jasim proffered grimly. 'He was a bitter loss.'

Elinor had felt sad when she had read about the older man's demise and then rather guilty when, soon afterwards, she had gone out and sold the diamond engagement ring she had inherited from her mother, Rose. The eye-watering value of the ring had astonished her and she had used the proceeds to buy the flat she currently shared with her friends. The security of a decent roof over her head had made single parenthood seem less intimidating.

She entered the crèche at a smart pace. The manageress, Olivia, had been pre-warned and was waiting at the entrance for them. Jasim was quick to engage her in well-bred conversation.

Elinor, however, was in panic mode. Spotting Sami reclining in a baby seat and playing with a brightly coloured toy, Elinor went straight to her son and released his safety belt to lift him. Sami chortled with pleasure and opened his arms wide. Anxious tears prickled the back of Elinor's eyes as her arms closed round his precious weight and warmth.

'Elinor…' Olivia called. 'You can go into my office if you like.'

The older woman's eyes were bright with curiosity. Elinor evaded them, pacing back towards Jasim's tall, darkly handsome figure with extreme reluctance. But he wasn't looking at her. His entire attention was welded to the little boy she held and when she got close he startled her by reaching out. 'Let me hold my son,' he urged with unconcealed impatience.

Elinor saw comprehension fly into Olivia's face, only to unleash an even more avid expression of curiosity. Although she had no desire to let go of Sami, she did not want to risk a scene that might upset her child. And Jasim, she registered as she clashed with his expectant dark eyes, was very likely to fight hard for what he wanted. She waited until she was inside the older woman's office before handing Sami over. Jasim's hand inadvertently brushed her arm and she was so aware of him that she was vaguely surprised not to see fingerprints left behind on her skin. Jasim clasped the little boy with care and held him out to examine, keenly scrutinising every inch of Sami's fearless little face. There was a quality of bemusement and wonder in Jasim's stern gaze that unsettled Elinor and made her feel very uncomfortable. Brown eyes sparkling, Sami smiled at Jasim and made no objection when Jasim brought him closer. His father's confident handling made it clear that he was no stranger to young children.

'He is the only boy born in my family for many years,' Jasim said gravely. 'It is a crime that we have been unable to celebrate his birth.'

A...*crime*? Well, that was certainly letting her know how he felt and more than hinted at the weight of blame he intended to foist on her. Resentment stirred like a knife twisting inside her and her soft mouth compressed into a mutinous line. 'If Sami wasn't present, I would tell you exactly how I feel about you—'

Jasim elevated a sardonic ebony brow, for he was astonished by the attack. 'Do you think I am interested in such a dialogue after you walked out on our marriage?'

An involuntary sour laugh fell from Elinor's lips. 'Marriage?' she repeated drily. '*What* marriage? It was as much of a fake and an insult as your supposed interest in m—'

'Meaning?' Jasim queried, angling his handsome head back as Sami sank an inquisitive little hand into his father's luxuriant cropped black hair and yanked hard.

'Sami, stop that…' Elinor instructed, leaning forward to detach Sami's grasping fingers from his father's hair.

'He can do as he likes with me,' Jasim countered squarely.

Elinor slung her child's father a look of flagrant loathing.

'Like you do? Your brother's wife comes to you with some absurd tale of her husband being led astray by the nanny and you leap right in and seduce me to order? Were you proud of the lines you spun me to get me into bed?' she condemned in a voice that was starting to shake with betraying emotion. 'What sort of a *real* man uses a woman like that? How could you sink that low?'

The healthy glow of his complexion had receded while his fabulous bone structure clenched taut. His dark deep set eyes flared bright as flames and he did not back down an inch. 'You eavesdropped on Yaminah that day. She was hysterical. I did wonder if you had overheard something—'

'I wasn't going to stay with you anyway,' Elinor told him vehemently. 'Not with the way you were treating me! I've got more pride than that, pregnant or otherwise, Your Royal Highness, and the last thing I needed was a reluctant liar of a bridegroom!'

'Silence!' Jasim bit out with ferocious disdain, every inch of his rigid bearing telegraphing his outrage at the abuse she was unleashing on him. 'I will not tolerate being spoken to like that!'

In the smouldering silence that stretched, Sami suddenly burst into noisy tears and stretched his little arms out pathetically to Elinor for comfort.

'Now look what you've done!' Elinor shot at Jasim furiously as she summarily snatched her son from his grasp. 'You've frightened him.'

'Your lack of control and manners did that,' Jasim contradicted without hesitation.

'*Manners?*' Elinor gasped. 'You can talk about manners after what you did to me?'

'Enough,' Jasim told her with icy restraint. 'I'll see you at the town house at seven this evening. I'll send a car for you.'

Elinor banded both arms round Sami in a protective gesture as she recognised in dismay that he clearly already knew where she lived. 'Don't bother. I won't come.'

'You're my wife,' Jasim breathed in a low-pitched growl.

Elinor spun away from him over to the window. 'We're still married?' she prompted tightly.

'Of course we are still married.' A lean hand curved to her slim shoulder to turn her back to him. Brilliant dark eyes assailed hers with cool purpose while the achingly familiar scent of his citrus-based cologne drifted into her nostrils. 'And I want my wife and my child back.'

'That's out of the question.' Elinor rested her chin on Sami's fluffy black curls and studied Jasim wide-eyed over her child's head because she didn't understand where he was coming from. Why would he say such a thing? He could only be saying it because he wanted Sami. As the silence deepened his shrewd gaze looked directly into hers.

Her mouth ran dry and her heart rate speeded up. Images of the night they had shared infiltrated her mind. Instantly she relived the feel of his lean, bronzed, perfect body, hot and urgent against hers, and the insatiable need he had roused and then satisfied over and over again. Her cheeks burned as her nipples tingled and lengthened beneath her clothing and a sensation like warm honey flowed between her thighs.

The atmosphere was thick with sensual tension. Jasim was rigid and strenuously resisting a powerful urge to touch her. 'I believe I will also enjoy the wedding night you denied me,' he murmured huskily.

Elinor shut him out by the simple dint of closing her eyes. She was so hot inside her clothes she felt as if she were burning up, but shame that she could be so wanton followed closely in the wake of her body's treacherous responses to him. 'It's not going to happen,' she told him flatly.

Jasim vented an unappreciative laugh and at the sound of it her eyes flew open. 'You're my wife,' he said again, as if that very fact outranked everything else and rendered even her hostility meaningless.

'Hopefully not for much longer,' Elinor traded on the way back into the nursery.

A brooding presence, Jasim watched Elinor tuck Sami back into a baby seat and was then distracted by a nursery assistant while his mother made good her escape.

On the way back to her desk, Elinor was taken aback by the tumult of emotions swamping her and bringing overwrought moisture to her eyes. Dimly she acknowledged that she was very much in shock at Jasim's descent and what it might mean to her and Sami. She had few illusions about the challenge she faced. Jasim was a Crown Prince with friends and contacts in government circles and big business and he enjoyed unlimited wealth and power. He could easily afford to hire top lawyers and launch a custody battle. Whether she liked it or not, she was going to have to share Sami with him.

It was not a compromise she found it easy to even consider, for she hated Jasim bin Hamid al Rais. She had believed herself to be strong and he had made her weak. It was degrading to acknowledge that she could have fallen in love as easily as a daydreaming teenager. But, worst of all, Jasim had cruelly misjudged her moral fibre when he'd given credence to Yaminah's fears that her husband was paying too much attention to the nanny. That was all such ridiculous nonsense, Elinor reflected bitterly. With the exception of their first meeting and their final one at Jasim's apartment, Elinor had never been alone on any other occasion with Prince Murad. Their few conversations had taken place in either his daughter's presence or that of other staff. Nothing said during those brief harmless dialogues had been in any way improper or even mildly flirtatious. Her pride and her principles revolted against the knowledge that Jasim and goodness knew who else had chosen to believe she could be capable of any other kind of behaviour.

But consternation swept away her angry thoughts when she picked up her son at the end of the day. Two bulky bodyguards were now stationed outside the nursery.

Olivia advanced towards Elinor uncomfortably. 'The prince insisted there must be a security presence to watch over his son while he is in our care. He also asked me not to mention their relationship to anyone else. Naturally I'm not going to breathe a word to anyone. I want to keep my job.'

'I'm sure this is just a temporary arrangement,' Elinor declared with more confidence than she felt, particularly when the same men followed her from the nursery and the older one informed her that a car was waiting to take them home. Rather than get involved in a dispute, Elinor acquiesced, but when she finally reached her apartment she was deep in troubled thoughts that were laced with a dangerous urge to simply pull up sticks and flee before Jasim sought to impose any more rules and restrictions.

'My goodness, you're back early,' Alissa commented when she entered the apartment.

And Elinor shocked them both by bursting into floods of tears. She hadn't let herself cry when she'd walked out on her sham of a marriage or during the unhappy aftermath while she struggled to build a new life rather than wallow in pointless regrets and self-pity. She hadn't even let herself cry when she'd given birth to Sami alone. But Jasim had taken her by surprise and all of a sudden and without the slightest warning the world had become an intensely threatening place.

'What on earth has happened? This is not like you at all,' Alissa muttered in dismay just as Lindy came through the front door and demanded to know what was going on.

There and then, Elinor let down her barriers and told the truth about Sami's conception and the secret marriage that had broken her heart and smashed her self-esteem.

'Sami's father is your husband? And a prince? Does that mean Sami is a prince as well?' Alissa enquired in a daze.

'I haven't a clue.' Elinor blew her nose and lifted her head again. 'About the only thing I do know is that I couldn't face going on the run with Sami—it wouldn't be fair to him.'

'Of course, you're not going to do anything daft like that,' Lindy interposed. 'That's only your panic talking.'

'I want a divorce. I assumed that Jasim would already have taken care of that!' Elinor erupted in a helpless surge of resentment over that fact.

'You can discuss that with him tonight,' Lindy replied.

Alissa frowned. 'Shouldn't you at least *try* being married for Sami's sake ? I mean, what was the point of getting married in the first place?'

Elinor paled before that uncompromisingly direct enquiry. 'Everything changed the minute I heard Jasim talking to Yaminah—'

'Basically I think you only really heard Yaminah raving and what she said could well be hogwash,' Lindy commented. 'Anyway, don't you think that the idea that Jasim deliberately set out to seduce you is a bit, well…improbable?'

Alissa nodded quiet agreement with the other woman's assessment. 'You're a very beautiful girl, Elinor. It's more likely that Jasim was simply attracted to you and the relationship was ruined by you falling pregnant when you had had virtually no time together as a couple. So dealing with the pregnancy took centre stage. Whatever you say about Jasim, he was very keen to stand by you and support you.'

Elinor groaned out loud and raked a frustrated hand through the auburn curls on her brow, her green eyes clouded by the growing confusion that had replaced her earlier certainty. 'You two have a totally different take on the whole situation.'

Lindy laughed. 'Of course we do. We're not personally involved and we're being wise after the fact, which is always easier. But I do think Jasim sounds like the sort of guy who might have deserved more of a chance than you were willing to give him.'

Elinor didn't want to hear assurances of that nature, particularly from Lindy, who always saw the best in people and invariably argued on the side of kindness and common sense.

'I also think…' the more shy and less outspoken Alissa ventured, 'that you need to make allowances for the fact that you didn't marry into an ordinary family—'

'Yes,' Lindy chipped in with her agreement. 'They're

fabulously wealthy and royal, and Sami isn't just an ordinary little boy either if he's in the line of accession to the throne. So how can you possibly expect to keep him to yourself?'

After that conversation Elinor had plenty to think about. She was in shock at an unbiased view of events that was very much different from her own. She wondered if she had been guilty of licking her wounds in silence for too long and if, during that process, her decisions had been unduly influenced by her bitterness, hurt and resentment. Had she overreacted on her wedding day? Should she have confronted Jasim there and then?

Those were the questions Elinor was tormenting herself with while she showered and changed. Shortly after she had bathed and fed Sami and left him in Alissa's care for the evening, the car arrived to collect her. Casually and comfortably dressed in black leggings and a colourful purple top that finished mid-thigh, she climbed into the limo and breathed in deep. One way or another she would sort everything out and *without* getting upset. After all, it was eighteen months since their disastrous wedding and it was time she rose above resentment and wounded pride and moved on, she told herself squarely.

CHAPTER FIVE

JASIM, on the other hand, was not in the mood to move on anywhere. The past still had too strong a hold on him and his estranged wife's dismissive approach to him earlier that day had outraged him. He would not have cared to relive the eighteen months of hell that her disappearance had put him through. A male who had long prided himself on his discipline and equanimity, Jasim could not comprehend why he was suddenly suffering from fierce surges of pure caustic rage.

When Elinor walked into the drawing room at the town house, Jasim was immediately struck by only one fact. 'Where is my son?' he demanded.

'I didn't bring Sami. I left him with my flatmate.'

'Didn't it occur to you that I would want to see him again?' The lean bronzed angel's face that had so often haunted her dreams was taut with annoyance. Jasim settled censorious dark eyes on her slender figure. She was dressed like a teenager, he thought impatiently, his attention lingering on the skin-tight leggings that defined her long coltish legs, shapely knees and slim supple thighs and the bright top that revealed the tantalising valley between her high, full breasts. Perfect breasts, he recalled, and his mind was suddenly awash with detailed erotic images, which had a predictable effect on his libido and only contrived to set his temper even more on edge.

Immediately on the defensive and responding to the smouldering atmosphere, Elinor blanked out his tall, powerful presence as much as possible because she hated the reality that she still found him wildly attractive. And, even as she stood there infuriated by his attitude, her mouth was dry and her pulses were quickening in treacherous response to his proximity.

'Why didn't you bring our son?' Jasim pressed.

Elinor bridled at the tone he employed, which suggested that he was dealing with someone rather slow on the uptake. 'There's too much tension between us. I didn't want to plunge Sami into the middle of another argument.'

'I have a nurse here ready to take care of him.'

The fact that Jasim was already thinking ahead to make childcare arrangements on Sami's behalf totally unnerved Elinor and roused her protective instincts. 'I wouldn't want Sami to be with a stranger—'

'Thanks to your selfishness, my entire family and I are strangers to Sami—are we *all* to be excluded from knowing him on that basis?' Jasim slung at her with biting derision.

Elinor did not appreciate being called selfish and she flashed him an accusing look. 'You're the one who created this situation.'

'How so? I made you my wife in good faith.'

'I don't accept that. I heard Yaminah talking,' Elinor reminded him with spirit while she noted the black density of the eyelashes that enhanced his stunning dark golden eyes. 'She got some nonsensical idea in her head that I was after her husband and that he was interested in me. Her suspicions were completely without foundation.'

'When my late brother gave you a ring that was a family heirloom worth a fortune, he made his interest in you *very* clear,' Jasim condemned, a slight tremor rippling through his lean, powerful frame as he recalled his repugnance at that more recent discovery. In his eyes that discovery had delivered a damning indictment of Elinor's morals. Yaminah's fear that she might lose her husband to the nanny had been soundly based in fact, for Murad would never have given a ring from the royal jewellery collection to a woman he only planned to have an affair with.

At his comeback, Elinor's eyes had flown wide in dismay and she swallowed awkwardly. 'How did you find out about that ring?'

'How do you think I finally found you?' Jasim demanded with a sardonic laugh. 'The inside of the ring was stamped with symbols that marked its history and ownership. When you sold it—for a tithe of its true worth—it eventually passed into the hands of a jeweller who recognised its provenance and importance. He contacted our embassy to make discreet enquiries.'

Elinor was stunned that the diamond ring she had sold had ultimately led to her being tracked down. 'Your brother did not give that ring to me personally. He gave it to my mother,' she protested in a rush.

Jasim's ebony brows pleated. 'Your *mother*?' he jibed.

'When my mother was a student, Murad fell in love with

her and asked her to marry him. Your father, however, wouldn't allow it and they broke up. Your brother wouldn't take the ring back.'

Jasim was still frowning, his incredulity palpable. 'If you are telling me the truth, it is not a story that I have ever heard before—'

'Probably because it happened over thirty years ago!' Elinor interrupted without apology. 'But the point is that it *did* happen and a couple of years ago, when he was re-visiting his old college at Oxford, Murad decided to look my mother up again. He had heard that she had married a professor in the history faculty, but not that she had died several years ago.'

'Naturally, I will check this extraordinary story out.' But Jasim remained resolutely unimpressed by the past connection she was suddenly proclaiming between their families. It stuck him as fanciful and unlikely in the extreme.

'Your brother simply turned up at my home and I had to tell him that my mother had passed away. He was very disappointed and sad and I asked him in. When he found out that I was a newly qualified nanny, he urged me to apply for the job of looking after his daughter.'

'Why didn't you share these facts with me before?'

Her gleaming green gaze narrowed, Elinor searched his darkly handsome features, absently admiring his classic bone structure. 'Your brother asked me not to mention the connection to anyone in case it was misinterpreted. And when I met you I had no idea that you were suspicious of what my relationship with him might be. You *did* think he had some sort of inappropriate interest in me when you came to Woodrow, didn't you?'

His brilliant eyes were level and unapologetic and his strong jaw line had an aggressive slant. 'It was possible. In the past Murad had indulged in a series of extra-marital diversions.'

'Well, I wasn't one of them!' Elinor lifted her head high, defying his unimpressed appraisal. 'For goodness' sake, you know you were the first man I slept with!'

Jasim shifted a broad shoulder in a manner of dismissive assent that incensed her.

'What the heck is it going to take for me to convince you that my dealings with your brother were entirely platonic?' she threw at him furiously.

'We are neither of us stupid. A clever ambitious woman would have been careful not to offer intimacy in advance of a more serious and profitable relationship,' Jasim pointed out flatly.

That alternative interpretation of the facts was the last straw for Elinor's temper. Focusing indignant emerald-green eyes on him, she snapped, 'How *dare* you insinuate that I was some gold-digging schemer ready to break up another woman's marriage? I hate you...I can't wait until we get a divorce!'

'You'll have to wait a long time. I have no intention of giving you a divorce,' Jasim informed her stonily. 'I want you to live up to the promises you made when you went through that marriage ceremony with me.'

Elinor folded her arms in a sharply defensive movement. She was livid at the manner in which he was standing in judgement over her while refusing to believe her side of the story. 'No way!' she told him baldly.

Jasim lifted his imperious dark head high and rested his

attention on the ripe curve of her soft pink lips. 'I am prepared to stand by my promises and give you another chance.'

'I don't *want* another chance from you!' she bawled at him, her pride bristling in revolt from that condescending offer. 'Do I strike you as that much of a doormat?'

'Sami needs both of us. He also needs to be living in Quaram where he can learn the language and culture of the people whom he will one day rule. That requirement is not negotiable,' Jasim imparted with steely cool.

Elinor's response to feeling threatened was to go straight into attack and she took an angry step forward. 'I'm not prepared to live abroad and certainly not with you, so we have a major problem. I don't trust you…I don't trust you at all!' she blazed back at him without hesitation.

Jasim closed lean brown fingers round her wrist and tugged her to him. His sardonic dark golden gaze flared down into hers. 'You may not trust me but you still can't take your eyes off me.'

'That's a ridiculous lie—how can you be so vain?' Elinor raged, although a tide of colour had flooded her cheeks and sexual awareness was like a firework flaring through her body, sending a chain reaction through every skin cell. Memory was taking her back and stealing away her resistance; it was a very long time since that night of passion.

He closed an assured hand into the tumble of her Titian curls and tilted her face up to his. Scorching eyes raked over her and she trembled, maddeningly conscious of the tightening of her nipples and the surge of heat and moisture at the apex of her thighs. At an almost scornfully slow pace, he tugged her up against him and traced the fullness of her lower lip with his fingertip. When that finger slid between her parted lips it was the most erotic thing she had ever known and the tightening knot low in her pelvis made her press her thighs together in an effort to contain the tingling sensation of immediate arousal.

The silence sizzled as their eyes collided. He kissed her with smouldering sexual skill and she quivered violently, fighting the tiny ripples of arousal currenting through her body with all her might. His tongue delved deep in a sweeping reconnaissance that tensed her every muscle.

'Am I vain?' Jasim husked against the swollen pink contours of her mouth. 'I don't think so. I excite you.'

And that was the taunt that finally gave her the strength to do what she should have done much sooner and push him away from her. On legs that were distinctly unsteady she stalked over to the window, where she stood struggling to catch her breath. But he had hit her problem right on the head, she acknowledged with bitter self-loathing. *Excitement.* He filled her with it and seduced her with it. She could not resist that wild charge of electrifying excitement or the explosive high ignited by his touch. Even standing there with her hands curled into defensive fists, she could still feel the magnetic pull of him and the painful aftermath of a desire that had to go unsatisfied.

'Have you nothing to say?' Jasim drawled smooth as silk.

Affronted by the knowledge that he knew her weakness, Elinor spun back to face him, a hectic flush staining her delicate cheekbones. 'Sami is much more important to me than excitement!'

'If that is true, I honour you for it, but you should also have the ability to foresee our son's needs both now and in the future,' Jasim asserted. 'As a boy grows he will need a father more and more. All of my family will cherish him, as will I—'

Elinor tore her attention from him. 'I don't want to be your wife.'

'But you *are* and for Sami's sake that must not change. A divorce would create a great scandal in my country and would be a lifelong source of shame and embarrassment for our son.'

At that news, her heart sank inside her. She could feel the bars of a steel cage of restraint tightening round her. If Sami's standing could be damaged by their divorce how could she push for one? Could she be that selfish? Could she think only of what she wanted now at this point in time? Or should she be willing to compromise? From below her feathery lashes she studied Jasim, her gaze wandering over the proud slash of his bold cheekbones, the classic hollows beneath, the arrogant jut of his narrow-bladed nose segueing down into the chiselled perfection of his well-formed mouth. She remembered the silky feel of his hair beneath her fingertips, and, more dangerously, the heat and urgency of his strong lean body against hers. She tensed in rejection.

He was gorgeous and she was married to him, but he was also utterly without conscience and ruthless when it came to getting what he wanted. A chill like an ice cube melting settled low in Elinor's stomach. He wanted Sami…

CHAPTER SIX

THE following afternoon Jasim strode out of the office he had picked to work in for its proximity to the nursery. He paused by the glass barrier to look down into the crèche on the floor below.

Sami was in a high chair just within his father's view, his dark curly head turned towards an assistant, who was serving snacks. Jasim's ebony brows drew together in a frown. His son appeared to spend too much of the day strapped into seats and play equipment like a miniature prisoner in perpetual physical restraint. He was safe but bored, his freedom to explore severely curtailed, and all elements of fun and even learning denied him by such a restrictive care regime.

A troubled light in his keen gaze, Jasim reluctantly recalled his own desolate childhood. He had never known his mother and he had not even been able to put a face to his father until he was over ten years old. Nobody had ever swept Jasim up in a hug when he cried; the guidelines for his upbringing had been exceedingly strict. He had been schooled from an early age at a military academy abroad where he had learned rigid discipline and self-command as well as how to handle the beatings and pranks that the younger boys endured behind the backs of the staff. His father had been a distant royal figure of unimaginable power who had censured his second son at a distance through the medium of an aide whenever school reports had showed Jasim to be anything less than top-notch at any academic subject or sport. Thankfully, Jasim had been born both clever and athletic and he had excelled. Even so, his many achievements had won him neither praise nor affection.

Having suffered such a tough upbringing, Jasim was eager to ensure a very different childhood for his son. In Quaram, Sami would not spend a good part of his day anchored in one place. He would be free to roam with attentive staff in tow to ensure he didn't get hurt. He watched as Sami lifted his toast and then, having knocked his elbow on a toy on the tray, accidentally dropped it again. The bread fell to the floor and Sami strained and strained a short arm to recapture it. Sami looked around then, visibly seeking attention, but no one appeared to notice what had happened. Finally the little boy flung back his curly head and started to cry.

Jasim found himself on the stairs without remembering the decision to go there. Huge fat tears were now rolling down Sami's red cheeks. Never had a baby looked so wretched to Jasim. An assistant gave Sami a toy in an attempt to distract him. Sami flung it away in an expression of hot temper that surprised his father. But the little boy's anger was short-lived. From the foot of the stairs, Jasim saw tears overflowing again from Sami's big brown eyes while tempestuous sobs shook his solid little body. His son was the very picture of misery and nobody was even trying to comfort him. Several children were in need of attention and it was a challenge for the assistants to take care of them all. Jasim could not bear to stand by and do nothing for his son. He was pierced to the heart by the sight of Sami's unhappiness. He strode into the nursery, sidestepped the startled manageress, and headed straight for Sami. It took the matter of a moment to release the sobbing baby from his restraints and hoist him up into his arms. Sami clung to his father and continued to sob inconsolably.

'I am taking my son home early,' Jasim informed the manageress.

He lifted another piece of toast from the plate abandoned nearby and presented Sami with it. The child stopped mid-howl, grasped the bread frantically between his short fingers and began to cram it into his mouth. He behaved as if he'd been brought up in a Stone-Age cave, Jasim reflected in appalled wonderment, his immaculate business suit and even his hair bespattered with crumbs.

Jasim emerged with Sami from the nursery to find his security team and his aides awaiting his next move in frank astonishment. Any kind of hands-on parenting in the Rais masculine bloodline had never, ever featured in the annals of the family. But Jasim, in delighted receipt of Sami's beaming two-toothed gummy smile of gratitude, was experiencing an enlightening high of relief and accomplishment and he was impervious to his shocked and uncomprehending audience.

Elinor worked doggedly through the afternoon, in spite of the fact that she was terrified that she would simply fall asleep over her computer. She had barely slept the night before and had awakened with a headache. It had taken great motivation to go to work and the doubts that had kept her awake during the night continued to interfere with her concentration. She continued to torment herself with questions that she couldn't answer. Did she owe it to Sami to give her marriage a second chance? Was that the best thing she could do for her son? Sacrifice her needs and wishes in favour of his taking his rightful place as an heir to the throne of Quaram? For how long would Jasim stay in London?

There was little point bewailing what could not be changed now, she told herself heavily. Jasim was who he was—as was Sami. But she loved Sami to the very depths of her soul and feared his father's interference in their lives. Olivia, thankfully, had kept the secret of Sami's paternity. A few people had asked Elinor what Prince Jasim was like and why he had been so keen to view the crèche, but nobody suspected that Elinor had been selected as guide for any reason other than that she had a child using the facility.

At finishing time, Elinor caught the lift down to the ground floor. She was relieved to see that Jasim's security guards were no longer stationed outside the crèche. Had he realised how much comment their presence would cause once enough people noticed them? Walking through the door, her eyes automatically scanning the room for Sami, Elinor stiffened at the look of surprise in Olivia's face.

'What's wrong?' Elinor questioned.

The older woman drew her off to one side. 'The prince took Sami after lunch. I assumed you knew,' she admitted worriedly.

'*Took*…him?' Elinor queried, the words slurring together on a tongue that suddenly felt too clumsy to vocalise words.

'He said he was taking him home.'

Perspiration beading her pale brow and gripped by complete overwhelming panic, Elinor pictured desert sand dunes and the power in her legs gave at the same time as the world around her folded into darkness. For the first time in her life, Elinor fainted. She recovered consciousness to find that she was in a seat with her head pushed down low.

'Take a deep breath,' Olivia was urging her in a stressed undertone. 'Elinor, I assumed it was okay because he's Sami's father.'

'Yes.' Elinor recalled that conversation in the older woman's presence and snatched in a shuddering breath. With all her courage she fought off the nausea and the dread that were making it impossible for her to think normally. Would Jasim just snatch Sami and fly him out to Quaram? She suspected that her estranged husband was heartless enough to stake his claim in an aggressive manner. Possession, after all, was nine-tenths of the law and who knew what the law on child custody was in Quaram? She was willing to bet that it would favour the ruling family rather than a runaway wife.

Somehow in the background people were talking and she struggled to regain her focus. 'Are you feeling any better?' Olivia prompted hopefully. 'The prince has sent a car to collect you.'

Elinor glanced up and saw two of Jasim's security team awaiting her at the door and the sense of relief that swept her then was so immense that she felt weak enough to pass out again. Jasim would scarcely have sent a car for her if he had removed Sami from the country behind her back. But how dared he have taken Sami from the crèche without telling her? She was outraged by an act that had reduced her to a state of sick, almost petrified, fear and an even more terrifying awareness of her own impotence. If Jasim decided to fight dirty rather than talk, what was she going to do to hold her own?

Her nerves honed to a fine edge of impatience, Elinor stalked into the book-lined luxury of Jasim's library where he greeted her from behind his desk. She noted in some dismay that Sami wasn't in the room.

'Where's Sami?'

'He's asleep upstairs. I will take you to him—'

'I want to speak to you first.' Elinor wasted no time being relieved that her son was still safe in London. She got between Jasim and the door and stared up at him, apprehension and resentment combining in a fiery combustible mix inside her. Indisputably sexy blue-black stubble was beginning to shadow his strong jaw line and roughen the skin round his handsome mouth. Tipping her head back even further, she clashed with the cool topaz challenge of his level gaze.

'You had no right to remove Sami from the nursery without my permission!' she condemned forcefully.

Ice chilled his hard dark gaze. 'I am his father. I will act as I think best. Sami was upset and he was not receiving the level of care that I would expect. That is why I removed him from the nursery,' he responded with measured calm.

'You had no right. Have you any idea how I felt when I found out you'd taken him?' she demanded half an octave higher. 'I was afraid you'd taken him back to Quaram and I'd never see him again.'

'Fortunately for you I have more scruples than you have,' Jasim said drily. 'I wouldn't do that to you or Sami.'

'But you should have warned me of your plans.'

'I did try to phone you.'

Elinor dug out her mobile and switched it on, seeing that several missed calls had been logged. Some of her anger ebbed away. He had at least tried to contact her.

But Jasim had not finished with her yet. 'As for seeking your permission, why should I have done? Did you seek my permission when you deprived me of all contact with my child for almost a year?'

Elinor moved restively away from the door, her angry colour dulling as he hit her on her weakest flank. 'That was different. I had good reason for acting as I did then.'

'No, you did *not*,' Jasim countered without hesitation, his assurance in contradicting her like a slap in the face. 'Only if I was an abusive parent would you have had an acceptable excuse for ignoring my parental rights. When you walked out on our marriage on our wedding day, you were thinking only of yourself and how you felt at that moment. I refuse to credit that you considered how that decision would affect our child or me.'

Consternation at the accuracy of his accusations increased Elinor's tension. She had backed away as far as the edge of his desk and she leant back against it now for added support. When she looked at him, however, her anger was like a hard bitter knot inside her. His face still had a devastating beauty that cut through her defences. But, even more disturbingly, Jasim also had the proud demeanour and aloofness of a statue set in bronze. He seemed untouched by events that had torn her apart. His self-containment mocked her emotional turmoil and she hated him for it.

Was there any way of overcoming the sense of humiliation and shame she always felt in his presence? Once she had fallen head over heels in love with him and made no attempt to hide it. She had surrendered her virginity within hours of meeting him and that knowledge still marked her as painfully as a whiplash on tender skin. She had failed her own standards and made a fool of herself and those were truths that replayed constantly in her mind when he was around, reviving unwelcome memories of her weakness.

'How did you expect me to feel after I heard what Yaminah had to say to you on our wedding day?' Elinor demanded fiercely. 'Was I really supposed to swallow my disgust at the way you had taken advantage of me to think about whether or not you would make a good father?'

'I didn't take advantage of you. Clearly you were incapable of judging the most important issues at stake. You are too keen to remind me of my supposed sins while ignoring your own,' Jasim intoned with sardonic cool. 'When you staged your vanishing act you put me in an appalling position with my family. I had to tell my father that I had married you but I was unable to produce my wife.'

'Any woman would have walked out after that ghastly wedding!' Elinor launched at him helplessly. 'You hated every minute of it and you couldn't even be bothered to hide how you felt!'

His dark eyes were cold as black ice. 'I was conscious that I was acting without my father's knowledge and I was ashamed of the fact.'

'I offered you a get-out clause before the ceremony even began,' Elinor reminded him with spirit.

'Empty useless words,' Jasim derided. 'To deny our child the status of legitimate birth would have condemned him to a lifetime in the shadows. He could never have known my family or claimed his rightful place among them. I could not have lived with that option. Presenting my elderly father with our marriage as a fait accompli was a lesser evil but not an act I can take pride in.'

'Of course it would have helped had you simply explained all that to me at the time,' Elinor argued bitterly. 'But you kept me at as much distance as you might have kept a stranger, so I'm not about to apologise for the fact that I had no idea what was going on behind the scenes! You showed no consideration to how I felt and I am never, ever going to forgive you for that!'

Troubled by her continuing defiance on the score of an event that he considered trivial, Jasim surveyed her. Why were women so irrational? A wedding was a wedding; they were still married, still legally husband and wife. Anger had banished her pallor, accentuating the jade-green brilliance of her eyes against her flawless skin. Her tumbled Titian curls were equally vibrant and drew his eyes against his will. His gaze dropped to the dewy pout of her mouth and then to the tantalising swell of the lush breasts that stirred with her ragged breathing. Strong and insistent desire surged with ravenous force through Jasim's lean, powerful length.

'Don't you dare look at me like that!' Elinor warned him, fully aware of the tension building in the atmosphere and the wicked coil of heat already forming low in her pelvis.

'You're my wife,' Jasim drawled. 'And I haven't been with a woman since I was last with you.'

Elinor was stunned by that information, while the intimacy of the declaration cut through the distance she was trying to achieve and made her face burn with hot colour. She had believed that their marriage was a mere formality on his terms and had not expected him to stay faithful during their separation. Indeed she had assumed he would divorce her. While she had struggled with a body made clumsy and weary by the later stages of pregnancy, she had miserably pictured Jasim wining, dining and bedding more sophisticated women, turning their heads with his charisma as he had once turned hers. The knowledge that he had practised celibacy just as she had was, nonetheless, a sudden source of immense satisfaction to Elinor. It would have been quite a challenge for him to rein in that high voltage sex drive of his, she reflected sourly, reluctantly prompted to recall the one night she had spent with him.

'I knew I'd find you,' Jasim intoned in husky addition.

'I'd like to see Sami now,' Elinor said eagerly, desperate to escape the charged atmosphere and the wickedly potent sexual images she was already struggling to wipe from her thoughts. She wondered if that was what she hated most about Jasim: his ability to transform her into a sexual creature, alien to the sensible self that she had long known and depended on. But her body was indifferent to such fine principles and she was painfully aware of the hollow ache at the heart of her and the slick moisture gathering there in a response that she could not seem to suppress.

Engaged in watching the wild fluctuation of colour in her cheeks, Jasim was amused until he wondered if she was faking a show of shy unease to impress him. After all, a husband who appreciated her would be much more easily manipulated than one who saw through her wiles. But his suspicions about her true nature no longer added up as neatly as they had once done. Surely a gold-digger would never have walked out on a marriage to a male as wealthy as he was and stayed away without failing to launch a lucrative alimony claim? Of course, she had had a very valuable diamond ring to sell, but she had not netted sufficient funds from that to enable her to survive without seeking employment. The modest office job she had taken didn't fit his cynical view of her either, he acknowledged, while he questioned how deep her attachment to Sami really ran. Did she really love his son? Or was Sami simply a weapon to be used?

He accompanied her upstairs to a room outside which a nurse sat on a chair ready to instantly respond to the little boy's first cry. Zahrah's needs had been equally well catered for, Elinor remembered. Sami was fast asleep in an abandoned sprawl. Elinor looked down at her sleeping son with a lump forming in her throat. Sami was unaware of the struggle of wills created by his very existence. The very thought of losing him terrified her. In such a short time Sami had become the centre of her world and the very reason she lived. Her eyes stung and she blinked rapidly. Sami, she was convinced, was infinitely more deserving of her love and loyalty than any man would ever be.

'How can we possibly resolve this?' she asked Jasim painfully.

'We have only two options. I take Sami to Quaram alone or you accompany us there as my wife,' Jasim proffered smoothly, a light hand at her spine urging her back towards the stairs again.

'You believe that those are the *only* options I've got?' Elinor exclaimed in a tone of angry rejection as they reached the hall.

A manservant pressed wide the door of the library where Jasim invited Elinor to take a seat. 'Of course, if you chose to remain in London where you could discreetly lead your own life, I would naturally compensate you for giving Sami into my care. You would be a very wealthy woman,' Jasim informed her, determined to test the level of her attachment to their son.

Elinor glowered at him in disbelief. 'You honestly believe that I might be willing to *sell* my son to you?'

'It's your decision and sell is an unnecessarily emotive word,' Jasim replied softly.

'No, it's a word as offensive as your offer. I gave birth to Sami, I brought him into this world purely because I loved and wanted him. I will never give him up to anybody else's care and, believe me, no amount of money will make me change my mind!' Elinor proclaimed heatedly.

Jasim strode forward and closed his hands round hers. 'I am happy to hear that assurance. Naturally Sami needs his mother. You must come to Quaram with me—'

Elinor winced, her brow furrowing as she tried and failed to slide her hands free of his without making a production out of it. 'Does it have to be *with* you? I mean, maybe I could travel out to Quaram and stay somewhere and you could see Sami as often as you liked—'

Jasim frowned. 'I will not even dignify that foolish suggestion with an answer.'

'Well, if I ask foolish things that irritate you, whose fault is that?' Elinor demanded between gritted teeth. 'You're the guy who set out to charm me and who hauled me off to bed where you didn't use protection!'

'Haven't we got beyond the stage of hurling recriminations yet?' Jasim demanded, smouldering dark golden eyes welded to the bewitching vivacity of her lovely face and the inner glow of emotion that she could not hide. 'Let us leave the anger behind and move forward. I live in the present and when I look at Sami I do *not* see a mistake, I see the future of my family—'

'But what about when you look at *me*?' Elinor slung helplessly. 'I'm a mistake who doesn't belong in your world!'

A lean masculine hand curved to her hip to ease her closer. Against her stomach she felt the hard swell of his erection and the insistent strength of his potent masculinity. '*I* think you belong,' he breathed huskily.

'That's just sex!' Elinor proclaimed, so full of emotion and frustration she could almost have burst into tears. Her heart was pounding, her mouth bone-dry.

Jasim pinned her to him in that intimate connection with impatient hands. She trembled, fighting the magnetic draw of him as well as the treacherous weakness of her own body. Stunning topaz eyes held hers and a breathtakingly beautiful smile tilted his beautiful mouth. 'You like sex too, *aziz*.'

Her skin burned beneath that confident pronouncement and she had to still an instinctive protest. She wanted more from him than his body, and even as she surprised herself by thinking that thought she wondered where her hatred had gone and loathed herself more than she had ever loathed him. 'We would need a lot more than that to make a marriage work,' she said tightly.

'Stay with me tonight,' Jasim urged, his breath stirring the vibrant curls on her pale brow. 'Let's make a new beginning.'

All atingle inside and out and with goose bumps marking her skin in response to the strong deep tone of his rich dark drawl, Elinor pulled free of his hold before her self-control wavered and let her down again. Once burned, twice shy, she rhymed inside her head. Sex was not that important to her, sex could *not* be that important to her that just the sound of his voice sent receptive shivers down her spine. 'That's out of the question.'

'I have to fly home within forty-eight hours,' Jasim imparted gravely. 'My father's health is very poor and I can't stay abroad for much longer. I must have your answer quickly.'

The speed with which he had snapped back into businesslike mode had taken Elinor aback. But then what more had she expected from him? Persuading her to accompany him home to Quaram was an easier option for him in the short term than trying to wrest custody of her child from her. Jasim bin Hamid al Rais was very practical and far from averse to manipulating her into doing his bidding. When he had described Sami as the future of his family she had truly understood the strength of the opposition she was facing. Unfortunately, a reluctant husband willing to offer her a new beginning on the basis of a night of rampant sex wasn't a tempting proposition. At least not to a sensible woman with some pride, Elinor affixed to the stream of her feverish thoughts. She might have made a total idiot of herself over Jasim eighteen months ago, but that should not mean that she had to spend the rest of her life paying for that act of bad judgement.

Resolved to fight for what best suited her needs, Elinor squared her slim shoulders. 'You were educated here in England, weren't you?'

His ebony brows elevated. 'Not fully. I began my education here when I was sixteen.'

'I don't want to be your wife any more than I believe you want me to be your wife,' she declared tightly. 'I have every respect for your background, your family and Sami's importance to you, but I intend to raise my son here in England. When he's older he can make his own decision about where he wants to live.'

Jasim's bone structure had set taut below his bronzed skin and his thickly lashed dark eyes were grave and cold. 'That is not an acceptable arrangement. I may have been educated abroad, but I was born a second son and my upbringing was very different from Murad's. Sami is the firstborn and my heir. I cannot allow you to keep him here.'

Her nerves succumbing to the terrible bite of tension in the air, Elinor was trembling. 'I'm not asking you to *allow* anything, I'm telling you that I do not *want* to live in Quaram!'

His hard gaze glittered gold with anger. 'You will not dictate terms to me. I hold diplomatic status here and I could fly Sami back home today without your permission. It was a courtesy to offer you a choice. Sami is vitally important to the succession and the stability of Quaram and I will not rest until I can bring my son back to my country because that is my duty.'

'Are you threatening me?' Elinor questioned fiercely.

'I am insisting that you consider your position and

Sami's future with simple common sense, rather than through some fluffy veil of foolish emotion and selfishness,' Jasim drawled in a raw tone of contempt. 'Sami will not be accepted as a future ruler if he is a stranger to our people. He cannot learn our culture and language at a distance and still expect to understand our ways and belong. If you deny him that experience, you will make him an outsider.'

Reeling from that crack about fluffy, foolish emotion, Elinor folded her arms in a sharp defensive gesture. 'I truly hate you for putting so much pressure on me!'

'I do what must be done,' Jasim countered with sardonic cool. 'You have to face reality. Sami is *not* an ordinary little boy. Some day he too will have to learn that responsibility goes hand in hand with great position and privilege.'

Elinor was anything but grateful for those home truths. She felt that Jasim had cruelly plunged her into an intolerable situation, where either she sacrificed her own needs or her son's. Was her son ever likely to forgive her if she denied him easy access to his father and his heritage? Separating Sami from a parent who would one day be a King could well foster uncertainties and divisions that would make Sami's life more difficult as an adult. How could she possibly act against what might be Sami's best interests?

'I want to go home now with Sami,' she breathed stiltedly.

A few minutes later she watched as Jasim bent to lift Sami from the cot. Although awake, Sami was still drowsy from his nap and his little face took on a cranky look when he registered the strangeness of his surroundings. Jasim was amazingly gentle with the little boy and Sami slumped against him and rested his heavy head down trustingly on his father's shoulder. 'He's getting to know me,' Jasim remarked with satisfaction.

At that same moment Sami stole his thunder by espying his mother and throwing his arms wide in a demonstration of enthusiastic welcome. In spite of her stress level, Elinor managed to smile and give her son a hug, while Jasim told her about the toast that Sami had dropped at the crèche. His very choice of words helped Elinor to appreciate why he had intervened and removed Sami—'I could not stand to see him cry like that.' Elinor realised then that she was getting to know Jasim as well, or at least another side to him that she could not have dreamt existed. When it came to Sami, it seemed Jasim was anything but cold, detached and harshly judgemental. Elinor wondered with some bitterness how it would feel to have the same power her son had to stir Jasim's emotions.

But, in the absence of that emotion, she had to consider what was best for her son. She recognised that, unless she was prepared to go out on a limb and risk damaging Sami's future prospects in his father's country, she did not have a choice to make. Moving to Quaram was a necessity, not another option.

'If there is no other way and it has to be done for Sami's sake, I will agree to live in Quaram,' Elinor breathed in a driven tone as she reached the foot of the elegant staircase.

'That is the right decision and it will not be one which I give you cause to regret,' Jasim asserted softly.

'You know very well that you might as well have turned a gun on me when you warned me that you could easily have flown Sami out of the country today without me!' Elinor snapped, compressing her soft mouth into an indignant line.

Yet Elinor also appreciated that, although Jasim was a ruthless, heartless rat, she still had unresolved feelings for him, feelings composed of maybe fifty per cent resentment and distrust, forty per cent sexual fascination and ten per cent hope for a fairy-tale happy ending in which he fell madly, deeply, hopelessly in love with her. But, as her late mother had taught her to have little faith in happy endings, she wasn't about to hold her breath on that score.

She went home and drew up lists of things she had to do before she could leave London for Quaram and she sat up late discussing events and making plans with her friends. The next morning she quit her job and Jasim insisted on taking Sami and her shopping for clothing more suited to a hot climate. She was startled by the number of outfits he deemed necessary and increasingly perturbed by his evident knowledge of what women liked in the wardrobe department.

'You've had an awful lot of women in your life, haven't you?' she opined, while he calmly selected garments that were displayed by a team of sales personnel for their appraisal and announced that he thought she suited bright colours like green and blue.

'I have a certain amount of experience,' Jasim responded with measured cool. 'But it would not be appropriate for me to discuss that side of my life with you.'

Her fingers curled into talons, her nails marking her palms with sharp little crescents. She hated the idea of him *ever* having been with another woman and felt sick at the concept of him being intimate with anyone else but her. Registering just how confused her emotions were around him, she felt her discomfiture increase. 'I didn't say I wanted to discuss it precisely. But the way you swept me off my feet—*literally*—at Woodrow the first day we met was educational,' she murmured soft and low. 'With hindsight I can see I was dealing with an expert womaniser.'

'You're entitled to your own opinion on that score,' Jasim remarked without heat, refusing to argue the point in public.

While it was true that Jasim had enjoyed many women, he was not ashamed of the fact. His affairs had always been discreet and conducted on candid terms. He had learned that most women were delighted to give him their company and sexual pleasure in return for a glittering social life and expensive gifts. Sex had never been complicated for him, but he was beginning to suspect that sex within marriage might well prove to be his biggest challenge yet. He glanced at Elinor, noting the tension still etched into her delicate profile. In his extensive experience all women loved to be spoiled. Not unnaturally, he had assumed that a major shopping trip would lift her mood and please her.

But the pursuit had failed to work its usual magic. It was slowly dawning on him that he had very little idea what went on inside Elinor's head. She gave him wildly conflicting signals. What was the matter with her? Why did he please her less than he pleased other women, who were enthralled and eager to reciprocate when he expressed an interest? Why was she sitting beside him watching the parade of beautiful designer garments with the expression of a puritan invited to an orgy? Sudden devilment gleamed in his dark deep-set eyes. If that was her attitude, he should meet her expectations head-on…

Frustration was filling Elinor to overflowing. As usual, Jasim had ignored her questions and slammed a door shut in her face and he was raising barriers to keep her at a distance. He didn't want her to know him any better. Evidently her role was to be more Sami's mother than a wife to Sami's father. It was an assumption that was to take a thorough beating at their next port of call—a highly exclusive lingerie boutique filled with tiny frilly pieces of satin, silk and lace that shocked Elinor to her unadventurous core. While she stood frozen with mortification by his side, Jasim examined what was on offer and made generous selections of frivolous items of underwear that Elinor could not even imagine wearing. She was outraged by his nerve. How dared he make such intimate purchases on her behalf?

Temper bubbling up in her like a natural spring, Elinor dealt him a furious appraisal when they were back inside the limousine.

'I wouldn't be seen dead dressed in underwear of that sort!' she snapped at him.

Unholy amusement turned his dark brown gaze to simmering gold chips of enticement in the lean dark lineaments of his handsome face. 'Such lingerie would certainly provide a novel look for your departure from the world…but I would much prefer to see you wear them while you were very much alive and kicking, so that I could show you my appreciation.'

'Never in this lifetime!' Colour ran like a betraying banner as high as Elinor's hairline as she recoiled from that riposte and the hot masculine appraisal that accompanied it. As if he was already imagining her prancing about a bedroom in those minuscule confections of satin and lace, designed to enhance and display the female body for a man's gratification!

Jasim skated a teasing forefinger down over the back of her tautly clenched hand. 'Never is a long time, *aziz*. Who can tell what the future holds?'

Elinor snatched away her hand. 'Certainly nothing of that nature, I assure you!' she rebutted furiously, squirming from the suspicion that he was accustomed to provocative displays in the bedroom and trying to encourage her to make an effort in the same direction.

Blissfully unaware of the tension in the air, Sami tugged off a sock and chuckled while he explored his bare toes. Elinor compressed her lips. Not for worlds would she have admitted that the promise of Jasim's appreciation lit a wicked little flame of longing inside her, while the prospect of dressing down in wispy nothings for his benefit had a decadent allure that carried sudden shocking appeal for her starved senses.

Instead she sensibly concentrated her mind on the packing she still had to do and the wisdom of getting Sami to bed soon to compensate for the early hour of their departure the following morning. Tomorrow she would be arriving in a foreign country and she knew that she would need all her wits about her as well as a good deal of adaptability to handle that challenge…

CHAPTER SEVEN

'You wish to know what you should wear to meet my father?' Jasim echoed with a frown of surprise. 'He won't take fright at the sight of your legs, if that's what you mean. There is no dress code, although I would aim at the conservative.'

Elinor vanished back into a small cabin on Jasim's private jet where she had been rifling through a suitcase, and wished she had made her mind up about what to wear before she travelled. Jasim certainly wasn't much help! With a sigh she shook out a blue silk dress and jacket, light enough to keep her cool and plain enough in style to suit any occasion. Sami was fast asleep in his sky cot, all the nonsense drummed out of him after an energetic and noisy hour of play with his father. Elinor was still shaken by the recollection of Jasim, careless of the damage he might be causing to his immaculate and beautifully tailored designer suit, getting down on his knees to play hide-and-seek around the seats in the main cabin with his enthusiastic son. It was obvious to her that Jasim already had a huge wow factor for Sami. Without any encouragement from her they were bonding like mad.

The diamond ring on her wedding finger caught her attention and she stiffened. It was the very ring with which Murad had once proposed to her mother, and which she had recently sold. Jasim had returned the magnificent diamond cluster, together with the wedding ring that he had given her, when she'd boarded the jet, insisting that she start wearing both.

'But why?' she had argued, uncomfortable with the engagement ring's sheer screaming opulence and the unhappy history that related it to her mother in her own mind.

'That ring is always worn by the Crown Prince's bride.'

'Your brother didn't give it to his wife,' Elinor could not resist reminding him.

Jasim gave her a grim look. 'But he *should* have done. It was hers by right.'

'You still don't believe what I told you about my mother and Murad, do you?' Elinor prompted tightly.

'I'm sure my father will confirm the story…if it is true,' Jasim completed in a sceptical tone that set her teeth on edge. 'Your own father neglected to mention it.'

Astonished by that casual comment, Elinor snapped, 'When did you meet my father?'

'Soon after you staged your vanishing act. Naturally I traced your father to see if you had been in touch with him.' Jasim recalled the obsessively tidy house and the absence of a single photograph of Elinor. He had not been impressed by the older man's lack of concern for his only child. 'He promised to contact me if he heard from you.'

'My father would never have acknowledged that his first wife enjoyed a romance with one of his students before their marriage. It always annoyed him, particularly as their marriage wasn't very successful. Did he tell you how stupid I was in the academic stakes?'

Jasim froze. 'No—why would he have done?'

'Because I was a major disappointment in that field.'

'When you disappeared, I was worried sick about your welfare,' Jasim admitted flatly. 'Enquiries were made at all the agencies dealing with nannies—'

'While I was pregnant I took an office skills course as retraining. I thought the hours would suit me better after my baby was born. My flatmates became my friends,' she confided. 'Alissa and Lindy were marvellous.'

'I am grateful that you had their support but had you given me the choice,' Jasim breathed, '*I* would have been there for you.'

As the private jet landed Elinor noticed the crowd of people outside the airport. 'Why are all those people standing outside?'

'Our arrival is quite an event. Sami's existence has been formally announced and it is probably safe to say that he is currently the most popular baby in Quaram,' Jasim shared with an amused smile. 'My brother's death was a great shock to everyone and the continuity of the royal line means a great deal to our people.'

Several rows of smartly dressed soldiers teamed with a military band, as well as a smiling collection of dignitaries, greeted them on their descent from the plane. A stirring musical score backed the formal welcome while just about everyone craned their necks to get a look at the baby in Elinor's arms. Rested from his nap, Sami, his big brown eyes sparkling, was looking around with great interest. From a polite distance and only at an affirmative nod from Jasim, cameras flashed to capture the royal party.

A limousine decorated with flags and ribbons collected them from the runway. Surrounded by police vehicles and preceded by motorcycle outriders, they were wafted from the airport into the city and port of Muscar. Everything was much more contemporary and western than Elinor had somehow expected and she scolded herself for not having done more research on her future home. The wide streets of the city were packed with people waving at the caval-cade as they drove past. Jasim gave her a running commen-tary, directing her attention from the stunning ultra-modern skyscrapers and landscaped green spaces that marked the business district to a conservation area, known as the Old City, where ancient mosques, souks packed with craftsmen and listed buildings were proving a strong draw to the tourist industry.

Soon after he pointed out the main government offices, he added quietly, 'There is the palace.'

The limousine rounded a vast fountain before turning down a huge imposing drive lined with trees. Gardeners were industriously watering the lush lawns. Ahead loomed a vast structure with a very strange-looking wavy roof that was the ultimate in avant-garde design.

'It's…er…very unusual,' Elinor remarked.

'Murad commissioned it and it won several design awards. I think it looks more like a hotel than a home and my father detests it, but this will be our home when we are in Muscar. I still believe that the old palace outside the city could have been successfully renovated.'

A throng of people were waiting outside the imposing

front entrance. Jasim explained that the crowd was composed of the household staff and he took charge of Sami to make it easier for Elinor to get out of the limo. Perspiration beaded her short upper lip at the same moment that she left the coolness of the car. The heat from the sun beat down on her. Within seconds she felt hot and uncomfortable. She was also starting to feel rather overwhelmed by the level of interest and attention and exceedingly nervous about meeting Jasim's father, King Akil. All the women hung over Sami with intense interest and admiration while Jasim translated the appreciative comments. It crossed her mind that Murad would have been less gracious and patient with such humble employees.

It was wonderful to step into the air-conditioned cool and shade of the palace. It was built on a very grand scale: the vast main hallway, walled and floored in pale gleaming marble, would have passed muster at an airport. She lingered below the refreshing blast of the air-conditioning until her silk dress no longer felt as though it was sticking to her skin and she had rediscovered her energy.

Jasim rested questioning dark eyes on her. 'Are you feeling all right?'

'It's incredibly hot out there,' she muttered apologetically, wishing she could retrieve the foolish words almost as soon as she spoke them, for what else could it be but very hot in a desert kingdom in mid-summer?

'It will take time for you to get used to the higher temperatures. Do you want to take a break before you make my father's acquaintance?' Jasim queried.

'No, let's just go ahead now.' Elinor swallowed back the additional words 'and get it over with,' which would have

been less than tactful. But she really wasn't looking forward
to the coming meeting. She was the pregnant foreign wife
Jasim had married behind his father's back, a wife who had
then disappeared for well over a year. She could hardly
expect King Akil to look on a humble nanny with that
history as a worthy match for his only surviving son.

They trekked a long way through the building. Footsteps
and voices echoed to create a noisy backwash of sound.
Eventually they reached a set of double doors presided
over by armed guards. The doors were thrown wide, an announcement made by a hovering manservant, and finally
they were ushered into the royal presence.

Elinor was shocked by her first view of Jasim's father,
who was resting on an old-fashioned chaise longue that
seemed ludicrously out of place against the extreme mo-
dernity of his surroundings. White-haired, clad in traditional robes and as thin as a rail, King Akil was much older
than she had expected and he looked very frail. Formality
ruled as greetings were quietly exchanged and then Jasim
broke the ice by carrying Sami over for his grandfather's
examination. An immediate smile chased the gravity from
the older man's drawn face.

'He is a fine handsome boy with bright eyes,' the King
commented approvingly to Elinor in heavily accented
English. 'You named him after my great-grandfather as
well. You have excellent taste.'

Elinor went pink with pleasure at that unexpected compliment. She had picked her son's name from the potted
history of Quaram on the royal website. Sami's much-
revered ancestor had been a renowned scholar and diplo-
matist credited with uniting his country's warring tribes.

She didn't bother to admit that she had also chosen that particular name because it sounded conveniently like an English one—Sam—that she thought suited her child.

With an imperious dip of his head, the King switched back to his own language and engaged his son in dialogue. As the older man spoke at length and with much solemnity, Jasim seemed to become a good deal tenser and his responses sounded a little terse. Indeed Elinor could not help but notice the rise of dark blood to Jasim's cheekbones and the revealing clenching of his lean brown hands and guessed that it was a challenge for him to retain his temper. Momentarily, the discussion or possibly what could have been an unusually polite dispute halted while a servant was summoned to escort Elinor and Sami from the room.

Full of fierce curiosity though she was, Elinor was nonetheless relieved to escape the uptight atmosphere. Even so, having noticed the extreme formality that reigned between father and a son, she was wondering why the relationship between the King and Jasim was so strained. An instant later, she was furious with herself for being so obtuse. Jasim had married her without his father's permission and her behaviour as a runaway wife could hardly have added gloss to her reputation. Most probably *she* was the root cause of the trouble between the two men!

A strikingly attractive young woman in an elegant black and white designer dress was walking towards her. A diamond brooch that Elinor thought was rather flashy for daytime wear glittered at her neckline. She paused to admire Sami.

'Your son is adorable. I am Laila, Jasim's cousin, and I have been asked to help you settle in,' the brunette announced, pearly white teeth glinting between raspberry glossed lips as she smiled. She had a wonderful head of thick black silky hair that curved round her heart-shaped face and fell down to her shoulders. Almond-shaped, slightly tilted brown eyes gave her an exotic quality and the heavy lids lent her face a voluptuous aspect that Elinor thought men would find highly attractive.

'Thank you. This is a rather new environment for me.'

Laila led her down a corridor. 'I imagine it is and you must be *dreading* making so many adjustments.'

Elinor tensed. 'No, I'm not quite that intimidated,' she parried.

'Life in the royal family can be very constrained,' Laila continued with an expressive roll of her eyes. 'When I'm in London I can do whatever I like, but it's different here. The King runs a very tight ship.'

Reluctant to get involved in that sort of conversation with a stranger, Elinor murmured instead, 'Murad's death must have hit your family very hard.'

'Jasim already enjoys more popular support than his older brother. Murad's extravagance offended many and his reputation was poor. You and the little boy are definitely the jewel in Jasim's future crown,' Laila quipped. 'A son at first go and when you were only just married—congratulations! We're all impressed to death.'

'I didn't appreciate how much Sami would mean to Jasim's family.'

'And our entire country. I believe history is about to be made on your behalf,' Laila remarked. 'I hear Sami is to be shown off to the television cameras and you are to be interviewed. Such media access to the royal family is unprecedented.'

Elinor, suddenly feeling much more daunted by her role as Jasim's wife than she was prepared to admit to her companion, said nothing.

'This is the royal nursery. An entire household has been designed around Sami,' Laila explained, crossing the threshold of a large room crammed with toys and baby equipment. Half a dozen servants streamed through other linked doorways to dip their heads very low while at the same time striving to get a first look at the child in Elinor's arms. 'I won't try to introduce you because few of the staff speak English. Let them look after him while I show you where you will be living.'

Elinor swallowed hard at the challenge of having to hand over care of her son.

'Sami will be spoiled rotten by everyone,' Laila told her with a hint of impatience as Elinor lingered in the doorway. 'Next to your husband he's the most important person in the palace.'

'Aren't you forgetting the King?' Elinor commented.

Laila guided her back into the corridor. 'That my uncle has lived this long is a tribute to his strength of character, but his illness is steadily gaining on him and Jasim is already taking on many of his father's responsibilities.'

Elinor was somewhat unnerved by the suggestion than King Akil was living on borrowed time. She had known the older man was ill but not that there was no hope of recovery. The suggestion that Jasim might soon have to assume the huge responsibility of becoming Quaram's next hereditary ruler brought a sober expression to her face and concern to her thoughtful gaze. Laila led her across a lushly planted courtyard to another building. The front door opened immediately and a servant bowed very low and ushered them in.

'This is where you will live with my cousin. It's very private.' Laila issued instructions to the servant in her own language. 'I've ordered refreshments.'

Elinor walked into a beautifully furnished reception room. Two servants hurried in bearing laden trays. Clearly their arrival had been well prepared for in advance. She sank down into a richly upholstered armchair and her only concern was the distance between the building and Sami's nursery. She knew she was going to have to speak to Jasim because she could see no reason why Sami had to be housed separately. Indeed she was already wondering if it was a deliberate attempt to make her son less dependent on her.

'You're very quiet. Are you nervous at the idea of becoming Queen?' Laila questioned in surprise as delicate glass cups of fragrant tea were offered. 'I wouldn't be—I would love every moment of being queen and, of course, if you hadn't caught Jasim's eye, I might well have been!'

It took a few seconds before the meaning of that startling announcement penetrated Elinor's troubled thoughts about her son. Green eyes widening, she frowned at her companion in some discomfiture. 'Were you and Jasim—?'

Laila sipped her tea and laughed without any sign of animosity. 'It was my uncle's dearest wish that we marry. But, like most men of his generation, Jasim preferred to enjoy being single for as long as he possibly could…and then you came along.'

Elinor gave the gorgeous brunette an uneasy glance. 'Yes.'

'And now my hopes are in the dust.' Laila shifted a

shoulder in a fatalistic shrug. 'Unless, of course, you would be willing to *share* your husband?'

The question was voiced so casually that Elinor could only loose a surprised laugh at what she could only assume was a joke. 'I don't think that would be my style, Laila.'

'But some women *do* share their men in the Middle East and quite happily, believe me,' Laila murmured soft and low. 'A virile man will never complain about having more than one wife to meet his needs and he will be less likely to stray.'

Elinor was so shaken by that revealing little speech that she struggled to absorb it, refusing to credit that the other woman could possibly be suggesting what Elinor was believed she was. Deeply uncomfortable and feeling very much out of her depth, she snatched up a tiny cake from the plate in front of her and began to nibble at it to occupy her hands. She tasted nothing because her taste buds seemed to have gone into hibernation.

'Now I've really shocked you. I'm sorry,' Laila groaned, setting down her tea and rising to her feet in a fluid motion. 'But such arrangements have worked very well for many marriages. You're a foreigner. There is so much you will not be able to share with Jasim. You don't even speak our language. Yaminah would not agree to Murad taking a second wife and their marriage began to fail soon afterwards.'

Green eyes gleaming with a feisty light, Elinor lifted her head high. 'I'm afraid I'll have to take that risk, Laila. I'm a firm believer in the value of monogamy. Jasim is off the market and I have no plans to share him with anyone.'

'And yet there are already rumours within the palace that that is the arrangement which Jasim is hoping you will consent to,' the exotic brunette advanced, her assurance not even slightly dented by Elinor's tart response.

'I'm sure I can rely on you to quash those silly rumours,' Elinor countered firmly, having reached the reluctant conclusion that Jasim's beautiful ambitious cousin was as poisonous as a scorpion. As for her suggestion that Jasim was hoping for a polygamous marriage, that had to be nonsense. Nonsense spouted by a jealous little cat, who had had her calculating eye on Jasim for herself! As Laila took her leave, however, Elinor was already recalling a truly ghastly story that she had once read about an Arab wife whose once happy marriage had been destroyed by a husband who had demanded and exercised the right to take other wives.

Alone, she was given a tour of the house by the senior manservant, Zaid, who spoke excellent English. The house was enormous and she was relieved by the discovery that there was ample space in which to set up a nursery for Sami. The interior, however, was as stark and contemporary as any within the main palace building. The floors were marble and occasionally wood. The windows had blinds rather than drapes. There were entertainment systems everywhere and elaborate switches to control the temperature, the lighting, the blinds and the music. Although a dressing room packed with male apparel was witness to the fact that Jasim lived there, there were no photos or anything more personal lying around. In fact the rooms had all the personality of a bland hotel.

Elinor was freshening up when she heard a door slam shut downstairs. Hurriedly drying her hands, she sped to the top of the stairs. 'Jasim!' she called.

Jasim strode out of the drawing room and looked up at her. His lean strong face was set in harsh lines and he took the stairs two at a time. 'My father expects us to go through another wedding,' he told her grittily.

'Oh, dear. Did you tell him how much you would enjoy going through that experience again?'

There was no answering humour in the angry dark eyes that met hers as he drew level. 'It is not a laughing matter. He does not consider the civil ceremony which we underwent without his agreement to be legal. He has already made all the arrangements for a second ceremony here and we have no choice but to go along with his wishes. It is to take place tomorrow.'

'My word, that's quick. Can we retrieve Sami before then?' Elinor asked.

'Why? Where is our son?'

Elinor explained about the nursery situated deep within the palace.

His ebony brows knit together. 'The household is half a century out of date when it comes to babies.' He pressed a bell in the wall and Zaid reappeared to receive the stream of instructions that Jasim aimed at him. The older man nodded eagerly and sped off. Jasim turned back to Elinor. 'From now on, Sami will sleep in the same quarters as his parents.'

Elinor followed him into the bedroom and watched him discard his jacket. His movements were oddly stiff and constrained, lacking in his usual grace. She studied his grim profile, the strain etching angularity into his classic profile. 'Was this wedding idea the reason you argued with your father?'

'It wasn't an argument—it was a mild difference of

opinion,' Jasim contradicted, unbuttoning his shirt. 'My father has made many plans for us. I am not accustomed to having my life organised for me. After the second wedding, we are to spend a month in seclusion while we become accustomed to being husband and wife.'

Elinor blinked. 'I beg your pardon?'

'Your disappearing act has made my father very nervous about the likely longevity of our marriage,' Jasim explained with an audible edge of derision. 'He believes that a divorce between us would be a disaster for the monarchy. He is convinced that our marriage will only last if I now take a long holiday from my responsibilities to spend time with you and our son.'

Surprised and dismayed by his explanation, Elinor found herself staring as he snaked free of his shirt, revealing a sleek brown torso rippling with whipcord muscle and marked by a black triangle of curls across his powerful pectoral muscles. 'Oh…'

Jasim tossed aside the shirt in a gesture of fuming impatience. 'I don't have time for such self-indulgence. My father is very ill. I am doing what I can to lighten the burden of his duties, but if I am not available he will try to do too much. He is not strong enough to survive another heart attack.'

The anger that she could see repeatedly bubbling up in him was making Elinor feel uneasy, and the atmosphere was explosive. 'Wouldn't he listen to your advice?'

'Obstinacy is a family trait.' Jasim had fallen still and outrage lightened his gaze to scornful accusing gold while he studied her. 'While lying appears to be your fatal flaw and I must be honest—I cannot stand the prospect of living with a liar because it means that you cannot be trusted.'

'Lying?' Elinor repeated in complete bewilderment. 'What are you accusing me of lying about?'

'I checked out your stupid story about a romance between Murad and your late mother. My father had not the slightest idea what I was talking about!' Jasim informed her in a savage undertone. 'My brother had never approached him with a request to marry anyone before he agreed to marry Yaminah.'

Elinor was astonished by that statement. 'But that's not possible. I mean, my mother told me about what happened. It was a major event in her life and she had no reason to lie—'

'*You're* the liar,' Jasim fired back at her with harsh emphasis. 'Why can't you just admit the truth? Murad gave *you* that diamond ring because you had a relationship with him!'

'That's absolutely not true!' Elinor hurled back at him.

In the simmering silence, Jasim yanked off his boxers. A lithe, incredibly male figure, his strong, hard body would have drawn any woman's attention. Elinor's cheeks were very pink. Even in the midst of a row, she found his sleek bronzed nudity an impossible distraction.

'If I didn't know for a fact that you were a virgin when I had you first, I would throw you out of the palace!' Jasim growled at her, the blaze of his wrath increasing at her refusal to come clean. 'What sort of a slut accepts a ring of that value from a married man and then, not content with that piece of brazen scheming, jumps into bed with his brother?'

'Don't you dare call me a slut!' Elinor flung at him furiously, stalking into the spacious limestone bathroom in his wake. 'You're the one who made all the running in our relationship, not me!'

Jasim switched on the water in the wet room and stepped beneath the refreshing gush. He was disgusted that she had lied to him and that he had had sufficient faith in her unlikely tale to actually broach the subject with his father. Naturally he had wanted to believe her story, for the truth he was facing now was a good deal less acceptable. His wife was a greedy, deceitful and immoral liar, who had used her sexual allure to manipulate his brother. There was nothing to celebrate in that fact and much to be ashamed of.

Even so, he noted without surprise, there was no hint of shame in Elinor's stance. Glorious red hair framed the pale beauty of her face and her emerald green eyes were bright with umbrage. She was fizzing with impotent rage at his condemnation and the sight in no way cooled his deep abiding anger with her. She had tried to take him for a fool and deserved everything she had coming to her. She needed to understand that it was time to clean up her act. If she did not, she was likely to find life very hard, for he had no intention of tolerating her devious ways.

'Well, you did make the running,' Elinor repeated afresh when he failed to respond.

'You didn't exactly fight me off, did you? Why would you have done?' Jasim derided as he washed. 'I played right into your hands. I was a better bet than Murad because I didn't have a wife. Of course you were willing to sleep with me!'

'I can't believe that you're insulting me like this—'

'No?' Water streaming down his lean bronzed physique, Jasim treated her to a lethal look of contempt. 'My brother was much softer with women than I will ever be.'

'You're supposed to be my husband—are you ever going to behave like one?' Elinor hissed, green eyes livid with anger.

'Not while your dishonesty is still fresh in my memory. I want the whole truth from you now,' Jasim decreed in a tone of steely command. 'How far did your tempting of my brother go? It must have been pretty intense if he gave you that ring.'

'You've got it all wrong and I'm not answering your stupid demeaning questions.' Her breasts heaving as she dragged in a deep breath to sustain her struggling lungs, Elinor glowered at him. 'Nor am I willing to go through some crazy second wedding with you…once was enough!'

'You're in the wrong country to issue a threat like that,' Jasim delivered with chilling bite as he sauntered out of the shower and reached for a towel. 'Place me in that kind of position and I swear I will tell my father about your sordid flirtation with Murad. If I do there will be no wedding and you will find yourself flying back to London alone.'

Elinor was chilled to the marrow by that warning, for she was in no doubt of how ruthless he could be. 'You can't threaten me like that.'

Smouldering dark golden eyes clashed levelly with hers. 'Don't tempt me. In Quaram I can do just about anything I want to do, *aziz*.'

'Does that include taking a second wife?' Elinor demanded with stinging scorn, for in the mood he was in she saw no reason to approach the topic with greater tact.

Jasim froze, his smouldering dark golden eyes narrowing and darkening to view her with questioning censure. 'Is that your idea of a joke?'

'No, not at all. It was your cousin, Laila, who suggested that you might be hoping for an arrangement like that…'

Jasim lifted his damp dark head high, an expression of

incredulous outrage stamped in his lean, darkly handsome features. 'She would not dare. Only you would have the bravado to subject me to such an offensive piece of salacious prejudice. It is more than a century since anyone in Quaram took more than one wife,' he spelt out rawly.

'I am *not* prejudiced!' Elinor shot back at him furiously.

Jasim dealt her an unimpressed look and strode out of the bathroom regally, as though he were not wrapped in a towel. Elinor shot after him, unwilling to let the matter lie, even though his shocked reaction was already beginning to make her suspect that she might have fallen headlong into a nasty little trap that Laila had set for her. Having filled her head with melodramatic drivel, Laila had set her loose to either worry herself sick about Jasim's supposed plans or confront her husband with the issue and deeply offend him.

'What a distasteful thing to say to me,' Jasim breathed, his beautiful dark eyes cold as black ice as he cast aside the towel and went into the dressing room. 'You should be ashamed of taunting me with such a tawdry accusation. I'm dining with my father this evening and I won't see you until tomorrow.'

Elinor folded her arms and compressed her lips. She was still very angry with him for misjudging her, but at the same time she was so worked up and upset that she could as easily have burst into floods of tears as shouted at him. 'Why should I care what you do or where you go?' she demanded mutinously, determined not to show weakness.

'Clearly I need to ask you to watch your manners and to avoid controversial subjects like culture with my relatives tomorrow,' Jasim spelt out flatly. 'Remember your behaviour reflects on both Sami and I.'

'I'll try not to embarrass anyone,' Elinor breathed tightly, mortified to death by that request and reminder.

Frozen to the spot, she stood by the window, only dimly aware that he was dressing in traditional robes similar to those his father had worn. As he strode out of the dressing room she turned to look at him. The white cotton *thoub* he wore below the black gold-trimmed cloak was buttoned, embroidered and immaculate. With his head covered and a double black cord binding the *gutrah* in place, his transformation into a regal desert prince was complete.

Twenty minutes after his father's departure, Sami was returned to Elinor's care accompanied by a gaggle of chattering attendants and a long procession of nursery furniture and toys. He was installed in the big room across the corridor from the master bedroom. Once he had gone down for the night, wonderfully impervious to all the excitement that was centred on him, Elinor accepted the light meal Zaid had had prepared for her.

She felt absolutely wretched. Laila had set out to trip her up and had succeeded beautifully with her booby trap of a reference to Jasim's fictional plans to take another wife. Now Jasim was affronted and convinced she had been making fun of him on the score of a delicate cultural issue. He also thought she was a shameless liar; if his father could not confirm Murad and her mother's romance thirty years earlier, there was nobody else to perform that feat for her. Had the King forgotten his elder son's university romance? Or did he genuinely not know about Murad's youthful relationship with an Englishwoman?

Whatever, Jasim continued to believe that Elinor had wantonly schemed to destroy his brother's marriage and take

Yaminah's place, only to surrender that ambition when a more accessible member of the royal family strode into her firing line. If that was what he thought of her, what sort of a relationship could she possibly have with her son's father…?

CHAPTER EIGHT

AT SOME timeless hour before daybreak, voices wakened Elinor. She had not slept well. Her argument with Jasim had kept on replaying inside her head and she had thought of other words she might have thrown, last words, final words, more cutting words, even the *ultimate* putdown. Having run the gamut of those pointless replays she had finally questioned the sheer level of ongoing anger that was preventing her from finding peace. Now her head was heavy, her body weary and her eyes swollen. She felt awful and could hardly credit that this was her *second* wedding day.

Frowning, she sat up in bed, registering from the dim glow penetrating the curtains at the window that the sun had not yet fully risen. She fumbled for the light by the bed.

'Allow me.' It was Jasim's voice and the unexpectedness of his appearance startled her.

'*Yes?*' Elinor prompted tightly when the lamp flooded the room with light and illuminated his tall figure by the bed. He was no longer wearing robes and he bore little resemblance to his usually immaculately groomed self. He was clad in faded jeans and a T-shirt, his black hair was tousled and he was badly in need of a shave. But it was his brilliant ebony-lashed dark eyes and the strain etched there that captured and held her attention.

He spread lean brown hands in an expressive movement that was remarkably eloquent of his mood. 'I'm sorry for waking you but I couldn't sleep. We parted bitterly, which is not how it should be today of all days,' he breathed tautly. 'I lost my temper. I was rude. I was cruel…'

'Yes…' Elinor could barely breathe that word of confirmation because conflicting feelings were at war inside her. He was so serious and full of guilt that she could not maintain her distance and still hate him. With all her being she wanted to reach out to him at that moment and indeed even as she spoke she stretched out a hand to him.

His lean, stunningly handsome face grave, he immediately closed his hand over hers. 'When I have to picture you flirting with Murad, something twists inside me and I am filled with such anger I cannot hold it in,' he admitted in a driven undertone.

As it dawned on her that it was jealousy and possessiveness he was describing her defences gave and she pulled on the hand holding hers to bring him down on the bed beside her. 'But there wasn't any flirting with Murad… *ever*,' she stressed earnestly. 'Your brother talked to me as if he was my father. He never said anything that couldn't have been said in front of his wife or indeed anyone. He was kind to me but that was all.'

Beautiful dark eyes locked to hers, Jasim exhaled slowly. 'I will try to accept that. It is not that I want to disbelieve your story about your mother…'

'But it was that story that brought me into your family's life in the first place,' Elinor pointed out.

Jasim met her clear green eyes, which bore not a shadow of constraint, and resolved to settle the issue by having it investigated. He knew he should have talked to his brother about Elinor, but he had not been able to make himself take that sensible route to enlightenment and then Murad had died. For the first time, however, Jasim was wondering if he could have totally misunderstood Elinor and Murad's relationship, which he had never had the opportunity to observe for himself.

'Please don't think I'm saying something I shouldn't,' but when you mentioned that Murad had had extra-marital affairs, I realised why his wife travelled with him every-where he went,' Elinor admitted uncomfortably. 'I may be wrong, but I suspect that your brother's wife was insecure and more likely than most to be jealous and suspicious of her husband's behaviour around other women—'

'You are saying that Yaminah saw something that was not there,' Jasim remarked without expression.

'I remember her staring at me once when she saw Murad and I laughing at something Zahrah had said. She didn't speak any English, which was awkward. I think your brother was fond of me in a mild way because my mother had once meant a great deal to him. Perhaps that was misinterpreted, I don't know. What I do know was that there was never any suggestion of sexual interest in his attitude to me.'

Jasim was still challenged to credit that his womanis-ing brother could have been unreceptive to Elinor's looks and appeal. But he was equally determined not to allow the issue to divide them. 'I too suffer from a suspicious nature when it comes to women,' he confessed, lifting a hand to stroke a forefinger along the alluring pout of her full pink lower lip. 'Three years ago, I was seeing a woman called Sophia who belonged to one of your country's titled families. I thought about marrying her. I believed she was a woman of good character and integrity and then the tabloid press exposed her for what she really was…'

'Oh…' Elinor said tremulously, her mind only half on the conversation as his finger slid into her mouth and she laved it with her tongue, heat blossoming between her thighs while she dizzily met his intent gaze. 'And what was she?'

'She'd been a real party girl, who had dabbled in drugs and had countless affairs. She had also had surgery to restore her long-lost virginity for my benefit,' he advanced with a roughened laugh, his attention sliding against his will to the neckline of her nightgown where the shadowy cleft and the peach smooth slopes of her full, firm breasts were on tantalising display. 'Yet that was of much less importance to me than all the lies she had told and I had swallowed. She had me fooled.'

And Elinor heard the lingering bitterness and hurt pride in that admission and recognised how afraid he was that he might fall into the same trap again. 'But you can't possibly believe that all women are the same,' she whispered, her breath feathering in her throat.

'Right now, I don't know what I believe…or that I care, *aziz.*' The hot blood settling heavily in his groin, Jasim brought his mouth down with a driven groan on hers, his tongue plundering the sweetness from between her readily parted lips with an urgency that made her heart pound like a drum within her ribcage.

Jasim jerked back from her with a look of frustration.

'I can't stay. It's almost dawn and it takes hours to prepare a bride for her wedding.'

Elinor was shocked by a desire to pull him back to her and wish her bridal duties to perdition if it prevented them from being together. As he sprang off the bed she raised an abstracted hand to rub her cheek where his stubble had scratched her. What shook her most was the intensity of her desire for him. He was teaching her things about her own needs that she would never have guessed and that she suspected she might never have known with another man, for Jasim's raw passion had lit a similar passion inside her.

'We'll be together later,' Jasim husked. 'But I'm afraid I need a few minutes of grace before I can be seen in public.'

Colour washed her face as she appreciated that he was lingering by the window while he waited for the visible bulge of his arousal to subside. But that she could affect him that way was a source of pride and satisfaction for her as well. He switched out the light before he left and she sank back into her warm comfortable bed and stretched luxuriantly at the prospect of a day that was now shorn of fear and insecurity.

Elinor was wakened again by a slender girl in her teens. Gamila introduced herself and told Elinor in English that breakfast awaited her.

'Lovely, thanks.' Elinor slid out of bed and slid her arms into the wrap she had left out beside the bed. Her attention rested on the untouched pillow beside hers and an ache, an uncommonly painful ache, stirred inside her. It bothered her that she missed Jasim so much. How could someone she had recently believed she hated have come to matter so much to her?

'Prince Jasim ordered a wide selection of food for you,' the girl added.

'I'd like to see my son first,' Elinor said apologetically.

'It's still very early. The little prince is still asleep,' Gamila explained. 'I went in to see him. He is a beautiful baby.'

A warm smile curved Elinor's mouth. 'I think so too.'

Downstairs she entered a dining room where the table groaned beneath the weight of a vast array of food. Elinor discovered that she was extremely hungry and enjoyed orange juice, cereal and two toasted muffins spread with honey. Even while she was eating the house seemed full of activity, with feet passing up and down the stairs and the chatter of many female voices. There was no sign of Zaid or any other man.

Having eaten, Elinor was escorted back upstairs to have her hair washed. It was conditioned and rinsed several times and then piled into a towel while a bath was run for her. She watched as an aromatic bath potion was swirled through the water and rose petals were scattered on the surface. Settling into the warm fragrant water and relaxing her stiff muscles was the purest of pleasures. It was an effort to get out again and swathe herself in a fleecy towel.

Once her hair was dry, Gamila suggested that she dress in casual clothes to head over to the main palace. There on the second floor she found a full-size beauty parlour awaiting her. She knew what the fashion was and consented reluctantly to a waxing session. It wasn't quite as painful as she had feared but she didn't think it was a procedure she would ever want to volunteer for. She agreed to a massage and lay on a narrow padded table where she was pummelled and rubbed with fragrant oil. Slowly the

stress drained out of her body. At some stage she fell asleep
and wakened without the slightest idea of where she was
or how much time had passed to find that she was being
given a manicure and pedicure. Relaxed after that nap, she
began to take an interest in the proceedings. Her nails
glossily perfect, she sat watching while intricate henna
patterns were painted onto her hands and feet. She
wondered if Jasim would enjoy that traditional touch and
smiled. She was relieved that there was no sign of Laila in
the gathering of female attendants because she was not sure
that she could have kept the peace.

Sami was brought to her while her hair was being
straightened and smoothed. He gave her a huge sloppy
kiss and settled into her lap like a homing pigeon, intrigued
by the amount of activity around her. Her companions
looked on Jasim's son with unreserved adoration and when
he got down from her knee to crawl off in exploration he
was petted and fussed over. Sami lapped up the attention
to the manner born and Elinor found herself wondering
how her son had ever managed with only his mother to
admire him.

Her make-up was done last and then she was guided into
another room to be shown the Western wedding dress,
which she was apparently to wear. Astonished, for she had
expected to be presented with a traditional Quarami bridal
outfit, Elinor stared at the white wedding dress, which glittered as though stars had been sewn into the fine fabric.
Thousands of crystals caught and reflected the light. It was
a wonderfully romantic dress, and when she had put it on
she could only marvel at her image in the mirror: her every
wedding-day dream was fully satisfied by the magnificent

gown. Her henna decorated hands and feet didn't quite match in style, but she didn't think that mattered as she eased her feet into delicate crystal-studded sandals with high heels. A short veil was attached to a silver coronet of flowers on her head.

A magnificent jewel case was brought to her.

'It is a gift from your bridegroom,' Gamila explained and tangible excitement filled the room when Elinor lifted the lid on a fabulous diamond necklace and drop earrings that quite took her breath away. Oohs and aahs of admiration sounded all around her. The necklace was the perfect complement to the boat-shaped neckline of her gown.

With her companions laughing and chattering she travelled down in a lift to the ground floor. When she stepped out a bouquet of white roses was handed to her by a giggling little girl. Moments later she saw Jasim, dressed in a snazzy grey morning suit that was a perfect tailored fit to his tall, well-built frame. She collided with brilliant dark eyes and her tummy flipped and her heartbeat thundered in her ears. The instant she saw him a helpless surge of relief and pleasure engulfed her.

You look amazing. He didn't say it; his mouth framed the words in silent appreciation and she lip-read them with an inner glow of happiness that she could not suppress. She had so many questions that she wanted to ask him. Where had the fairy-tale dress come from at such short notice? Why had he given her the diamonds? Why all the fuss when she had dimly expected a short ceremony? But there was no opportunity for her to speak to Jasim in private. They were ushered into a room crowded with guests and married all over again. Throughout the ceremony, an interpreter stood

by her elbow carefully translating every solemn word that
was spoken. They exchanged rings. Her ring, at least, was
not new and when it was returned to her finger it somehow
felt more right on her finger than it had before. The formalities over, she posed with her hand resting lightly on
Jasim's arm for several ceremonial photographs.

'Where did my dress come from?' she whispered.

'Italy. I called in favours and described what I wanted
for you. It was flown in this morning.'

'I love it. And the diamonds?'

'A traditional gift from the groom.'

A pair of antique sedan chairs was brought in and they
were each assisted into them. There was a lot of laughter.
Hoisted high, the bride and groom were carried to a flower-
bedecked room for the wedding party. Jasim helped Elinor
out and her attendants hurried forward to rearrange the
folds of her dress. Then, the bride and groom stood at the
head of the room to greet their guests. Elinor was astonished when she espied her father working his way through
the crush towards her.

A tall bearded man with grey hair and spectacles, Ernest
Tempest clasped his daughter's hand and frowned. 'Jasim
insisted that I come. Your stepmother couldn't make it. She
can't stand the heat in places like this. Well, you've done
very well for yourself,' he pronounced. 'Who would ever
have thought it? I never thought you'd amount to anything.'

It was over two years since Elinor had last seen her
father and he had not altered one little bit. She was amazed
that, even with Jasim's encouragement, he had chosen to
fly out to Quaram to attend her wedding. Evidently she had
her marriage to a royal to thank for that feat.

'I'm really pleased you were able to come,' she said pleasantly. 'Are you staying for long?'

'A few days. There are a couple of very interesting archaeological sites in the north of the country and your husband's organised a tour guide for me,' the older man explained. 'Quite a forceful, managing sort of a chap, isn't he?'

Elinor tried not to laugh at that description of Jasim as her father took himself and his opinions very seriously. 'Yes, he is.'

That rather impersonal dialogue complete, Elinor's father moved off again. In a daze she turned to Jasim. 'I certainly wasn't expecting to see my father here.'

'He's the only family you have, but I would never have pressed him to attend if I had known he was likely to tell you that he thought you would never amount to anything,' Jasim admitted, his annoyance on her behalf heartening. 'I wanted our wedding to be special in every way this time.'

Impressed by that statement and the kind of temperament that prompted healing rather than divisive moves, Elinor would have liked to discuss it further with him. It was at that inopportune moment that Laila, sheathed in an azure-blue evening gown that showed off her fabulous curves, glided up. Tossing a brazen smile in Elinor's direction, the beautiful brunette engaged Jasim in a low-pitched conversation. He laughed a couple of times. The friendly familiarity of their relationship was obvious and it set Elinor's teeth on edge.

'You get on very well with your cousin,' Elinor commented when Laila had finally moved on after a lengthy show of reluctance and many heartfelt sighs.

'We grew up together,' Jasim parried lazily. 'She hopes

you'll forgive her for the joke she had at your expense yesterday.'

'The sharing-you-with-a-second-wife joke in extremely bad taste!' Elinor remarked acidly, indignant at the manner in which the other woman had smoothly contrived to excuse her behaviour.

'Laila has always loved to tease and let's face it—you seem to have been a very easy mark,' Jasim informed her with rueful amusement. 'Do you always believe everything people tell you? No matter how ridiculous it might be?'

Hot-cheeked, Elinor had to bite her tongue to rein back a tart and resentful response. She knew she had been credulous and the mortification of it still stung painfully. 'You took it equally seriously last night,' she reminded him drily.

Jasim inclined his proud head in acknowledgement of that reminder and they sat down side by side in throne-like seats while a meal was served.

'Is it true that your father wanted you to marry Laila?' Elinor could not resist asking in a feverish undertone. 'Did you *think* about it?'

'Of course I did. In many ways she would have been perfect, but I was only twenty-six at the time and although she is very attractive I didn't want to marry anyone,' Jasim fielded.

Perfect and *very attractive* were the words that lingered on Elinor's mind. No, she definitely could not kid herself that Jasim was blind to his cousin's charms. It was an unwelcome reminder that Jasim had only chosen her as his wife because she had conceived his child. While she agonised over that fact the celebration trundled on. Speeches were made, songs were sung and poems of inordinate length about great battles and tragic love were recited. Arabic music was played and several traditional dances, which included a lot of waving of swords and cracking of whips, were performed. As evening fell they went out onto a balcony to watch an amazing firework display.

In the middle of it, Jasim closed a hand over hers and tugged her through a door into another reception room, which was empty. 'We will leave now…' he breathed, one hand lifting to nudge a stray auburn strand of hair back from her soft cheek, his fingers lingering to stroke the delicate ear lobe stretched by the weight of a diamond earring. 'You're the perfect height for me,' he murmured lazily.

She looked up into smouldering dark golden eyes and her breath convulsed in her throat while her anticipation climbed ever higher. He reached for her with purposeful hands and crushed her slender, yielding length to his lean, hard body. The fiery passion with which he drove his sensual mouth down hard on hers thrilled her to death, while the erotic dance of his tongue inside her sensitive mouth made her quiver. Even through their clothing she could feel the insistent swell of his arousal. He shuddered against her, hot and eager with desire, and at the very core of her body she melted with liquid heat.

'You're treating me so differently today—why?' she prompted breathlessly.

'I offered you a new beginning and failed to deliver. That wasn't fair to you or Sami,' Jasim conceded tautly. 'I don't want to sabotage our marriage before it even gets off the ground. Sometimes I can be my own worst enemy.'

'And mine,' she completed unevenly.

'Not any more.' He escorted her out to the lift, assuring

her that her luggage was already on board the helicopter awaiting them.

'What about Sami?' she asked anxiously.

'He will join us first thing tomorrow—'

'Why can't he come with us now?'

'My father has asked that Sami and I do not use the same mode of transport in case there is an accident,' Jasim explained wryly. 'It will be inconvenient for us but I can see the wisdom in his request.'

Her skin went clammy at the mere mention of an accident although she knew they happened every day. She thought it was understandable that Murad's unexpected death should have made the King more nervous.

'Did you enjoy the day?' Jasim pressed.

'Very much,' she said truthfully, her mouth still tingling from the exhilarating pressure of his. 'I was surprised by how westernised it all was though.'

'Western-style weddings are currently the height of fashion in Quaram. I pushed the boundaries further by requesting a mixed-sex party afterwards,' Jasim admitted as he urged her outdoors into the balmy heat of evening. 'My father witnessed the ceremony but the party would have been a step too far for him and he conserves his strength as best he can.'

In the powerful lights that lit up the waiting helicopter, Jasim scooped her up into his arms. The full skirts of her gown foamed up round her slim body as he put her on board. 'You haven't even told me where you're taking me!' she exclaimed in the midst of her laughter.

'A villa on the Persian Gulf that used to belong to Murad. Yaminah asked me to take all her Quarami property off her hands because she has moved back to France to be near her family.'

'How are she and Zahrah managing?' Elinor enquired.

'Rather better than anyone expected. I understand that Yaminah has already acquired an admirer, a former friend from her youth, and Zahrah has always been very attached to her maternal grandparents.'

'Life goes on,' Elinor quipped, cheered by the idea that the older woman might find happiness again.

'Ours has barely begun, *aziz*.' As the noise of the propellers drowned out any prospect of further conversation, Elinor met Jasim's dazzling golden-as-topaz eyes, gloriously fringed by black lashes, and her heart skipped an entire beat.

Suddenly, exasperated by the level of her response to him she closed her hands tightly together on her lap and urged herself to use her head. Jasim had dropped the aggro and made peace with her for a very good reason: he didn't want a divorce. His elderly father had no doubt decided to accept his foreign daughter-in-law for much the same reason. Sami lay at the very heart of her acceptance as a wife and it would be foolish to overlook that reality. Jasim might still suspect that she had attempted to lure his brother away from his wife—and that she'd accepted a very valuable ring in the process—but from now on, he would probably keep his reservations on that score to himself. Why? For the sake of their marriage and the image of the monarchy in a small country, where such matters were still of vital importance.

So, Elinor reflected, it was time for her to jump off the bridal bandwagon that had given her starry eyes and reconnect with the ground. What was it about Jasim that could make her behave so foolishly? Last night's insane attack of insecurity after Laila's jibes about his taking a second wife? It had not been her intellect that spawned her reaction, but the tumultuous emotions that Jasim still aroused in her. He had the power to make her jealous and possessive, to lift her to passion and drop her into the depths of despair. The day she had walked away from him she had almost drowned in that sense of despair, until she had picked herself up and focused on her baby rather than her broken heart. If she didn't want to be badly hurt again, she needed to regain that emotional control and distance, because Jasim was never likely to give her the love that she secretly craved from him, was he?

The leader of a large contingent of security staff met them off the helicopter. The villa was a palatial, ultra-modern structure embellished by a verandah, extensive grounds and every possible interior extravagance. 'The views in daylight are spectacular,' Jasim told her, and then he swept her up into his arms to carry her over the threshold.

'You don't have to do fake stuff like this to impress me or make me happy,' Elinor told him uncomfortably. 'I know and accept that this is a very practical marriage. I've got no illusions.'

'It's not fake,' Jasim protested, lowering her down the hard length of his muscular body to lead her upstairs.

'I don't want to get into another…er…difference of opinion with you,' Elinor selected, borrowing his terminology, 'but you never really wanted me. You didn't *choose* me. You were only interested in the first place because you thought that your brother—'

Jasim rested a brown forefinger against her parted lips in a silencing gesture that stilled her tongue. 'Don't go back over that ground again, particularly if you're about to make another set of wrong assumptions,' he instructed. 'This is our wedding night.'

'I know,' Elinor reminded him dolefully, moving into a lamplit bedroom adorned with an over-generous number of flower arrangements. 'But facts are facts—'

'You are a very stubborn woman,' Jasim intoned. 'But we are two different people. Your facts are not my facts. How could they be?'

Blinking warily, Elinor looked back up at his bronzed features, her senses singing against her will at his dark, sleek perfection. His stunning dark golden eyes were sombre and serious. 'How do your facts differ from mine?'

'The first time I saw you, even though I was prejudiced against you and you had been drinking, I still thought you were the most gorgeous woman I had ever seen,' Jasim breathed in a driven undertone of urgency that suggested that practising such candour was still a challenge for him. 'Although I have never found redheads attractive, I really love your hair.'

In tune with that unexpected confession, Jasim meshed long fingers into the tumbled, scented depths of her luxuriant mane. 'I love your hair,' he said again, knuckles brushing her cheekbone, her lips and the curve of her breasts to emphasise the point he was determined to make. 'Your face, your mouth, your very beautiful body. I wanted you as soon as I saw you and with a powerful desire beyond any I have ever known before. That reaction had nothing whatsoever to do with anything I had been told about you...it was private and personal to me and concerns only you—'

Elinor was gripped by the edge of fierce urgency in his dark, level drawl. 'If that's true, I—'

'You must accept that it is true. You must also understand that that reaction was not at all welcome to me,' Jasim stated with a frown. 'Naturally I didn't want to be that attracted to you.'

Elinor had gone from feeling like the consolation prize in the wedding lottery to the most desirable of women. On that issue, at least, his sincerity was highly persuasive, right down to the assurance that he had never previously found red hair pleasing. Her slim shoulders lifted a little, her spine straightening. Her hands sliding up to his broad shoulders, she began to help him out of his jacket.

A surprised laugh fell from his lips. He shrugged off the jacket, dealt with his tie and smiled down at her while she undid the buttons on his dress shirt with unsteady hands. 'You know what you want,' he murmured thickly.

And she knew she wanted him; for the first time in well over a year, she wanted him without any sense of guilt or shame. She knew now, and without any shadow of a doubt, that he genuinely wanted her too. It was a simple truth but an immensely important one for her peace of mind. She parted the edges of his shirt and ran her palms down slowly over the warm, hair-roughened wall of his muscular torso, delighting in the heat and masculinity of him. His breathing quickened audibly when her fingers dipped below his waist. He took her hand and pressed it against the hard contours of his surging erection.

'This will be a night of unforgettable pleasure,' Jasim

promised huskily and he turned her firmly round and began to unfasten her gown.

Pink spots of colour adorning her cheekbones, Elinor stepped out of the rucked-up folds of her beautiful dress. She had never felt more exposed than she did then, with her slender body clad only in the ivory satin underpinnings of her bra, panties and lace-topped stockings.

'I have never seen anything more exquisite,' Jasim swore, studying her with scorching golden eyes of deep appreciation.

A slow burn started in her pelvis as he undid her bra and slid it off.

'You have the most wonderful breasts, *aziz*.'

He moulded his hands to the full firm globes, catching the swollen stiff nipples between his fingers and then backing her down onto the bed to put his mouth there instead. The feel of his lips and his tongue on her sensitised flesh fanned the slow burn at the heart of her into a blaze of tingling heat. He tormented the tender buds until her hips were arching off the bed. Stepping back from her, he shed the remainder of his clothing.

Elinor could hardly breathe for desire and the joy of looking at him. There was a pagan glory to his lean, hard body and his rampant arousal. He pulled her down onto the white linen sheets with him. Her tapering fingers skimmed like butterflies over a powerful hair-roughened thigh. Newly confident, she was touching him as she had long yearned to touch him and the very intimacy of her erotic exploration and her pronounced awareness of how she was affecting him stimulated her even more.

A tremor ran through his big frame and he murmured her name. Her fingertips found him, traced his towering

potency and practised a delicious friction before her lips
engulfed the most sensitive part of all. She elicited a groan
from him and then a protest.

'That's enough,' he told her thickly, lean fingers
plunging into her hair as he gazed wonderingly down at
her. 'I want to make love to you.'

'And do you always have to have top billing?' Elinor
whispered playfully, prepared to stop the sensual torment
only in the knowledge that she had him all to herself for a
month. And, by royal command, she thought with satisfaction. It was only now when she was starting to appreciate
how much Jasim respected his father that she understood
how much courage it must have taken for him to marry her
without the ailing King's approval.

A wolfish grin slashed his beautiful mouth and he
hauled her up to him to kiss her with a fierce, wild
thoroughness that answered the hot surge of blood through
her own body. Her heart pounded as he arranged her back
against the pillows.

'I want you to remember our wedding night for ever,'
he murmured silkily.

And much, much later, she knew she would never forget
it. He began at her feet and she discovered that places that
had never previously been erogenous zones had surprising
possibilities, not one of which he overlooked in his
devotion to detail. By the time that her heart was racing and
every inch of her was damp and wildly sensitive to the
skilled caress of his mouth and his hands, she knew her
honeymoon was going be a sensual delight from start to
finish because he seemed to take so much pleasure from
her eager response.

Her entire skin surface was tingling, her straining nipples moist from his attention when he finally deigned to touch her where she was most desperate to be touched. He commented on the waxing that had left her bare and sensitised and she was so excited by that stage that she couldn't even find her voice. Her excitement was growing and growing at an uncontrollable rate. He parted the plump swollen lips that were slick and moist and she gasped out loud, squirming and rocking against him in frustration for more. The hollow ache between her thighs had become unbearable.

'Jasim…*now*!' she pleaded.

He closed his hands to her ankles and tipped them back and took her willing body with all the urgency, strength and passion she yearned for. He plunged hard and deep into her tender core and waves of intense pleasure claimed her with his every thrust. It was gloriously passionate and primal and exactly what she needed. When contractions were rippling through her he groaned as her body tightened round him. She cried out when the explosive ecstasy of climax engulfed her and held him tight while he shuddered and reached his own shattering release in her arms. There were tears in her eyes in the aftermath and a new willingness to face her deepest emotions. She was still crazy about him, she acknowledged. Love had bitten her deep and there was no longer any hope of her escaping its bonds.

Elinor pressed her lips to a smooth brown shoulder, drinking in the warm familiar scent of his skin with intense appreciation and a sleepy smile of contentment. 'Being married definitely has its compensations,' she told him with satisfaction…

CHAPTER NINE

'WERE you in love with Sophia?' Elinor asked, tossing out the question in haste before she could lose her nerve.

Jasim dealt her a look of consternation, as well he might have done at that sudden intimate question. Previously they had been discussing his recent decision in a boundary dispute causing trouble between local Bedouin tribesmen.

Mortified by her own lack of diplomacy, Elinor went pink. 'I'm just curious,' she told him as lightly as she could manage and she was lying through her teeth. In truth she wanted to know every tiny detail of every relationship he had ever had with a woman, which was more than a little sad in her own estimation and likely to leave her disappointed since Jasim was not given to chatting freely about such things.

The early morning silence was broken only by the crunching footfall of their horses' hooves in the sand. They often went riding at dawn when Elinor found the heat easiest to handle. The sun had risen and the peach and pink splendour of the skies was colouring the sand to shades of ochre and red. The arid landscape of stony plains broken by rocky outcrops and vast sloping dunes had become familiar to her, as had the surprising number of animals and the wide range of fauna that survived there.

'Why do you want to know?' Jasim enquired.

Primed to find significance in his every word and hesitation, Elinor said instantly, 'So, obviously you *did* think you were in love with Sophia—'

'No, I did not—'

'But you were thinking of *marrying* her!' Elinor exclaimed in disbelief.

'I was not brought up to regard love as a necessary component of marriage,' Jasim imparted grudgingly. 'She was beautiful, elegant, well educated and spoke several languages. I saw those as important qualities.'

Elinor turned shocked eyes on him. 'I can't believe how cold-blooded you can be!'

'I am not cold-blooded, but love can cause a lot of grief,' Jasim declared in what she could see she was supposed to accept as the closing argument of the discussion. 'A wise man chooses a wife with more than love on his mind.'

'My goodness,' Elinor sighed heavily. 'You'd never have picked me in a million years!'

'But I'm delighted with you now that I've got you, *habibti*.' With those irreverent words, Jasim sent her a wicked slanting grin that made her heart hammer hard inside her. It was a grin that, like his laughter, she was becoming increasingly familiar with and it transformed his invariably serious demeanour. Three weeks of privacy at the villa had given them the chance to discover a lot about each other and had laid a firm foundation for a much deeper relationship than she had ever hoped to have with him.

'Did your parents have an arranged marriage?' she

asked with a frown as she struggled to understand his outlook, which was so very different from hers.

His dark gaze narrowed, his whole face freezing, and then he swiftly looked away, murmuring in a taut response, 'No, but my father's first marriage to Murad's mother was arranged and it was happy, as well as lasting almost thirty years.'

'You know,' Elinor commented in a tone of discovery, while wondering why on earth her question should have created so much tension, 'you never ever mention your own mother.'

Jasim vented his breath in a pent-up hiss of impatience. 'And you are only just noticing? It is considered bad taste to mention her. She ran off with another man when I was a baby and I don't think my father has ever recovered from the disgrace of her desertion.'

Elinor blinked in shock and then shut her eyes in mute discomfiture. The unevenness of his usual quiet, steady drawl told her what an emotive subject she had stumbled on and also how very unaccustomed he was to having to make such an explanation. She said nothing just then. She could only imagine how horrific a scandal must have been caused by his mother's behaviour in so old-fashioned a society. She had seen Jasim's shame as he told her and compassion stirred in her that he should still feel so strongly about something that had happened so long ago, particularly when it was an event he could have had no influence over. But that new knowledge added another telling dimension to her awareness that he found it hard to trust women. At the same time her mind overflowed with questions that she was too tactful to ask him to answer.

'I believe my father is considering another visit today,' Jasim imparted. 'His interest in Sami is heartening.'

'Yes.' Elinor, however, did not find it that easy to sit on the sidelines of those visits. The King and Jasim walked on verbal eggshells in each other's presence and extreme politeness ruled until Sami did something silly and broke the ice. She had often wondered and never dared to ask why the older man and his second son treated each other like strangers.

'I've been surprised by the amount of interest my father has taken in Sami,' Jasim shared with the abruptness of a male striving to reward her with a confidence in gratitude for her not having pursued the more controversial topic of his mother.

'I think your father is trying to get to know you better as well,' Elinor admitted.

'Nonsense…why would he do that?' Jasim countered with distinct derision.

Elinor counted to ten and said nothing. From the corner of her eye she noted that Jasim was still regarding her with expectancy. Having cut off her opinion at the knees, he still wanted to know what had made her think that his father might be trying to mend fences with him. Amused, she held her peace. She still found it extraordinary that Jasim was so volatile beneath that sober, serious exterior of his.

Beneath the safe surface, he had an explosive temper and he seethed with dark, deep emotion. At some stage, however, he had learned to suppress those feelings and make self-discipline and duty his twin gods to be obeyed. Sometimes she marvelled at how controlled he was, rarely showing emotion except in unguarded moments or when he thought he was unobserved. She had first seen the cracks in his smooth outer surface when he played with Sami.

His love and pride for their son shone out. With Sami, Jasim relaxed, and when he played with their little boy he discarded his reserve and dignity. Sami was very much an energetic boys' boy and he made a beeline for Jasim whenever he saw him. In fact every time Elinor saw her child in his father's arms she knew that she had made the right decision when she had decided to give her marriage another chance. Sami adored his father.

And Elinor had come to appreciate that she adored Jasim too, although she was a little more critical than Sami was. But there was no denying that the love she had once refused to acknowledge now ruled inside her, for Jasim had made a great deal of effort to ensure that she was amazingly happy. The guy who was waited on hand and foot, and whose staff revered him for his interest in their more humble lives, brought her breakfast in bed almost every morning. Her eyes sparkled. Once he had fed her to restore her energy he often got back into bed as well. No complaints there, she thought, getting a little breathless just stealing a glance at her handsome husband.

While they had been sent to the villa for privacy, daily flights came in carrying government ministers and courtiers. Jasim was consulted about just about everything that happened in Quaram. She had once read that a man could be judged by the company he kept and, in Jasim, she saw the evidence of that. His opinions were held in high regard, his gravity admired, and everyone was delighted that he now had a wife and child.

'But what must people think about us after that wedding when we already had a baby?' Elinor had asked anxiously during their first week at the villa.

'They think that I married you without my father's permission and kept quiet about you until it was safe to bring you out into the open after Murad's death. While disrespect towards a father is a serious matter, the romance of forbidden love, a secret marriage abroad and a baby son win that contest hands down,' Jasim had explained with unhidden amusement. 'Our second wedding here in Quaram was regarded as a sign of my father's approval and acceptance.'

Since their arrival, he had taken her on several trips into the desert where they had enjoyed the hospitality of the local tribesmen in villages and in goatskin tents. He was very well informed and often in demand to settle disputes. He could sit hour after hour with the tribal elders and listen patiently to arguments, such as what was the correct compensation to be paid for a goat that had strayed into a herb garden, and still give the matter his full attention. She had sat in the back of the tent with the women and children drinking strong sweet tea while a television running off a car battery supplied the entertainment. In the process she had also become hopelessly addicted to a madly melodramatic Quarami soap full of sobbing women, swashbuckling men and disaster.

One evening it had rained and he had taken her out the next day to see the amazing sheets of beautiful wild flowers that had come up overnight on the sand. Her pale skin burned easily in the sun and he was assiduous in ensuring that she was slathered in sunscreen and covered up when the light fell on her. She felt safe with him, cared for, appreciated, she acknowledged reflectively as she dismounted from her horse at the stables.

'I should have told you about my mother before this,'

Jasim admitted without warning over breakfast. 'It is easier for you to hear such a story from me than to embarrass someone else with questions.'

'It's not that unusual a story, though,' Elinor told him gently.

'It is in Quaram, particularly in the history of my family.' Lean, strong face taut, Jasim frowned. 'My father was a widower in his fifties when he met her. She was the daughter of a Swiss doctor and half his age. He fell in love with her and married her very quickly. By the time I was born two years later, I understand the relationship was already under strain as she disliked the restricted life she led here.'

Elinor stopped eating to listen. 'And then?'

'She met another man when she was visiting her family. There was an affair which my father discovered and she fled, leaving me behind. She married her lover. I never had any contact with her.'

Elinor frowned. 'Did you ever *try* to have contact?'

'No, nor did she ever try to contact me. She married several times, had no more children and died a few years ago. I don't think she had a maternal streak. I had no cause to thank her for anything other than the gift of life,' Jasim proffered. 'My father couldn't bear to look at me—the son of the woman who had humiliated him in the eyes of our whole country. He sent me off to a military school abroad as soon as he could.'

'That was cruel!'

'He once told me that he was concerned that I might have inherited my mother's moral weakness. Some years later, however, I learned the *true* reason why my father rejected me. He feared I might not be his child and I was

DNA-tested without my knowledge as soon as the tests first became available.'

Elinor shook her head, distressed by what she was finding out about his disturbed and unhappy childhood. 'How could he be so blind? You look so like him.'

'A physical likeness was not enough to satisfy a man tortured by his suspicions.'

'He punished you for your mother's desertion!' she proclaimed with angry heat.

Jasim shrugged a broad shoulder in a dismissive gesture. 'If that is what he did, it was not deliberate for he is not a vengeful man. I was the unfortunate casualty of a broken marriage and his bitterness. No one has the power to remake the past.'

But that afternoon when King Akil arrived for his third visit, Elinor was convinced that Jasim's father was finally trying to bridge that difficult past with his only surviving son. Unfortunately the older man was too proud and Jasim too accustomed to maintaining formal relations for any advance to be easily made. Elinor remained troubled by the awareness that Jasim had been denied the love and affection of both his parents as well as being exiled to a foreign school as a child to toughen up. She saw the proof of his sad upbringing in the warm affection he continually poured on their son. She was now also wondering if he had ever been in love with any woman or if, indeed, he had the smallest idea of what that kind of love would feel like. Certainly there was nothing in his past experience likely to encourage him to trust a woman enough to love her. Jasim, Elinor recognised then, was likely to prove a long-term project in the love stakes.

In the heat of the afternoon, Elinor often lay down for a nap. She was undressing when Jasim strolled into the bedroom. As he came to a halt, dark golden eyes openly engaged in appreciating the picture she made in a turquoise satin bra and knickers, she went pink.

'I was about to invite you for a swim,' Jasim husked, moving closer and turning her round to fold her back against his long powerful body in a confident movement. 'But you might burn in the water and I would prefer to burn you with the fire of my passion in here.'

He eased her rounded breasts free of the satin cups and stroked the straining pink nipples between his fingers. A tiny clenching sensation in her groin made her gasp, feel the race of arousal flame through her while he brushed her hair off the nape of her neck to press his mouth there. She quivered, arching her spine and moaning as his clever fingers teased the tender skin between her thighs. His touch burned through the taut, damp fabric stretched there and with a sound of impatience he stripped the knickers off, bracing her against the side of the bed and parting her legs.

Trembling with wanton eagerness, she heard him unzip his jeans and waited. He drove into her hot wet sheath with molten urgency and an earthy groan of deep satisfaction.

'You are perfect for me, *aziz*,' he told her hungrily, his hands taking advantage of her position to knead her lush nipples and torment the tiny sensitive bud below her mound.

The surge of her excitement was intense. He ravished her with sensual force. Melting ripples of explosive pleasure seized a hold of her and she cried out at the height of her climax at the strength and wonder of that glorious rush of ecstasy. In the aftermath he dragged her shaking weak body onto the bed with him and held her close, pressing his mouth gently to hers.

'That was incredible,' she framed unevenly.

Jasim smiled lazily down at her. 'It always is with you.'

Releasing her to vault off the bed, he dug into the pocket of his jeans and presented her with a little box.

Propping herself up on one elbow, she opened it to reveal a glittering emerald ring. 'My goodness…it's exquisite.'

'It reminded me of your eyes, *aziz*.' Jasim slid it onto her finger. 'We must make the most of our last week here. I will be very busy when I return.'

She admired her ring. He had dropped his guard, shared his secrets with her. She wanted to tell him she loved him but worried that it might make him feel uncomfortable and her feel something less when he could not return the words. The silence stretched and she curved back into his arms, seeking the warmth and familiarity of him as a reassurance.

On the final day of their honeymoon, Jasim, who had spent odd hours going through his late brother's papers in his study, filled a box with documents and some rare old leather-bound books that more properly belonged in the palace library. Two helicopters sat outside in readiness for their return to Muscar. One of the pilots was ill and in bed in the staff quarters, but it was not a problem because Jasim was a pilot after training for several years with his country's air force.

'I'll be with you in a couple of hours when we have landed,' Jasim vowed as Elinor hovered anxiously. 'Stop looking so worried. I'm qualified to fly fighter jets.'

Elinor nodded agreement and wondered if she was turning into an awful clingy woman who had got too

attached and couldn't bear her husband out of her sight.
She boarded her helicopter. Smiling at Sami, who was
kicking his feet in excitement in his seat, she did up her
belt. As the unwieldy craft rose into the air she saw a
hurrying manservant bump into one of the gardeners and
drop the box he was carrying.

In the act of striding past to get into the other aircraft,
Jasim was quick to notice the photograph that had fallen
out of one of the books and he bent to scoop it up. It was
a faded picture of his older brother as a young man with a
woman in an evening gown. She was blonde and small with
a wide sweet smile that had a strong tug of familiarity for
him. He reached for the book and pulled out the folded
sheet of paper also protruding from its pages. It was a
letter. The harsh light of the sun at noon illuminating the
still crisp copperplate English script, he began to read and
it wasn't very long before Jasim was being rocked by an
appalling sense of guilt...

CHAPTER TEN

'YOU MUST BE BORED witless after spending a month at the beach, hemmed in by the sea on one side and the desert on the other!' Laila opined, all smiles and pleasantries as she sauntered into the sitting room where her mother, Mouna, was drinking tea with Elinor.

'Laila,' her gentle mother scolded. 'That was impolite.'

Laila rolled unconcerned eyes. 'There are no shops at the beach and Englishwomen are said to be very fond of shopping.'

'But all Englishwomen are not the same,' Elinor responded as she stretched out a hand to restrain Sami from climbing into a large plant pot. 'I like fashion but I get bored trailing round shops. I enjoyed the desert as well.'

'Ninety-nine per cent of women would enjoy the desert with Jasim in tow,' Laila remarked, lowering her voice to prevent her mother from hearing that sally.

Lifting a drowsy Sami onto her lap, Elinor gave the beautiful brunette a serene smile. 'You're probably right. He made a wonderful guide.'

'I hear you have been invited to open the new hotel and leisure complex and that the King has agreed.'

Rocking Sami, who was tired and getting cross, Elinor concealed her surprise at what was news to her and simply inclined her head to the brunette in acknowledgement. Until Laila appeared, uninvited and looking quite ravishing in a white shift dress that hugged every curve, Elinor had been hoping Jasim would get back. Then, aware that the other woman would linger to take advantage of his presence, she had wished Laila away. Now turning a discreet eye to the watch on her wrist for about the fourth time, Elinor was more concerned that Jasim was so late and wondered what was holding him up.

'Perhaps you're about to become the figurehead for our new media-savvy modern monarchy,' Laila commented, with an envy she could not hide, just as an older man in a business suit knocked on the sitting room door.

'Your Highness,' he greeted Elinor, who was still striving to adapt to her new title. 'The King wants to speak to you.'

Totally taken aback by that announcement, Elinor scrambled to her feet clutching Sami. Zaid, always a step ahead in questions of what was required within the household, had already summoned the baby's nurse and the young woman hurried in to take charge of the little boy.

On the way to see the King Elinor was a bundle of nerves, for she could not think of anything that Jasim's father might have to discuss with her and her companion was as unresponsive as a block of wood to her curious questions. Could it be about the opening of the new leisure complex that Laila had mentioned? She would have expected any such request to be passed on to her by Jasim. Almost inevitably she began to wonder if she had done or said something wrong and if his father could be taking advantage of his son's absence to tell her about it.

The King was sitting in the ornate reception room where he conducted most of his meetings. The instant Elinor laid eyes on his stony face and grey pallor, her heart gave a sick thud inside her and she forgot the protocol she had learned from Jasim and spoke first. 'What's happened?'

With his hand he urged her to make use of the chair that had been set beside his. Her legs feeling wobbly, Elinor sank down heavily, her eyes glued to the older man's deeply troubled face.

'Jasim has had to make an emergency landing and the rescue services are trying to locate the site as we speak,' he said in a low fierce voice.

Elinor felt the blood drain from her shattered face and her stomach gave a sick somersault. A horrible jumble of frightening images filled her mind. 'Did he crash?' she asked in a wobbly voice.

'We don't know—only that the helicopter developed a fault. He is an accomplished pilot. He passed out top of his year from the military school,' the older man informed her heavily. 'He will know what to do.'

'He'll be all right...he *has* to be,' Elinor mumbled shakily, terror threatening her desperate attempt to maintain her composure. Had she been alone, she knew she would have crumbled and sobbed out her fear.

The older man was sitting with lowered head and closed eyes, his lips moving as though he was praying.

'He is not answering his cell phone,' he revealed.

Elinor stopped breathing. Jasim had boasted that there was not a corner of Quaram that did not enjoy good network coverage and she knew he never went anywhere without his phone. She stared into space while the seconds ticked by and she prayed harder than she had ever prayed in her life before. Now when she had found such happiness with Jasim, she could not bear to imagine life without him. She heard the buzz of voices beyond the doors and realised that word of the accident was spreading inexorably through the palace; a crowd of people was gathering in the hall. The voices grew louder until she heard the slap of running feet against the marble floor. One of the doors opened with noisy abruptness.

Two of the King's aides erupted into the room closely followed by a couple of Jasim's. They raced down the room and burst into animated speech. Elinor had not a clue what they were saying but was convinced they could not be delivering bad news with so much animation and excitement.

'Jasim has been located,' his father announced grittily, reaching out to grip her hand in a supportive move. 'He is well.'

'*How*…well?' Elinor demanded helplessly.

'Scratches, bruises, but he is whole in limb and he will soon be here with us,' the King proclaimed tremulously, waving both hands in urgent dismissal of his hovering aides, who were staring at him and then swiftly averting their eyes from their elderly ruler.

Elinor turned worried eyes to Jasim's father. Unashamed tears of relief were streaming down the older man's face. He looked at her with anguished eyes of regret. 'He was always good and worthy of praise and I ignored him.'

'It's not too late to change that,' she murmured feelingly. 'It's never too late.'

They sat there together in a surprisingly companionable silence while they waited for Jasim's return. A curious calm had descended over Elinor. She was thinking that she too would have had regrets had Jasim been taken from her without warning. He might have died without knowing that she loved him and that awareness distressed her.

The palace guard in the grounds discharged their guns in long noisy bursts to announce Jasim's return. The King hurried down the long room to the doors to await his son. Elinor had already decided to leave the two men alone to talk, but she needed to see Jasim in the flesh to fully believe that he was safe and unharmed. He strode in, black hair tousled and dusty, the sleeve of his shirt missing and a bandage on his arm.

'I thought you weren't hurt!' she exclaimed in dismay.

'It's only a scratch,' he barked, an expression of shock and incredulity crossing his lean dark features as his father suddenly wrapped both arms round him and enveloped him in a hearty emotional hug.

Although it hurt Elinor to walk away when she too longed for that physical contact to vent her relief from intense fear and concern, she slipped out of the door behind Jasim and left him in peace with his father while she headed back to their corner of the palace. She still felt dizzy and physically weak at the merciful reprieve from her worst possible fears. Jasim had become as precious to her as Sami and she was still in shock from the fright she had had. Ruefully conscious that stress and heat had left her clothing sticking to her damp skin, she went straight upstairs for a quick shower.

She was wearing only a bra and pants when she heard

Jasim return. Snatching up her wrap, she pulled it on and hurriedly knotted the sash before leaving the room to greet him.

'I'm sorry I was so long,' he groaned, 'But my father had a great deal to say to me—'

'I thought he might,' Elinor confided, hauling him closer with two possessive hands, drinking in the familiar musky scent of his skin and the rich honeyed aroma of the frankincense smoke that the staff were always wafting ritually over him. 'He was very upset. That's why I left you alone.'

'I am married to an angel of tact and intelligence,' Jasim drawled softly, holding her back from him to gaze down at her flushed and anxious face with unashamed appreciation.

'What happened to your cell phone this afternoon?'

'I was in such a frantic hurry to follow you back to Muscar that I left my phone behind at the villa.'

Elinor frowned. 'Why were you in such a hurry?'

'I knew I had to offer you a grovelling apology for ever having believed that you would lie to me.'

Her brows pleated. 'What are you talking about?'

Jasim dropped an arm round her slim shoulders and walked her into the bedroom. He dug into his shirt pocket and removed a photo and a sheet of paper. He gave her the photo first. 'I believe that this woman may be your mother, Rose.'

Elinor stared down in surprise at the photograph, which she had never seen before. It depicted her late mother with a much younger and slimmer Prince Murad, both of them clad in evening dress. 'Yes, it is. Where did you get it from?'

'It fell out of a copy of the Koran that Murad cherished…along with this letter.' He passed her the letter.

It was a letter written by her mother to Murad, telling him gently that they had to get on with their lives since they could not be together and that staying in contact would only make that more difficult. 'It's very sad,' Elinor whispered.

'Murad must have loved her very much to keep the photo and the letter for so many years. When I saw the date I understood why my brother did not ask for his father's permission to marry your mother. It was the same year that my mother deserted my father and clearly Murad saw no point in requesting the King's blessing for his marriage with a foreigner. My father was so bitter over what he saw as his own mistake that he would have refused. I'm afraid that if my brother told your mother that he was threatened with disinheritance, he was lying.'

Elinor was shaking her head in rueful comprehension. 'It's awful how something one person does can affect so many other lives in different ways.'

'But I misjudged you and insulted you,' Jasim reminded her darkly, brilliant dark golden eyes welded to her. 'I believed Yaminah's melodramatic suspicions and I kept on crediting her take on your relationship with Murad, even after I should have accepted that you were telling me the truth!'

'Yes, but you do tend to see wheels within wheels where none exist. You're jealous and possessive by nature,' Elinor pointed out ruefully. 'You make everything complicated—'

'No, I don't.' Jasim gave her a look of reproach.

'Well, you have since I met you. You always seem to expect the worst from women—'

'Yet I have received only the *best* from you,' Jasim interrupted, closing lean hands over hers. 'You are everything that I ever dreamt of finding in a woman. I know that now yet I almost lost you for ever. I feel sick at the thought that I might never have found you and Sami again.'

'You're hurting my hands,' Elinor told him apologetically. It did seem a very prosaic comment to make in the midst of that emotional flood of appreciation.

He lifted her crushed fingers to his lips and kissed them, massaging them to restore her circulation after the ferocity of his grip. 'It took me a long time to realise that I loved you. I didn't think I *could* fall in love and then I was too slow to recognise it when I did.'

Bemused by that declaration, she stared at him, scarcely daring to believe that he could mean what he was saying. 'I never thought I'd hear you say those words.'

'Neither did I,' Jasim confided, gathering her close to his lean, powerful frame. 'But I love you very much and I feel amazingly lucky to have you, *hayati*—'

'I love you too.' Elinor allowed her fingertips to trace one hard, angular cheekbone in a tender caress. 'I honestly believed that you were never going to feel the same way.'

'You must have suspected when I took you out to see the wild flowers,' he breathed in wonderment. 'I've never done anything like that in my life before with a woman.'

'I must have been slow on the uptake as well. I simply thought that you were trying to teach me about Quaram.'

'I believe I fell for you the first time I saw you on a horse.' His irreverent grin slashed his lean, strong face. 'You looked like a wild warrior woman: sexy, strong—'

Highly amused, Elinor smiled up at him. 'Whatever turns you on.'

'Unfortunately, my jealousy of the bond I believed you had already formed with Murad coloured everything,' Jasim admitted flatly. 'It clouded my reasoning. I couldn't wait to take you to bed because only then would you be really mine.'

Elinor linked her hands round his neck, loving the fact that he was just so basic and masculine in his reactions. 'Everything with you happened way too fast for me and I don't adapt well to things like that,' she murmured. 'We barely had five minutes together as a couple before I discovered that I was pregnant, and then playing a leading role in a shotgun marriage didn't make me feel any better about myself or the decision I was making.'

'I should have explained to you how I felt about marrying you behind my father's back. But I should also have looked to the future and made it a more joyful day.' Jasim frowned. 'I can see how my attitude gave you the impression that I was a reluctant husband and contributed to your lack of faith in me later that day when you overheard Yaminah.'

'It was just the last straw, but you weren't the only one of us who got it wrong. I should have confronted you, rather than just walk out.'

Jasim held her fast to him and tugged up her chin so that their eyes met. 'The worst of your sins was failing to get in touch even to tell me that you were well and safe. You were pregnant. I was afraid that you might have decided not to continue with the pregnancy.'

Her eyes widened in consternation. 'Jasim, *no*, I wouldn't have done that.'

'But I didn't know that,' he reminded her ruefully.

'I'm sorry I didn't phone you. I was horribly bitter. For a long time I thought I h-hated you.' Her voice faltering to a halt, Elinor wrinkled her nose. Her eyes were prickling with tears, the weight of stress she had borne earlier taking its toll on her, and she buried her face in his shoulder, needing the warmth and security of his closeness. 'But I think I still loved you and only hated you for hurting me.'

'I'll never hurt you again,' Jasim swore huskily. 'We have found so much together. I could not bear to lose it.'

'I was scared you would try to take Sami away from me when you found me again,' she confessed.

'I grew up without a mother and I would not have sentenced Sami to the same experience. But I was ready to put on the pressure, pull him away a little and make a lot of noise if it meant that you followed him and came back to Quaram with me.' Dark golden eyes vibrant with amusement as he made that frank admission, Jasim looked so gorgeous he made her mouth run dry. 'I wanted *both* of you back in my life full-time. For the eighteen months you were missing, you were all I thought about and other women didn't exist for me, *hayati*.'

'I wish I'd known,' Elinor lamented.

'Maybe I needed to lose you to fully appreciate you.' Tiring of talk, Jasim captured her mouth in an intoxicating kiss and her world went into a sensual spin. Gathering her yielding body into his arms, he urged her down on the bed.

The lingering edge of fear from the afternoon made her as eager for him as he was for her. They shed their garments in a tangled heap and rolled across the mattress welded to each other like magnets. But the act they shared was slow and sweet and joyful with love and mutual appreciation. Afterwards she lay replete and content and very weary in his arms, revelling in the tenderness in his eyes and the way he kept on telling her how much he loved her, words she knew she would never tire of hearing.

'Some day I'd like another child,' Jasim murmured

huskily, one hand splayed across her flat stomach. 'I would be there right from the beginning and I would not leave your side until the baby was born, *habibti*.'

Elinor was almost asleep, a dreamy smile on her lips. 'Some day, I might take you up on that,' she whispered.

Almost three years later, Elinor entered the nursery at Woodrow Court wearing a beautiful green satin evening gown and a magnificent set of emerald and diamond jewellery that glittered fierily below the lights.

Sami was tucked up in bed clutching a toy racing car. His sister, Mariyah, a dark-eyed toddler with her mother's ready smile, was fast asleep, and the newest addition to the family, Tarif, at four months old, was mesmerised watching the cot mobile above him with big drowsy eyes as it turned and played a lullaby. He was a laid-back good-natured baby who only cried when he was hungry. She was the mother of three children, Elinor reflected in bemusement, still amazed by the speed with which her life had changed and flourished. Mariyah, if truth be known, had not been planned, but the pregnancy had been easy and the delivery quick and Elinor had decided she would like her third child to be born within the same age range as the other two.

It was their fourth wedding anniversary and Elinor was content to look back on the three wonderful years she had shared with Jasim. They were rarely apart for, as his father's heir, Jasim travelled a great deal less. King Akil had outlived all the gloomy forecasts and, although he was by no means a well man, he had regained his appetite and a little weight and was certainly looking a good deal better. Jasim and his father often worked together now and had grown a great deal closer and that improved relationship had brought Jasim peace after his turbulent, unhappy childhood.

Elinor too led a very busy life. She had been asked to open the new hotel and leisure complex in Muscar. Soon afterwards she had agreed to help raise funds for a charity for premature babies, an interest that had led to countless hospital visits and other requests for her support. When Jasim was so much in demand she felt it was important that she had her own concerns and, between those and her desire to spend as much time as possible with her children while they were still so young, her daily schedule was pretty packed. Whenever she was in England she met up with Alissa and Lindy and she loved escaping the pomp and ceremony of life in Quaram to be treated just as a friend.

How had she dealt with Laila? Elinor's eyes sparkled at the recollection. She had leant on Jasim to issue invitations to palace functions to every eligible man he knew and, before very long, romance had worked its magic and Laila had been married and swept off to Oman by a very rich and besotted sheikh. Elinor got on very well with Laila's mother, Mouna, who looked on her as an extra daughter and adored the children.

Elinor had seen very little of her father in recent years but that was only what she had expected. Ernest Tempest had little interest in his grandchildren, and once he had satisfied his curiosity about the ancient history of Quaram further visits had had little appeal for the older man. Elinor believed she had already received more warm appreciation and encouragement from Jasim's father than she had ever received from her own.

At the King's instigation, the old rambling palace in the

desert outside the city had been renovated from top to bottom and the royal household had moved back there. Murad's monstrous noisy marble palace was now being used by the government as a conference centre, a parliamentary building and a museum. Yaminah had remarried and become stepmother to several children with her second husband. She had attended Jasim's birthday party the previous year. Elinor had enjoyed seeing Zahrah again and Yaminah had been scrupulously polite and pleasant as though all her wild suspicions had been laid in the grave with her first husband.

'What a picture you make,' Jasim breathed from the doorway.

In a whirl of fabric as her glamorous gown spun out round her, Elinor sped over to him. 'I thought you were going to be late—'

'For my anniversary dinner with my beautiful wife? Never!' Jasim teased, dark golden eyes smouldering with sensual appreciation over her before he curved an arm round her and walked round the nursery, bending down to say goodnight to Sami, laughing at the way Mariyah was curled up in one corner of her cot and smiling down at Tarif. 'But before we eat, I have something to show you. Unfortunately you're rather overdressed for our destination.'

'Shall I change?' Elinor asked.

'No, you look fabulous and I want to feast my eyes on you.'

'The emeralds are way over the top,' she sighed, her fingertips brushing the superb necklace.

'That was my father's gift,' he reminded her. 'And he doesn't do cheap or ordinary.'

She giggled like mad when he carried her out of the

house and stashed her in the Range Rover parked out front. 'Where on earth are we going?'

Jasim turned the car in the direction of the stables and she sat up straight, her level of interest growing, for the year before Jasim had given her a superb mare and she was a good deal more interested in horse flesh than she was in jewellery.

He helped her out and guided her over to the stables while she gathered her skirt up in one hand to stop it trailing. 'I have a surprise for you.'

'If it's got four legs, I'll love you for ever…well, I'll love you for ever whatever you do but more particularly if it's a live present.'

'Hush, *habibti*,' Jasim urged. 'She's been a little neglected and she's rather nervous, so the staff haven't subjected her to a decent grooming as yet.'

'Who?' Elinor was now nestling under his arm like a purring cat, for whenever he called her *habibti*, which meant 'beloved', she just melted inside.

A shaggy greyish-white head poked anxiously out over the stable door. The elderly animal in no way resembled the pedigree, perfectly groomed horses that usually occupied the boxes. Elinor stared at the homely mare with huge rounded eyes. *'Starlight?'* she whispered in disbelief, her voice cracking with emotion. She moved closer. 'My word, you've found Starlight for me! Is it any wonder that you're the love of my life?'

Jasim stood back watching while she petted the horse she had adored as a teenager and which her father had sold. He told her something of the mare's history since then and her eyes glistened with tears. After she had coaxed Starlight into trusting her again, she turned back to Jasim and flung herself at him in a passion of gratitude, hugging and kissing him with abandon.

'You really are wonderful,' she told him with shining eyes.

'You're the wonder in my life, *habibti*. I have you and I have three beautiful children, and I feel as though you have given me the whole world,' Jasim murmured huskily, studying her with quiet adoration.

Happiness bubbled up inside Elinor. 'I love you,' she whispered. 'And every day I'm with you, I love you a little more.'

* * * * *

RUTHLESS MAGNATE, CONVENIENT WIFE

Lynne Graham

CHAPTER ONE

OIL billionaire, Sergei Antonovich, travelled behind tinted windows in a big black glossy four-wheel drive. Two car-loads of bodyguards flanked him, in front and behind. Such a sight was worthy of note en route to a remote Russian village like Tsokhrai. But everyone who saw the cavalcade pass knew exactly who it was, for Sergei's grandmother was well known locally, and her grandson always visited her on Easter Day.

Sergei was looking at the road that he had turned from a dirt track into a broad highway to facilitate the transportation needs of the coach-building factory he had set up to provide employment in this rural area. In the winters, when once he had lived here, the road had been thick with mud and often impassable by anything more sophisticated than a farm cart. When it had snowed, the village had been cut off for weeks on end. Sometimes even Sergei still found it hard to believe that he had spent several years of his adolescence in Tsokhrai, where he had suffered the pure culture shock of an urban tearaway plunged into a rustic nightmare of clean country living. At the age of thirteen, he had been six feet tall, a gang member and embryo thug, accustomed to breaking the law just to survive. His grand-mother, Yelena, had been barely five feet tall, function-ally illiterate and desperately poor. Yet Sergei knew that everything he had become and everything he had achieved in the years since then was down to the inde-fatigable efforts of that little woman to civilise him.

The convoy came to a halt outside a humble build-ing clad in faded clapboards and sheltering behind an overgrown hedge. The bodyguards, big tough men who wore sunglasses even on dull days and never smiled, leapt out first to check out the area. Sergei finally emerged, a sartorial vision of elegant grooming in a silk and mohair blend suit that was superbly tailored to his broad-shouldered powerful physique. His ex-wife, Rozalina, had called this his 'annual guilt pilgrimage' and had refused to accompany him. But his visit was enough reward for the elderly woman who would not even let him build her a new house. Yelena, Sergei re-flected grimly, was the only female he had ever met who wasn't eager to take him for every ruble she could get. He had long since decided that extreme greed and an overriding need to lionise over others were essentially feminine failings.

As Sergei strode down the front path towards the dwelling, villagers fell back from where they were gath-ered in its doorway and an awe-inspired silence fell. Yelena was a small plump woman in her seventies with bright eyes and a no-nonsense manner. She greeted him without fuss, only the huskiness of her voice and her use of the diminutive name 'Seryozh' for him hinting at how much her only grandchild meant to her.

'As always you are alone,' Yelena lamented, guiding him over to the table, which was spread with a feast of

food to satisfy those who had just finished practising a
forty-day fast in honour of the season. 'Eat up.'

Sergei frowned. 'I haven't been—'

His grandmother began to fill a large plate for him.
'Do you think I don't know that?'

The bearded Orthodox priest sitting at the table,
which was decorated with flowers and painted eggs,
gave the younger man who had rebuilt the crumbling
church tower an encouraging smile. 'Eat up,' he urged.

Sergei had skipped breakfast in anticipation of the
usual gastronomic challenge that awaited him. He ate
with appetite, sampling the special bread and the Easter
cake. Throughout, he was approached by his grandmother's visitors and he listened patiently to requests for
advice, support and money, because he was also the
recognised source of philanthropy in the community.

Yelena stood by watching and concealing her pride.
She was wryly aware that her grandson was the cyno-
sure of attention for every young woman in the room.
That was understandable: his hard-boned dark features
were strikingly handsome and he stood six feet three
inches tall with the lean powerful build of an athlete. As
always, however, Sergei was too accustomed to female
interest to be anything other than indifferent to it. His
grandmother had a fleeting recollection of the lovelorn
girls who had dogged his every step while he was still
a boy. Nothing had changed; Sergei still enjoyed an extraordinary level of charisma.

Sergei was mildly irritated by his female audience
and wondered how much Yelena had had to do with the
surprising number of attractive well-groomed young
women milling about. His concentration, however, had
only to alight on his grandmother, though, for it to occur

to him that she looked a little older and wearier every time he saw her. He knew she was disappointed that he had failed to bring a girl home with him. But the women who satisfied his white-hot libido in his various homes round the world were not the type he would have chosen to introduce to a devout old lady. He recognised that she was desperate to see him marry and produce a family. It would have surprised many, who saw Sergei solely as an arrogant, notoriously cold-blooded businessman, to learn that he actually believed that he *owed* it to Yelena to give her what she wanted.

After all these years, what thanks had Yelena yet reaped from taking a risk on her once foul-mouthed and defiant grandson? While her guardianship had turned Sergei's life and prospects around, life for her had remained very tough. His immense wealth and success meant virtually nothing to her, yet he was her only living relative. Her husband had been a drunk and a wife-beater, her son had been a car thief and her daughter-in-law an alcoholic.

'You worry about Yelena,' the priest noted sagely. 'Bring her a wife and a grandchild and she will be happy.'

'If only it were so easy as you make it sound,' Sergei quipped, averting his gaze from the excess of cleavage on display as a nubile beauty hurried forward to pour him another coffee.

'With the right woman it *is* that easy!' The priest laughed with the pride and good humour of a family man who had six healthy children.

But Sergei harboured a deep abiding aversion to the matrimonial state. Rozalina had proved to be a very expensive mistake. And, more significantly, even a decade after the divorce he could not forget the child she had aborted to protect her perfect body. He had never told Yelena about that, as he had known it would have broken her heart and troubled her dreams. He also knew, noting the depth of the lines on her creased and weathered face, that she was on the slippery slope of life and that time was of the essence. Some day there would be no one left to tell him that the noise of his helicopter landing nearby had traumatised her pig and stopped her hens laying. It was a bleak thought that made his conscience stab him. Who had done more for him and who had he rewarded least? If any woman deserved a bouncing baby on her lap, it was Yelena Antonova.

Sergei was still mulling over the problem that afternoon when his grandmother asked him if he ever ran into Rozalina. He managed not to wince. He was a loner, he always had been, and he found personal relationships a challenge. He loved the cut and thrust of business, the exhilaration of a new deal or takeover, the challenge of cutting out the dead wood and increasing profit in the under-performers, the sheer satisfaction of making a huge financial killing. If only marriage could be more like business with clear-cut rules and contracts that left no room for misunderstandings or errors!

An instant later, his high-powered brain kicked up a gear and he thought, *Why not?* Why the hell shouldn't he choose a wife and get a child by the same means in which he did business? After all, trying to do it the old-fashioned way had been catastrophic.

'Is there anyone?' Yelena asked with a guilty edge that told him she had been holding back on that question about his private life all day.

'Perhaps,' he heard himself say, holding out a thread of hope or possibly a foundation for a future development.

And, that fast, the plan began forming. This time around, Sergei decided, he would take the professional practical approach to the institution of marriage. He would draw up a list of requirements, put his lawyers in charge and urge them to use a doctor and a psychologist to weed out unsuitable applicants for the role he envisaged. Of course the marriage would be short-term and he would retain custody of the child. He immediately grasped the dichotomy of his preferences. He didn't want a wife who would do anything for money, but he *did* want one prepared to give him a child and then walk away when he had had enough of playing happy families for Yelena's benefit. But somewhere in the world his perfect matrimonial match had to exist, Sergei reasoned. If he was specific enough with his requirements he would not even have to meet her before the wedding. Energised by that prospect, and once back behind the privacy of the tinted windows of his four-by-four, he began to make bullet points on his notebook computer.

When Alissa saw her sister, Alexa, climbing out of a totally unfamiliar fire-engine-red sports car, she was filled with a lively mix of exasperation, bewilderment and impatience. Even so, a strong thread of relief bound all those disparate emotions together and she hurtled downstairs, a tiny slender blonde with a mass of silvery pale hair and clear aquamarine eyes.

She flung open the front door of the cottage and the questions just erupted from her in a breathless stream. 'Where have you been all these weeks? You promised you'd phone and you didn't! I've been worried sick about you! Where on earth did that fancy car come from?'

Amusement gleaming in her eyes, Alexa strolled forward. 'Hi, twin, nice to see you too.'

Alissa hugged her sister. 'I was going out of my mind with worry,' she admitted ruefully. 'Why didn't you phone? And what happened to your mobile phone?'

'It broke and I got a new number.' Alexa wrinkled her nose. 'Look, things got very complicated and I kept on deciding to wait until I had something more concrete to offer you—and then when I finally *did* have it, I thought it would be easier to just come home and tell you face to face.'

Alissa stared at her sister, not understanding and not expecting to, either. It had always been that way because, although the girls had been born identical, it had been clear from an early age that below the skin they were two very different personalities. Alexa had always been the single-minded, ambitious one, quick to fight and scrap for what she wanted, and she made enemies more easily than she made friends. Alissa was quieter, steadier, occasionally tormented by an overdeveloped conscience and altogether more thoughtful. At twenty-three years of age, the sisters were less obviously twins than they had been as children. Alexa wore her long silvery blonde hair sleek, layered and shoulder length while Alissa's was longer and more usually confined in a ponytail. Alexa wore fashionable, often provocative clothing and revelled in the attention men awarded her, while Alissa dressed conservatively and froze like a rabbit in headlights when men homed in on her more understated charms.

'Where's Mum?' Alexa asked, flinging her coat down in a heap and walking into the kitchen.

'She's at the shop. I came home this afternoon to do the accounts,' Alissa confided, putting the kettle on to boil. 'I gather you got a job in London.'

Alexa gave her a rather self-satisfied smile and leant back against the kitchen counter. 'Of course I did. I'm a whizz at selling luxury cars and I've earned a lot of commission. How's Mum?'

Alissa pursed her lips. 'As good as she's ever going to be. At least I don't hear her crying at night any more—'

'She's getting over it? About time,' Alexa pronounced with approval.

Alissa sighed. 'I don't think Mum's ever really going to get over it—particularly not while Dad's parading his fancy piece round the village. Or with all this debt still hanging over her, not to mention having to sell her home into the bargain…'

Alexa gave her a wide smile. 'Well, I was going to ask you whether you wanted the good or the bad news first. On the way here I stopped off at the solicitor's and told him to go ahead and agree a financial settlement for the house. I also gave him enough money to settle the bills. Prepare yourself for a surprise: I've got the cash to pay off our bastard of a father!'

'Don't talk about Dad like that,' Alissa said uneasily while she struggled to accept the dramatic assurance that the other woman had just voiced. 'Although I agree with the sentiment.'

'Oh, don't be so mealy-mouthed!' Alexa urged tartly. 'Mum loses her son and my boyfriend in a ghastly accident, nurses Dad through his cancer scare and what's her reward? Dad takes off with a hairdresser young enough to be his daughter!'

'You just said you've got enough money to pay off

Dad and more for the bills—how is that possible? You've only been away three months.' Alissa was frowning. She wanted so badly to believe it was possible, but her native wit was telling her that even though Alissa was a terrific saleswoman she still didn't have that kind of earning power.

'You could say that I went for a new job with a big cash payment up front. As I said, there's enough to settle all Mum's bills and pay off Dad,' Alexa repeated, keen to make that salient point again.

Alissa was wide-eyed with disbelief. 'As well as enough to buy that car outside *and* renew your designer wardrobe?'

Alexa's smile evaporated as she gave her twin a cool accusing scrutiny. 'You've already noticed the label on my new coat?'

'No, it just has that look. That sophisticated look that expensive clothes always seem to have,' Alissa advanced ruefully. 'What kind of a job pays that much money?'

'Didn't you hear what I told you?' Alexa demanded thinly. 'I've saved our bacon—I have enough money to sort out *all* Mum's problems and give her back her self-respect and security.'

'That would take a miracle.' Alissa was convinced that her sister was wildly exaggerating the case.

'In today's world, you have to compete and work *very* hard and make sacrifices to bring about a miracle.'

At that reference to making sacrifices from a young woman who had never demonstrated the smallest leaning in that direction, Alissa stole a troubled glance at her sister. 'I don't understand.'

'As I said, it's complex. For a start I'm afraid I had to sort of *borrow* your identity.'

Alissa froze at that announcement. 'Borrow my identity? *How?*'

'You're the one with the university degree and I needed to use it on my application to meet the criteria,' Alexa revealed, lifting her chin in defiance of her twin's shaken stare. 'And because I had used it to make myself look educated I had to use your name as well. When they checked out my claims they'd soon have discovered that I was lying if I'd applied under my own name.'

Alissa was very shocked at her sister's casual attitude to what she had done. 'But that's…that's fraud, cheating…'

Alexa's indifference to what she clearly saw as a minor detail was striking. 'Whatever. I thought it was worth a try and so it proved, but then I started seeing someone.'

'You're dating again?' Alissa gasped in surprise and excitement. After her sister's boyfriend, Peter, had died in the same car crash that had taken their brother's life—a tragedy that had soon been followed by their father's shocking defection—Alexa had become so angry and bitter that she had sworn off all men. Alissa had understood the level of her sister's heartbreak for, as their next-door-neighbours' son, Peter had been as much a part of their lives as any member of the family.

'Were you too busy looking at the coat to notice *this?*' Alexa extended a hand on which an opulent ruby and diamond ring glowed on her engagement finger.

Alissa gaped. 'You're engaged…*already?*'

'And preggers,' Alexa confided.

'Pregnant as well?' Alissa stared as her sister turned sideways but it was evidently early days for her stomach still looked perfectly flat. 'My word, and you never said a thing about all this until now?'

Alexa grimaced. 'I told you that things had got complicated. I was in the running for that job and I didn't want to tell Harry about it…yes, that's *his* name. He's quite well off—a gentleman farmer who runs his family estate. They're thrilled about me and the baby, not a bit bothered that I'm not one of the county set. But neither he nor his family would understand what I signed up for before we met…or that I could have accepted all that money for the right reasons.'

Her smooth brow furrowing, Alissa stared. 'Alexa, what are you talking about? This job? What money did you accept?'

Alexa sat down at the kitchen table and sipped her tea before she replied. 'I never thought I'd get it. I went through the whole application process out of curiosity. Strictly speaking, it's not really a job,' she admitted in an undertone.

Alissa sank down into the chair opposite. 'Then what is it? It isn't anything, well…immoral, is it?'

'Before I tell you, you think very carefully about what that money will do for Mum,' her sister urged sharply. 'It's her only hope of rescue and I've already paid out most of it on her behalf. All I had to do to get it was agree to marry a very rich Russian and act like his wife.'

'But why would any man want to pay you for doing that? These days I thought most rich Russians were beating off gold-digging women with sticks,' Alissa remarked drily.

'This guy wants it all done on a business basis, with money paid up front, signed contracts and a settlement agreed for the divorce at the end. He wanted an educated attractive Englishwoman and I stepped forward. I almost told his lawyers that he could have two of us for the price of one!'

Alissa wasn't amused by that rather tasteless joke. 'So, let me get this straight—you decided you were willing to marry this man just for the cash?'

'For Mum!' Alexa contradicted loudly. 'I was only *ever* willing to do it for her sake.'

Alissa sat there tautly and thought about this explanation. Everything she herself had done of late, from resigning from her comfortable librarian's job in London to coming home to help out as best she could, had also been done for her mother's sake. Both young women adored their parent, who was currently stressed out of her mind and desperately depressed, a mere shadow of the cheerful and energetic woman she had once been.

A kinder and more loving and supportive parent or wife than Jenny Bartlett would be hard to find. Unfortunately, over the past two years, the twins' once close and contented family circle had been cruelly smashed by a series of disasters. The death of their brother, Stephen, and of Alexa's boyfriend, Peter, in a car crash one wintry evening had only been the first calamity to strike them. That storm had barely been weathered before their father's cancer was diagnosed. Long months of anxiety and debilitating medical treatment had followed. Throughout all those events their mother had been the strongest of them all, refusing to allow her family to sink into despair. She could never have guessed then that, within months of his recovery from cancer, her husband of thirty years would desert her for a much younger woman and then claim half of their home and business to finance his new lifestyle. Watching those awful proceedings unfold from the sidelines, Alissa had felt her heart break alongside her mother's.

Alissa had learned a new insecurity when she had finally realised that she could not even trust her father to be the honest and decent man she had always believed he was. Although he was an accountant on a good salary, he was pursuing his wife for a share of the home that had originally belonged to *her* parents and of the small business that she had set up and ran entirely on her own. Money and the lust for more of it, Alissa thought fearfully, could turn people into strangers and make them do inexcusable things. Now it seemed to her that Alexa had got caught up in the same dangerous toils.

'Pay the money back,' Alissa urged tightly. 'You can't marry some foreigner you don't even know for money.'

'Well, I can't marry him *now,* can I? I mean, I'm carrying Harry's baby!' Alexa pointed out flatly. 'And Harry wants us to get married in the next couple of weeks.'

Alissa nodded, unsurprised by that sudden announcement. Alissa always did everything at supersonic speed. That she had fallen in love and fallen pregnant within months and was racing equally fast into marriage was the norm for her. She had never learnt patience and if common sense threatened to come between her and her goals she would ignore it.

'*You* must go ahead and marry the Russian in my place,' Alexa continued, 'or I'll be forced to consider an abortion…'

Shattered by that announcement, Alissa pushed her chair noisily back and leapt upright. 'What on earth are you talking about? *Me* marry this weird guy? An *abortion?* Is that what you want?'

A petulant expression traversed Alexa's face. 'No, of

course it's not what I want, Allie, but what choice do I have? I signed a legal binding contract and I accepted a huge amount of money on the strength of it. Most of the money has been spent so I can't give it back. So where does that leave me?'

Alissa was once again aghast at that admission. '*Spent?*'

'Mostly on Mum. Okay, so I bought the car and a few other little things. At the time I thought that with the sacrifice I was making in agreeing to marry the guy, I had the right to spoil myself a bit. After all, it was me, not you, riding to Mum's rescue!' her twin vented, treating her sister to a scornful appraisal. 'I mean, here you are, acting all shocked at what I've done. But what have *you* done, but sit here wringing your hands and checking bank statements? It took me to take action, so don't you dare look down on me for being willing to marry a stranger for money. Money and lots of it is the only real cure for the problems here!'

The louder Alexa's angry voice got, the paler Alissa became and she sat down heavily again. 'I'm not looking down on you in any way. You're right. You have pulled off something that I couldn't have and, yes, we are desperate for money—'

Her sister clasped her hand in a fierce plea for understanding. 'Don't I deserve to be happy?'

'I've never doubted it.'

'But I never thought I'd be happy again after Peter died. I thought my life was over, that I might as well have died in that car with him and Stephen,' Alexa confided in a pained tone. 'But now I've met Harry and everything's different. I love him and I want to marry him and have my baby. I've got my life back again and I want to enjoy it.'

Touched to the bone by that emotive speech, Alissa clasped both her hands round her sister's in a warm gesture of understanding. 'Of course you do…of course you do…'

'But Harry won't want anything more to do with me if he finds out what I signed up for—it will *destroy* us!' Alexa sobbed, swerving from furious defensiveness and drama to a noisy bout of self-pitying tears. 'He would never understand what I've done or forgive me for being so mercenary. He's a very straightforward, honest man.'

All of a sudden, Alissa was feeling as though she was on old familiar ground. When they were children, Alexa had often got into tight corners and Alissa had usually got her out of them. More than once Alissa had shouldered the blame for Alexa's wrongdoing, as even then she had dimly grasped that she might be the less adventurous twin but she *was* the stronger and the least likely of the two to break down when life became difficult. Alexa might be more daring, but she was also surprisingly fragile and could never cope once she made a mess of things.

'Surely Harry doesn't have to know about all this?' Alissa said, even though she felt guilty for suggesting that Alexa keep secrets from her future husband.

'Listen, Allie,' Alexa breathed. 'If I don't show up and marry the Russian, I'll have to repay the money and I can't. Do you honestly think a guy like Sergei Antonovich is going to let me get away with defrauding him of that amount of cash?'

'Sergei Antonovich? The Russian billionaire?' Alissa queried in consternation. 'He's the guy who wants to hire a wife? For goodness' sake, he's always knee-deep in supermodels and actresses. Why would he have to *pay* a woman he doesn't know to marry him?'

'Because a long time ago he was married and it didn't work out. This time around he wants a marriage of convenience on a strict business basis. I don't know any more than that,' Alexa replied, her eyes swerving abruptly from her sister's questioning gaze to rest fixedly on the table instead, her whole face taut and shuttered. 'That was what the lawyer told me and he said I didn't need to know any more and that it was just a job; maybe a little different from other jobs, but a job nonetheless.'

'A job,' Alissa repeated, widening her expressive eyes in emphatic disagreement.

'If you marry Antonovich instead, I'll be able to go ahead and marry Harry, we'll keep the money and Mum's life will go back to normal. You know, the Russian hasn't met me yet, so he won't know we've switched and he's never going to guess that you're not the woman who was selected—'

'It doesn't matter…it's crazy and I couldn't do it,' Alissa framed unevenly, feeling the weight of the pressure her twin was heaping on her shoulders and firmly resisting it.

'I applied in your name,' her sister reminded her. 'It's you the lawyers will come after if you don't follow through on that contract.'

Alissa, usually slow to lose her temper, was finally getting angry. 'I don't care what you did—*I* didn't sign any contract!'

'Well, you might as well have done because I forged your signature,' Alexa informed her wryly. 'I'm sorry, but we're both involved in this up to our throats. Short of a lottery win, we can't return the money and why would you want to anyway? We've no other way of saving this house for Mum. At the moment, it's impossible to get a loan—'

'But Mum couldn't have afforded to pay it back anyway. And now there's not even anything left to sell,' Alissa acknowledged.

The few valuable pieces of furniture and jewellery that had been in the family had already been sold to shore up her mother's finances. The cottage had long been mortgaged up to the hilt when Jenny had borrowed against the property to buy premises in the village and open up a coffee and craft shop there. Although the cottage was currently for sale, there had been few viewers and little interest shown; times were hard and the property was definitely in need of modernisation.

In the uncomfortable silence that stretched, Alissa stood up. 'It's raining—I promised I'd pick Mum up if it was wet.'

Alissa climbed into the elderly hatchback car that belonged to her mother and drove off. As she pulled into a parking space outside the shop, she saw a curvaceous brunette emerging and unfurling a bright yellow plastic umbrella. She wore a skirt short enough to shock a burlesque dancer. At the sight of her, loud alarm bells rang with Alissa because the woman was her father's girlfriend, Maggie Lines. As Maggie sped on down the street Alissa scrambled out of the car in haste and knocked on the shop door when she found it locked.

'What was that woman doing in here?' she demanded of the small blonde woman who let her in.

Her mother's eyes were reddened and overbright, her level of stress palpable in her fearful expression and trembling hands. 'She came to talk to me. She said she didn't like to come to the house and at least she waited for closing time—'

Alissa was rigid with outrage on her gentle mother's behalf. She felt that it was bad enough that her father had had an affair but it was unspeakably cruel that he should allow his partner in crime to harass the wife he had deserted. 'You don't need to talk to Maggie. She's Dad's business, not yours, and she should keep her nose out of what doesn't concern her!'

'She says that fighting it out between the lawyers is only increasing our legal bills,' Jenny muttered tautly.

'What did she want?' Alissa prompted, carefully removing the dishcloth that her mother was twisting between her nervous hands.

'Money. What she said is your father's due,' the older woman explained in a mortified undertone. 'And although I didn't like hearing it, what she said was right. It *is* the law that he has to get his share of everything, but there's not a lot I can do when we haven't even had an offer for the house, is there?'

'She shouldn't have come here. You shouldn't have to speak to her.'

'She's a very determined young woman but I'm not scared of her, Alissa. And you shouldn't be getting involved in all this. Your father may well marry Maggie and start a second family with her. It happens all the time, so it would be wiser if you didn't take sides right now.'

Her troubled eyes glistening with tears, Alissa gripped the older woman's hands tightly in hers. 'I love you so much, Mum. I hate to see you being hurt like this.'

Jenny Bartlett attempted a reassuring smile. 'In time I'll get over it, "move on" as Maggie likes to say. But right now it's all too fresh. I *still* love him, Alissa,' she muttered guiltily. 'That's the worst thing about all this. I can't seem to switch off my feelings.'

Alissa wrapped her arms protectively round her slight mother. Her own heart felt as if it were breaking inside her as a swell of memories from happier times engulfed her. It was not right that the mother who had loved and supported her all her life should lose her home and business as well, for it would leave the older woman with absolutely nothing to survive on. 'Alexa's home, Mum, and she's got good news: she's met a man and it's serious—'

The older woman turned startled eyes on her daughter. 'Has she…*really?*'

'Yes, and Alexa and I have sorted out something on the money front too,' Alissa heard herself say with deliberate vagueness. 'You may not have to sell the house after all.'

'That's not possible,' Jenny exclaimed.

'Miracles do happen,' Alissa commented, thinking up fantastic stories of special financial arrangements that could be made and secured on her and her twin's earning power.

And she was stunned by her own audacity. She was the sensible twin, the one who was never impulsive and didn't take risks. But family came first and she was desperate to help and bring the ghastly divorce settlement to a dignified conclusion for her mother's sake. She watched the older woman lock up. So, did that mean she was willing to marry Sergei Antonovich? Or had she just been guilty of offering her mother false hope? During the short drive home Alissa tussled mentally with herself.

A few minutes after she walked through the front door, however, Alexa helped her to make a final decision. 'I got a call from the Russian's lawyer while you were out,' her twin whispered in Alissa's ear while Alissa was busy preparing supper. 'Sergei Antonovich has decided to meet me before the wedding. You have to decide whether you're going to help Mum or not!'

Put on the spot, Alissa thought first about the baby that her twin was carrying and doubted Alexa's readiness to continue that pregnancy if her relationship with the father ran into trouble. In comparison Alissa had no relationship that such a marriage could interfere with.

A long time ago, she had suffered considerable heartache when she'd secretly fallen for Alexa's boyfriend, Peter. Since then she had made occasional forays onto the dating scene, only to retreat when she met up with the impatient sexual expectations of the modern male. Those who had failed to press her panic buttons on that score had signally failed to impress her on any other level. Unlike Alexa, who scalp-hunted with almost masculine enthusiasm, Alissa preferred quality over quantity and was more often alone than involved in a relationship.

Indeed her family meant much more to Alissa than anything else in her life. Having had to stand by powerless while that same family had all but disintegrated had tortured her. But now Alexa had put the power to alter that situation into Alissa's hands. Did she have the strength to go against her every principle and make a mockery of marriage by using it as a means of making money? Did the fact that she had no plans to profit personally make it any less of a sin? And now that she had that option, could she honestly turn her back on the only chance she was ever likely to get to settle most of her mother's problems?

On the other hand, Alissa reasoned, money would not bring her father home or cure her mother's pain, but it would certainly help the older woman to adjust to her altered future if it allowed her to remain in her childhood home and retain her business. On that optimistic thought, Alissa squashed the doubts bubbling up frantically to the surface of her mind. Pretending to be some man's wife would be a challenge, but the return of some semblance of normality to her mother's life would be worth it. On reaching that conclusion, Alissa came to a swift decision and gave Alexa the answer she most wanted to hear…

CHAPTER TWO

FROWNING, Sergei surveyed the studio photo for at least the tenth time that morning. Taken feature by feature, Alissa Bartlett was very attractive but regrettably she didn't *do* anything for him.

Sergei, who had never suffered from indecision, was fighting a galloping attack of cold feet. Having noted that his lawyers hadn't done much research into his bride-to-be's background, he had already resolved to have that omission rectified before he went any further. But, if he was honest, his main objection to her was a good deal more basic: in a nutshell, the skinny blonde turned him off big time.

He had read the transcripts of her interviews and studied her psychological profile and, the more he found out about her, the less he wanted to marry her, even temporarily. The trouble was that she *did* tick all the boxes he had demanded be ticked. In that respect, his staff had done an excellent job. He could not deny that she was attractive, educated, sophisticated and elegant. But then he had failed to lay down the right criteria for the role. He had thought too much about what was on the outside and not enough about what was on the inside, for it was plain Alissa was also selfish, extremely vain, rather stupid in spite of that education and cold as ice in the emotional department.

However, since when had he wanted emotion involved in a relationship with a woman? Sergei asked himself with derision. But then, never before had he been confronted in advance by so many unpalatable facts about a woman's character. Furthermore, Yelena was nobody's fool and was almost certain to spot the ugly truth below the pretty surface show of such a wife. That was why Sergei had decided that he *had* to meet his chosen bride in the flesh rather than risking compounding his mistake by marrying her sight unseen in a week's time. He didn't want to leave anything to chance. He could always cancel the contract if she didn't come up to scratch in the flesh. He cursed under his breath, wondering if all his carefully laid plans were about to come to nothing…

'This just isn't me,' Alissa sighed, studying her reflection in the mirror with critical and uneasy eyes.

'You're not supposed to be you, you're supposed to be *me*—at least to look at!' Alexa argued vehemently. 'And you can't show up in some cut-price dreary outfit when I was supposed to choose a new wardrobe in time for the wedding and given the money to do it. I'm going to have to give you almost all my clothes to go through with this masquerade.'

Recognising the resentful note in her twin's voice, Alissa breathed, 'I don't want your clothes because they're not my style—'

'You don't *have* a style,' her more fashionable sister retorted tartly. 'You wear cheap comfy clothes and that's not what a rich man expects. If you're going to carry this pretence off, you have to get the image right.'

'If you added a set of wings I'd look just like a fairy off a Christmas tree!' Alissa exclaimed in mortification, twirling so that the short skirt of the black dress flew out and exposed the cerise-pink layers of net edged with lace beneath. The net was scratchy and uncomfortable and the towering pink peep-toe shoes she also wore forced her to walk in little mincing steps. Plus, she was a good deal curvier than her sister and her breasts were straining against the snug fit of the bodice. 'This dress is too small for me!'

'It's fine. I have a much slimmer figure. You can't expect the dress to look anything like as good on you as it does on me. Try to remember that it's not cool to stuff yourself if there's food around,' Alexa reprimanded her. 'You're welcome to my clothes. After all I am pregnant and they won't fit me much longer. Make sure you don't lose that coat by leaving it down somewhere. There are thieves everywhere.'

A towering man, who was as tall as he was broad, came to the door of Alexa's apartment to announce that a car was waiting downstairs for Alissa. Alexa was careful to stay out of sight. He had a heavy accent and minimal English at his disposal, so Alissa's initial chatty efforts to find out what his name was, how long he had worked for his employer and where she was going fell on stony ground. During the journey, however, he turned in the front passenger seat, eased open the partition and pointed carefully to himself. 'Borya,' he told her, having worked out what she wanted to know.

'Alissa,' she responded cheerfully, striving not to surrender to the nervous chill steadily spreading through her.

The vehicle came to a halt outside a nightclub where a sizeable gathering of stylish people were already queuing for entry. A protective presence by her side, Borya swept her in past the doormen. Mindful of her twin's strictures about the coat she wore, Alissa came to a halt at the cloakroom check and removed the garment, determined to take no risks with it. Borya broke into a voluble speech but she was none the wiser as to what he was telling her and she passed over the coat.

'Are you feeling all right?' she asked the attendant, who was coughing into a handkerchief and shivering in the corner behind the counter.

'I've got a rotten cold and it's freezing in here,' the girl spluttered miserably and Alissa felt desperately sorry for her; while she had been a student she had often worked in low-paid part-time jobs to make ends meet.

Surrounded by his aides and his entire security team, Sergei was in a private room watching football on a giant wall television plasma screen. But the instant his bride-to-be walked through the door backed by Borya, he shook himself by totally forgetting the game. Indeed unfamiliar words like exquisite and dazzling briefly shone a glow of inspiration over Sergei's more usually prosaic thoughts. He was initially off-balanced by the reality that Alissa did not seem to bear much resemblance to her photo. In the flesh she was so much more than merely attractive. In fact she was incredibly feminine with a beautiful heart-shaped face, delicate features and aquamarine eyes as blue-green and mysterious as the sea. Long golden blonde hair tumbled halfway down her back. She was also tiny, the dress drawing attention to her minuscule waist and the pouting upward swell of the surprisingly full curves above it. His attention rested on her lush Cupid's bow mouth and the firm rounded globes of her breasts. The tightness at his groin shifted into the heaviness of solid arousal and his galloping attack of cold feet just vanished there and then. Somehow the photo had lied: she was gorgeous and very beddable.

When Alissa saw the big dark male sprawled on the sofa, she fell still and had to be urged forward. In slow motion he came fluidly upright, well over six feet of long, lean, powerfully built masculinity unfolding before her intimidated gaze. He was a stunningly handsome guy. Black hair was brushed back from his lean bronzed face, which was dissected by the arrogant blade of his nose and complemented by high carved cheekbones and an aggressive jaw line. Her ability to swallow and breathe was arrested while she stood there staring. He was blatantly male in an age when that primal attribute was becoming more and more rare. Glittering, very dark eyes flared down into hers and her heart succumbed to a nervous bounce behind her ribcage.

'Come and sit down,' Sergei murmured, his accent purring over syllables that took more concentration than usual to pronounce. 'I'm watching my club play. Do you follow football?'

'No, not at all,' Alissa admitted, scanning his appearance. He wore a black striped designer shirt, the sleeves of which he had pushed up his arms, and well-cut black trousers. The jacket of his business suit lay in a heap and his silk tie was in the process of falling off the coffee table onto the floor. She could tell at a glance that he was untidy and that he most probably had a low tolerance threshold for any kind of restriction. His tightly leashed energy hummed in the air like a building storm while he automatically took up a strong stance of authority.

Sergei, who was accustomed to women who raved about football for his benefit, was stunned by that careless response. 'You don't like football?' he repeated, giving her another chance to reconsider and ingratiate herself.

'I've never thought about it one way or the other. I wasn't one of the girls who wanted to play it at school anyway,' Alissa confided as she lifted his jacket, folded it and set it neatly aside so that she could sit down. The tie on the floor irritated her but she struggled not to pick it up. After all, she wasn't his maid. 'I wasn't the sporty type.'

She was small-boned and fragile and the idea of her on a football pitch struck him as ludicrous. He snapped imperious fingers like a potentate presiding over a court and the waiter hovering by the door hurried over to take his order for pink vodka. A tall bottle arrived and drinks were poured. Alissa accepted a glass and wished she were able to ask some of the dozen questions brimming on her lips, but she could not afford to expose her ignorance and risk blowing her cover. Trying not to wince at the strong taste of the drink, she sipped.

'You don't like vodka either?' Sergei quipped, wondering why she was so uptight, sitting perched on the very edge of the sofa and maintaining a careful distance from him.

At that comment, which strongly suggested that she was not meeting his expectations, Alissa deemed it wisest to tip her head back and down what remained in the glass in one go. It was like swallowing flames and she thought her burning throat would never be the same again. Another bottle arrived with a fresh pair of glasses.

'Try this one and see if it is more to your taste—it's made in Scotland,' Sergei informed her lazily.

'I'm okay—I don't drink an awful lot.' Alissa continued to clutch her empty glass to make it easier to avoid the offer of another.

'You should enjoy alcohol while you still can,' he told her.

Alissa wondered what on earth she was supposed to make of that piece of advice. What did he mean? That if she signed on the dotted line as his wife she would no longer be allowed to drink? The sudden outcry from the men in the room accompanied by a full-throated roar from the spectators of the game on the television stole her attention.

'Oh, someone's scored, have they?' she commented brightly, forgetting that odd remark of his in her eagerness to make conversation. Nobody needed to tell her that her sister, Alexa, would not have been sitting there by his side as quiet as a little mouse. 'How exciting…'

'Alissa,' Sergei said gently, 'it was the other team, *not* mine, which scored.'

Colour flamed in her cheeks. 'Oh, dear…'

Sergei closed long fingers round the small hand curling into the sofa by her side and used that connection to propel her across the space separating them.

'What are you doing?' Alissa gasped, instant panic flooding through her.

Unperturbed, Sergei drew her right up to him and brushed the golden hair back from her cheeks with confident fingers. All big eyes and fluctuating colour, she was breathing rapidly. It was not the flirtatious or amused reaction he expected to receive from an experienced woman and he was intrigued. 'What do you think?' he mocked.

She collided with dark eyes flaring lustrous gold and a tight clenching sensation in her pelvis made her shift

uncomfortably in her seat. She gazed up at him, terrified that any attempt to go into retreat or call a halt
would have the same provocative effect on his intrinsi-
cally dominant nature as a gauntlet thrown down in
challenge. As her nipples tightened into stinging prominence she sucked in a ragged breath and pressed her
thighs tensely together. She knew what was happening
to her and she didn't like it at all. Her body was attracted
to him, not her brain, she told herself angrily. Her brain
had nothing to do with the desire that was assailing her
in a seductive tide.

'You're very sexy,' Sergei husked, a long finger trac-
ing the voluptuous raspberry-tinted curve of her lower lip
while his hungry body reacted with almost painful enthusiasm to the sensual pull of her fragrant body so close to
his. 'Come home with me tonight. Why should we wait?'

Her aquamarine eyes flew even wider and she lowered
her lashes hurriedly in self-defence. They had only met
a few minutes ago and he actually thought she would be
willing to sleep with him tonight? He *expected* her to
sleep with him? He could only be asking why they should
wait for the wedding. If Alexa had been sitting beside her
at that moment, Alissa would definitely have strangled
her twin. Exactly what kind of an arrangement had Alexa
signed up for with this man? And how could Alissa challenge his assumptions without revealing her ignorance
and running the risk of being unveiled as an impostor?

The atmosphere vibrated like a tautly strung musical
instrument. In the midst of the frantic thoughts racing
inside Alissa's head, Sergei tugged her to him and
brought his wide shapely mouth crashing hungrily down
on hers. It was sweeter than sweet in intensity and hotter
than flames. Fireworks of response were set off like a

chain reaction of energy snaking through her slender body. She had never before got a charge like that from a kiss and the power of it shocked her. He parted her lips with his tongue and delved sensually deep in the moist interior of her mouth and she shuddered with the wicked, wanton pleasure of it. The smouldering prickle of heat between her thighs raised her temperature even more. Her fingers were lodged in the luxuriant thickness of his black hair, but she craved much closer contact than she already had. She wanted to press herself fully against his lean, hard body.

'Enough, *milaya moya*.' Sergei set her back from him with urgent hands while he scanned her hectically flushed face and the lack of focus in her eyes with satisfaction. She was seriously hot and passionate. He liked a woman who could forget herself so totally in his arms. He was already picturing that tiny lush body splayed across his bed, and the wedding he had begun to dread finally acquired a strong source of appeal. Getting his wife pregnant did, at the very least, promise to be a highly entertaining pursuit.

Disorientated, Alissa blinked, not quite ready to accept that she could have let him kiss her breathless while making no attempt to end their embrace. She was in a state of complete bewilderment.

'The game,' Sergei murmured succinctly as if it was the only thing in the world that mattered at that moment.

Alissa almost lifted one of the bottles off the table and brained him with it. He was talking about football! The football was more important than she was? Her soft swollen mouth snapping shut like a steel strap, Alissa murmured sweetly, 'I like a man who has his priorities in the right place.'

Sergei would have suspected sarcasm if it were not for the fact that women were invariably too busy trying to impress him to snipe at him. He turned his attention back to the television screen. 'I'll take you down to the nightclub when the game is over.'

The colour in her cheeks high, Alissa stared at the television screen and childishly hoped his team would lose. She had let him kiss her in front of a room full of men. She had completely forgotten where she was, who she was with and who she was supposed to be pretending to be. How could she have behaved like that with a man she barely knew? And would he just have pushed Alexa away and gone back to watching his stupid game? Why, all of a sudden, was she thinking like a jealous insecure teenager? Wouldn't she be better engaged wondering *why* Sergei Antonovich had suggested she spend the night with him? Most jobs, even unusual ones, were conducted in a more professional and considerably less intimate manner.

Sergei could feel her boredom and it irritated him. It was bad enough that his team was losing. Indeed, in spite of the millions he had poured into his football club, it was a bloodbath on that pitch! He began to explain the game to her, astonished by a level of ignorance that ensured that she even had to ask the meaning of the simplest of terms. No, she definitely wasn't sporty and she had clearly made no effort to discover his interests and prepare for them so that she could be a good companion. He was annoyed that she had been so lazy. No Russian woman would have made such a cardinal error when it came to pleasing a man. On the other hand he was convinced she would please him very much in bed and he was strong enough to mould her like wax into what he wanted in every other field.

Alissa accompanied him into the lift. 'This place is enormous.'

'I extended it to provide VIP rooms. It's very popular. The staff are trained to deliver the service that Russians expect,' Sergei advanced, taking advantage of the mirrored walls to study her from all angles and finding no view that disappointed him. There was no denying that she was little, but in all the right womanly places she was deliciously rounded, which compensated for her lack of height.

'You own this club?' Alissa said in surprise.

'Yes. There wasn't a club in London able to offer the level of facilities that I expect.'

She had never met a man of such blazing assurance. She sensed that that confidence defined him. He expected the very best and refused to accept less, which was why he had bought his own nightclub and personalised it to suit his needs. So demanding and confident a male must have found an unsuccessful first marriage intolerable. Did that explain why he had chosen to opt for a businesslike approach for his second marital venture? It was unlikely, Alissa decided when she recalled the salient fact that this proposed marriage was only to last a couple of years at most. Normal marriages didn't take off with the divorce date already in place. So, why was he bothering to get married?

'You're very quiet,' Sergei commented as the lift doors purred open, letting in a flood of voices and pounding music.

From that point, there was no further opportunity for speech. Men she recognised now from his security team were standing by an empty table, keeping it reserved for their employer. But no sooner had Sergei stepped onto the dance floor to approach that table than the front-runners in a surge of excited women engulfed him. Alissa had never seen anything like it. She was nudged back by the tide, pushed aside, left standing while various women giggled, reached out to try and touch him and performed dance steps as though they were auditioning for Sergei's benefit. It was no wonder that he exuded the air of a man accustomed to being the centre of attention for he very definitely was, just as there was no doubt that he could have walked away from his admirers had he so desired.

Alissa lifted her head high and left him to it, taking a seat behind the table where Borya was stationed. With two beautiful women on either side of him and visibly hanging on his every word, Sergei appeared to be in his element. And he *was,* Alissa acknowledged, because Sergei Antonovich was a notorious womaniser or, depending on one's outlook, a famous connoisseur of her sex. Over the years he had appeared in a lot of tabloid pictures, always with a different gorgeous woman clinging to him as he emerged from nightclubs, stood on yacht decks or posed in front of the impressive Antonovich building that housed his business empire in London. Although he was not known for fidelity or for the longevity of his affairs, a long list of fabulous beauties had still accepted him on those demeaning terms.

Sergei looked around for Alissa and could barely credit that she had simply walked off and sat down. In all his life a woman had never treated him to such a display of indifference and it infuriated him. They were getting married in a week! He had just organised the publicity release on that score and there was his bride ignoring him, demonstrating her inability to meet the demands of the role she had been hired to play. No normal woman in love with a man would leave him with a bevy of willing and seductive beauties milling around him.

Stony-faced and unimpressed, Alissa sipped vodka through compressed lips while Sergei danced and flirted with the collection of truly shameless and determined women. There was the fatal flaw in all that wealth, power and potent male beauty, Alissa reflected with simmering scorn. Sergei Antonovich had no manners and not the smallest idea of how to behave in public with the woman he was planning to marry. That was undoubtedly why he had to *pay* a woman to take on the job. No woman with any pride or dignity would tolerate such treatment, not to mention the arrogant assumption that she would be happy to watch a bunch of footballers chasing a stupid ball round a muddy pitch at their very first meeting. If it had been a real date, Alissa would already have labelled him a loser and headed for home. Now she was wondering how long she was obligated to sit in public letting him make a fool of her while he dallied with the deferential type of oversexed woman he clearly preferred.

Alissa's fingertips began to drum a little tattoo on the table top while she watched Sergei and she decided that she was leaving within the next ten minutes. She was irritated when someone blocked her view and she glanced up in surprise as a handsome blond man in a suit spoke to her in spite of Borya's attempts to head him off. He was asking her to dance. Well, why not? Why should she sit bored, like a prisoner at her guarded table? Alissa rose from her seat, slid out from behind the table and off she went.

Sergei, who had little experience of women who

fought back on his own level, was astounded to be forced to witness the reality that his future wife could dance in a very suggestive manner with another man. Dark eyes colder than a Siberian winter, he watched Alissa wriggle her curvaceous hips and turn, short skirt flying up to reveal the pink lace-edged net and a pair of very shapely, slender legs. He strode across the floor and, with an aggressive jerk of his head at her partner, he cut in, lifting his hands to rest them on her slight shoulders.

'What the hell do you think you're playing at?' he demanded rawly in the interval when the music paused before coming back again on an even more deafening beat.

Alissa was stunned by the level of aggression in his behaviour and was not at all surprised that the man she had been dancing with beat a safe sensible retreat, for she suspected that Sergei was quite capable of getting physical. In an abrupt movement that took him by surprise she shrugged off his hands and stalked off the floor. She was going home and she didn't care how he felt about it. She wasn't prepared to spend one more minute in a domineering brute's company!

Sergei's anger was laced with outrage and a profound and lingering sense of disbelief because her defiant refusal to conform to his expectations was the direct opposite of the treatment he was used to receiving from a woman. He strode off in her wake, snatching out his cell phone to answer it when it buzzed. It was the owner of the firm he used to do background screening calling to tell him that it would take much more time than was available before the wedding to do the usual full in-depth check on Alissa. Sergei studied the tiny stalking figure ahead of him, the swirl of her short skirt, the defiant angle of her little shoulders, and told his caller to forget about the check altogether. Just then he knew that, whatever happened, he intended to have her in his bed and to hell with the risk!

Alissa stopped at the coat-check facility, for she had no intention of drawing down Alexa's ire by abandoning her sister's much-prized coat.

'What do you think you're doing?' Sergei growled from several feet away.

'I'm going home. I don't date Neanderthal men and the only place you belong is a cave!' Alissa sizzled back at him without hesitation.

'You're not on a date,' Sergei reminded her with biting cool, reluctantly amused by the 'Neanderthal man' crack, but also offended even though nothing would have made him betray that crucial fact.

In an impatient movement he stepped forward and addressed the coat check attendant. 'Get a move on,' he urged. 'We are in a hurry.'

'Don't be so rude!' Alissa launched at him. 'She's not feeling well. She doesn't need you barking orders at her like she's in the army.'

All amusement evaporating, Sergei drew in a long slow breath and suppressed his volcanic temper with some difficulty. Borya and his men were already stationed by the exit, transfixed by the scene being enacted fifteen feet from them. What sort of a woman dared to tell him how to behave? Criticised him? Threatened to walk out on him? He flicked a glance at the shocked coat-check girl, who was coughing noisily into a hanky and simultaneously trying to shrink into the back of her cubbyhole. What sort of a woman cared about the health or the feelings of a menial employee? A kinder woman than the more selfish type he usually spent his time with, he conceded grudgingly. Her altruistic concern reminded him of Yelena, who had long been the first port of call when neighbours fell sick or needed someone to mind their children. Here was a woman who might, with his guidance, turn into exactly the kind of wife he wanted to produce for his grandmother's inspection.

Alissa watched Sergei settle a high denomination banknote down on the counter in a silent apology. Oh, how she wished the girl would fling it back in his handsome teeth and demand the words instead, but of course she didn't. In obvious awe of him, she stammered heartfelt thanks and pocketed the money at a speed that shook Alissa. He took the coat and extended it with a flourish for Alissa.

She dug her arms into it and froze as his lean warm hands lifted her hair from her nape where it had caught beneath the collar. The gentle brush of his fingertips against her skin burned through her sensitised body like a match flame lighting dry crackling straw. That fast she remembered the raw, demanding sensuality and pressure of his mouth and her body reacted to the memory with an instantaneous rush of heat and moisture between her thighs. Unbearably aware of her body's wanton vulnerability, she froze.

Sergei eased her back against his big powerful frame and ran lean, sure hands down her sleeves to lift and enclose her hands in the warm, firm grip of his. Unable to maintain her rigid stance and wildly aware of his proximity, she trembled.

'The press are waiting outside and you are about to enjoy your fifteen minutes of fame,' he murmured lazily, the rich dark tone of his deep voice feathering like a caress along her spine. 'It's time to start acting and look happy to be with me.'

Alissa was bemused by that information. The press? She felt out of her depth and knew that, most ironically, her sister would have loved such a moment in the public eye. 'So I can't slap you, then?'

Sergei vented a roughened masculine laugh that made her more than ever conscious of his sexual pulling power. 'No.'

'Or sulk?'

'I wouldn't put up with it, *milaya moya*. Just like I won't stand another man laying a single finger on any part of you while you're supposed to be mine,' he added with a studious casualness that somehow made what he was saying all the more riveting. 'With me there are boundaries and you *must* respect them. Do I need to say any more?'

Picking up on the intimidating chill in his intonation, Alissa almost shivered, but she was bone-deep resistant to domination of any kind. 'Were you born a bully? Or do you find you have to work at it?'

Sergei was utterly poleaxed by that impudent comeback. Black brows descending over grim dark eyes, he stared down at the shining blonde head that barely reached the centre of his chest, his long brown fingers still instinctively engaged in stroking the fine-boned fragility of her wrists. She was the size of a doll and she was fighting him every step of the way. He could not even begin to credit her bravado.

'Your silence tells me that it comes naturally to you,' Alissa answered for herself and even she was wondering why she was going out on a limb to hit back at him. Was it the effect of the vodka? Or his behaviour with female admirers, which had paraded his total lack of interest in her feelings? Or the ghastly embarrassing truth that she found him stupendously attractive in spite of his overpoweringly masculine ways?

Sergei bent to clamp his hands to her waist and then he lifted her bodily around to face him. 'By the time I'm finished with you, you will *love* football—'

Seriously vexed at being lifted off her feet and treated like a child, Alissa focused on him with blazing aquamarine eyes. 'Dream on!'

'And once you get used to me you'll be jealous and clingy and adoring just like all the other women I've ever known,' Sergei completed with raw conviction.

In the hold of his hands, her fingers balled into furious fists. 'I don't think you can ever have met a woman like me before.'

His brilliant dark eyes flamed golden as the heart of a fire and he looked dangerous, his lean, dark, handsome face taut. '*Stoy*…stop!' he spelt out with critical cool. 'Have you forgotten why you are here with me?'

Her lashes lowered and she was suddenly still and fighting to get a grip on her angry discomfiture. His reminder had been timely: she *had* forgotten. He had hired Alexa to carry out a role and so far Alissa had annoyed him, disagreed with him and argued with him. She breathed in slow and deep to calm herself.

'That is better,' Sergei pronounced and he lowered his arrogant dark head and pressed his lips gently to her lush pink mouth.

And for the merest fraction of a second she resisted the urge to part her lips before the throb of the blood in her veins and the acceleration of her heartbeat combined to vanquish her defences. Suddenly, without even being aware of the prompting, she tipped her head back and let him taste her again, glorying in the shimmering, prickling mist of coming-alive sensation surging through her again. The flick of his tongue against the tender roof of her mouth made her shiver and press forward, instinctively wanting more.

'Now we will go outside,' Sergei breathed, lifting his handsome dark head and tugging her beneath one arm.

The bank of cameras and shouted questions that greeted their appearance made her shrink back against the arm locked to her slender spine. Aquamarine eyes huge, she contrived an uncertain smile while his bodyguards fanned out around them to prevent anyone from getting too close. She didn't breathe again until she was safe inside the limousine and invisible behind the tinted windows. She was in a daze, unable to credit that she had let him kiss her again and that, in truth, she could hardly wait for a repetition. It was as if one little taste of him had created a terrifying craving she could not suppress.

'You didn't enjoy the attention,' Sergei remarked, his questioning gaze locked to her pale face. 'It frightened you—why?'

'I suppose I'm rather a private sort of person.'

'That is not the impression you gave in your interviews.'

Alissa had felt safe from detection in his presence because he had never met her sister. But evidently her sister's interviews had been recorded in some way and he was aware of the content and had formed advance opinions about her personality on that basis. Suddenly she was very tense. 'Everyone puts their best foot forward in an interview situation.'

Sergei made no comment but he noticed her evasiveness and wondered what lay behind it. 'You have to learn to relax with me. In less than a week we're flying to Russia for our wedding.'

'Russia,' Alissa echoed weakly, plunging into even deeper consternation at the concept while she asked herself if she could possibly go through with the role her twin had agreed to play.

'This is for you.' Sergei handed her a parcel. 'We'll be able to keep in touch now. I've been too distant from this process, *milaya moya.*'

It was Alexa who took the trouble to rip the wrapping off the parcel twenty minutes later. Goggle-eyed, she studied the mobile phone she had extracted and she let out a sudden whoop. 'Oh, wow, I can't believe it. He's given you only one of the most expensive phones in the world! See those…' She extended the phone to her sister. 'Those are real diamonds.'

'Are they?' Alissa was unable to share her excitement for, while she could admire the glitter of the diamonds, she could not see the point of such decoration on a mobile phone. Indeed that level of adornment struck her as an embarrassingly pretentious display of wealth.

'This is worth thousands and thousands of pounds and I'm more entitled to it than you are!' Alexa suddenly concluded, shooting Alissa a resentful glance. 'I'm the one who won this job and now you're getting all the stuff that should have been mine—'

Alissa was less interested in the phone than in the wedding on the horizon. 'Why do you think Sergei Antonovich wants a wife in the first place? Aren't you curious?'

Alexa's face shuttered and she pursed her lips. 'Not really. As long as it's nothing illegal, I couldn't care less why. Maybe it'll give him some sort of tax or business or inheritance advantage, or perhaps he wants a wife to give him a breathing space from all the pushy women who target him.'

'Sergei certainly didn't strike me as the marrying type,' Alissa confided. 'He also asked me to spend the night with him—'

Eyes rounding in shock, Alexa studied her twin with a dropped jaw. 'He *did*? He found you that attractive? I bet you thought all your Christmases had come at once. Why did you leave him to come back here, for goodness' sake?'

Her face hot in receipt of that revealing response, Alissa murmured, 'The point is…why did he ask? Since when was sex part of the arrangement?'

Alexa was still engaged in playing with the phone and, although she tensed at her sister's question, she did not lift her head for several seconds. Blue-green eyes scornful, she looked over at Alissa. 'Think about what you're saying. How are you planning to pretend to be his wife without ever sharing a bedroom with him?'

That angle hadn't occurred to Alissa and she compressed her lips in dismay. 'I didn't realise that the job entailed carrying on the pretence that we were a couple behind closed doors.'

'You can't be that naïve. He must have a lot of staff and he wants everyone to think it's the real deal, not just a select few. Of course what happens behind those closed doors would be your choice entirely.'

Alissa's rigid expression of disapproval had eased a little. 'So there was no *prior* assumption that there would be…er…intimacy of that nature?'

'Of course not. What do you think I am?' Alexa demanded sharply. 'But put a young and attractive man and woman in the same room and nature tends to take its course, if you know what I mean.'

The trouble was that Alissa genuinely didn't know, for she had as yet no experience to equal her twin's.

'You can't *still* be a virgin!' Alexa exclaimed, interpreting her sister's embarrassment with a look of disbelief.

In a defensive movement, Alissa threw back her slim shoulders. 'Why shouldn't I be?' she asked with quiet conviction. 'I just haven't met the right person yet and I'm not ashamed of that.'

'Sometimes I just can't believe we're twins. We are *so* different!' Alexa carolled in frustration. 'Why do you make sex such a big deal? Is it any wonder you're still on your own? A guy has to tick every box on your checklist to get anywhere near you. This exchange is just not going to work.'

'What do you mean?'

'I'm the one who was picked to be Sergei's wife and it looks like I'm the only one of us capable of carrying it off,' Alexa breathed flatly. 'Since we can't repay the money, I'll have to get an abortion.'

In horror, Alissa leapt to her feet. 'I won't let you do that!'

'We only have two options,' her twin reminded her doggedly. 'You marry him in my place so that we can keep the money, or I terminate this pregnancy and stick to the contract—'

'I *said* I would do it,' Alissa retorted, unnerved by her twin's mood, for she knew how impulsive her sister could be and she was very much afraid that Alexa might still press on with her idea of a termination.

'But you're baulking at every little thing!' Alexa flung angrily at her.

'I don't call sharing a bedroom with a guy I hardly know a "little" thing…'

'That's right, go ahead and make me feel like a total slut just because I wouldn't have made a big fuss about it when he's so gorgeous! All right, I've had a lot of men in my life and you haven't, but do you have to be so superior and smug about it?'

'I'm not superior or smug,' Alissa protested in dismay. 'Anything but!'

'Well, you'd better make your mind up fast. Do you want to help Mum or not?' Alexa demanded coldly.

And did she also want to be an aunt to the baby that her sister was carrying? Alissa added inwardly. She had met the baby's father, Harry, only that day when he'd arrived to take both young women out for lunch. Alissa had liked him very much and was satisfied that he genuinely loved her wilful twin. Right now, Alexa, however, was less easy to read or predict. Her sister was all over the place emotionally, one moment sentimental about her approaching motherhood and marriage, the next feeling threatened by the awareness that her freedom would be curtailed. Alissa could see the manner in which her twin was still retaining a possessive grip on the ridiculously expensive phone. She also knew how easily tempted her sister was by luxury goods. More than once Alexa's love of designer labels had got her into serious debt. Alissa also fully understood that, confronted by that outrageous diamond-studded phone, Alexa was wondering if she had made a serious mistake when she had surrendered the chance to marry a billionaire, regardless of how brief and fake the alliance was to be.

Alissa was determined to stay with the solution that promised her sister the best chance of happiness and she rammed down a lid on all her own reservations and breathed in deep. 'I want to help Mum more than anything. I'll go ahead with it, whatever it costs.'

CHAPTER THREE

ONLY a few hours after that conversation, Sergei snatched up a towel and strode out of the wet room where he had cooled his hot blood under a long cold shower. He snatched up a towel. It was four in the morning and he had barely slept. He had tossed and turned, as overheated and hungry for a woman as a sex-starved teenage boy. He was not amused by that reality and he was bewildered and frustrated by the sexual intensity Alissa Bartlett had fired in him.

A brooding frown stamped on his lean strong features, he logged onto his notebook PC and brought up the photo of his bride-to-be. It was a source of irritation that the woman in the picture somehow contrived both to look like Alissa and yet *not* like her. In the flesh, her face was softer, rounder, her eyes brighter, her smile full of appeal. How were those differences possible? Obviously it was an old photo, taken when she was thinner, and it wasn't a flattering representation.

Desire, however, did not blind Sergei to more obvious facts. In every way, he reflected grimly, Alissa Bartlett had proved to be much more of an unknown quantity than he'd expected. She had demonstrated quirky autonomous traits that made him distinctly uneasy. He had thought the marriage plan was pure perfection with every detail settled in advance of the ceremony and the margin for error reduced to almost nothing. He had believed she was a safe choice. But when he endeavoured to slot that defiant little blonde, who had danced with another man, into his game plan he saw dangerous ripples spreading as though a large boulder had suddenly been pitched into still water. Gut instinct now warned him that Alissa was a bad bet, more likely to give him trouble than a smooth and successful conclusion.

He should bail out now, Sergei acknowledged grittily. Unfortunately he found her hugely attractive and that advantage would be almost impossible to find elsewhere. An overlong procession of greedy, cunning lovers had made Sergei exceedingly choosy about the women he took to his bed. It was ironic that even though Alissa had infuriated him she had also ignited a stronger level of pure driven lust in him than he had experienced in over a decade.

Alissa had also resurrected his appetite for risk. So what if he was taking a chance on her? He pictured her in her little black dress, firm breasts rising above the scooped neckline in a tantalisingly voluptuous display as she spun on the dance floor, revealing glimpses of her slender thighs. His body reacted with maddening enthusiasm to the image. He had liked that dress but it would have shocked Yelena. The outfit had been too revealing for anything other than private consumption. He would have to take her shopping to ensure that she acquired more sedate clothing, while also ensuring that some day soon she would put on that dress especially for him so that he could strip it off and enjoy the delights of the body that lay underneath.

If he was so hot to taste this forbidden fruit he had to take the risk of marrying her. Such powerful desire demanded and deserved satisfaction. He was willing to sacrifice his freedom and marry to please his grandmother, but he saw no reason why he shouldn't make every effort to ensure it was, at least, a pleasurable and entertaining experience.

Alissa wakened with a start when her shoulder was roughly shaken. A phone was ringing and she sat up on the sofa, where she had spent a most uncomfortable night, and looked woozily at Alexa, who was extending her diamond-studded phone.

'Answer it, for goodness' sake!' her twin urged. 'I can't answer it for you. It's sure to be *him* and it's safer if he doesn't know I exist.'

Alissa answered the phone.

'I want to take you shopping,' Sergei announced without any preliminary greetings. 'I'll pick you up at ten.'

And that was that. It was not a request, but an order. As she shared both that opinion and the outing mentioned with her sister Alissa studied the phone with disfavour, convinced that it was more of a convenient command line for Sergei than a gift.

'Of course he's going to be bossy!' Alexa snapped crossly. 'He didn't make all that lovely cash by acting like a wimp. He's rich and powerful and he knows what he wants and when he wants it.'

'I haven't got much time. I'd better get dressed.'

Alexa released a heavy sigh of irritation. 'And I can't trust you to do it on your own.'

Her sister's annoyance permeated the atmosphere as she insisted on putting together an outfit for Alissa to wear.

'What is really wrong?' Alissa pressed anxiously.

'I feel like you're stealing my life,' Alexa confided, shocking her twin with that accusing statement. 'A billionaire is taking you shopping and it should have been me!'

Alissa gave her aggrieved sister a troubled appraisal. 'You're going to marry Harry soon. He loves you and you love him and you have a baby to look forward to. Everything with Sergei is fake and it won't last,' she reminded her.

'When I look at a photo of Sergei Antonovich I'm still jealous,' Alexa said tightly. 'And I'm not used to being jealous of you. What man ever looked at you when I was around? I've always been the prettier, more popular twin.'

The bell buzzed. Alissa was tense, hurt and nonplussed at her sister's admission. Alissa longed to suggest that Alexa take her place but, of course, that option was no longer possible. Borya accompanied Alissa downstairs. She was lost in her thoughts, acknowledging that it was true that Alexa had always enjoyed the status of being the more attractive of the two of them. She was thinner and wittier, always beautifully groomed and she drew men like bees to a honeypot. What was true now had also been true, more painfully so, in their adolescence.

Alissa winced at the secret knowledge that she had once fallen hard for their neighbour, Peter, but had never truly existed for him except as Alexa's sister and a friend. She had gone through agonies of guilt where Peter had been concerned, because she had known that loving her sister's boyfriend was disloyal and shameful.

As a result, she had never told anyone how she'd felt about Peter, not even when Alexa had deceived him with other men, revelling in the other opportunities and passing flirtations that came her way. Alexa had always had a somewhat elastic approach to fidelity, for she had reserved the right to be outraged when their father had gone off with another woman.

Alissa's train of thought was derailed with startling abruptness when she first caught sight of Sergei ensconced in the back seat of the opulent limousine. He was even bigger, darker and more gorgeous than she remembered. One glance and her mouth ran dry and a flock of butterflies broke loose in her tummy.

'Alissa.' Sergei scanned her with laser-bright dark golden eyes that missed nothing. She looked tense and miserable, which could only irritate a man accustomed to female smiles and gushing appreciation. She was dressed in yet another mistake, he noted, watching with unashamedly hypocritical male appreciation while she endeavoured to take a seat in a short tight skirt and high-heeled boots without showing him her undergarments. But, mood and wardrobe errors aside, she still looked fabulous. He was already trying to pin down exactly what he found so irresistible about her.

Was it those big aquamarine eyes that, according to the light, went from the sea-blue to mysterious, deep-forest-green? The delicacy of her bone structure? The exceptionally feminine appeal of her tiny fragile proportions? Those delightfully unexpected curves?

'Why are we going shopping?' she asked.

'You have a final fitting for your wedding dress…and I believe we should also take the opportunity to extend your wardrobe.'

Alexa had already had dress fittings? Why on earth had her twin failed to warn her of that fact? The prospect of trying on a wedding dress intimidated Alissa, while Sergei's concluding comment simply surprised her. 'But why do I need more clothes?'

'Those you wear are too revealing,' Sergei informed her bluntly.

Her face flamed as though he had turned a blowtorch on her and her fingernails dug crescents into the skin of her palms as she swallowed back a tart response. She could easily have agreed the point and it annoyed her that she could not shrug off responsibility for the outfits he had so far seen her in. Her full curves at breast and hip made fitted tops and short skirts seem much more daring than Alexa's ethereal slenderness ever had.

Sergei shifted an expressive hand. 'You look very sexy but I want a more upmarket conservative image for my wife.'

Thirty minutes later, Alissa underwent one of the most mortifying experiences of her life as the designer and her assistants endeavoured without success to get a toile—a sort of understudy to a real bridal gown—to fasten on her.

'I think I may have put on a little weight,' Alissa said tightly as their combined efforts to cram her into the too small garment were constricting her lungs.

As that confession was made the toile went slack again and her attendants backed off. An uneasy silence fell.

'I'll take your measurements again, if I may?' the designer asked with commendable brightness.

Red-faced with embarrassment and feeling the size of a heifer, Alissa withstood being measured and could not avoid seeing the designer's mounting anguish as the numbers expanded.

'Don't worry,' the older woman finally murmured with rigid calm. 'The dress will be altered in time for the ceremony.'

Alissa guessed that the lack of open lamentation was down to the small fortune that Sergei was undoubtedly paying for the gown. But she was mortified by her companions' astonishment. After all, brides usually got thinner before their weddings.

'That took a long time,' Sergei remarked when she rejoined him. He cast aside his copy of *The Financial Times* with a strong suggestion of relief.

'The dress will have to be altered,' she admitted.

Sergei frowned, black brows pleating in surprise. 'You've lost weight?'

Biting at her lower lip, Alissa said the only thing she felt she could say in the circumstances. 'No, I've put it on. I'll have to starve from now on—'

'Not while you're with me, *milaya moya*,' Sergei quipped. 'I won't allow you to shrink your assets.'

It was impossible not to notice his downward glance that paid homage to the swell of her breasts beneath the sweater she wore. In receipt of that all-too-male look of appreciation, Alissa went so red she was vaguely surprised she didn't spontaneously combust. 'I like food too much, particularly chocolate,' she heard herself respond inanely while she strove valiantly to ignore the sexual spark in the atmosphere.

It was a novelty for Sergei to be with a woman who admitted to enjoying food. He was more accustomed to ladies who demanded the calorie count of a dish before they would even consider eating.

Back in the limo, Alissa wondered how on earth he managed to make her so painfully aware of him as a man. Or was she oversensitive to his potent male aura? Whatever, she was conscious of every breath he drew.

In yet another exclusive designer salon they were served with champagne while a large collection of clothes was presented for scrutiny. Alissa tried on a scarlet dress and jacket. It was a perfect fit and very much more conventional in style than anything her sister would have chosen. Feeling ridiculously self-conscious, she emerged from the cubicle to let Sergei see it. He, she was starting to appreciate, liked to be in charge more than was good for him *or* her.

'I like that,' he breathed in sudden amusement. 'Add some fur and you could be a very cute female Santa Claus…'

'No fur, please,' she replied, then queried, 'Do you have Santa Claus in Russia?'

'*Ded Moroz*…Grandfather Frost, and he comes in the New Year with a female sidekick called the Snowmaiden,' Sergei told her. 'But you can celebrate Christmas any way you want while you're with me. I didn't even know the festival existed until I went to live with my grandmother.'

While you're with me; a subtle little reminder that she would be a temporary wife rather than a real one, Alissa assumed. Christmas was only seven weeks away. Where would she be living then? Feeling extraordinarily vulnerable, she stood still while his smouldering dark eyes raked over her. An inner glow spread through her pelvis, tightening her tummy muscles and leaving her insanely aware of his raw sexual power.

At his behest, she tried on outfit after outfit. Half the time he was on the phone, delivering terse commands in his own language, but the whole time his attention seemed to be on her. It bothered her that she got a thrill out of his obvious interest and she had to resist a shameful urge to preen and pose. It was becoming harder and harder for her to view their approaching marriage as just a job, since he was personalising everything. An hour after their arrival, a package was delivered to him by his chauffeur.

Alissa made her final appearance in an opulent full length turquoise silk evening gown.

One glance at her and the exquisite pain of rampant sexual arousal assailed Sergei in a tidal wave. The fabric cupping her breasts was too fine to conceal her nipples which protruded like ripe cherries. Expelling his breath in a slow hiss of restraint, he sprang upright and signalled her.

'Come here,' he told her when she stopped a few feet away from him.

With care, Sergei employed a tissue to wipe her lips clear of tinted gloss. 'Less is more,' he murmured in a roughened undertone.

Alissa gazed up at him wide-eyed and was ludicrously unprepared for the kiss that followed. Long fingers meshing with her hair, he pried her lips apart and took her mouth with erotic force. His hunger exploded through her and her head spun and her stomach lurched with excitement as if she were on a fairground ride. The tight knot in her tummy clenched hard and with every fibre of her being she craved more intimate contact.

'Right moment, wrong place, *milaya*,' Sergei quipped, setting her back from him, and she almost screamed and stamped her foot with frustration. While he called every shot and maintained supremacy, he also made her feel controlled and helpless. Nothing, it seemed, took the edge off her intense craving for him. 'Open your mouth.'

'Why?' she framed stonily, annoyed that he had kissed her again and left her feeling things she barely understood and certainly didn't want to feel. Her body was humming and all churned up in a very uncomfortable way.

'You can't have me right now but you can have… *this*,' he murmured playfully, sliding a chocolate between her lips.

The meltingly rich taste of chocolate reached Alissa's taste buds in a gastronomic tide of sensation. It tasted so good, she almost closed her eyes to savour it in full. 'That is to die for,' she whispered.

Sergei got an erotic buzz just watching her. She was a wonderfully sensual woman and she could wind him up like a clock. He wanted to scoop her up into his arms and take her somewhere private where he could sink deep and hard and repeatedly into her lush little body until he had satisfied the fierce hunger he was restraining with such difficulty. But on another level he was enjoying that unusual edge of anticipation driven by a level of moderation he had never practised before.

Somewhere close by a phone rang insistently. Alissa broke free of the spell holding her in stasis. 'That's mine.'

One of the assistants brought her the mobile phone from the changing room. It was Alexa calling, words gushing from her in a breathless tide. 'Mum's found out that you're marrying Sergei next week. One of her friends brought in a newspaper with a picture of you together. She's in deep shock—'

'Oh, my word,' Alissa exclaimed in consternation, uneasily conscious of Sergei's proximity. 'What did you tell her?'

'Well, that you'd been seeing Sergei when you were still working in London but that it hadn't worked out and that's why you never mentioned him,' Alexa explained. 'And now he's back and it's all on again. What else could I say?'

'This just goes on getting more and more complicated,' Alissa lamented.

'What's going on?' Sergei demanded, and one glance at his lean, taut features was sufficient to tell her how much he hated being left out of the loop on any issue.

'My mother saw a photo of us together in a newspaper and she's in shock—'

'Is that her you're speaking to? No?' he queried. 'Then get her on the phone so that I can speak to her.'

And although Alissa tried to argue with him, nothing else would satisfy him. Alissa dialled the number of her home and broke through her mother's anxious and reproachful questions to ask her to speak to Sergei. Sergei then took the phone from her damp grasp and proceeded to stun Alissa by selling himself as the perfect son-in-law, who couldn't wait to meet his future mother-in-law. While Alissa hovered, taut with growing incredulity and resentment at the ease with which he dealt with the situation, he insisted he would send a car to pick her parent up and ferry her back to London to dine with them that same evening.

When he had finished talking, he passed the phone back to Alissa.

'I do understand why you got swept away by him,' Jenny Bartlett told her daughter in a dazed voice. 'Sergei really *does* know what he wants, doesn't he? I can't wait to meet him, darling.'

'I seem to recall that your parents are getting a divorce,' Sergei remarked when the call had finished.

'Yes,' Alissa confirmed with a flat lack of expression, shying away from that controversial subject while dimly also wondering why he had never known about Christmas until he went to live with his grandmother. Had his parents died? What age had he been? She decided it was no business of hers and that if she wanted to survive their fake marriage she had to learn to keep a sensible distance from him.

She didn't go back to Alexa's flat that evening. Meanwhile, Sergei dropped her off at his indescribably chic apartment to get changed while he returned to his office to attend a meeting. Alissa wandered round the penthouse admiring the fabulous art works on display, before selecting an elegant green shift dress to wear. The prospect of trying to deceive her mother into crediting that she was in love with Sergei seriously unnerved her.

But she need not have worried for right from the start Sergei took centre stage and it was soon clear that her mother was much impressed by his calm and assurance. Alissa, however, was taken aback when the older woman let drop that Alexa had picked the same day to marry Harry that Alissa had to marry Sergei. As quickly Alissa assumed that Alexa had chosen that date deliberately to ensure that Sergei did not have an opportunity to meet her.

'An extraordinary coincidence,' Sergei commented.

'A disaster because I can't be in two places at once,' Alissa's mother opined in a pained voice, her distress unconcealed at that clash of dates. 'I'm heavily involved in organising Alexa's day and, because she's pregnant, I can't possibly abandon her to see to it all on her own—'

'Of course not,' Alissa broke in and squeezed her mother's hand soothingly. 'We understand…'

'But I really would like to see both my daughters get married.'

'Unhappily our arrangements are too advanced to allow the date to be changed,' Sergei said in a tone of apology.

'But there is a solution,' Jenny told him hopefully. 'Would you consider a double wedding with Alexa and Harry here in the UK?'

Alissa's eyes opened very wide at that startling suggestion and she froze in dismay; if Sergei met her sister, he would learn that Jenny's daughters were identical twins and he might well become suspicious!

'I'm afraid such an arrangement would not be possible.' Sergei then explained that he had an elderly and frail grandmother who had never left Russia in her life and who was eagerly looking forward to attending their traditional wedding in St Petersburg.

Alissa assumed it was a polite lie, but she was impressed by his inventiveness when put on the spot. She reckoned that the presence of her mother at her own bogus wedding would only make the occasion more of a strain. When it occurred to her that she was already in the very act of deceiving her mother, guilt pierced her deep.

Sergei then went on to suggest that he and Alissa should have a church blessing, followed by a party at which he could meet Alissa's friends and family, in London the following month. Her mother's disappointed face slowly warmed to that prospect and it was easy to tell from the suggestions she went on to make for the event that she was, not only charmed by the idea, but also equally charmed by the man who had voiced it.

When the meal was over, Alissa opted to return home with her mother. Sergei's steely glance warned her that he was displeased by that choice, but Alissa had no intention of spending time alone with him at his penthouse. Their marriage was supposed to be a legal arrangement and a job, nothing more, and if she wanted him to respect those boundaries she needed to keep some distance between them. In addition, Alissa was in no hurry to return to Alexa's apartment laden with piles of expensive clothes that would be likely to awaken her twin's bitter envy again.

'I expected to see you again before the wedding,' Sergei revealed, standing on the pavement beside the Mercedes that contained Alissa's mother and awaited Alissa.

'I'm sorry—I'd like to spend some time at home before I go to Russia.' Pale and taut, Alissa collided head on with smouldering dark golden eyes heavily fringed with lush black lashes. Her tummy flipped as if she had been flung up in the air. Surely no man had ever had such compellingly beautiful eyes? Her fingers clenched into her palms as she stepped back from Sergei, uneasily aware of the phalanx of bodyguards hovering around them.

'You make it sound so reasonable, *milaya*.' Sergei reached out and closed a hand round hers as she brushed a skein of gold silky hair back from her brow. He eased her inexorably closer. 'But you know that's not what I want.'

The lashes above her aquamarine eyes fluttered down to conceal her strained gaze. Her heart was racing like an overwound clock behind her breastbone. His mesmeric pull was almost more than she could bear. Even the timbre of his rich dark drawl slivered through her like the lick of a flame. But that tide of physical response infuriated her and stung her pride.

'Surely there's some part of the day when I can have

my own free time?' Alissa queried, throwing her blonde head high, a gleam of challenge in her bright eyes.

'Your own free time?' Sergei countered, his lean dark features tensing.

'Isn't this a job? I can't be on duty twenty-four-seven.'

Sergei froze, all warmth ebbing from his gaze leaving it winter-dark and cold. In that instant she could have done nothing more offensive than voice a cool and emotionless reminder of the legal agreement that had brought them together He marvelled that for a little while he had somehow contrived to forget that fact. Her words had grated on him, striking the hard calculating note that he was all too accustomed to hearing from her sex. Evidently he had not yet been generous enough to keep her sweet.

'I don't think you can have read the small print on your contract,' he breathed in an icy cutting tone of distaste. 'From the moment you wear my wedding ring, you *will* be on duty twenty-four-seven.'

Sergei walked away, leaving Alissa paralysed on the pavement with nervous tension. She was torn between regret and relief. A terrifying part of her wanted to run after him, to douse the aggression she had awakened and luxuriate in the kiss that she had subconsciously longed to receive. But the rest of her rejoiced in saying no to that weaker part of her nature. She wasn't a toy for him to play with as and when he fancied. She was too proud and intelligent to behave like the women who had fawned on him at his club the night when they'd first met, wasn't she? But just at that moment pride was a cold companion filling her with disappointment rather than a sense of achievement…

CHAPTER FOUR

WHEN Alissa returned from her walk, Alexa, her face flushed with annoyance, pounced on her twin the moment she entered the house. 'Where have you been?'

'You were still in bed when I got up. I had a few things to buy and then I went for a walk…'

'A walk?' Alexa wailed in disbelief. 'You're flying to Russia this afternoon and all you can think to do with yourself is go for a stupid walk?'

Alissa compressed her lips. 'I don't know how long I'll be away. I'll miss this place.'

'Mum came home at lunchtime. She's guessed where we got the money from!' her sister told her abruptly.

Alissa studied her twin in dismay. 'How could she possibly have guessed?'

'Naturally she doesn't know about the marriage-as-a-job angle,' Alexa breathed impatiently. 'But even though I'm the one who gave the money to the solicitor, she's convinced that *you* must have got the money from Sergei to pay off Dad.'

Alissa groaned. 'My goodness, how am I supposed to talk my way out of that?'

'Well, you don't need to bother. Sergei's loaded and

he's about to become Mum's son-in-law and one of the family. I said that he'd given the money to you and it was up to you what you did with it. I talked her out of phoning him to discuss it.'

Alexa's ability to talk her way out of a tight corner was legendary. Alissa regarded her with wry bemusement.

Her twin widened scornful aquamarine eyes. 'So once again, *you* didn't need to do anything; *I* saved the day.'

Anger flashed through Alissa and she had to grit her teeth to hold it back. In spite of the fact that Alexa was marrying Harry in twenty-four hours, her sister was behaving as though she were the wronged party. 'No, I'm the one saving the day this time around,' Alissa contradicted. 'You signed the contract in my name without my knowledge, but I'm marrying Sergei.'

'Whoopee-do, and what a sacrifice that is!' Alexa exclaimed with stinging derision. 'He's absolutely gorgeous, fantastically rich and incredibly generous. Look at the presents he keeps on sending you, never mind the flowers! Anyone would be forgiven for thinking you're marrying him for real tomorrow.'

Her face tight with discomfiture, Alissa went upstairs to escape the argument. It hurt to be at odds with her twin, to be forced to accept that Alexa's love of money and luxury currently seemed more important to her than Harry, or even her baby. Over the past five days, Sergei had sent Alissa flowers every morning as well as several unexpected gifts. Alissa wondered if he was trying to convince her mother that they were a normal bride and groom, for she couldn't think of any other reason for his munificence. She was now the bemused owner of a diamond-studded watch, an extensive set of designer luggage and a diamond solitaire ring that had made Alexa so jealous she had snapped at Harry when he had collected her for their wedding rehearsal that same evening.

Was Sergei simply getting into the role of keen bridegroom? He had phoned her every day as well. But he talked as though words came at a premium price that he was too stingy to pay. He would mention briefly that he was in New York or had just closed a deal, or he would talk about his football club or the players. Alissa found herself chattering about nothing in particular to fill the awkward lulls and afterwards she would cringe at the memory of her more inane comments. And, sometimes, Sergei would ask questions that were more terrifying than encouraging.

'How many men have you had in your life?' had been one blunt and bold enquiry that had shaken her.

'One or two,' she had told him grudgingly and, to punish him for his inappropriate curiosity, she had counter-attacked with, 'Have you ever been in love?'

'That is when you get excessively attached to one woman? No, I've never even come close,' he had informed her with a distinct note of satisfaction, as if falling in love was something *real* men didn't do.

'Then why did you get married that first time?' she had heard herself demand before she could think better of getting so personal—especially when she was trying to set an example by being impersonal with him.

A yawning, uneasy silence had greeted her query.

'She was the most beautiful woman I had ever seen,' he had finally imparted in a discouragingly gritty response. *But that's so superficial,* Alissa had wanted to tell him, though the tense atmosphere had kept her quiet.

Those phone conversations had brought Alissa no nearer to knowing the man she had agreed to marry. If anything he had become more of an enigma than ever. He could be very unpredictable. He was still a closed book in every way that mattered and curiosity was starting to kill her. She needed to know what made Sergei Antonovich tick, what made him angry, what made him happy. With each day that passed the big black hole of her ignorance only irritated her more.

That afternoon, Alissa parted from her mother and her sister in the privacy of their home. Alexa was brittle and moody and Alissa wished her twin and her prospective bridegroom well before she left alone for the airport. Of course, while she was involved with Sergei she could never be truly alone, because he had insisted that she accept the presence of a pair of bodyguards, who had collected her from home.

Her mobile phone rang on the journey. When she answered it, she was taken aback to hear her father's voice. 'Your mother told me at the weekend that you're leaving this afternoon. I'm at the airport and I need to talk to you—'

'At the airport?' Alissa repeated in surprise.

'Meet me for coffee,' Maurice Bartlett urged. 'I'm only here to see you. It feels like half a lifetime since we last met.'

The formalities of travel complete, Alissa, a slim elegant figure clad in a full length black coat and boots, went to meet her father. When he saw her he rose from his table and hurried into the concourse to greet her. As he approached her her bodyguards came between them.

'It's okay. I know him. You can take a break,' Alissa urged her bodyguards in some embarrassment, making vague shooing motions with her hands as if she were dealing with a flock of hens.

The two men exchanged uneasy glances and backed off with reluctance. Appraising her troubled face with a frown, Maurice Bartlett closed both his hands round hers as if he feared she might suddenly decide to walk off again. He was a handsome blond man who looked a good deal younger than his age. 'Thanks for coming. I knew you couldn't be as hard and unforgiving as your sister has been.'

'I'm not forgiving you for the past six months—just now I couldn't,' Alissa admitted gruffly half under her breath. 'But you're still my father.'

'I can't believe how long it's been since I saw you.'

She was appalled to feel a surge of childish tears sting her eyes. 'That's not my fault. You left us—'

'No, I didn't. I left your mother,' he argued, wrapping his arms round her to pull her close as her tears overflowed and rolled down her cheeks. 'I can't bear to lose you and Alexa as well. These last months haven't been easy for me either—'

He urged her into a seat and sped off to get coffee. Being with him felt wrong to Alissa, like straying into the enemy camp. The pain he had caused all of them was still too fresh. She breathed in deep and blinked back the tears, hoping that her mascara was waterproof.

Her father sat down beside her and gripped her hand in his. 'If it makes you feel any better, it's not working out with Maggie,' he confided heavily.

Alissa swallowed hard, for that news was not a comfort. It only made her wonder if all the heartbreak had been for nothing. 'I've only got a few minutes,' she warned him.

'So how did you fall in love with a billionaire?' he quipped. 'Now if it had been your sister, I would have been less surprised.'

Alissa was grateful for the abrupt change of subject. 'Harry, Alexa's man, is lovely. He adores her.'

'For his own sake, I hope he can stand up to her as well. Alexa's headstrong and I can't quite picture her settling down to be a wife and mother,' the older man confided ruefully.

Alissa looked at her father and without even meaning to heard herself say accusingly, 'We used to be such a happy family.' As soon as she said it and saw him recoil guiltily, the tears welled up in her eyes again. Both happy and sad memories tore at her. She would never have dreamt that the breakdown of her parents' marriage would cause her so much grief as an adult.

She was swallowing back a sob when she noticed a pair of photographers standing nearby with cameras angled in their direction. Anxiety gripped her because Sergei had warned her that she needed to be on the lookout for the paparazzi now to avoid them. 'I've got to go,' she said abruptly and stood up.

Her father hugged her and dropped a kiss on the top of her head. 'I'm sorry,' he said despondently. 'I'm really sorry. Sometimes you don't know what you have until you lose it.'

Alissa eased gently free again. Moisture still glittering on her pale cheeks, she moved away, noting the relief of her security team as they fell in either side of her. Her father was a weak man who didn't seem to know what he wanted any more. Only a couple of months ago he had told them all that he could not live without Maggie Lines and that he had to be with her. Did he want to go back to her mother now? Or was that a fanciful idea?

Alissa's first experience of travelling in a private jet

soothed her fractured emotions. She revelled in the peace and tranquillity and all the space while the cabin crew attended to her every need. She watched a film and skimmed through several glossy magazines before enjoying a very pleasant meal followed by a box of Belgian chocolates, which she found impossible to resist. She had one chocolate and closed the box feeling very virtuous, but was eventually tempted into eating more. Sergei phoned her during the flight.

'Thanks for the chocs,' she murmured, 'but I shouldn't be thanking you, I should be complaining. I've already eaten half of them.'

'Didn't I tell you that I'm fattening you up for Christmas?' Sergei teased.

'That's not a joke, Sergei. When it comes to chocolate you have to be cruel to be kind,' she warned him. 'I'm not great with will power.'

'I have a meeting this evening, so I won't see you before the ceremony,' he told her.

Stark disappointment flashed through Alissa and took her very much by surprise. Why was it that she had to constantly remind herself that she was deceiving her family to play a paid role in Sergei's life? Why did she keep on forgetting that basic fact? Why the heck couldn't she stop thinking about Sergei Antonovich? What was she? An immature adolescent or an adult? His attraction ought to be outweighed by his 'Neanderthal man' approach to women, she told herself sternly.

Mid-evening the jet landed at Pulkovo Airport in St Petersburg. It was much colder than it had been in London. A limo wafted her slowly through the city streets. She had never seen so many fabulous old buildings grouped in one place, so she was less surprised than

she might have been when she was deposited outside a
splendid classical property and informed that she had
arrived at Sergei's home. She mounted the steps, her
breath like puffs of smoke in the icy air, and walked into
the merciful warmth of a superb big hallway with an intricate polished wooden floor. The lemon-coloured
walls, stucco work and restrained furnishings were su-
premely elegant and quite unexpected after the edgy
modern design of Sergei's London apartment.

The stylish décor continued upstairs and into the
green and gold guest room where her luggage was deposited. She turned down the offer of food and stifled
a yawn. It had been a long day and she was very tired.
A pair of maids arrived to unpack for her and she took
refuge from all the attention in the stunning bathroom.
Lying back in the hot water while jets pummelled her
weary limbs was wonderfully relaxing and she stayed
there longer than she had planned and indeed was beginning to drift off to sleep when a loud rata-tat-tat
sounded on the door and made her sit up with a start.

'Yes?' she called in dismay, clumsily scrambling up
and clambering out to grab a towel.

'It's Sergei…I want to speak to you.'

Aquamarine eyes flying wide with surprise in her
flushed face, Alissa snatched the white towelling robe
off the back of the door and hastily put it on. It was not
a flattering garment but it was better than a bath towel.

Barefoot and hesitant, she emerged, feeling naked
without her make-up on. She had not even had the time
to run a brush through the tousled damp hair she had
piled on top of her head.

One glance at Sergei, looking impossibly tall and intimidating as he strode forward, stole the breath from

her lungs. In a charcoal-grey business suit, he was a spectacular sight, but his expression paralysed her in her tracks. His lean, darkly handsome face was hard and taut with anger as he slung a couple of photographs down on the bed in an aggressive gesture. 'Explain yourself!'

Stiff with astonishment, Alissa collided with scorching dark golden eyes and then bemusedly turned her attention to the pictures on the bed. She moved closer and frowned down at the grainy images, her bewilderment only increasing when she realised that they depicted her with her father at the airport café. 'What is there to explain?'

Sergei dealt her a look of pure black fury that made her lose colour. 'How can you ask me that?' he seethed in a raw undertone.

Alissa went rigid with indignation at his attitude. 'Don't you dare raise your voice to me!' she launched back at him angrily.

Sergei surveyed her in disbelief. 'Is that all you have to say to me?'

Alissa shrugged, strands of golden hair sliding down from her topknot to curve to her pink cheeks. 'I've got nothing at all to say to you. You barge in here when I'm in the bath—'

'I knocked on the door!' Sergei grated.

'The very fact that you think that that is something to boast about says it all really, doesn't it?' Treating him to a disdainful look that would have shrivelled a less assured male, Alissa carefully worked her way round to the other side of the bed. 'How dare you shout at me?'

'If I see you holding hands with another man and weeping over him, shouting is the very least of what you can expect from me!' he raked back at her without hesitation, clearing the foot of the bed in one long stride to close the distance between them again.

'I will not be threatened.' Breathing in short agitated bursts, Alissa reached for the crystal vase of flowers on the occasional table beside her. 'If you come one step closer to me, I will thump you with this!'

His ebony brows snapped together in a smouldering frown of incredulity. 'Are you crazy?'

'I can look after myself,' Alissa declared with bristling outrage.

'Why the hell would you try to thump me?' Sergei demanded. 'I'm not threatening you with violence.'

Alissa made no attempt to loosen her white-knuckled hold on the vase. *'No?'*

Sobered and set back by that condemnation, Sergei looked grave. 'Of course, I'm not. I would never hurt a woman.' He reached down faster than she could react and deftly removed the vase from her hand to set it back on the table. 'You scare really easily, don't you?'

'And you're *surprised*?' Alissa bawled back at him full volume, rage and embarrassment combining inside her. 'You roar in here like a hurricane…'

With a ground-out curse in Russian beneath his breath, Sergei snatched up one of the photos. 'Stop trying to avoid the issue. Who is this man?'

Alissa tightened the belt on her towelling wrap and folded her arms. 'My father—'

'Don't tell me a stupid lie like that!' Sergei snapped, out of all patience at that response as he stared down at the photo in his hand. 'This man looks no older than I am—'

'I'm sure Dad would be very flattered to hear that opinion, but I'm just bored with the whole subject. Why don't you check your facts before you attack people?'

'I don't make a habit of attacking people,' Sergei asserted grimly, well aware that for once in his life he had let his temper rip before he had investigated the cold hard facts. That was not how he usually operated and he could not explain the sudden absence of logic and cool that had afflicted him. He only knew that he felt out of kilter and that made him uneasy. 'If that man is your father, why are you holding his hand and crying?'

'It was an emotional moment and I hadn't seen him or talked to him for weeks.' Alissa was still angry with Sergei and she shot the crystal vase a look of regret, for thumping him with it might have released some of her pent-up fury. 'Going by the way you're behaving, you're obviously used to women who play around behind your back—'

'I am not,' Sergei cut in to dismiss that insulting charge while wondering why the instant he saw those photos of her with another man a red mist of rage had enveloped him to the exclusion of every other thought and prompting.

'You're not even my boyfriend,' Alissa pointed out.

'But tomorrow I will be your husband—'

'I hope you'll forgive me for saying that right at this moment that doesn't strike me as a very appealing prospect,' Alissa retorted with a challenging lift of her chin.

'I'm not trying to appeal to you.' Aggressive to the last, Sergei flung his arrogant dark head high. 'I am what I am and I'm unlikely to change.'

'Well, that's certainly telling me, isn't it?' Alissa quipped. 'You're not even bright enough to learn from your mistakes.'

The silence screamed. His lean, powerful length taut with shock at that comeback, Sergei viewed her with burning disbelief.

Conscience smote Alissa. Why was it that when she began fighting with him she could never resist the urge to top his last remark? It was a bad habit and a dismal way to embark on their relationship; he would keep on fighting because he didn't know any other way. 'That was rude, not a fair comment—'

'When was a woman ever fair?' Sergei drawled between clenched teeth of outrage.

'Giving me another opening like that is just asking for trouble,' Alissa warned him ruefully, gazing at him and silently marvelling at the lush black luxuriance of the lashes that accentuated his beautiful dark eyes. 'Okay, I'm at fault for not just giving you a straight answer.'

Sergei had never met a woman capable of giving him a straight answer and he was grudgingly amused by that statement.

'But obviously my dad is my dad and I couldn't credit that anyone would think we might be a couple,' she protested in her own defence. 'And since my parents broke up, my relationship with him has really suffered, so it was a very emotional meeting.' Her throat thickened and her voice wobbled a little on that admission.

'Why?'

'*Why?*' Alissa wailed, bewildered by the question.

'You're an adult. What your parents do is their business.'

'Maybe you're not from a close family but we *were* really close and loving,' Alissa countered thickly, appalled to hear tears clogging her diction again and wondering when she had turned into such a watering pot. 'And then it all just went within twenty-four hours. It was such a shock. Dad announced that he'd fallen in love with another woman and, a few hellish weeks later, he moved in with her…'

With a sense of wonderment, Sergei stared down at the twin tracks of tears glistening on her cheeks. She was so emotional and that contradicted her psychological profile. She also seemed to sympathise with everyone *but* him. She'd gone from shouting at him to threatening him with a vase. His hard mouth curved ever so lightly at that comical recollection and he bent down suddenly and scooped her up easily into his arms.

'What are you doing?' Alissa yelped, fingers clutching wildly at a broad shoulder for balance.

'I think it's called being supportive. I'm not sure. It's not a field I'm experienced in,' Sergei confided, settling down on the bed with her slight frame cradled on his lap and deciding that, after all, there was something to be said for this supportive stuff.

'Mum's so unhappy and I can't fix it,' Alissa mumbled tearfully, wiping angrily at her wet eyes, finally acknowledging that she was exhausted by the day she had endured.

'She'll meet someone else and be happy again,' Sergei forecast, lowering his handsome dark head, nostrils flaring as he breathed in the soapy, peachy aroma of her hair and skin. The neckline of the robe had dropped lower and wider to reveal the smooth, tantalising upper slope of her firm breasts. That view stoked his hunger for her by a factor of ten.

'She loves Dad. Life's not that simple…'

'Only because you want to make it complicated,' Sergei cut in, tilting her head back and nuzzling his darkly shadowed jaw rhythmically against the tender skin of her throat. She quivered in his grasp, every sense leaping into sudden awareness. '*Ti takaya nezhnaya…* you are so soft, *milaya moya.*'

Alissa knew she had to pull away and respect the boundaries that she knew she needed to impose with him, but the physical ability to resist Sergei's dark allure was terrifyingly absent. He was being so gentle and she sensed that that didn't come naturally to him. Her nipples were tingling into straining prominence, sending an electrifying message to the swelling dampening tissue between her thighs. That sensual awakening was an exquisite pain.

His mouth closed over hers in a wildly intoxicating kiss. Fireworks of response blazed inside her, sending her temperature rocketing while her hunger climbed. She let her fingers sink into his cropped black hair with a muffled moan of satisfaction. She couldn't get close enough to him. He felt as necessary to her as air to breathe. The fierce intensity of his hard mouth on hers was devastatingly erotic. He slid his hand through the gaping neckline of her robe and captured a pouting rose-tipped breast, skilled fingers stroking the velvety tip into throbbing rigidity. A gasp of response erupted from her as sensation piled on sensation. He kissed her breathless and her heart was hammering so hard she felt dizzy and clung to him.

The buzz of a mobile phone proved to be the wake-up call she needed. She pushed him away with both hands and tugged the edges of the robe back together. Trembling, she slid back to the floor, shunning the bed and him and the deceptive intimacy that had almost betrayed her. He answered his phone, his dark drawl rough-edged with huskiness.

When the dialogue finished, she breathed, 'What happened to the meeting you said you had this evening?'

'A London tabloid newspaper editor sent me those photos, obviously in the hope that I would dump you and call off the wedding and so give them an even bigger scoop,' he explained with rich cynicism. 'I skipped the meeting.'

Her body was a riot of nerve-endings sizzling with a sense of loss and disappointment. He was making her want things she had never wanted before and he was teaching her to want him with a depth of longing that physically hurt. The atmosphere was explosive, undertones swirling beneath the uneasy silence that intimidated her.

Sergei always played it cool, but he was fighting a very powerful urge to just yank her back into his arms. He hated the idea that she had any kind of a hold on him, for that was not his style. 'You want me to leave,' he murmured.

Alissa stared back at him, knowing that that was not what she wanted at all, but also that it was what she should want. His lean, darkly beautiful features dazzled her, commanded her attention, and locked her gaze to him. His very interest thrilled her and made her feel special. He was the sort of guy she had never expected to meet and she knew she would never meet his like again. To be an object of desire to a male who had been with some of the world's most beautiful women just blew her away.

'Alissa..?' he prompted.

'Yes.' The word of rejection was forced from her by fear, for she felt insanely out of her depth.

As self-assured as ever, Sergei strolled over to her and rested a lean bronzed forefinger against the pulse flickering below the pale purplish hollow of her collarbone, betraying her tension. 'Tomorrow, you will be mine. Twenty- four-seven, *milaya moya,*' he reminded her silkily. 'I can hardly wait.'

Even after the door thudded shut on his departure, Alissa stayed where she was, frozen between consternation and anticipation. Some minutes later she got into bed in a daze and tried to find sleep rather than relive the forbidden delight of his hands on her body…

CHAPTER FIVE

ALISSA WAS WAKENED early the following morning and treated to breakfast in bed. Her mother phoned her to wish her well. In the background she could hear a hubbub of bridal activity and she was hurt when Alexa professed to be too busy to come to the phone and speak to her sister personally.

After she'd had a shower, Alissa found a beautician and a hairdresser awaiting her. Clearly, a strict schedule was being observed. The professionals took charge and her hair was styled, her nails painted and her face made up. She could not escape the surreal sense that none of what was happening really had anything to do with her. It was not until the wedding gown was reverently brought in by one of the designer's assistants that she began to feel involved and intimidated at one and the same time.

The white dress was an elegant column design, lifted into the extraordinary by the shimmering crystals that glittered on the gorgeous fabric like thousands of stars below the lights. Alissa was hugely impressed and equally so with the cobweb-fine lingerie and the shoes ornamented with pearls. She suffered a moment's fear that the dress would not fit, but it skimmed her curves to perfection and she dared to breathe again. The delicate tulle veil falling from the wreath of real flowers encircling her head was very pretty. When she finally saw herself in a mirror, she knew she had never looked better.

She was ushered downstairs and tucked into a limousine. When she was deposited in front of a public building, she had to fight the urge to shiver in the icy air. A young woman, who spoke fluent English, greeted her in the busy hallway and introduced herself as Lukina, one of Sergei's aides.

'Where are we?' Alissa asked.

'ZAGS—where the civil ceremony takes place.' The question seemed to surprise the brunette. 'Didn't you receive the information I sent you a few weeks ago? It contained a complete breakdown of everything that would be happening today as well as some useful pointers.'

Alissa reddened and realised that once again her twin had neglected to keep her up to speed on things that she needed to know. 'Sorry, I forgot.'

'Mr Antonovich is keen for you to make a particular effort to be pleasant to his grandmother, Yelena,' Lukina informed her anxiously. 'He's her only grandson and this is a very special day for her.'

Alissa's flush deepened at the offensive suggestion that she might have to be told to be nice to Sergei's grandmother. So it was that her eyes were sparkling when she entered the room where the ceremony was to take place. Bridal music was playing in the background as, heartbreakingly handsome in a superbly tailored dark suit, Sergei strode up to her and presented her with a dainty bouquet of rosebuds that was incongruous in his large hands and which he patently could not wait to relinquish.

Every choice concerning the wedding had been based on what Yelena might like or expect. Sergei had ordered an extremely feminine and romantic wedding dress, as he had guessed that Yelena, who had never enjoyed frills in her own life, would enjoy such a spectacle. What he had not foreseen was how well the shimmering dress and simple floral wreath would frame and enhance Alissa's fair, delicate beauty. She looked like a fairy princess from an old storybook, and although he wanted to laugh at that comparison he was disturbed by the discovery that he could not take his eyes off her.

Meeting Sergei's dark smouldering gaze, Alissa tensed. Sexual awareness and the first renewed flickers of desire stole back into her slender body. He reached for her hand and she saw a small elderly woman in a bright blue dress and jacket keenly observing them and smiled, immediately guessing who she was.

The brief ceremony was highlighted by an exchange of wedding rings and she learned that in Russia the wedding ring was worn on a woman's right hand. Afterwards they signed the register, whereupon Sergei introduced her to the woman she had noticed earlier. Yelena, as cheerful as a spring flower in her suit, glowed with energy and good humour.

Yelena shared the limousine that ferried them to the church and Sergei translated his grandmother's rapid-fire questions.

Asked if she liked children, Alissa declared that she adored them and hoped to have two or three. Yelena followed up that response with others of a more housewifely note. Did she cook? Yes, but she didn't bake very well. Did she sew? Not really, the ability to sew on a button was Alissa's only talent in that field. Did she embroider or knit? No, she didn't embroider, but she had loved knitting ever since she created tiny garments for a friend's baby. Sergei was accustomed to women without domestic skills and he was quick to assume that Alissa had decided to lie to impress Yelena. But struggling to translate a more technical exchange on knitting for the women's benefit, he began to doubt that conviction and he was pleased to see his grandmother beaming at his chosen bride.

'She took the trouble to knit for her friend's baby. That's a good woman. You've done well,' Yelena pronounced with approval, straightening her grandson's tie for him before he could assist her from the car. 'She's very pretty as well. Give as much time to your marriage as you give to business and you will be together for a lifetime.'

Taken aback by that blunt advice on how to hold onto a woman when he had much more trouble getting rid of them, Sergei escorted his bride and his grandmother into the church, which was packed with guests. Awesomely aware of being the centre of attention and recognising the buzz of curiosity as she passed by, Alissa was tense and nervous and very much afraid of making a wrong move in public. She was also striving to understand why Alexa had begged her to marry Sergei in her place while withholding all useful information about the role. Had her sister secretly wanted her twin to fall flat on her face?

The priest blessed their rings and they were given candles to hold. They held hands as the slow ritual proceeded, reaching its climax when they were crowned and followed by the sharing of a cup of wine and a final blessing.

'I really, *really* feel married after all that palaver,' Sergei growled like a bear on the way out again.

'You've been through it all before,' Alissa pointed out, less comfortable with the knowledge that she was faking a marriage in the aftermath of a solemn religious service.

'I only went through a civil ceremony the last time. This day will last for ever,' Sergei groaned. 'We still have the reception to get through.'

'Don't you enjoy socialising?' Alissa was wryly amused by his mood and grateful she was not a genuine bride, liable to feel hurt by his indifferent attitude.

'That's not the problem.' In the rear seat of the limo, Sergei gripped her hand to turn her round to face him. Black-lashed, dark golden eyes raked hungrily over her in a look that was purebred primitive. 'You make the most exquisite bride. I just want all the show and fuss to be over quickly so that I can be alone with you, *milaya moya.*'

Her face warmed, and habit almost made her voice a protest to remind him that she was only a fake bride and that his being alone with her wasn't about to change anything. But when she looked at his devastatingly handsome features and felt the pull of his potent masculinity, her heartbeat hammered in her eardrums and the griping words shrivelled on her tongue and died in her throat. The truth was that Sergei Antonovich absolutely mesmerised her and, even though she knew that the relationship could go nowhere, temptation was biting deeply into her resolve to keep things platonic.

After all, no man had ever made her feel the way Sergei made her feel and it was perfectly possible, given the level of Sergei's attraction, that no other man ever would. How was she supposed to live in close proximity to him and pretend to be his wife, while at the same time totally resisting his attraction? Piece by piece, hour by hour, he was contriving to weaken her will power and destroy her defences. Alexa's scornful words about her twin's lack of sexual experience had also left their mark on Alissa, making her feel foolish, outdated and ignorant. Perhaps it was true that she was guilty of making sex too much of a big deal, she reasoned uncertainly.

Unaware of the mental moral tussle his bride was engaged in, Sergei was now in an excellent mood while he mentally ticked off boxes with a great deal of satisfaction. Most importantly of all, Alissa had hit it off with Yelena. Strangely, he acknowledged, Alissa seemed to bear no resemblance to the woman described in the psychological profile he had had done on her. How was that possible? Did it mean that such profiles could be so inaccurate that they were not worth the paper they were written on? Or was it simply that Alissa was an excellent actress, well up to the challenge of concealing her less engaging traits of character?

But why on earth was he splitting hairs when she was putting on a wonderful performance? Evidently he had picked the right woman for the role and now all he had to do was get her pregnant. Not a challenge he was likely to shrink from, he conceded with dark sexual amusement. The arousal that always assailed him to some degree in Alissa's presence was already charging his lean powerful body with erotic expectancy.

Outside the hotel doors being spread wide for their entrance, Sergei scooped Alissa up into his arms and carried her over the threshold to the accompaniment of the shouts, cheers and comments freely offered by the guests grouped in the foyer. Perhaps that was the first hint that Alissa received that Russian weddings were often a good deal less sedate than English ones. Everything seemed rather more colourful and informal.

As soon as they were seated a man stood up to toast the newly-weds and moments later there was an outcry of, *'Gorko! Gorko!'*

'Now we kiss for as long as we can,' Sergei told her, brilliant dark eyes frowning at her bewildered expression. 'Didn't you bother to read the information you were sent?'

Alexa had struck again, Alissa recognised in frustration, and annoyance filled her. That was the moment that Sergei chose to pry her lips apart with the tender pressure of his slow, sensual mouth. That more subtle approach wasn't what she expected from him and ironically she initially tensed in surprise. But when he dipped his tongue between her lips, her knees developed a responsive wobble and her hands crept up round his neck to steady herself. The guests were chanting but she didn't know what they were saying. Indeed the presence of an audience could only be a source of discomfort when Sergei was making love to her mouth with a sweet shattering eroticism that made mincemeat of her resistance. It seemed a very long time later when he finally freed her and she dropped back down into her seat dizzily, still drunk on the hot hungry taste of him and the thrumming of her awakened body.

Only a moment later when she was studying the assembled guests she was astonished to realise that she actually knew one of them. Her brightening eyes dimmed, however, when she failed to pick out the man's wife at the same table. Without a word she got up and went over to speak to him.

Crown Prince Jasim was already rising to greet her

approach with a wide smile of welcome. 'Alissa, what a great pleasure it is to be at your wedding. When the invitation arrived, I'm afraid I paid no attention to the bride's identity, for it never occurred to me that I might already know her.'

'Elinor isn't here with you?' Alissa queried just as Sergei drew level and curved an arm to her slender spine.

'Sergei…' The handsome heir to the hereditary desert throne of Quaram delivered his congratulations before turning back to Alissa to answer her question about her friend and former flatmate. 'Sami has a bad dose of chickenpox and Elinor could not bring herself to leave him.'

Alissa fully understood that maternal decision on her friend's part. 'Of course, she couldn't. If Sami's miserable he'll need his mother for comfort.' She asked after Jasim and Elinor's little daughter, Mariyah. When Alissa had last seen the royal children, Mariyah had been a newborn baby.

'How did you get to know Jasim's wife?' Sergei asked, amazed that such an association had escaped his knowledge.

'I met her when she was pregnant with Sami and living in London. I was a student then and Elinor and I, along with another girl, shared a flat for a while,' she explained. 'But it's been months since I last heard from Elinor. We always meet up when she visits London. She's still one of my closest friends but since she married Jasim she's become incredibly busy. I must phone her and catch up. What's your connection with Jasim?'

'We see each other regularly at OPEC meetings. I've never met his wife but I've heard that she's a beauty.'

A warm smile lit up Alissa's heart-shaped face. 'She

is. And I learned to knit purely for Sami's benefit. He was the most gorgeous baby,' she told him softly.

Someone else was toasting them and the same chant of *'Gorko! Gorko!'* started up again. Dark eyes locked appreciatively to her smiling face, Sergei took her into his arms to kiss and she was more than ready for the experience the second time around. It was like falling from an exhilarating height and burning up in the process. In the aftermath, her pulses were racing. When the wedding breakfast was served, she drank champagne and picked without much appetite at the first course she was served while an internationally famous singer took to the floor to entertain them.

In a party atmosphere that ensured that there was a good deal more drinking than eating going on, Alissa enjoyed several drinks and felt a little dizzy when she got up to dance with Sergei. She was wondering how a man she barely knew could have such a massive impact on her. Around him her body had a life of its own. She was short of breath without running and when he drew her close and the evocative scent of his skin and the cologne he used assailed her, butterflies went mad in her tummy. Inwardly she was already regretting that, with vodka flowing like literal water, she might have accepted too many of the drinks pressed on her.

'Tell me,' Alissa asked as she ditched her usual caution while they danced, 'was a wish to please your grandmother the reason you wanted a wife?'

Sergei tensed and glanced down at her with cool dark eyes.

Alissa tilted her chin. 'There's no need to look at me as if I'm about to run off and tell the newspapers!'

His aggressive jaw line clenched. 'You had better

not,' he murmured with chilling bite. 'I will not have Yelena hurt.'

'I wouldn't hurt her. She's so happy you've got married,' Alissa whispered, noting the old lady's animation as she chatted to her companions at the table. After a bad first marriage, Sergei had been understandably reluctant to take the plunge a second time. That made perfect sense to her. His caring so much for an elderly relative, however, touched her heart and showed her another side to his tough character. But her smooth brow furrowed because she could only consider his solution to Yelena's desire for him to remarry downright quixotic and blind in the short term. Surely his grandmother would only be more upset when his second marriage broke down as well?

'To ensure that you don't cause a scene, *milaya moya*,' Sergei murmured lazily, 'I will warn you that you are about to be snatched away from me. It's a tradition. I ransom you back.'

So, Alissa made no protest at being hustled out of the function room by a noisy crowd of well-refreshed guests and thrust into what she at first took for a cupboard but which, on lengthier scrutiny, she realised was a housekeeper's storage room. She leant back against the shelves and wondered how long it would take for him to pay the ransom.

Only minutes later she had her answer when the door flew open framing Sergei's tall, powerful frame. He snatched her into his arms again and kissed her, all the raw energy and white hot sexuality of his temperament poured into that potent sensual assault. As he whirled her away to a chorus of approval someone trod on her dress and she heard a worrying ripping sound.

'My dress is torn!' she exclaimed, her hands clutching the sparkling fabric over her thighs in dismay.

Sergei crouched down to examine the frayed remnant of fabric now trailing. He leapt up again and signalled someone. Ten minutes later she was standing in the bedroom of a fabulous hotel suite, clad only in her lingerie while her dress was carefully repaired in the reception room next door. She flinched and spun round in dismay when the door opened without even the hint of a warning knock.

Sergei focused on her small slender figure and the laughing comment he had meant to make fell from his memory there and then. She whipped her arms protectively round her scantily clad body but not before he had had the opportunity to enjoy an enchanting glimpse of her pale rounded curves. He leant back against the door and snapped home the lock, his dark eyes flashing hot gold at the sight of the pouting breasts encased in white gossamer-fine lace that revealed her delicate pink nipples. Her tiny waist, the feminine swell of her hips and the elegant sweep of her slender thighs only heightened his interest.

'Why are you hiding yourself? Let me see you properly, *milaya moya*,' Sergei urged, discovering to his amazement that he was as eager as a boy to see her naked. The pulse at his groin, which had kept him simmering on the edge of full arousal for hours, accelerated.

Her aquamarine eyes widened, her body quickening with a desire she couldn't stifle. His heated look of masculine appreciation flattered her, making her unexpectedly proud of her body. But innate common sense told her that such a thought was brazen and likely to get her into trouble. Furthermore she could not credit that her rather ordinary shape could compare to that of the international selection of well-known beauties he was accustomed to being with. Embarrassment and discomfiture attacked her then in a blinding wave. She sat down at the foot of the bed and crossed her arms, concealing her lightly clad body as best she could.

Sergei had had more than enough of waiting. Ever since the first night with her at his club, he had been ablaze with fierce sexual need and impatience. For a man with no concept of female reluctance or of pleasure deferred, that wait had proved a tough and thankless challenge. Now, with his lean muscular body honed to a raw edge of desire by the kissing, the dancing and the lack of privacy that had enforced rigorous restraint on his strong libido, he was intensely hungry for her and in no mood to hide it. In a sudden movement, he pitched off his jacket and yanked loose his tie.

'What on earth are you doing?' Alissa asked, wide-eyed.

'You're not very good at following through on orders, are you?' Sergei murmured in his deep, dark, accented drawl. 'That wilful independent streak is something we can work on together—'

'We can't...er...get involved,' Alissa protested, her voice taking on a slightly shrill note that carried a hint of panic.

'There's no point in saying that we can't do what we've *already* done,' Sergei countered with fierce conviction and he reached for her hands to tug her up off the bed without further ado. 'I've been involved from the first moment I saw you. It's not what I planned; it's definitely not what I wanted. I never mix business with pleasure—'

'This *is* business,' she reminded him shakily, having

discovered that those scorching golden eyes of his had sufficient impact to hold her as securely still as handcuffs and leg irons. She wanted to pull back and stay connected to him at one and the same time.

'But it's also an exception because it embraces you and I want you more than I've wanted any woman in a very long time,' Sergei imparted with charged urgency.

'You're only trying to justify yourself,' Alissa reasoned in growing desperation.

'Of course I am, *dorogaya moya*,' he responded with immense assurance. 'I've made my fortune from being a very adaptable man. We are together for the foreseeable future and will be living in the most intimate of connections—what is logical and reasonable should guide our behaviour.'

As his masculine gaze flamed over her Alissa snatched in a sharp breath, for his keen appraisal was making her feel as self-conscious as if she were already naked. And she saw no logic whatsoever in being wildly attracted to a guy so far removed from her in terms of wealth and status. Indeed, she saw only disaster. 'It would just complicate things,' she muttered in feverish rebuttal.

Sergei knew women. She couldn't stop staring at him, Her pupils were dilated, her lips moistly parted, her breathing audible. He could sense how close he was to victory. 'I don't do complicated. Trust me I'll keep it straightforward.'

Confident as ever, he lowered his handsome dark head, his luxuriant black hair gleaming in the light of the lamp she had lit to chase the wintry darkness of late afternoon. He pressed a teasing kiss to the corner of her tremulous lips. Instantly, revealingly, she turned her head straight into the kiss, lips parting in readiness for the exhilarating plunge of his tongue. Low in her throat she moaned when he gave her what she longed for in that first kiss and a knot of gathering sexual tension clenched tight in her pelvis, leaving her awesomely aware of her body.

How could she possibly trust him? He was notorious with women. If a supermodel or a famous actress couldn't hold him for longer than five minutes, what hope had she? But his unashamed single-minded desire for her excited Alissa and ensured that she felt truly feminine and attractive for the first time in her life. Even so she was uneasily conscious of her inexperience and suspected that it might shock him, possibly even repulse him. He shifted against her, one hand cupping her hips to tilt her to him so that she could feel the urgent vigour of the erection tenting the fine fabric of his trousers. A quiver of pure hunger, as sharp as it was painful in its intensity, slivered through her.

Sergei unclipped the bra with one hand and drew it down her arms before succumbing to the temptation of looking at her beautifully formed breasts. He cupped the pert mounds in reverent fingers. 'You are a work of art.'

His fingers brushed the lush pouting buds that crowned the full swells. He was already as hard as steel and he vented an earthy groan of appreciation and backed her down on the bed, his mouth swooping down to capture a quivering nipple to tease it with the slick of his tongue and the edge of his teeth.

That sweet torment of sensation arrowed straight down to the hot damp place between her thighs and raised her temperature to a tingling height. Her hips squirmed in a rhythm as old as time. She dragged him up to kiss her again, rejoicing in his passion but desperately hungry for more. Her untried body was soaking up every new sensation like a sponge and responding with increasing demands.

The level of her response astounded Sergei. He reeled back from her to haul at his shirt and she leant over him, tugging frantically at buttons with an eager lack of sophistication and dexterity that he found tremendously attractive.

The shirt finally conquered with the loss of only one button, Alissa studied his golden-toned torso and the pelt of curling black hair accentuating his pectoral muscles and felt weak with longing. She let her hands run unsteadily down over his stomach, felt his taut muscles contract in reaction and pressed her lips to a masculine nipple, headily drinking in the familiar smell of his skin.

'*Yizihkom,*' he breathed thickly.

'In English?' Alissa gasped.

Sergei tipped up her chin, dark golden eyes smouldering with sexual heat. 'Use your tongue,' he translated thickly, wondering at her tentative caresses and the way in which his advice caused immediate hot colour to rise in her cheeks.

Knowing she needed all the help she could get, Alissa obliged, keen to please him as much as he had pleased her and driven on by the fire of craving at the heart of her. He tasted every bit as good as he looked and had he not pushed her back onto the mattress to torment the hard buds of her sensitised nipples, she would certainly have become more daring. Her downfall was complete when he employed a seeking hand below the lace panties and found the precise spot to tease, destroying what remained of her self control.

With a helpless cry she arched up to him and he crushed her mouth below his, his tongue meshing with hers in an erotic dance.

'Please…oh, *please*!' Alissa moaned, burning with all-encompassing need and beyond thought.

With a roughened curse half under his breath, Sergei ripped off her panties and discovered the warm wet welcome awaiting him with a savage sound of overpoweringly male satisfaction. Springing upright, he dispensed with his own clothing while she looked up at him with dazed eyes of need.

He was so beautiful—a pagan vision of bronzed muscular power and energy. He was also very aroused and her first sight of a fully erect male was daunting.

'We'll never fit!' she told him before she could think better of it.

Sergei laughed out loud, for it struck him as such a naïve and irrational comment from a woman who had stated in an interview that she considered herself very much a woman of the world and comfortable with men. 'I am so hot for you, I am in pain,' he confessed, coming down to her again.

He entered her hard and fast and she yelped and flinched with pain.

An incredulous look in his hot golden gaze, as he had felt the resistance of her flesh to his invasion, he growled, 'You cannot be a virgin…'

'Why? Is there a law against it?' Alissa countered, her low voice raw with embarrassment and the lingering shards of discomfort still throbbing through her tender flesh.

'Do you want me to stop?' Sergei was frozen with frustration and a hunger that made him tremble because the lush, tight fit of her tiny body round him was extraordinarily pleasurable.

He was already trying and failing to replace the image of the woman he had thought she was with the woman she now appeared to be. He had picked a wife he'd believed would spring no surprises on him. Better the devil you know, he had decided, and who had more experience than he of shallow, unemotional and mercenary women? Instead he had found himself a virgin and suddenly he understood the blushes and the awkwardness and the confusing signals she gave him. He studied her from below the screen of his ink-black lashes and the rarity of the gift she had given him finally struck him. She was his wife and no one but him had ever got this intimate with her. It was a thought that had strong appeal for a male as discerning as he was. The disturbing surprise suddenly became a cause for celebration.

'Don't stop,' she breathed, helpless in the grip of the erotic heat and intensity still roaring through her.

Expelling his breath in a hiss of relief, Sergei began to move again while exerting every atom of control that he could muster. He responded well to challenge and he was determined to exceed whatever expectations she had of the event. His fluid increase in tempo sent excitement flashing through Alissa faster than an express train and fuelled her need. She bucked under him and sobbed with startled pleasure when he employed slow subtle movements that tormented her with sensation. She couldn't control anything that she was feeling and what she was feeling was incredibly powerful. The hunger stoked by his passion reached a frantic height when every part of her was pitched to an unbearable degree of longing and then in a breathless heartbeat she reached an ecstatic climax. As she writhed under him in frenzied abandonment, wave after wave of pleasure convulsing her slender body, Sergei enjoyed the longest and most stupendous release of his life. His superb body shuddering over her, he tasted the ecstasy.

A split second later, he was wondering with an amount of alarm that shook him whether that single act of stunning sex might get her pregnant. And he didn't want her carrying a child too soon, did he? Momentarily, Sergei, who never, ever deviated from a goal once he was set on it, was plunged into genuine bewilderment by his own change of heart on the baby issue. But when she conceived, it would surely be a case of game over as far as the bedroom was concerned and he really did not want to put her out of commission in the first month. That said, however, his priorities were unchanged, he re-assured himself confidently: he was simply taking a rain check on that objective. Why shouldn't he want to enjoy his bride for a while? There wasn't a man alive who would not want to make the most of a woman who gave him that much pleasure between the sheets, he reasoned, his tension ebbing again. Releasing her from his weight, he anchored her to him with an appreciative arm.

'Bihla chudyesna…that was amazing,' he told her with husky satisfaction, landing a haphazard kiss on her cheekbone and then backing off so fast in discomfiture at having given her that salutation that she almost fell off the bed. 'But we have a reception to get back to.'

Shot back to reality with a vengeance by that reminder, Alissa slid off the bed as if she had been jabbed by a hot poker. Realising in mortification that, aside of a wispy bra and a pair of torn knickers, she had no clothes to put back on, she snatched at the bedspread and yanked violently at it to haul it from under the big bronzed length of him where he lay in an infuriatingly relaxed post-coital sprawl. Concealing herself within its folds, Alissa was furiously aware of Sergei's unashamedly amused scrutiny.

'What is hidden is always more intriguing, *angil moy*,' he murmured with silken approbation. 'And much more appealing to a man like me than a short skirt and a low neckline—'

'Intriguing you is the very last thing on my mind!' Alissa almost spat at him, a tempestuous fury building behind her embarrassment.

With his brilliant dark eyes gleaming, his black hair ruffled and blue-black stubble beginning to shadow his strong jaw line and highlight his shapely mouth, he was a pagan vision of male beauty and magnetism. And she hated him, absolutely hated him for taking advantage of her the very first chance he got! Or the very first chance she had *given* him, she rephrased bitterly, loathing herself even more than she loathed him. But then what else had she expected from Sergei Antonovich? He was programmed to take advantage. He was a billionaire buccaneer in business, famous for his unpredictability and ability to move fast on a choice deal.

'How much did I hurt you?' he enquired with lazy assurance.

Her face burned. 'I'm not going to discuss that—I'm not going to discuss anything that happened in that bed because there's no need. It's never going to happen again!'

Sergei was happily engaged in admiring the way the silk spread poured over her ripe little curves to cradle a pouting breast and define a deliciously voluptuous buttock. That green shade threw her aquamarine eyes into prominence as well. He was hugely relieved to hear that she didn't want to discuss anything. Particularly anything that related to how their business contract had suddenly expanded to include sex for pleasure.

Unusually for him, he wasn't quite sure why the business angle was taking more and more of a back seat, but he suspected it had a lot to do with the reality that he had wanted to bed her from the first instant he laid eyes on her tiny curvy frame. Why should that be a problem? She was proving to be a very worthwhile investment and there was no reason why he shouldn't keep her as an indulgence for as long as he wanted. By the time she had given him a baby, she would no longer be a novelty, he reckoned with cynical conviction. An awareness of his own notorious track record warned him that familiarity would soon breed, not only contempt, but also boredom, and he would be glad to see her go.

'You took advantage of the fact that I had had too much to drink!' Alissa launched her attack without warning.

'Had you?' His black brows drew together. 'When you were ripping off my shirt you struck me as an equal partner in every respect,' he mused with the aura of a male recalling that act with satisfaction. 'Don't spoil it by being childish.'

'Childish?' Alissa parroted in a rage.

'Why does the timing matter?' he demanded in sincere incomprehension, for he had baulked at the prospect of a child conceived by artificial means in a Petri dish and sex had always been part of the package deal. 'We wanted each other and we went to bed—'

'We didn't even make it *into* the bed!' Alissa snapped accusingly, wondering why he was talking about timing, since she could not see what that had to do with anything.

An almost imperceptible darkening of colour high-lighted Sergei's high cheekbones. He was willing to admit that as encounters went it might not have been the idealistic stuff of a virginal fantasy. But then, he was well aware that she was not a romantic woman. No romantic woman would accept a huge amount of money to marry a stranger, give him a child and then walk away from that child.

'It's too late for regrets,' Sergei pointed out with innate practicality.

Outraged by his attitude, Alissa stalked into the en-suite bathroom to stare shell-shocked at herself in the mirror above the vanity unit. Her wreath of flowers was crushed, her veil creased and her make-up smeared all over her face. She looked like a car-crash bride and the illusion of perfection was long gone. Tear tracks streaked her face while she stood there recognising that she had just totally changed her relationship with Sergei. Sex had smashed the boundaries she had known she had to retain if she was ever to win his respect. Her body ached with her every movement. She showered as best she could without getting her hair wet.

A knock made the door bounce in its frame and she spun round and opened it a mere crack, because she knew exactly who had to be behind that too-powerful knock.

'I'm going for a shower in the other bedroom.'

Consternation made Alissa open the door wider and note the fact that he was only wearing his trousers with his shirt hanging open. 'For goodness' sake, put on all your clothes before you step out of this room!'

'Why?'

Her mouth snapped into a compressed line at what she saw as a very stupid question. 'Because if you don't the women out there fixing my dress will realise exactly what we've been doing!'

'*So?*' Sergei prompted very drily, thinking not for the first time that Alissa's attitudes and declarations frequently defied all logic and reality. 'We got married, we shagged, so far, so normal...'

Alissa breathed in so deep she was afraid that she would burn up with the internal heat of her vexation. 'If you don't put your clothes on, I'll never forgive you!' she snapped in dire warning.

'They'll know anyway,' Sergei told her with impatience. 'You've wrecked your hair and the flowers in the wreath, so I asked the beautician and the florist to come up and sort you out.'

Scarlet to her hairline, Alissa gave him what could only be described as a very aggressive and freezing nod, before shutting the door in his lean, darkly handsome face. Later she could never work out quite how she managed to handle the reappearance of the support team, entrusted with licking her back into bridal shape, because inside herself she was cringing. The knowing looks when she reappeared at the reception by Sergei's side ate her alive with mortification. His reputation went before him, she reflected ruefully. When Sergei disappeared with a woman, no one, it seemed, had any doubt of his intent.

Intercepting a warm smile from Yelena, Alissa went over to talk as best she could to Sergei's grandmother. The grizzled bearded man by her side revealed that he was a retired professor living in Yelena's village and he translated to enable the two women to communicate. Alissa was surprised to find that she was confiding in Yelena about her parents' separation.

Sergei joined them and spoke at length to his grand-mother before closing a hand over Alissa's and guiding her onto the dance floor. She glanced up at his lean, breathtakingly handsome face and her heart thumped heavily in her eardrums. She felt so vulnerable, so unsure of what to do next, for the passion they had shared had wrecked the framework of their relationship and she had no idea what would replace it.

'We're leaving,' Sergei explained only when she questioned why they were leaving the function room and by a side door. 'Yelena's right. You look ex-hausted…like a little white ghost, *angil moy*…'

CHAPTER SIX

PINK colour swam up below Alissa's fair skin in a revealing tide.

In the limo, Sergei slid a long brown forefinger below her chin to tip up her face. 'You're still angry with me,' he noted in apparent surprise.

'No, I'm not. I'm not a child either. I do appreciate that I was equally responsible for what occurred,' she said woodenly, long feathery lashes veiling her aquamarine eyes from his scrutiny.

Unholy amusement lit up Sergei's smile; he was in an unusually good mood. She was still furious with him and couldn't hide it and he loved that transparency of hers for its rarity. Her refusal to meet his eyes and her rigidity spoke for her. Women didn't treat him that way and her nerve in doing so intrigued him. She was a novelty and so far the exact opposite of the woman described in that psychological profile. She was warm when she was supposed to be cool, passionate when she was supposed to be indifferent and deeply attached to her family when she was supposed to be selfish and detached. Even so, whatever conundrum Alissa presented, she had put on a marvellous show for his grand-mother's benefit.

'I have a gift for you.' Sergei presented her with a jewel case.

'*Another one?*' Alissa asked in disbelief and she was annoyed when that tart response only made her feel rude and ungracious.

'I always reward excellence and you surpassed my highest expectations today,' Sergei drawled as smooth as glass.

'At the wedding…or on the bed?' Alissa queried in a frozen little voice of supreme scorn.

Her tone was wasted on Sergei, who merely vented an appreciative laugh that emphasised how far apart they were in terms of humour. 'You were a triumph everywhere, *angil moy*.'

With pronounced reluctance Alissa flipped up the lid of the case to reveal a diamond necklace that would surely have been worthy of the Crown jewels exhibited in the Tower of London. In spite of the fact that she was determined not to be impressed, her lips fell wide as she gazed at the river of perfectly matched glittering stones embellished by a magnificent pendant with a huge opulent emerald at its heart.

'Well, thank you very much,' she muttered finally, re-minding herself that Alexa would have snatched it up, put it on and wrapped her arms gratefully round his neck in reward for such generosity.

'Don't you like jewellery?'

'Oh, very much,' she hastened to declare, steeling herself to remove the necklace from the case and behave as he almost certainly expected her to and wrap it straight round her neck. 'But you really don't need to give me stuff like this.'

Sergei did up the clasp. The stunning pendant was heavy and cold on her skin. *Her reward for excellence.* Alissa remembered that wild raunchy coupling on the bed, which had evidently pleased him very much. Her tummy clenched with a disturbing combination of intense shame and equally intense excitement. Her virginity hadn't repulsed him in the slightest and, although what she had allowed to happen between them felt indisputably wrong and her pride lay in ashes round her feet, Sergei *still* didn't repulse her. What was the matter with her? Where had her values gone?

The limousine wafted them back to his imposing city residence. He took her hand in the hall and directed her up the sweeping staircase.

'Where are we going?' she queried when he walked her past the room she had slept in the night before.

'Your new room.'

'Is it your room as well?' Alissa enquired tightly.

'No, I'm not into that joined-at-the-hip cosy couple stuff,' Sergei imparted with perceptible recoil at the idea. 'Not my style. I have my own suite next door.'

Alissa's tension eased at the news that she was not expected to share a room with him. Surely with that sensible demarcation line in place there was less chance that she would be tempted by him again?

Sergei opened the door. He escorted her across the depth of a superb large bedroom and paused on the threshold of the en suite where odd flickering shadows were lighting up the walls. Alissa moved past him to gape in astonishment at the sunken bath already filled with steaming water and encircled with candles.

Sergei rested both hands on her narrow shoulders. 'This has been a stressful day for you but you rose wonderfully to the challenge. I want you to relax now.' He flipped her gently round, detached the wreath and veil, cast them carelessly aside and began without hesitation to unfasten her dress.

'I can manage fine without help!' Alissa exclaimed.

'I don't think so.' Sergei breathed in the warm and already familiar scent of her. She smelled of the perfume he had bought her in London, a light but lingering floral fragrance that suited her so much better than the more exotic cloying concoction she had sported at their first meeting. He pressed his sensual masculine mouth against the soft skin of the fine-boned shoulder he had bared, his lips moving in a caressing trail to her sensitive nape while he slowly eased the fitted sleeves down her arms. Alissa quivered in response as though he were touching much more intimate places. Never ever had she dreamt that it was possible to be so insanely aware of a man. As her knees threatened to buckle and her stress level rose like steam in a tightly lidded pot she fought her treacherous weakness with all her might. And then suddenly without warning it was all too much for her and she sagged back into the shelter of his strong arms, tears burning the backs of her troubled eyes.

'Don't do that,' she told him shakily.

'But you like what I do to you,' Sergei asserted with husky assurance, sliding his hands below the loosened bodice to nudge her lace bra out of his path and cup the soft silken mounds of her breasts in his palms. Her nipples tightened into tingling erection below the skilled stroke of his thumbs.

'Whether I like it or not is irrelevant!' Alissa argued wildly.

'How can it be?' Sergei urged, turning her round to face him. 'It's the icing on the cake for both of us. But you should have warned me that I would be your first lover. If I'd known I would have been more patient and I might have hurt you less.'

Alissa wanted the tiled floor to open up and swallow her. She snatched at her bodice before it could tumble lower and expose her bare breasts. Her hands were trembling, for she was remembering that wild passion when his impatience had only been matched by her eagerness and the pain had drowned in the hot sweet tide of pleasure. Her face burning, she stepped back from him. 'I'm fine,' she said flatly.

Sergei dealt her a flashing smile of such intrinsic charisma that her gaze stayed glued to him. 'We'll eat together in an hour.'

Relieved by his departure and wrung out by the day's events, Alissa shed her dress in the bedroom and finally sank into the bath with a heartfelt sigh of pleasure. Rose petals floated on the surface of the fragrant water. Sergei, she acknowledged in wonderment, had actually pre-arranged the candlelit bath for her and she was impressed, much more impressed than she had been by the gift of the extravagant diamond and emerald necklace. She shifted position and the dulled throb of her still tender flesh mocked her. So she was fine, was she?

She had had a lust-fuelled sexual encounter for the very first time and, while she was still ashamed of herself, she was even more worried that it would take very little effort on his part to persuade her into a repetition. The whole situation ran against her every principle and just then she could not work out how she had got caught up in it. She was his wife, his bought and paid for wife, who had already agreed to let him go without a fuss when he wanted his freedom back. He saw no reason why they shouldn't make the most of the attraction between them in the meantime. Alexa would probably have laughed and settled for a short-lived casual affair, Alissa reflected uncomfortably. Why did she want more from Sergei than that fleeting sexual interest?

What did she like about Sergei Antonovich? It amazed her that she had disliked him so thoroughly at their first meeting. But then she had learned more about him since then, she reasoned.

He was very fond of his grandmother and so determined to make the older woman happy that he was willing to fake a marriage for her benefit. Alissa believed that he had made the wrong decision on that score, but she couldn't fault his good intentions. She also liked the fact that for all his wealth and power he didn't take himself too seriously. And his manners were faultless. He opened doors, held out coats for her, asked if she was cold and generally practised the kind of courtesy that had fallen out of fashion with so many men. He made her feel incredibly feminine as well. And although he was extremely blunt she preferred honesty to hypocrisy and evasion. Besides, while he was indisputably arrogant and bossy, he could also be surprisingly thoughtful and considerate, she conceded, resting back in the sunken tub with a dreamy smile blossoming on her face. When a maid rapped on the door to deliver a box of handmade chocolates to the very side of the bath, Alissa's smile shone even brighter. She let a chocolate melt against her taste buds and sighed in bliss while she allowed her thoughts to drift for long timeless moments.

I really really fancy him. I want to sleep with him tonight. I'm falling in love with him like some silly infatuated schoolgirl!

Eyes wide with shock and dismay at the thoughts suddenly chasing without warning through her bemused head, Alissa sat up with a start, water sloshing noisily around her. Conscious that the water was cooling by then, she got out of the bath and wrapped her slender figure in a white fleecy towel. Only taking the time to remove her make-up and comb her hair, she returned to the bedroom just as the phone by the bed buzzed.

'Come and join me,' Sergei urged lazily. 'I've just had to sack the manager of my football team!'

Alissa rummaged through the drawers in the dressing room for nightwear. Everything had been unpacked and neatly put away for her. Sliding into a turquoise nightdress in haste, she pulled on the matching wrap while chanting a firm mantra to herself. I am not going to have sex with him again. *I am not going to have sex with him again under any circumstances. We're just going to talk about football. But I do hope I don't have to watch any.*

Sergei, his lean, beautifully built body clad solely in a pair of black silk designer boxers, was pacing the floor of the room next door and talking on the phone in a foreign language. He was also gesticulating with a good deal of force to express his feelings. With the fingers of one brown hand he indicated the trolley of food by the bed in an invitation for her to help herself.

Alissa only then realised that she was actually ravenously hungry and she lifted a plate and selected choice morsels of food from the sizeable assortment of hot and cold dishes on offer. Forcing her attention away from the clothes discarded untidily on the carpet, she curled up on the bed and munched happily through a selection of chicken, salad and fresh baked bread. Sergei completed his phone call, treated her to a spirited speech about unreliable temperamental staff and embarked straight away on another phone call. She didn't quite grasp what all the fuss was about and truthfully didn't much care. Halfway through her own meal she set it aside and filled a plate for him, placing it where he could reach it while he paced back and forth.

'How many languages do you speak?' she enquired between calls.

'Six or seven and enough to make myself understood in basic terms in another couple,' he breathed as if the talent were nothing unusual. 'When I do business, I like to be able to talk to people direct rather than through intermediaries.'

'I speak French and Spanish but not fluently,' she told him modestly.

'You have to learn Russian,' he replied.

'Do I?'

His black brows drew together in a frown at the question. 'Of course, *milaya moya.*'

Sergei studied her, striving to dissect the precise source of her ever-growing appeal because, just at that moment, she looked more like a teenager than an adult. Her face shone with cleanliness and her hair was tucked untidily behind her ears. Natural and unadorned, she bore no resemblance to the high maintenance women who normally shared his bed. She had beautiful eyes though, very clear and expressive. They were by far her best feature, although that soft, full-lipped mouth was worthy of note too, he conceded, while at the same time noting the fine smooth grain of her skin and the appealing delicacy of her bone structure. His appetite for food dwindled to be replaced by another kind of hunger while he appraised her and recalled more intimate images that sent the blood pounding through his veins.

Struggling to appear unaware of that lengthy all-male scrutiny, Alissa asked herself what she was doing sitting on his bed. Was that being standoffish? More businesslike in her approach? Discouraging? Shame sat like a lump of lead in her stomach but she didn't budge. Without warning the prospect of keeping her distance from him and restoring platonic limits had all the appeal of a heavy rainstorm on her horizon.

'I like that you're completely sober,' Sergei commented.

'I learned to leave my glass full and everyone stopped pushing more drinks in my direction,' she confided with a comical expression.

Charmed by that cheeky smile, Sergei switched off his phone, tossed it aside and reached for her with purposeful hands. She came up on her knees and he knotted one hand in the heavy fall of her golden hair and slowly, sexily ravished her mouth while he pushed the wrap and the straps of her nightie down off her slim shoulders. As the garments fell to her knees he captured her breasts and kneaded the quivering tips until she was gasping, shaken by the immediate surge of heat between her thighs.

'I can't stop wanting you,' Sergei growled, long fingers dropping down to part the golden curls on her mound and gently tease the sensitive bud of her clitoris before venturing to stroke the lush damp lips she would have hidden from him.

Her breath was rattling in her tight throat. She parted her thighs for him, awkwardly balancing herself with a hand on his shoulder until he hauled her up into his arms and tipped her back on the bed. Her body was humming, as desperate for every caress as though their earlier encounter had never happened. He kissed a tormenting passage down over her writhing, shifting length.

'I want to make love to you the way I should have this afternoon,' Sergei breathed thickly. 'I can't wait to drive you crazy with pleasure.'

And just as he knew what he was doing, she did as well. Later she would make herself acknowledge that shameful fact, but while he was doing gloriously arousing things to her weak and easily tempted body she was a complete pushover. What she was feeling was impossibly strong and left no room for questions of right and wrong. He pleasured her with his mouth and his tongue and his fingers until she was a trembling, overheated heap of excited nerve-endings crying out for more.

Hot and ready, she watched him as he donned protection. When he finally sank into the tight wet sheath of her womanhood, the sheer excitement of his entrance sent her careening headlong into violent orgasm. Her sobs and convulsions of delight almost made Sergei lose control as well. Fierce strain etched in the hard, handsome contours of his face, he lifted her knees to hold her still and drove his hard male heat into her yielding flesh with insistent hunger.

Her excitement never once dropped by so much as an atom and she soon hit another high, a climax ripping through her like fireworks blazing up. Afterwards she thought she would never move again. Her limbs were heavy, her body languorous and the most amazing sense of well-being and peace engulfed her. Sergei rolled over, keeping his arms wrapped round her so that he carried her with him.

'You are so hot, *angil moy*,' he intoned, his stunning dark golden eyes glittering with rich appreciation, his heart still thundering against her, his bronzed length damp with sweat. 'I may never let you get out of this bed again.'

Alissa was so exhausted that she had no strength left to move. She consoled herself by dabbing kisses on whichever part of him she could reach and he stretched indolently and this time around he stayed close, letting her have her way.

'Yelena told me you're still stressing about the breakdown of your parents' marriage,' Sergei murmured. 'That's crazy—'

Alissa stiffened. 'Why is it crazy?'

'You lived in a happy united family for over twenty years. You should appreciate how lucky you were.'

Alissa blinked in shock at that rebuke from an unexpected quarter. 'Why? What was your experience?' she snapped, mortified by his criticism.

'A father in and out of prison for stealing cars—he was a thief and a stupid one. I also had to put my mother to bed drunk every night,' he breathed wryly. 'My father was shot dead in the street for stealing a local gangster's car and a year later my mother's liver finally quit and she died…'

Caught up in the dark story of his childhood, Alissa wriggled round in the circle of his arms to look at him wide-eyed with disquiet. 'What age were you then?'

His lean strong face bore no emotion. He might have been talking about someone else's life. 'Thirteen. Yelena insisted on giving me a home with her. We were strangers because my father was a lousy son as well,' Sergei recounted levelly, grim dark eyes meeting hers. 'She was my only experience of family life and I gave her a hard time. I was as feral as a wild animal.'

Alissa traced the stubborn shape of his sensual lower lip with an admiring fingertip. 'I can imagine that.'

Sergei released a spontaneous laugh of disagreement. 'No, you can't. We grew up in different worlds. Yours was cosy, middle class and protected. I bet you got just about everything you ever wanted.'

'No, I didn't!'

'Tell me one thing you didn't get,' Sergei challenged, absorbed in the constant play of animation across her heart-shaped face, while he wondered why he was talking to her when he never wasted time doing that with a woman.

'I fell in love with someone else's boyfriend once,' Alissa admitted, offended by his apparent belief that she had been spoiled and cosseted with good fortune all her days. 'I had to get over it, but it was a very unhappy time for me.'

'Didn't you make a play for him?'

Alissa gave him a shocked look. 'Of course not. He was my sister's boyfriend.'

'If you weren't prepared to fight for him, you can't have wanted him that much, *milaya moya*,' Sergei quipped, wondering darkly if she would fight for him or whether she was guilty of being as shallow as her profile beneath that surface show of niceness.

'Sergei…' she said ruefully. 'There are such things as family loyalty and moral standards.'

'I wonder if our child will inherit your outlook.' His

dark brows drew together in a slight grimace. 'I'm
very cold-blooded when it comes to protecting my own
interests. One or two of your genes mightn't do too
much damage but too many would make him or her
weak in my world.'

In receipt of that speech, Alissa blinked in bewilderment and jerked back from him. '*Our child?* What are
you talking about?'

Scanning her perplexed face with a frown, Sergei
loosened his hold on her, allowing her to break the connection. 'If that's a joke, it's not a very good one.'

'Why would it be a joke? I agreed to marry you…'

'And have my baby, as you are very well aware,'
Sergei countered with impatience. 'But if you agree, and
I don't see why you shouldn't, I'm willing to push the
time frame back a month or two.'

And have my baby. That fatal assurance rang like a
clarion call in Alissa's head and froze her to the marrow.
Alexa could not possibly have agreed to such an iniqui-
tous contract. It couldn't be true, it *couldn't* be!

CHAPTER SEVEN

'WHAT are you doing?' Sergei demanded as Alissa slid soundlessly off the side of the bed like a wraith trying to avoid detection. In almost the same movement she reached for her discarded nightdress.

Alissa's upper lip was damp with perspiration. She had broken out in a literal cold sweat. Why would Sergei lie? Nor had there been anything teasing about his voice or manner. Indeed he'd had been terrifyingly matter-of-fact when he mentioned putting back the time frame for a while. A baby? She was to give him a baby as part of the contract? He had to be out of his mind!

She pulled on her nightie with shaking hands, for the nakedness of intimacy seemed more wrong than ever now that she was being forced to confront the reality that to protect her sister she had deceived him. Was it possible that Alexa could have set out to deceive her as well? It was after midnight and Alissa was incredibly tired. There were no bright ideas in her mind to inspire her and no magical escape hatch in sight. So desperate was she to know exactly what Sergei was talking about that she felt that her only option was to come clean.

'We need to talk,' Alissa breathed tautly.

Wondering what on earth she was up to, Sergei had already sat up to view her with narrowed and intent dark eyes. 'It's late,' he responded, wishing he hadn't broken the habit of a lifetime and started sharing confidences with her. Somehow she was getting under his skin and he didn't like that.

Alissa laced her hands together. 'I'm afraid we've got to talk because when you mentioned having a baby I genuinely didn't know what you were talking about—'

'Bearing in mind the contract you signed and the legal advice you had beforehand, that's an impossible claim for you to make.' Brilliant dark eyes now glinting with cold incredulity, Sergei thrust back the bedding to spring out of bed. 'What are you trying to do to me?'

Alissa hovered while he strode into what appeared to be a dressing room similar to hers and disappeared briefly from view. She listened to doors being opened, drawers being rammed in and out with a force that defeated their smooth gliding mechanism. The tension in the air was already making her tummy queasy. The sheer scale of the deception she had engaged in was suddenly hitting her for the very first time. It seemed to her that she could only have walked blindfold into marrying him with her brain on hold. Only now, when she had to break the silence of secrecy, was she able to fully contemplate the enormity of what she had done.

Sergei emerged, sheathed in well-worn jeans and a black T-shirt. Barefoot, every inch of his long muscular physique taut, he surveyed her, his lean dark features set in forbidding lines. 'Explain yourself.'

Her heart beating very fast, Alissa breathed in deep, wondered where on earth to begin and decided to go straight to the crux of the matter. 'It was my sister who initially applied for this…er…role. She went through the whole interview procedure using my name and my educational background…'

His bronzed skin stretched taut over his proud bone structure. A hint of pallor was detracting from his healthy colour. 'Your…*sister*? Are you seriously trying to tell me that you are not the woman who was vetted to become my wife?'

The tension was so fierce that her spine was rigid. 'Yes. I know it must sound awful to you, but there was truly no malicious intent involved in the exchange.'

Taut with savage disbelief at that either excessively naïve or excessively stupid assessment of the damage done, Sergei's hands slowly coiled into fists of restraint by his side. He could not immediately credit the possibility that he could have spent a fortune recruiting the perfect wife and the future mother of his child only to end up being duped by a complete con artist and her accomplice in crime. The very idea of it enraged him. Transgressions of that nature didn't happen to Sergei. He had little experience of monumental foul-ups because he employed a large staff of the very best professionals available to protect him.

Alissa was torn between relief at his silence and terror of what he might be about to say to her. She made a slightly clumsy pleading movement with one hand and took a step forward. 'My sister, Alexa, is my twin—my identical twin.'

Comprehension hit Sergei like a punch in the stomach. He immediately recalled the sour skinny version of her in the photograph. He had got the little, smiley, curvy virgin one instead when he might well have rejected the original in the flesh. Recalling his misgivings over Alissa's failure to match his initial expectations and, even more gallingly, the background check he had cancelled out of pure lust, he cursed and only half under his breath. He should have insisted that she be checked out. He had only himself to blame on that score. Why had he let her sex appeal overrule the shrewd intelligence and preservation instincts that until now had kept him safe?

'You do realise that you and your sister have committed fraud?'

Alissa turned very pale indeed at that charge and busied her trembling hands in picking up her wrap and putting it on. *'Fraud?'* she queried unsteadily, sheer horror at the assurance that she was guilty of a crime scrambling her ability to think straight.

'Who went through the elimination process for this role?'

'Alexa.'

'For the entire process?' Sergei prompted.

Alissa nodded confirmation, her eyes full of anxiety.

'Who signed the contract?' he continued

'Alexa…in my name. She forged my signature,' Alissa told him unwillingly.

Reining back a burst of volcanic rage that would have blown her out of the room, Sergei allowed himself to wonder whether, in the light of those facts, she was still his legal wife. He levelled hard dark eyes of purpose on the bird he had in hand and knew that, impostor or otherwise, he had no intention of letting her out of his sight for longer than five minutes lest she make a run for it. Fired up by the danger of that risk, Sergei lifted the phone to speak to his security chief, Borya, and gave the older man a ream of detailed instructions. He commenced with an order for background reports on Alissa and her twin sister and concluded with the directive that his wife's phone calls be recorded and her every move watched.

Breathing in short shallow bursts, Alissa waited for Sergei to turn back to her. Fraud was a hard, scary word and she felt incredibly stupid for not having expected it to be thrown at her.

'You're an impostor,' Sergei told her with icy precision.

Alissa nibbled worriedly at her lower lip. 'Yes.'

'A liar—'

'I haven't had to tell any lies!' she protested.

'From the first night we met you've been lying to me by pretending to be your sister,' he rephrased his charge grimly. 'Why?'

Alissa had never been so conscious of his size as she was standing in that lamplit bedroom with his dark shadow falling across her. His anger was like a physical entity in the room, for the atmosphere was explosive. She breathed in deep and slow.

'While Alexa was going through the application, she started dating someone and she fell pregnant by him. So, of course, then she couldn't go through with marrying you, but she'd already spent the money you gave her—'

'What? All…' Sergei quoted a massive head-spinning amount of money and suddenly it was Alissa's turn to gape at him in disbelief. 'Even the biggest spendthrift would find it hard to spend that much in so short a period.'

'You *can't* have given Alexa that much money!' Alissa exclaimed in astonishment.

'Don't act the innocent. You and your sister were playing for very high stakes and you got away with the cash. But pause and consider your predicament for a moment. I have never allowed anyone to get away with cheating me,' Sergei informed her softly.

A quiver of cold alarm was trickling down Alissa's tense spine while anger was beginning to spark inside her. 'There was never any intention of cheating you—'

'Then how come I paid and got an impostor and a liar who expects me to believe that she doesn't even know what was in the contract her sister signed in her name?' Sergei angled harshly at her.

'I never got the chance to see the contract!' Alissa slammed back at him defensively.

In answer, Sergei swept up the laptop on the chest near the bed and hit several buttons on the keyboard before angling it in her direction. 'Here…your recommended bedtime reading. It's the contract. If you're telling me the truth, which I doubt,' he said coldly, 'don't you think that neglecting to read what you were signing up for was very foolish?'

'But I didn't sign up for it originally…'

'Who got the cash?'

'Alexa used it to help Mum keep her home and business and pay off Dad's claim on them.'

'What a saint of a daughter!' Sergei derided. 'Are you planning to play the same violins for my benefit? Save your breath. Sob stories leave me cold.'

Clutching at the laptop, Alissa lifted her chin. 'I've none to tell you. But Alexa was totally honest. If she hadn't been pregnant she would have gone ahead and married you!'

'Try some joined-up thinking,' Sergei advised with stinging scorn.

'And what's that supposed to mean?' Alissa shot back at him.

'According to what you've told me your sister used your name from the outset in this scam,' Sergei reminded her very drily. 'Obviously there was no way that she could *ever* have planned to marry me when she was masquerading under your name! That would have been a legal impossibility.'

In receipt of that shrewd and contemptuous assurance, Alissa dealt him a fuming appraisal, infuriated by his insinuations. Just then she was in the grip of shock and it was beyond her capability to compute that fact and doubt her sister's intentions when her own actions had always been powered by family loyalty. 'You've said enough—'

Sergei flung open the communicating door to her bedroom in a blunt invitation for her to leave. 'I've only just begun.'

'What are you going to do...now that you know?' Alissa asked nervously.

'I'm not about to be the loser in this scenario,' Sergei drawled, smooth as silk. 'Be assured of that. I may well prosecute you and your sister for fraud.'

Alissa twisted her hands together. 'Sergei...nobody meant to do you any harm. It was just the way things happened and Alexa was in a complete panic—'

His lean, darkly handsome face was cold and set, his dark eyes merciless. 'If you're not prepared to fulfil that contract in her place, I've been cheated and I won't accept that. I'll tell you what I intend to do tomorrow.'

That last assurance made her blood run cold but there was one question she just had to ask. 'Did Alexa really agree to have a baby with you?' she framed unevenly.

'Not so much with me, as *for* me. Study the contract,' Sergei instructed flatly. 'You're very lucky I'm not throwing you out on the street right now! As far as I'm concerned you're a lying, cheating con artist.'

That judgement hit Alissa hard. As the door snapped shut in her face she backed over to the bed and sat down to focus on the contract on the screen. It was very long and involved and by the time she had finished rereading the more complex clauses she was ashen pale and shattered by the lies and omissions her twin had employed to lure her into taking her place.

On one very telling issue Sergei had been hatefully accurate. Alexa *had* walked away with a fantastic sum of cash, far, far more than Alissa could ever have estimated. Furthermore it would only have taken less than a quarter of that money to settle their mother's financial problems, so Alexa had enriched herself considerably by signing that contract in her sister's name.

Alissa was in deep shock and questions she had never dreamt she might ask about her sister were now tormenting her. Had Alexa planned to use Alissa as a dupe from the outset? What else was she supposed to think? Trust Sergei to pick up on the fact that, having used Alissa's name to begin with, Alexa could never have followed through on the contract she had signed.

Devastating as that possibility was, Alissa was a good deal more appalled by the actual content of the contract. Sergei hadn't only wanted a wife to please his grandmother, he had wanted a child as well and, having spelt out those terms in advance, he was expecting the bride he had hired for the purpose to supply him with one. Where did that leave them both? She could not even countenance the idea of having a child with him, never mind giving that same child up wholly into his care. She curled up in her cold bed and shivered. How on earth could she have got herself into such a mess? All those years of stepping up to save Alexa from herself had clearly addled her wits, for they were no longer children and she had ignored the gravity of exchanging identities as adults and the threat of legal repercussions. She was filled with horror at the idea that she might have inadvertently broken the law.

It hurt even more, though, to accept that her sister had known all along about the baby issue and had deliberately concealed that aspect because she had known that Alissa would never agree to it. Obviously, Alexa had done it for the money, that extraordinary pile of cash that had tempted and finally persuaded Alexa into deceiving her own flesh and blood for the sake of profit.

While Alissa succumbed to exhaustion and tossed and turned her way through uneasy dreams for what remained of the night, Sergei was thinking. The fire of his anger, chilled and steadied by several hours of frustrating consultation with his lawyers, was still liberally laced with outrage. He had begun to believe in Alissa, he registered in sardonic disbelief. He, who had not trusted a woman since Rozalina and who had countless experiences of female greed and dishonesty, had nevertheless mysteriously warmed to Alissa's girl-next-door warmth and seeming innocence. And yet she was clearly a fake, a lying, cheating little fake whose dazzling sex appeal just so happened to have stopped him dead in his tracks.

Her sins and his oversights had come home to roost and he had to forge a new path to his goal or he would lose everything. Losing was never an option for Sergei. He could not even contemplate such a demeaning conclusion. He studied his bruised knuckles with hard dark eyes. Some time during the night, when the endless wrangling of the lawyers during conference calls had breached his tolerance level, he had punched the wall in frustration, but now ice-cold logic was ruling him once again. He had no plans to lose *anything*, least of all the right to keep his ravishingly sexy wife in the marital bed.

When the maid entered the room and opened the curtains the next morning to let wintry daylight flood in, Alissa came awake immediately. She had a headache and a jarring jumpy sense of stress that was new to her. The very first thing she did was text Alexa, warning her twin that Sergei knew the truth and that they needed to talk urgently. Breakfast was served to her while she sat frozen in place against the pillows, recalling that ghastly confrontation with Sergei during the night.

A bitter laugh bubbled in her throat when she remembered her dizzy introspection during that candlelit bath. Hands up who was impressed to death by the gorgeous Russian billionaire who had swept her to the altar! She had sat in that bath with a diamond and emerald pendant worth thousands still clasped round her neck and she had eaten handmade chocolates while nourishing romantic ideas and feelings that could only make her shudder in retrospect. Of course she was not falling in love with Sergei Antonovich! Of course she did not admire him!

He might be her every fantasy come true in bed, but that did not excuse her for getting so carried away with her role that she had started acting like a real bride on her wedding night. Shame sat like a brick at the foot of her throat and strangled her appetite at source. At some stage, she dimly appreciated, all sense of reality had forsaken her and she had forgotten that she was virtually an employee hired to do a specific job.

And now she knew that it was a job she could never, ever fulfil. Sergei had been willing to pay a fortune for a discreet woman, willing to give him a child and then walk away without any hassle. What did that say about him? Her soft mouth trembled and she dug her fingers tightly into her palms. Not a guy who thought much of a woman's maternal instincts or even of a child's need for a mother. Not a guy who thought much of women as decent people full stop, she reckoned painfully. And all *she* had done was give him even more justification for his cynical attitude towards her sex!

Her eyes stung with tears and she blinked rapidly and sniffed, furious that her emotions were still out of her control. But she really did feel wretched and ashamed at what she had let herself get involved in. She was thinking about the man who had impassively admitted putting his alcoholic mother to bed every night as a child. Even his loving grandmother had not managed to alter Sergei's bleak view of family life. He'd had dreadful parents. And one bad marriage had evidently ensured that he was not prepared to give any woman a second chance.

Certainly not one who had already been exposed as a liar and a cheat, Alissa told herself doggedly. She mopped her face and blew her nose and struggled to pull herself back together to deal with life as it was, not as she would have liked it to be.

The phone rang while she was getting dressed.

It was not her sister as she had hoped, but Sergei. 'I'll see you downstairs in twenty minutes,' he informed her.

Alissa anchored her hair in a ponytail and stonily studied her reflection. She hadn't bothered with make-up and had pulled on jeans and a sweater. Her *own* clothes, not the borrowed glamour of the designer garments that Sergei had purchased for her. The transformation was complete and she looked ordinary again. But what was the point of gilding the lily for his benefit? Surely that would only make her feel as if she were still trying to pretend to be her more fashionable twin? She checked her mobile phone. Alexa had still not responded to her text. Impatient to talk to her sister, Alissa rang her direct and had to leave a message when the call wasn't answered.

'*Dobraye utra*…good morning.' Sergei surveyed his bride with sardonic cool when she appeared in the doorway of the elegant library he used as an office. 'Are the jeans your equivalent of sackcloth and ashes? I'm not impressed.'

Stung by his acerbic mockery, Alissa folded her arms in a defensive movement. Her struggle to maintain her composure was not assisted by the truth that, while her troubled sleep had left her pale and drawn with heavy eyes, Sergei looked as breathtakingly handsome and vibrant as a man who had enjoyed a full eight hours of undiluted rest. The leap of attraction and erotic response that slivered through her treacherous body mortified her pride. 'I hardly think that what I wear today makes any difference,' she said flatly. 'I don't feel that those clothes you bought are rightfully mine and that I should wear them.'

'Such a little puritan…' Sergei released a derisive sound of amusement that grated against her nerves in the tense silence. 'Let me see—you can marry me in a church in front of hundreds of people and allow me the freedom of your beautiful body, but your principles are too fine to allow you to wear the clothes I bought you?'

As he spoke a deep flush of humiliation slowly rose below Alissa's pale skin and washed up over her face, highlighting the sea-blue shade of her beautiful eyes. She was squirming. 'I didn't mean it like that—'

'Oh, I think you did but, as I have discovered, there's often a wide gulf between your principles and your actual behaviour.'

'Is this why you asked me to come down here? Just so that you can insult me some more?'

Sergei elevated an ebony brow. 'I don't do small talk. Or were you expecting praise for what you've done?'

Alissa drew in a sharp little breath and held it before shaking her head in grudging agreement on that point. Her gaze evaded his.

Satisfied to have put her out of countenance, Sergei lounged back against the edge of his desk to study her. Dressed like a teenager with her face bare of cosmetic enhancement, she looked outrageously youthful and innocent. He paid no heed to the aura of shame and worry that clung to her, for he was in no mood to trust such a show. He was no longer surprised that she had contrived to fool him. The greatest misogynist would have been challenged to pick her out as the calculating con artist she was, he conceded grimly. Hadn't he been taken in? Hadn't his lawyers been fooled by her sister? And hadn't he wanted Alissa so much that he had stifled his misgivings and cancelled the background check that would certainly have revealed that she was one half of a matching pair?

'What we both need to know now is—where do we go from here?' Sergei spelt out.

'I couldn't possibly meet the terms of that contract!' Alissa shot at him in a nervous rush. 'I had no idea that conceiving a child was part of the agreement. I was willing to act as your wife—'

'And share my bed with enthusiasm,' Sergei inserted silkily. 'Let's not forget that angle.'

Alissa flung her head back, her golden ponytail bouncing, her eyes very bright and reproachful. 'That just happened, for goodness' sake!'

Sergei dealt her an unimpressed look as hard as polished steel. 'In this scenario that is very difficult to believe. Sex oils so many wheels. When a man wants a woman he's more careless about the little things that don't add up.'

'Look, stop trying to make everything worse than it already is. I didn't use sex to *do* anything! I may have slept with you and I wish I hadn't,' she declared heatedly, 'but let's leave it at that. What are you going to do about all this?'

'If I do what my lawyers want me to do, I will prosecute you and your sister for fraud. One word of complaint from me and Alexa will be arrested. It is a criminal offence to deliberately sign a contract to defraud anyone of their hard-earned cash.'

Alissa met his contemptuous dark golden eyes in a horror-stricken collision. 'You *can't* do that!'

'I think you'll find that as the wronged party in this set-up I can do whatever I like.'

Desperation assailing her, Alissa was thinking frantically hard. 'But you wanted discretion and if you start prosecuting people it'll get into the newspapers. Surely you can't want that to happen?'

Sergei was impressed by the speed with which she

had brandished her only possible weapon. 'Why should I care? Yelena doesn't read newspapers and it is very unlikely that anyone close to her would find out about a legal case taking place in the UK. I have done nothing wrong and nothing that I am ashamed of and publicity, bad or otherwise, isn't a matter of concern to me. Throwing you and your sister to the wolves on the other hand would at least give me some satisfaction.'

Alissa was paralysed to the spot by that blunt speech. Stone cold fear chilled her tummy, for she knew he was capable of launching a prosecution. Hard enough, vengeful enough, ruthless enough to hit back hard and hurt. Her mind kept on dropping stupidly back to the candlelit bath and the chocolates and the change in him cut through her like a knife. The day before might never have been.

'But nothing would satisfy me quite as much as the fulfilment of the original contract, *milaya moya*,' Sergei informed her smoothly. 'You assure me that that is out of the question, but tight corners have a habit of pushing back the boundaries of what people find acceptable—'

'Nothing you could do or say would persuade me to give up my own child!' Alissa snapped back at him with not an ounce of hesitation.

'I will make you an offer, then. If the money is returned in full and you agree to maintain the marriage for at least a year, I will put all thought of contacting the police on hold for the moment.'

Return the money? Of course he would want the money back, a little voice cried inside her head. She shifted position uneasily. 'From what I understand, a fair proportion of it has already been spent—'

'From what you understand?' Sergei repeated very

drily. 'Are you trying to tell me that you don't have access to that money?'

'Alexa has it, but obviously I'll speak to her.'

Sergei surveyed his bride with burning disbelief. 'Your sister set up the scam, took the money and left you to deliver on the contract and face the music? And you let her do that to you? Evidently I got the dim twin, rather than the cunning, greedy one!'

Highs spots of colour burnished Alissa's cheeks. 'It wasn't like that. I'll admit that Alexa can be reckless and extravagant but she's *not* a thief—why won't you listen to me?'

'You've yet to say anything that either makes sense or is of interest to me.'

'There was no scam!' Alissa proclaimed in fierce protest.

'Then what was it? Where's my money? Or alternatively where's the woman I believed had signed a binding contract with me?' he countered harshly. 'Your sister used your name, backed out last minute and took off with the cash. You're the only hostage I've got. Isn't it time that you stopped disclaiming all responsibility and accept that you're in this up to your throat?'

In receipt of that blistering advice, Alissa swallowed hard and painfully. A tension headache was tightening like a band of steel round her brow. 'I'll try to get the money back—'

'I don't want "try", I want *will*,' Sergei emphasised. 'And don't try selling anything I've given you to pay me back with my own money.'

Alissa stiffened even more at that warning. 'I wouldn't do that. I know you probably won't believe me but I'm not a dishonest person.'

Sergei subjected her to an astringent appraisal. He was wondering if it was possible that her sister had duped her as easily as she had evidently duped his lawyers. He could see that Alissa was still in shock. He could see that she hadn't slept well. He could see that she was trembling and upset. His angular jaw line clenched and he averted his attention from her slight figure. He would have no pity for anyone who cheated him. She was in shock because she was being called to account and distressed because she feared punishment. And naturally she would want to awaken his sympathy.

Sergei straightened to his full commanding height. 'Do not doubt that I am prepared to bring the police into this.'

'I don't doubt it. But you did say that you wanted me to agree to stay as your wife for the next year,' she reminded him anxiously.

'I refuse to upset Yelena with the immediate break-down of our marriage,' Sergei said coldly.

'Okay…I'll stay,' Alissa mumbled, feeling that it was the least she could do in the circumstances.

'My priorities have changed, though.' Sergei studied the faithful fit of her sweater over the swell of her rounded breasts before raising his darkly appreciative gaze to the wide soft fullness of her mouth. Desire was already roaring through him like a hurricane force and he marvelled at the reality that he wanted her as fiercely now as he had wanted her before he had consummated their marriage. He was amazed by her continuing pull on his libido.

'How?'

'I want you in my bed whenever I want you, and with no more nonsense about not wanting to be with me.' Sergei lifted his arrogant dark head high, his glittering golden eyes hurling a challenge. 'If I'm not going to get a child out of this arrangement, that will be my compensation.'

Aquamarine eyes wide with alarm at that bold demand, Alissa was wildly aware of the burning heat of his sensual scan of her body and she slowly turned a painful pink shade.

'And that is not negotiable in any way,' Sergei intoned soft and low. 'I will only let you go free if you return that money.'

Alissa sent him an anguished look. 'I couldn't just go on sleeping with you as though nothing has happened!'

Sergei shrugged a broad shoulder in a show of outrageous nonchalance. 'I think you'll find you can, just like you did yesterday when you were the only one of us aware of the deception,' he reminded her with a sardonic curl to his handsome mouth. 'I'm leaving for London in an hour but you're staying here.'

'Why?'

'I'm giving you three days to decide what your next move will be. And if you're staying on my terms, I expect you in my bed waiting for me when I get back, *milaya moya.*'

Incensed by that cutting little speech, Alissa took a hasty step forward.

Sergei reached for her in almost the same movement. He hauled her bodily into his arms and tasted her parted lips with a hot, driving hunger that took her by shock and storm. She shivered against his unyielding masculine contours, her straining breasts crushed by his powerful torso, a firestorm of response flaring like a shameless fever in her pelvis and leaving her legs weak.

'I think that after you've considered your position

you'll make it a honeymoon to remember, *angil moy*,' Sergei breathed in a tone of strong satisfaction.

Her fingers crept up to touch her tingling swollen mouth. 'A honeymoon?' she echoed blankly.

'On my yacht, where we'll have perfect privacy. *Smile*,' Sergei urged with sudden raw impatience, exasperated by her lack of enthusiasm. 'Giving you a choice between a prison sentence and my bed is very generous of me, more generous than you deserve.'

And Alissa saw that he did indeed believe that her apparent wrongdoing fully excused him for using the most unscrupulous tactics against her. She also knew better than to call Sergei's bluff. He wasn't joking. He wasn't making empty threats. He would be within his rights if he made an official complaint to the police through his lawyers. She pictured her pregnant sister being arrested and charged, closely followed by herself. As the prime instigator, Alexa might well receive the heavier punishment, but what consolation would that be to either of them? The same cold fear infiltrated Alissa again. She *had* to persuade her sister to return the money she had received for signing that contract.

'Why did you want a baby? Just to make Yelena happy?' she asked Sergei on impulse as she turned to leave the room.

Sergei glanced at her in surprise. 'That was my main motivation when I first came up with the idea,' he admitted. 'But I do genuinely like children and I would like a worthy cause to work for, other than myself.'

Alissa went upstairs and phoned her sister again. When she received no response she called her mother instead and found herself having to talk at length about her wedding and the guest lists for the London party her mother was eagerly planning before she could ask how to get in touch with her twin.

'That could be a problem,' Jenny Bartlett replied ruefully. 'Harry and Alexa are staying in a Turkish villa and she told me not to expect her to ring.'

That night Alissa lay in bed thinking about Sergei, who wanted a family of his own even though he wouldn't admit it in those terms. *A worthy cause to work for, other than myself.* In the darkness she blinked back tears and wondered what on earth she was going to do and whether it would be possible for her to go on sharing a bed with Sergei without getting emotionally involved. She was convinced that eventually he would wake up to the awareness she was really nothing that special and his desire for her would die.

For the first time she was remembering that Sergei and his lawyers had chosen Alexa to be his wife, not Alexa's more ordinary twin sister. Alexa was the sophisticated, witty twin, the one the men always went for in Alissa's experience. How long would it be before Sergei suspected that he had been short-changed in the most basic way of all with a woman who could not equal his original choice? It was a very long time before Alissa got any sleep…

CHAPTER EIGHT

'SO WHAT'S all the fuss about?' Alexa demanded sulkily down the phone.

After a wait of almost thirty-six hours for a return call in response to her many messages, Alissa was so relieved to hear her twin's voice on the line that she felt momentarily dizzy and sank down heavily on the side of the bed while she spoke to her. 'For goodness' sake! Sergei has found out what we did.'

'I should have known you couldn't keep your mouth shut.'

'That had nothing to do with it! How could you not tell me that having a baby was part of that contract?' Alissa snapped back, angry disgust girding every syllable of her response. 'You must have known I would never agree to anything so outrageous.'

'You said you'd do anything to help Mum. And obviously you could have taken contraceptive pills to make sure it didn't happen.'

Alissa felt a surge of disbelief at that suggestion. 'How could you let me marry Sergei on false pretences? It was a rotten thing to do! It wasn't fair to me and it wasn't fair to him either!'

'Since when did being fair to Sergei become an ambition of yours?' Alexa demanded. 'Are you trying to make brownie points at my expense?'

'You're just not taking this seriously, are you?' Alissa censured tightly. 'Sergei is very angry and he is threatening to have us both prosecuted for fraud. What you did was illegal, Alexa…'

Alexa giggled. 'He's never going to go public with a story like this! Can you imagine how embarrassing that would be for him?'

'I think you should know that Sergei doesn't embarrass easily,' Alissa inserted sharply.

'He's just trying to scare you when he makes a threat about prosecuting us, Alissa. He doesn't mean it.'

Alissa realised then that the belief that Sergei would never risk the story of that contract getting into the newspapers had always been her sister's insurance policy against retribution. 'You're wrong. He's deadly serious and he wants his money back.'

'Well, he's got no hope of that!'

'Alexa, I now know that you got a *huge* amount of money for signing that contract. You landed me into this situation and you can get me out of it again. You have to sell that car and return as much of the rest of that money as you can put together to Sergei's lawyers in London.'

'Or what?' Alexa sniped.

'You cheated him, you cheated me. Don't you feel any shame about that? Sergei kept his side of the bargain but you didn't and I *can't*. Keeping that money when you didn't earn it is the same as stealing and I'm shocked that you can't see that!' Alissa condemned angrily. 'Sergei thinks we deliberately set out to defraud him and he blames me for it. What's got into you, Alexa?'

'What's got into you? You're my sister. Where's your loyalty?'

'Loyalty doesn't come into this. You have to repay the money!'

'You're being so stupid! I can't possibly repay all that I've spent. Don't phone me again, just leave me alone—this is supposed to be my honeymoon and I'm not about to let you wreck my marriage or my bank balance with your accusations and threats!' Alexa blazed back at her in a fury and the line went dead.

Shaken by that final exchange, Alissa breathed in deep and wondered if anything she had said had hit home hard enough to influence her headstrong sister. She had not said half of what she would have liked to have said. But then it would have been counterproductive to tear too many strips off Alexa at the same time as she was striving to persuade her twin to redress some of the damage she had done. Pushed too hard Alexa would only rebel and take easy refuge in geographical distance and silence.

Alissa went downstairs for breakfast and received a personal visit from the chef, who wanted her to choose meals for the rest of the week. He was quickly followed by the housekeeper, who had several concerns to discuss with her. With one of Sergei's aides brought in to act as an interpreter, Alissa realised that she really did need to learn enough of the Russian language to make herself understood if she was going to be in St Petersburg for much longer. She picked meals without knowing what they were and agreed, after a tour of inspection, to the redecoration of a smoke-stained bedroom damaged by a guest who had fallen asleep with a cigarette in his hand. Afterwards, she fingered the heavily etched wedding ring she wore. With Sergei on her mind night and day without cessation and his household staff coming to her for instructions, she was beginning to feel as if she was really and truly married to him.

And since there was nothing further she could do at present to change her current situation, shouldn't she be doing more in one of the most scenic cities of the world than sitting behind closed doors and worrying? That decision reached, Alissa informed Borya, who suddenly seemed to be constantly hovering around her, that she wanted to go out and where. She wondered why the older man hadn't accompanied Sergei to London. Having donned a purple wool dress and a ravishing full-length coat and boots, Alissa left the house with Borya and his team in tow and commenced her sightseeing tour.

The rest of the day just vanished in the vastness of the baroque green and white Winter Palace and the State Hermitage Museum. Countless art collections were housed within the magnificent cluster of buildings that overlooked the Neva River. Alissa wandered from room to room, dazzled by the priceless works of art and fabulous antiquities on display, grateful for the distraction from her troubled thoughts. In the gardens that lay opposite, she decided that it was too cold for a walk when it began snowing. Big, fat, fluffy snowflakes were drifting down. Even though she had carefully layered her clothing and taken every precaution to keep warm, the icy air pierced her to the bone. She was hurrying back to the limousine when someone shouted her name and she stilled in surprise and spun round, only to notice the camera angled at her too late to avoid it. Borya let out a roar and two of his team set off in hot pursuit of the paparazzo. She was relieved to get back to the house, where she delighted the chef by eating a substantial meal and slept like a log through the night.

The following day, determined not to sit around awaiting either Sergei's or Alexa's next move or phone call, she set off doggedly for Peterhof, a palace complex outside the city. The park of golden statues and elaborate fountains was white with snow and the temperature chilled her to the bone. Her security team had taken the hint from the day before and wore hats and heavy overcoats. When she slept that night she dreamt of wolves chasing her through the park and the endless ornate rooms.

The afternoon of the next day, she was flown out to Sergei's yacht, which was anchored at Antibes, where the weather was considerably milder. The long sleek craft was called *Platinum* and the crew was almost entirely English. She was given a tour of the incredibly opulent vessel and the name seemed peculiarly apt for the lavish décor. The facilities ranged from a home cinema to a gym and a disco bar and sunbathing area that boasted a swimming pool. The master suite in particular was an amazing space with private terraces and seating areas and a marble bathroom of such staggering opulence that she wanted to leap straight into the bath and pretend she was Cleopatra.

As soon as she boarded the yacht set sail. After dining at a table with panoramic views of the sea, she sat down on a sofa in the master suite and switched on the evening news on the wall-hung television screen. She tensed at the sound of Sergei's name and turned up the volume. A photo of their wedding was briefly shown, followed by a view of Sergei standing at a podium in a crowded function room while half a dozen journalists shot questions at him. Evidently he had just taken over some international company. The screen then flipped to a solo shot of Alissa in the snow in St Peterburg. She frowned as she realised it had to be the picture stolen by the paparazzo who had taken her by surprise earlier. The voiceover sounded serious and indeed Sergei was—a wedding one day, big business on the other side of the world the next…and his bride abandoned to find her own amusement…

Sergei flew in to the yacht later than he had planned. His ears were still ringing from Yelena's censorious phone call an hour earlier. His grandmother had seen Alissa on television alone in the park and had been aghast that Sergei could have left his bride to her own devices so soon after the wedding. Alissa had definitely been a big hit with Yelena, Sergei conceded wryly, for never before had Yelena attempted to interfere in his relationship with a woman.

A bottle of champagne and two glasses were brought out to the terrace where Alissa was watching the sun go down. The yacht was moored off a Greek island studded with little white buildings and arrow-shaped green cypresses. The sea glimmered in the fiery glow of sundown. By the time she heard a helicopter coming in to land, darkness had fallen and only the stars lightened the heavens.

Alissa sat as stiff as a stick of rock on her comfortable sofa. Sergei hadn't even bothered to phone her to tell her he would be coming, but the incredible industry of the crew rushing about cleaning and polishing throughout the afternoon had forewarned her of his arrival. And while she wasn't demeaning herself to the level of a nonentity by waiting in bed for him as instructed, she wasn't wearing jeans and a sweater and a scrubbed bare skin either. He had not given her a choice and she was playing it safe, not least for her mother's sake for, whatever else might have gone wrong, Alissa had not allowed herself to forget that her beloved parent's future had been secured by Sergei's money.

Powered by a strong sense of anticipation, Sergei strode away from the helipad and took the private steps up to the master suite two at a time. She was on the terrace, dressed in something glamorously long and blue and silky. Her golden hair was loose on her shoulders, framing an exquisite face dominated by her lucid aquamarine eyes and the rosebud perfection of her lush mouth. His desire ignited with satisfying urgency and he smiled down at her.

After the manner in which they had parted, his unexpected smile knocked Alissa for six as it lit up his stunning dark eyes and added a bucket of compelling charisma to his arrestingly handsome features. Sergei was always such a very unpredictable force of nature, she reflected ruefully. But his sheer physical impact pinned her to her seat. Everything about Sergei was larger than life and powerful. Crackling with high-voltage energy, he towered over her, all broad shoulders and lean hips and long legs. In a sleek black pinstripe suit that had the tailored perfection of fit that flaunted expense and exclusivity, Sergei Antonovich was as stunningly good-looking as he was white-hot sexy. Something tightened low in her pelvis and her nipples lengthened into straining points. Her mouth was dry as a bone and breathing was a challenge as she stared at him.

'Champagne?' Sergei uncorked the bottle and let the golden liquid cascade down into the elegant flutes before extending one to her.

'Are we celebrating?' Alissa enquired helplessly.

Sergei quirked an ebony brow. 'You tell me. I assume your presence here means you're staying for the foreseeable future.'

Alissa thought of a dozen replies, all of which would have pointed out that she really had very little choice unless she was prepared to sacrifice pretty much her entire family's future as well as her own. But just as quickly she recalled his insistence that she stop hiding behind what he regarded as excuses rather than admit that she found him wildly attractive. When she looked back at him, an awkward little silence had fallen. Her complexion reddened and the flute between her fingers shook a little. 'Yes,' she said flatly, suppressing all her misgivings as well as the pretences she was used to hiding behind.

'Common sense has triumphed, *milaya moya*,' Sergei quipped. 'We both have need of each other.'

Bubbles burst beneath her nose and dampened her skin as she sipped the champagne.

'But now you've deprived me of having wonderfully erotic dreams about chaining you up as a prisoner at the foot of my bed,' Sergei husked in completion, golden eyes glinting from below the luxuriant fan of his black lashes in raw sensual challenge.

Her heart hammered and her body quickened. It shook her that the very idea of being a prisoner in Sergei's bedroom roused a response from her body that she could not stifle.

'I've thought of nothing else,' he confided, sinking down beside her and setting his champagne flute down.

'Since you went away you've done nothing but eat, sleep and breathe business.' Alissa could not resist making that contradiction.

'The faster I closed the deal, the sooner I could return. You're the only reward I wanted,' Sergei told her thickly, pulling her to him to taste her ripe mouth with a warm sensual pressure enlivened by the deeply erotic dart and thrust of his tongue. Her fingers sank deep into his black hair while her senses leapt into awareness and she moaned beneath that onslaught.

While he kissed her, he let his hand roam over her silk-encased length, lingering on the firm swell of her breasts and the prominence of her taut nipples. Soon little responsive sounds trapped in her throat were escaping and she was trembling on the edge of an excitement so intense she feared it. With a hungry groan, he hoisted her up into his arms and strode indoors.

'Would I need to chain you up?' Sergei asked thickly, standing her between his spread thighs and lifting the robe she wore to explore the quiveringly ready body concealed beneath.

She could barely breathe for excitement but she had not forgotten his forecast that some day she would be as clingy and adoring as his other lovers. 'Yes, you would,' she told him even as she let her head fall back and her lips part on a helpless whimper of response as his thumb rubbed her clitoris and his skilled fingers probed the hot slippery heart of her femininity, sending delirious waves of delight pounding through her as wildly as breakers on a beach.

'*Patse luy min-ya*…kiss me,' he commanded roughly, lifting her and bringing her down on the edge of the table.

And, wanting his mouth again, she did as he asked and rejoiced in his passion. The wood of the table was cool beneath her overheated skin but she didn't care. She was pulling at his belt, wanting, needing with a strength that came close to pain. Sergei brushed aside her fingers and dealt with the clasp that had defeated her. With a guttural groan of relief and pleasure, he finally drove his engorged length into her hot damp sheath. A drowning, dizzying rush of honeyed sweetness and excitement surged through her as every sensation forced her closer and closer to a rapturous climax.

'Don't stop…*don't* stop!' she gasped wildly.

Holding her tightly to him, he pounded into her tender core with spellbinding passion. And when she went into orgasm, it was like a massive firework display going off inside her, her entire body burning and soaring with the all-encompassing high of ecstasy. The languor and peace of satiation finally followed.

'I can never get enough of you, *angil moy*,' he breathed raggedly into her hair, turning up her face to steal a scorchingly possessive kiss from her lips while smoothing her tumbled hair back from her damp brow and studying her with smouldering dark eyes. 'One minute after I come I want you again.'

Little tremors and aftershocks of pleasure were still quaking through Alissa's slight body. She was shattered by the force of need he had awakened in her and the mind-blowing pleasure he had given her. As the intense sensation faded she was aghast at the reality that he had enjoyed her on top of a table while still fully dressed. She watched him as he impatiently shed his clothes in an untidy heap.

'Aren't you ever tidy?' she sighed.

'I have more important things to do. But you're talking like a wife,' he commented in surprise and he laughed, dark golden eyes suddenly glinting with amusement.

'Isn't that what you want?' Alissa traded, lifting her chin.

'*Da*…yes. I want the full package. But right now we need a shower,' he told her, peeling the robe she wore off before he gathered her up into his arms.

'I can't give you the full package,' Alissa reminded him in an anxious warning. 'Don't you dare try to get me pregnant.'

Sergei frowned. 'Not without your consent. I've used a condom every time I've been with you…except the first time,' he mused, startling her with that admission. 'That was before I knew who you were and there seemed no point in taking precautions when the ultimate goal was a child.'

As Sergei lowered her down to stand on her own feet in the spacious shower Alissa was pale and tense. She had assumed that he had protected her the first time as well. She had been so out of control that she hadn't noticed and she was furious that she had failed to look out for herself. 'Let's hope we get away with it,' she remarked in a brittle voice.

'I was expecting it to take at least a year for you to conceive and the last thing I would want is for that to happen now, when we no longer have either an under-standing or an agreement in place. Of course, as you get to know me better, you may well change your mind on that issue—'

'No way!' Alissa asserted fiercely. 'I won't change my mind. A child needs a mother and my child will need me—'

'You're so sexist, *angil moy*,' Sergei censured, pulling her into the path of the multi sprays of water, laughing without reserve when she yelped as a needle-sharp spray hit a sensitive spot. He hoisted her up against him, her arms coiling round his neck as he braced her hips against the marble wall and wrapped her legs round his waist. 'What would you do with my baby? Use it as a weapon against me? Would you keep us fighting never-ending custody battles and constantly up the stakes to feather your own nest while hitting out at me?'

'Is that what you think women do?'

'I've watched a lot of my friends go through hell over access to their children by former partners. Even marriage is no protection. It's not a situation I will put myself or my child in with any woman. Women often want revenge when a relationship breaks down.'

Shocked by the strength of his opinions on the subject, Alissa just shook her head slowly. 'I would just love my baby and no matter what happened I would try to base all my decisions on what was best for my child.'

His lean dark features clenched hard. 'You say all the right things, *milaya moya*. You said them to your sister on the phone as well but unfortunately you don't always seem to live up to them.' He released her and strode out of the shower.

Alissa took a moment or two to get her thoughts straight and then raced after him to yell, 'How the heck do you know what I said to my sister on the phone?'

'I had your calls monitored. I wanted to know if you were telling me the truth.'

Alissa gave him an appalled appraisal. 'You had them monitored—you *snooped* on me? That's a dreadful thing to do!'

'Unlike you I didn't lie, cheat or set out to defraud anyone,' Sergei responded drily. 'You can always trust me to give you the truth, but I will not be kept in the dark about anything that concerns my interests.'

Belatedly becoming aware of the chilly evening air

striking her wet, dripping body, Alissa coloured and dived back into the bathroom for a towel. While she dried off her damp hair she struggled to recall what she had said to Alexa during that phone call and cringed at the awareness that Sergei must have heard every word. He was watching the business news when she reappeared. Ignoring him, she wriggled into silk pyjamas and got into bed.

'Are we actually going to share the same bed all night?' Alissa demanded abruptly. 'I thought you didn't do couple-type stuff.'

Sergei ran an appreciative hand down over the curve of her hip as she lay there with her back turned to him. 'You've taught me to see advantages I never saw before. For the next few weeks we are going to share everything like normal newly marrieds.'

But Alissa could not understand the reasoning behind that decision. If she was not about to give him a child what was the point of greater familiarity? And surely so much intimacy was not required to make their marriage look real from the outside? From what she could work out they were unlikely to see enough of his grandmother for there to be any need to put on such a show of being close.

'Stop agonising over everything. So, you're not perfect, but then I never expected you to be and my desire for you makes me more tolerant,' Sergei murmured with unnerving intuition. 'Relax, close your eyes, go to sleep.'

And somehow she did, waking at some stage of the night to find that she was closely entwined with Sergei's lean muscular body and far too close to him for comfort. Her squirming efforts to ease free without waking him roused him very thoroughly in a way she had not intended and her pyjamas did not last long as a barrier. Exhaustion kept her asleep until dawn when once again the touch of his expert hands on her sinfully sensitised body set ripples of tormenting need loose inside her and tightened every nerve ending to screaming point. When he finally entered her, slow and deep and sure, the breath left her body in a hiss of reaction and the flood of sweet, painfully intense sensation engulfed her. The yearning was more than she could bear and all control fell away as he sent her hurtling headlong into the burning, melting waves of irresistible satisfaction.

Afterwards, she twisted round in his arms and buried her face in a broad bronzed shoulder, breathing in the scent of his sweat-dampened skin as if it were the elixir of life while she hugged him close. Her body wasn't her own any more; when he touched her she could not resist him. That scared her. Too much exposure to Sergei was bad for her. She felt clingy, which appalled her, and she had no intention of letting that urge out to cause havoc with her self-discipline. She only hoped she wasn't pregnant, for she did not share his apparent conviction that one act of lovemaking without protection was insufficient for conception. And that was one complication they could certainly do without....

CHAPTER NINE

'*Ty v poryadka?*... Are you okay?'

A frown of annoyance mingled with concern stamped on his lean bronzed face, Sergei hovered on the threshold of the bathroom, held back only by Alissa's frantic hand signals warning him to keep a distance. 'Look, I'm calling a doctor. I think you've caught a bug.'

'I don't need a doctor,' Alissa protested, freshening up at the sink, her voice rather shrill because with every day that passed her anxiety was steadily mounting. Her period was well over a week late, her breasts were sore and attacks of nausea were making her throw up without good reason at odd times of the day. She had already worked out which diagnosis she most feared.

Ignoring her objections, Sergei got on his phone to arrange for a doctor to be brought out to the yacht as soon as possible. Alissa was a sickly green colour and he was convinced that she had succumbed to some ongoing bug or infection. He stared down at Mattie, the little scruffy dog frantically wagging his stub of a tail and licking at his shoes. He finally bent down to give Mattie a reassuring pat to prevent him from demanding attention from Alissa, who was clearly in no fit state to respond to needs other than her own.

Over three weeks had passed since Alissa had been ashore and had first seen the dog lying injured in the gutter. One minute she had been by Sergei's side looking in the window of a gold merchant in Corfu town and the next she had been racing across the busy road at great risk to her own safety and getting down on her knees to attend to the dog. A trying day for Sergei had followed while Mattie was treated by the local vet and identified as a stray and therefore homeless. In spite of a visit to an animal sanctuary, where Sergei had made a very generous donation, Mattie, with his three legs, his tatty coat and perennially anxious expression, had somehow contrived to move in with them on the yacht. Now as Mattie cried anxiously for Alissa in the doorway Sergei sidestepped the little animal to scoop up his wife and carry her back to the bed in spite of her vehement protests.

'Just lie there, *angil moy*,' Sergei instructed, out of all patience with her independence. 'Stop being so stubborn! You're sick and you should rest.'

In truth it was a relief for Alissa to lie down in comfort and close her eyes for a few moments. She still felt dizzy and nauseous, and she was torn between exasperation at her physical weakness and dismay that she might have fallen pregnant by a man who wanted to have a child and raise it *without* her.

Sergei surveyed the pallor of her face and the slightness of her body in the bed. He was convinced she had lost weight and her healthy appetite had noticeably dwindled. He was genuinely worried about her. Possibly he was guilty of having made her overdo things. She looked fragile and he should have been treating her accordingly. But being selfish came naturally to him, he acknowledged grudgingly, and he had insisted she go swimming and waterskiing most days. When Sergei cut his working hours his unlimited energy needed the outlet of physical activity. In and out of bed, theirs had been a very active honeymoon. He had taken her everywhere with him, regardless of the reality that she was no more into fishing than she was into football. On the other hand, he reflected abstractedly, she could add an excitement to a picnic in a deserted cove that no fish alive or dead could have delivered.

'I'm being a real drag,' Alissa sighed, fighting back her fatigue even to speak. 'I bet your last honeymoon wasn't like this.'

'Most days Rozalina was far from sober or nursing a heavy hangover and she stayed in bed until nightfall,' Sergei countered with unhidden distaste. 'You feeling off colour occasionally is nothing.'

Alissa had pushed herself up on her elbows to study him with bemused eyes. 'Didn't you appreciate that she was a heavy drinker when you married her?'

'I didn't notice. I was only twenty-two and the marriage was a joke. She was a party girl round the clock and it got on my nerves even before the honeymoon was over.'

'I can imagine,' Alissa murmured. She had noticed his caution with alcohol and he never drank very much. After his experiences with an alcoholic mother, a wife who couldn't stop drinking would have been a serious turn-off for him.

'Your addiction to chocolate is a lot easier to live with, *milaya moya*,' Sergei quipped, looking so astonishingly handsome as his sensual mouth curved into a charismatic smile that her heart skipped a startled beat.

A middle-aged doctor was collected at the harbour and brought out to the yacht within the hour. When Sergei showed worrying signs of wanting to stay for the consultation, Alissa persuaded him to leave. She wasted no time in telling the doctor that she thought she might be pregnant, but that she preferred to keep that private if he decided that her suspicions were correct. After an examination and an on-the-spot test, he was able to give her that confirmation and, even though she had thought she was prepared for that news, the acknowledgement that she had indeed conceived Sergei's child left her in a state of shock.

Sergei rejoined her and shifted his lean brown hands in a gesture of frustration. 'The doctor said the sickness would go away and that there's nothing to worry about. Shouldn't he have prescribed something for you to take?'

'I'm not that sick…maybe I've just got a little run-down,' Alissa suggested, swinging her legs off the side of the bed and gathering up the panting bundle of dog that hurled itself ecstatically at her knees. 'Mattie's so affectionate, isn't he? He just loves to be fussed over. You can tell that he's never had so much attention before.'

Sergei watched Mattie turn up his tummy to be tickled and suppressed a sigh. She was more concerned about the dog than about her own health. 'Stay in bed for a while—get some sleep,' he urged, snapping his fingers to bring the dog darting back to his heels as he left the suite.

A baby, Alissa thought in wonder, checking her still-flat tummy in a mirror while she ignored Sergei's advice and got dressed. Sergei's baby…that he wouldn't want to share. He didn't trust her sex and she had given him good reason not to trust her. What was she supposed to do now? When it occurred to her that out of distrust he might try to take her child away from her she just wanted to run and keep on running away from him.

And feeling like that was a great shame, she acknowledged heavily, after such a long happy run spending over three weeks together on board *Platinum*. In truth, she had become very deeply attached to Sergei, but nothing would have elicited that admission of deep love and even stronger caring from her. She had got so used to being with him...the sudden explosions when anything went wrong...the immense satisfaction when things went right. Without a doubt Sergei was a volcanic personality, but he absolutely fascinated her and he could make the most ordinary pursuits entertaining.

When had she reached the stage that she would sneak down to look through the glass wall of his office just to get a look at him while he spent several hours away from her to catch up with business? When the sight of him lying asleep by her side in the early hours could turn her heart inside out? Or when a glimpse of him covertly petting Mattie could make her eyes smart with stupid tears? He hadn't wanted the little dog at all at first and had been astonished when she had failed to leave the injured animal to recuperate at the sanctuary. But, day by day, Alissa had watched Mattie limping and hopping valiantly out of his basket to steadily wear down Sergei's defences and wheedle his way into full acceptance. It was becoming more and more of a challenge to keep her emotions under control around him.

But normal life was about to intervene. It was the last full day of their honeymoon and she was already wondering ruefully when she would next have Sergei all to herself. He had not yet told her when they would be leaving but *Platinum* was cleaving through the waves at a purposeful pace far different from the idyllic lazy cruising that had distinguished their exploration of the Greek islands.

She had spoken to Prince Jasim's wife, Elinor, several times in recent weeks. She had enjoyed catching up with news about Elinor's life and children and had found it a comfort to be able to chat to her friend, even though she had not felt able to confide fully in her.

'Where are we?' Alissa queried, peering through the salon windows at the picturesque harbour when the yacht dropped anchor late afternoon.

'It's a surprise. Are you sure you're well enough to go ashore?' Sergei prompted.

'I'm great…' Alissa executed a twirl, golden hair rippling in the sunlight, her purple sundress splaying round her slim figure. She was making a real effort to hide her tension and the growing fear that her only option was to walk out on Sergei before he realised that she had already conceived his child. Even he had admitted that he did not want that to happen without a legal agreement in place between them. And yet, in spite of those anxieties, Alissa was also experiencing an inner glow of awe and pleasure when she thought about the baby growing inside her womb.

They disembarked from the yacht at the busy marina where a Turkish customs officer stamped their passports and a four-wheel-drive awaited them.

'I had no idea we would be visiting Turkey,' she told Sergei as the vehicle hurtled through busy noisy streets before climbing into the lush green hills studded with villas.

'Didn't it occur to you that we weren't that far away from the Aegean coast?'

'No, geography was never my strong point. Sergei, where on earth are we going?' she demanded, desperate to know what the surprise was.

'To see your sister and her husband,' Sergei revealed.

Alissa, who had already considered and dismissed that possibility, spluttered, 'You can't be serious!'

'I've got to meet Alexa some time. Why not now?'

'But she's pregnant,' Alissa protested vehemently. 'She mustn't be upset.'

Sergei gave her a surprised glance. 'She's not pregnant any more. I assumed your mother would have told you but perhaps she doesn't know yet either?'

Alissa stared at him in consternation. 'Alexa's lost her baby—how did you find that out?'

'Harry told me. Your mother gave me his number and I've spoken to him a couple of times to arrange this meeting. Your sister doesn't know we're coming. Alexa's been what Harry calls…temperamental and I think he's hoping that seeing you will improve her mood.'

Outside a smart white villa with a glorious view of the marina and the sparkling Aegean waters far below, Alissa climbed out. She was as taut as a bowstring. The sun was warm on her shoulders and, with her heart heavy at the news that her sister had lost her baby, she was keen to see Alexa and offer what comfort she could. 'You can't say anything about that contract or the money,' Alissa warned Sergei anxiously. 'Promise me you won't say anything because Harry knows nothing about the whole business.'

Sergei nodded acquiescence with an inhuman cool that made Alissa even more suspicious and on the alert.

He had breathed fire like a dragon over Alexa's deception, yet now he was being calm and non committal. A stockily built attractive man with fair hair, Harry ushered them out to a shaded terrace where Alexa was reclining on a lounger. Her twin gave them a stunned appraisal and then she leapt up with a delighted smile. 'Alissa…I don't believe it!'

Alissa managed to say how sorry she was about the baby in an undertone before Alexa switched her attention straight to Sergei. Alissa watched as her twin relaxed into surprisingly copious giggles when Sergei said something droll and her tension began to evaporate. In turn she made an effort to talk to Harry.

'How has she been?' she asked.

'This is the brightest I've seen her,' Harry revealed. 'I hoped that seeing you would do the trick. I know how close you girls are.'

But Alissa could only be disturbed by the reflection that times had changed and she no longer felt so close to her twin. Although she felt as though too much water and too much hurt had gone under the bridge, her strongest urge was still a wish to ease her sister's pain over the loss of her baby. She had also decided that she would not mention her own pregnancy in case it proved too distressing a reminder for Alexa of the child she had miscarried.

CHAPTER TEN

ALEXA wasted no time in curving a managing arm round Alissa to march her indoors for a private chat. 'If we're heading out on the town tonight I need to get changed.'

'Sergei says the yacht club down at the marina isn't that fancy.'

'Don't you know that the yacht club is *the* place to be seen? It's where all the rich yachties and celebrities hang out. They're calling Bodrum the new St Tropez,' Alexa informed her drily. 'My goodness, you've been putting on the weight, haven't you?'

'Do you think so?' Alissa, who had not stepped on a set of scales in many weeks, gave her figure an anxious inspection in the mirror and belatedly noticed the way her breasts seemed to swell even in the comparatively modest neckline she was wearing today. She wondered whether the chocolate or the baby was responsible. 'Sergei likes curves,' she heard herself say defensively.

'Oh, men always say that when you ask them,' Alexa retorted with derision. 'But when they dump you, they always go off with someone half your size! So, tell me, what's it like being married to Sergei?'

Alissa perched on the edge of the bed while her twin

rifled through a packed wardrobe in search of an outfit. At that leading question she went pink. She did not want to incite her sister's scorn by launching into a panoply of praise that might even include the recent development of Sergei hurling his clothes in the direction of a chair instead of the floor. 'It's easier than I expected,' she breathed stiltedly. 'But I'm more concerned about you—when did the miscarriage happen?'

'When did the...*miscarriage* happen?' Alexa repeated, turning to stare at her sister with a frown of bemusement. 'Don't be silly, Allie. That story was only for Harry's benefit. There never was a baby. I was sure you would have worked that out for yourself by now.'

Alissa stared back at the slim blonde woman in stunned disbelief, for Harry had not been the only person affected by that inexcusable pretence. Alexa had even used the threat of an abortion to pressure Alissa into taking her place as Sergei's wife. '*Never?* You were never pregnant? I'm sorry, I find that very hard to believe after some of the things you said to me.'

'It suited me to pretend I was pregnant,' Alexa told her defiantly. 'And the worse thing about all this is that now even Harry suspects that I was lying all along.'

'My word, does he?'

'After a shotgun wedding, what man wouldn't be suspicious? I told him I had had a very early miscarriage that didn't require medical attention, but I'm not sure he's convinced.'

Alissa was sincerely appalled at the ease with which Alexa had lied and misled even her own family, behaviour that did not appear to have awakened her twin to either guilt or regret. 'Why on earth did you get us all involved in your lies? How could you have wept in

front of me and told me how much you longed to marry
Harry and have his baby when there never was a baby?'
she gasped in condemnation.

'For the money, of course!' Alexa gave her a look of
scorn. 'You do ask crazy questions sometimes. Once I
found out I'd have to get pregnant to fulfil that contract
with Sergei, I knew there was no way I could ever face
going through with it and that I would have to hand over
the opportunity to you. I mean, even the thought of
ruining my figure with a pregnancy turns my stomach!'

Listening to that frank confession, Alissa only contrived to hang onto her temper with the greatest difficulty. A fierce and bitter sense of betrayal gripped her
at the knowledge that she could so easily have been
taken in by the twin she loved and had trusted. Until
Alexa had admitted the fact, Alissa had had no idea that
her sister was revolted by the very concept of pregnancy.
'So all that stuff about you being pregnant was simply
a lie to pressure me into marrying Sergei in your place?'

'As I said, I handed the opportunity to you, and
haven't you done well out of it?' Alexa flung back
without shame while she treated Alissa's appearance to
a deeply envious appraisal. 'I did you a favour. A
gorgeous guy with a yacht the size of the *Titanic*? A huge
diamond on your finger? He never stops spending money
on you—obviously you're doing something right. You've
been shopping until you drop round the Greek islands
with the paps dogging your every move—be honest,
you're living the life most women would kill to have!'

'But I don't want Sergei because he's rich!' Alissa
yelled back at her sister in a positive passion of angry
distaste. 'I want him for the man he is, not for what he
has. I'd want him even if he was broke!'

'I don't believe it…you've actually been stupid enough to fall in love with a guy who chose to *employ* a woman to marry him.' Alexa studied her with disdainful amusement. 'Are you insane? As far as he's concerned you're not a real wife, you're just the hired help!'

The reminder sobered Alissa as nothing else could have done, because while such words were unwelcome she recognised the truth of them in her heart. Falling for Sergei had always been a major no-no and yet she had foolishly done it. Common sense had gone out of the window the first night she'd met him. And while Sergei's forecast that she would fall in love with the game of football was still being challenged by the effort it took for her to stay awake until the end of a match, she had fallen head over heels for him almost straight away.

'And I could take Sergei off you again in five minutes,' Alexa forecast with a patronising smile. 'After all, if he finds you attractive, he'll find me positively irresistible! Would you like me to give you a demonstration?'

'I don't think you're likely to get very far with Sergei until you return that money you accepted on false pretences,' Alissa said gently, anything but amused by her twin's nasty wounding assurance that Sergei would go for her more sophisticated charms the first chance he got.

'Watch me—I'll make it well worth his while to let me keep the cash. Don't you know how to please a man yet? It all starts and ends in the bedroom,' Alexa murmured suggestively, smiling with satisfaction at her reflection as she posed and preened in front of the mirror so that the brief silver dress she wore flashed into quicksilver folds against her long slender legs.

'That's not funny, Alexa,' Alissa said tightly.

'It wasn't meant to be. If it wasn't for me, you

wouldn't even be *with* Sergei. Don't forget that,' Alexa reminded her viciously.

When she was in such a mood there was never any talking to Alexa, and Alissa was grateful to get back downstairs again where the two men were chatting on the terrace. Alissa plonked herself down next to Sergei. She was feeling threatened enough by Alexa that she would throw herself bodily onto Sergei's lap in a very public demonstration of affection if he just gave her the smallest sign of encouragement. Hyper-aware of his every move, she was agonisingly conscious of the way he stared at her sister when the silver-clad blonde made her entrance.

'What do you think of Alexa?' Alissa asked, despising herself utterly for sinking low enough to pose that question to Sergei as soon as she was alone with him.

They were driving back to the marina with her sister and Harry following in their own vehicle. Dark eyes narrowing, Sergei drawled, 'She's very different from you—*amazingly* different considering that you're identical twins.'

It was not a response that Alissa could find any comfort in receiving. In her experience she had always been labelled the plumper, plainer twin, who lacked the fun, girly, sexy sparkle of the sibling ten minutes her junior. Being more clever and more popular with her own sex had never felt like a consolation when she was aware that nine out of ten men preferred girly sparkle and sexiness.

Alissa tried very hard not to be put in the shade during the evening that followed. Hugely conscious that she was carrying Sergei's child and worrying about that reality along with her very uncertain future as his wife, she discovered that stress knocked any sparkle she might have had right out of her. Long before then, however, she was being wounded by Alexa's behaviour, for her sister was flirting outrageously with Sergei.

Sergei had no need to do anything. Alexa switched on like a high-powered searchlight and focused all her attention on him. While Harry was clearly becoming more and more annoyed by his wife's provocative behaviour, Alissa was wondering unhappily if Sergei was already convinced that he had ended up with the wrong twin. Listening to the repartee zipping back and forth between them, she could tell that Sergei was very much accustomed to women like her sister. Indeed she had the hideous suspicion that if Alexa was to ask him to choose outright between them, Alexa could have walked right out of the club with Sergei, unconcerned at deserting either her sister or her new husband.

'Are you sure you don't want anything else?' Sergei prompted Alissa, who had asked yet again for a mineral water.

'Alissa's always preaching temperance at parties!' Alexa giggled, waving her sex-on-the-beach cocktail round like a fashion statement.

'I'm just not in the mood for alcohol.'

'Alissa has been unwell,' Sergei commented, brilliant dark eyes locked to Alexa's shimmering smile of indifference.

'Oh, dear, what a drag for you on your honeymoon!' Alissa exclaimed, all her sympathy angled in Sergei's direction.

The level of her discomfiture and tension was making Alissa feel horribly dizzy and nauseous again and she took refuge in the cloakroom. Was she a drag? She could not credit that her twin was making a play for Sergei right before her eyes, and Harry's. Sitting watching it from the sidelines was a uniquely painful and sobering experience, Alissa conceded wretchedly. Sergei had done nothing to shoot down Alexa's pretensions and Alissa could see that he found Alexa both attractive and entertaining. Suddenly she asked herself why she was tolerating her situation as a powerless bystander.

Wouldn't it be better to leave, bow back out of Sergei's life before everything got even more complicated? After all, she was going to have to leave sooner rather than later, in any case. Once her pregnancy began to show, Sergei would feel cheated if she wasn't prepared to hand her baby over to him. How could he feel any other way after that wretched contract? But she wouldn't deny him access to his child; she wouldn't use her baby as a weapon. No, not even if Sergei *did* take up with her sister!

Her tummy somersaulted at that horrible prospect, which she knew she would not be able to bear in long-suffering silence. Nor, she thought in anguish, would she ever be able to forgive Alexa for making a play for Sergei. Alexa knew that Alissa was in love with Sergei. Alissa was convinced that she would never, *ever* be able to forget the pain she had endured watching her sister charming Sergei before her very eyes.

Alissa made her mind up fast. Her passport was in her handbag. She would take a taxi to the nearest airport. Withdrawing a notebook and pen from her bag, she wrote Sergei a note, telling him that he was free and that it was better for them to part while they were still friends. *Friends?* Her soft mouth down-curved. She didn't want to be his friend, but it sounded much better than telling him that working up the courage to leave him was the hardest thing she had ever done. For a moment she almost panicked about leaving Mattie and then she added a line to the note to let Sergei know that she really, *really* wanted the little dog brought back to the UK on his pet passport.

She gave the note to a waiter along with a tip, pointing out their table, and contrived to leave the club in the wake of the departure of a large party of noisy diners. She had noticed the taxi rank earlier and it wasn't far to walk. She only had sterling notes in her purse but the driver said he was happy to accept them. It took a good forty-five minutes to reach her destination and for every minute of that time she was lost in memories of Sergei and fighting the inclination to go back.

How could she go back? What would be the point? With Sergei's outlook, the news that she had conceived his child would be bad news and he would fight her for custody, she *knew* he would. On the other hand, perhaps if she stayed a little longer and talked to him she might be able to get through to him and persuade him that a happy, healthy child ideally needed two parents. Unfortunately, after watching Sergei and Alexa together, Alissa couldn't face that option. She had to get away for her own sanity, she told herself urgently.

Buying a ticket for a flight to London was straightforward, but she had quite a few hours to wait. She bought a soft drink and sat down in a café to drink it. She was so miserable she wanted to put her head down on the table and sob. Images of the ghastly dinner she had endured watching Alexa and Sergei interact kept on returning to haunt her. But hadn't that always been her fear? That she was really second best and that if Sergei had ever got the choice, it would not have been her whom he chose? The proof of that humiliating conviction was tearing her apart. She did not think she would ever be able to look at her sister again. Didn't Sergei appreciate that all Alexa really cared about was his wealth and what it could buy her? That she had the attention span of a flea when it came to men?

A shadow fell across the table surface and she lifted her head, pushing back her blonde hair from her warm brow with a weary hand. She froze when she realised that it was Sergei standing over her, dark eyes smouldering hot as a volcanic core, his lean, dark, handsome face set in angry lines.

'Why did you follow me?' she whispered fiercely. 'It's easier if you just let me go.'

'But that's the one thing I can't do,' Sergei revealed, thrusting back the chair opposite and dropping down into it with all the force of a forest tree crashing to the ground in a storm. 'I can't let you go.'

So tense that she was barely breathing, Alissa focused on him with a treacherous surge of pleasure. She had thought she might never see him again, or at least that the next time she laid eyes on him it might be in a courtroom months from now. Just those thoughts had made her feel deprived and she had started missing him the same second she'd left his side at the club.

'You have to let me go. It's time,' she told him gruffly.

'I told you I can't do it,' Sergei delivered in a roughened undertone. 'If you try to walk away from me, I'll lift you up and carry you out of here.'

'You wouldn't do that, for goodness' sake…'

'It would probably get me arrested because no doubt you would scream and shout. But I would still do it,'

Sergei intoned. 'I won't stand by and let you walk out on me without fighting.'

'But why would you fight?' Alissa was so stressed she could feel the dreaded tears gathering behind her eyes, even though she was as mad with him as she was also very upset. 'Alexa's much more your type.'

Sergei studied her levelly. 'You're the clever twin. You've got to know better than that, *angil moy*. Maybe I made a mistake not spelling out my disinterest more openly this evening.'

'Your...*disinterest*?' Alissa echoed in a doubtful tone.

'But I wanted you to see exactly what your sister is like so that you won't let her take advantage of you again. Because she will try again and again to use you and I don't want that to happen.'

Alissa was frowning at a view of the interplay round that dining table that she had not considered. 'I wouldn't let Alexa take advantage of me...'

Sergei vented a sardonic laugh and gave her an expressive glance. 'I bet she's been taking advantage of you since you were children. I also bet that she was a very spoiled and selfish child, and that your parents found it easier to give in to her iron will than stand up to her. Alexa *expects* to get away with her offences.'

'Are you saying you *don't* prefer her to me?' Alissa prompted in amazement.

'I'd sooner get down and dirty with a shark. Alexa is everything I don't want in a woman and she repulses me.' Sergei grimaced. 'Exactly what would I find attractive about her? She's smothered in make-up and she dresses like a tart. She has to be the centre of attention and she has no manners. Surely you noticed the way in which she humiliated her husband this evening?' he prompted. 'That was another reason why I didn't obviously try to repel Alexa—if I pretended that I hadn't noticed how she was coming on to me it was less embarrassing for Harry.'

It was an analysis of Alexa that left Alissa bereft of speech, for she had spent most of her life feeling overshadowed by her twin's attractions and now the accepted order of things was being swept away by Sergei's bluntly offered opinions. 'I never thought of that angle,' she said numbly. 'Poor Harry—'

'That's one marriage unlikely to last long. They were fighting when I took my leave of them—even then she was blaming you for spoiling her evening and calling you a drama queen for walking out,' Sergei breathed in disgust.

'Maybe I am a drama queen.' Alissa sighed, the sturdy foundations of her resentment being destroyed with every word he spoke, because it was patently obvious even to a bitterly jealous and insecure person such as she was herself that Sergei not only wasn't attracted to her twin, but also actively disliked her.

'No. I should've appreciated that you read the situation the wrong way. Do you think we could find somewhere more private?' Sergei angled his handsome dark head in the direction of the family with noisy kids taking seats too close for comfort.

Alissa rose upright. 'Okay—where?'

'The yacht…'

Uncertainty made her frown. 'I'm not—'

'Or I carry you bodily out of here, *angil moy*,' Sergei completed, surveying her with stubborn determination.

And she knew he would, and suddenly she was laughing and the tears spilled over a little to mingle with her laughter. She sucked in a deep breath to steady her nerves as he walked her towards the exit doors. It was dark and cool outside and he shrugged out of his jacket to drape it round her bare shoulders.

'I didn't only decide to leave because of what happened this evening with Alexa,' she warned him stiffly.

'I wouldn't have gone ahead with the marriage or the contract if she had turned up that night before the wedding,' Sergei confided abruptly as he urged her into the four-wheel drive revving its engine by the kerb. 'Until I met you, I was ready to dump the project because I wasn't attracted by her photo and I didn't like what I heard in her interviews.'

'Is that the honest truth?' Alissa prompted in an urgent whisper in the rear seat.

Sergei nodded.

'So when you said that Alexa and I were amazingly different that's what you meant...'

'*Da*...yes. You had the X-factor, she didn't, *solnyshko moyo*.' Sergei closed an arm round her and drew her close.

Alissa spent most of the journey happily adjusting to the news that Sergei had picked her, not Alexa, to marry and that he preferred her in every way. In the moonlight his lean, strong face was a brooding arrangement of light and shade, hooded eyes dark and unfathomable. She wondered how he would feel when he realised that she was carrying his child. Was that revelation likely to divide them again?

'If you leave me, I'm keeping Mattie,' Sergei told her softly. 'That note of yours was priceless. You didn't devote one line to agonising over leaving me, but you lamented leaving Mattie behind for two and a half lines!'

'You can't have him,' Alissa asserted, fearful that he would take the same attitude over their child.

'I would have let you visit him occasionally.'

They boarded *Platinum* and Mattie raced to greet their return with panting, wriggling, doggy fervour and sharp little barks. When he had quietened down, Alissa breathed in deep. 'I have something to tell you…'

Sergei spread lean brown hands wide. 'I'm waiting—just tell me!'

'I'm pregnant—that's part of the reason why I left. I just didn't see how we could possibly manage—'

'*Pregnant?*' Sergei swept her up in his arms in an expression of exuberance that totally took her aback. Both arms wrapped round her, he gave her a wolfish smile. 'That's the best news I've ever heard…and we didn't even have to work at it! Not that having to work at it would have been a trial,' he acknowledged with an easy masculine laugh.

'You can put me down now,' Alissa advised in a daze.

'Why? So that you can put some sort of gloomy slant on this moment?' Sergei censured in full bossy mode. 'Don't you realise that the rule book on our marriage went out the window the same day I met you?'

'It wasn't a real m-marriage!' Alissa stammered that reminder as Sergei very deliberately spread a large hand across her stomach.

'How real does real have to be before you will believe in it?' Sergei enquired, stretching her out full length across his lap and flipping up her dress so that he could bend his handsome dark head and press his lips to the bare skin of her stomach instead. 'It's amazing to think our baby's in there.'

Alissa was frozen in place by the unpredictability of his reactions to her announcement. 'You're really pleased about the baby, aren't you?'

Sergei gave her a huge smile. 'Isn't it obvious?'

Sudden tears convulsed Alissa's throat. 'It's different for me. You married me according to a contract.'

'Which you broke,' he slotted in with amusement.

'Only a few weeks ago you were threatening to prosecute me!' she slung shrilly back at him.

'A couple of weeks back, I received background reports on you and Alexa and I didn't have to be a genius to work out that your sister has never been a nice person. I knew who to blame. You were thoughtless but there's no malice in you. I went from wanting to prosecute to giving you an extended honeymoon instead. Haven't the last few weeks we've spent together taught you anything about me?'

'Only that I don't know what you're going to do or say next!' Alissa was so worked up that she burst into tears and startled him. 'I don't even know what you want from me or if you're about to try and take my baby away from me!'

Sergei framed her face with firm hands. 'I wouldn't do anything that hurt you or the baby. I want you both together…for ever.'

'*For ever?*' Alissa gasped, tears still trickling down over her cheeks.

'For ever,' Sergei confirmed, claiming a kiss with a hungry urgency that sent an entirely new source of energy coursing through her slim body. 'Because I have feelings for you that I never thought I would have for any woman and I was overjoyed by my good taste when I heard you shouting at your sister this evening that you would want me even if I was broke!'

Alissa flushed crimson. 'Oh, my goodness, you *heard* that?'

'I heard it—the window was wide open behind the shutters. I love you,' he breathed huskily, stealing yet another kiss and an even more passionate one this time that sent her senses all reeling.

'Honestly?' she checked, scarcely able to believe that all her dreams were coming true at once.

'Honestly,' Sergei confirmed with mock solemnity.

Her fingers closed round his tie and pulled it loose. 'I'm crazy about you too,' she confided breathlessly.

Sergei carried her down the companionway to the master suite. She lay in his arms with a blissful smile. 'What made you love me?'

'The oddest things.'

'Like what?' she demanded, eager to know.

'When you told me off for shouting at the checkout attendant, it was a wake-up call. When you looked like an angel in the church on our wedding day. When you insisted I send Greek postcards to Yelena and you refused even to consider having a child and giving it away.'

'You liked that even though it meant I couldn't do what you wanted?' she queried in amazement.

'I'm naturally perverse and when you got all dirty and bloody rescuing Mattie I was even more impressed. You have a big heart and I love that side of you most of all, *angil moy*,' Sergei confided, unzipping her dress so that it fell at her feet. 'But I wasn't impressed when you ran out on me tonight without even telling me what was wrong.'

'I couldn't bear watching Alexa flirt with you—'

'I couldn't bear listening to her put you down,' he countered.

'I was scared to tell you about the baby. I sort of assumed it would end everything between us and just start up a horrible dispute about custody so I saw no point in staying to talk,' Alissa admitted ruefully.

Releasing the hooks on her bra, Sergei curved her back against his muscular chest, closed his hands to her breasts and breathed raggedly. 'I won't ever let you go. You're the woman I never thought existed, the woman I believed I would never find. When my lawyers told me to prosecute and divorce you, I ignored their advice. They thought I was insane, and love must be a kind of insanity because I didn't really care what you had done. I was too busy being grateful that I didn't get the wrong sister.'

'But you've forgiven me so much.' Overwhelmed by his generosity and understanding and the strength of his love, Alissa swivelled round in the circle of his arms. 'I really, really love you, Sergei.'

With all their defences down and their mutual joy in the baby she had conceived, they had so much to share. Alissa had never known such happiness could be hers. Sergei told her about the abortion that his first wife, Rozalina, had had without consulting him and how that discovery had led to their divorce and the loss of a good part of his wealth back then. Alissa wrapped him tight in her arms and fully understood his longing for a child, a family, a secure circle of people he could love and trust and work hard to support and spoil. They made passionate love and talked far into the early hours before Sergei decided that the honeymoon should be extended by one more week.

The next day she rang her mother just to tell her how deliriously happy she was and that she had conceived. Jenny, shaken by Alexa's recent announcement that she had lost her baby, was overjoyed by the discovery that she was going to be a grandmother after all.

Just over a year later, Alissa was putting the finishing touches to the giant Christmas tree she had had erected in the drawing room. She was humming a carol under her breath as she attached delicate baubles and ornaments to the branches.

Mattie was snoozing by the fire. Alissa and Sergei's infant daughter, Evelina, was in an equally restful mood and dozing in a baby seat. Evelina had the arresting combination of her father's luxuriant black hair and her mother's light eyes. Once Alissa had got over the nauseous phase, she had had an easy pregnancy. In every way it had been a very busy and eventful year.

They'd had a second wedding in London, for Sergei had confided that his lawyers were not one hundred per cent certain that their Russian marriage was fully legal when Alexa had forged Alissa's signature on certain documents. Alissa had fully enjoyed that ceremony and her mother had enjoyed it even more. The big glitzy party that had followed had proved to be the social event of the year. Jasim and Elinor had attended and their other friend and former flatmate, Lindy, had also put in an appearance. That had been very welcome, for neither Elinor nor Alissa had seen much of Lindy recently as the younger woman was very much focused on her small crafts business and worked long hours.

For a good deal of the year, Sergei and Alissa based their lives in St Petersburg, but they were planning to live mainly in the UK once Evelina reached the age for school. Alissa's parents had reconciled, although it had been quite a few months after her father's affair with

Maggie had ended before Jenny was prepared to invite her estranged husband to move back in with her again. Alissa's father had returned the money he had been given and in turn Jenny had insisted on returning all of it to Sergei. For a while Alissa had found visiting her reunited parents rather like walking on eggshells, but time had healed the worst wounds and the older couple currently seemed to be rediscovering happiness. She had also managed to regain her former closeness with her father after Sergei had pointed out that it really wasn't fair to punish people for being less than perfect.

Unhappily she had yet to reach the same accommodation with Alexa, whose own life had admittedly suffered a number of disastrous ups and downs in recent months. After a history of violent quarrelling with Harry and his family, and having had an affair with her married boss, Alexa was now in the midst of a bitter separation. While she had flatly refused to repay the money she had accepted for signing the contract with Sergei's lawyers, she now had to fight Harry's attempt to take a good share of it off her in a divorce settlement.

'What goes around comes around,' Sergei had commented cheerfully.

Alissa had not seen much of her twin over the past year but the sisters did make a point of being pleasant to each other when they met at family gatherings, for Alissa did not want her parents upset. Alexa had also made an effort to attend Evelina's christening while avoiding getting within thirty feet of Sergei's sardonic tongue. Alissa had found it easier to forgive her twin's flaws once she'd realised that Sergei was never going to be one of Alexa's admirers. At present, her strongest hope was that Alexa would stop rating the acquisition of money above everything else in her life and appreciate what was really important.

'It's good to be optimistic,' Sergei had quipped on that score, deaf to Alissa's protests. 'But please don't introduce her to any of our single male friends. I don't want anyone putting that on my conscience.'

Yelena was a frequent visitor and was arriving the following day to share her second Christmas with them. She would stay until the Russian New Year had been welcomed in. Alissa could now speak enough of her husband's native language to make herself understood and she got on very well with her husband's grandmother. Yelena positively worshipped Evelina and seemed to have no greater happiness than to sit quietly attending to her first great-grandchild.

The slam of the front door alerted Alissa to Sergei's return and wakened Evelina and the dog. Mattie trotted over to welcome Sergei home while Evelina kicked her legs in expectation of the attention she was accustomed to receiving from her father. As the door opened Alissa felt a leap of wicked anticipation flare and she studied the tall handsome male in the doorway with loving eyes and a wide smile. She had never known until she met him that another human being had the power to give her such happiness. Sergei stowed parcels on the table, contrived to pat the dog and scoop up Evelina on his way past, tucking his daughter deftly below one arm to keep the other free to reach for his wife.

'A week without you all is a week too long, *angil moy*,' he groaned, bending his proud dark head to steal a hungry kiss from her soft pink lips. 'I'll have to keep you in bed for a month before I recover from that amount of self-denial.'

Alissa moaned a little beneath the urgency of his sensual mouth, both thrilled and embarrassed by that candid warning.

Evelina let out a cry of complaint because she was being crushed and Sergei lifted the little girl playfully aloft to study her with loving attention before lowering her and smoothing her little dark head with a gentle reassuring hand. Replacing her in her seat, he turned back to his wife.

'I even missed the dog,' he groaned. 'What have you done to me?'

Alissa linked her arms round his neck and smiled up at him. 'We missed you too…'

He kissed her again, passion stirring so that her slim body welded to the lean, hard angles of his. 'I almost forgot,' he said, freeing her to lift the parcels.

Evelina got an ingenious toy to keep her amused and Alissa got a fabulous diamond eternity ring. 'It's an expression of my love and appreciation, *angil moy*,' Sergei breathed, turning the ring at an angle so that she could see the words *'For ever'* etched in flowing script on the inside with their names.

'It's wonderful,' Alissa sighed happily sliding the ring into place beside her wedding ring. 'I'll think of you every time I look at it.'

The last parcel contained a little box with a tree ornament that bore a remarkable resemblance to Mattie, or at least a four-legged version of him. Glowing with contentment, Alissa hung the thoughtful gift on the tree. Their nanny came down to collect Evelina for her bath and Sergei and Alissa enjoyed a leisurely evening meal catching up on news. Jasim and Elinor had invited them to visit Quaram in the spring and they were looking forward to the trip. On their return they would as usual be spending Easter Day with Yelena.

When dinner was over, Sergei closed his hand over Alissa's and murmured, 'I hate leaving you but I love coming back home to you, *moyo zolotse.*'

'What are you calling me?'

'Literally? "My gold", and you are.' Sergei closed her possessively into his arms, staring down at her with brilliant dark eyes warmed with love. 'When I met you, I struck a gold mine.'

Alissa smiled up at him, touched by his sincerity and grateful for the strength of the love they shared and the joy that Evelina had given them and their families. 'I'm incredibly happy with you, too.'

'I love you, *moyo zolotse.*'

* * * * *

GREEK TYCOON, INEXPERIENCED MISTRESS

Lynne Graham

CHAPTER ONE

As TWO of the more elderly directors of Dionides Shipping again pressed questions that had already been answered Atreus let his attention stray to the Art Deco bronze on the far side of the boardroom. It was of a voluptuous Spanish dancer, only half-clad in what might once have been a romanticised concept of gipsy clothing.

When Atreus had first taken over as CEO of the family business he had been stunned by the sexy statue, which had seemed so out of step with his grandfather's stern, old-fashioned outlook on life.

'She reminded me of my first love,' the old man had confided with a faraway look in his faded eyes. 'She married someone else.'

Atreus could not imagine such a disappointment happening to him. The women he met these days were financially astute and a challenge to shake off. Ever since he'd been a teenager he had been relentlessly hunted by gold-digging beauties who would throw themselves in his path in attempts to ensnare him and his wealth. Black-haired, with eyes dark as sloes, and six foot three inches in height, Atreus had always been an object of desire. By the time he had twice become the unhappy focus of false paternity claims he had decided that he would only marry a woman with a fortune and social standing to match his own. His late father, Achilles, had set his only son a chilling example by living an exemplary life until the age of forty, when he had inexplicably gone off the rails by abandoning his wife and only child to run off with an artist's model famous for dancing on tables. From then on wild self-indulgence and extravagance had ruled the lives of both Atreus's parents, and he had lost his early childhood to their excesses. After that, raised almost entirely by his strict paternal uncle and aunt, Atreus had been deeply suspicious of any inner prompting to step off the straight and narrow. That had been his father's fatal flaw; it would not be his.

Regardless of that fact, the Art Deco bronze had contrived recently to acquire a strange significance for Atreus. It reminded him of an episode some weeks earlier that had taken place on his country estate. On a warm summer afternoon while he had been walking through the woods he had come upon a curvaceous brunette skinny-dipping in the river. Her presence on private land had infuriated him. After all, he had paid a fortune for the seclusion of his large estate, and he employed numerous staff to guard his privacy from trespassers and camera lenses. Ironically, ever since then the memory of the brunette's indescribably lush and creamy curves had had an extraordinarily erotic hold on him—awake and asleep. Yet she had been a woman who had borne not the slightest resemblance to the slender elegant blondes who usually attracted him…

In fact she had not been his type in any way, Atreus acknowledged impatiently. According to his estate manager, Lindy Ryman was an eccentric animal-lover who scratched a living making and selling pot-pourri and candles. A regular churchgoer, she was also a well-respected member of the local community, who hid her remarkable curves beneath drab long skirts and wintry woollens. Atreus had been tough on her in the woods, for at first he had been convinced that she had deliberately schemed—like so many women before her—to set up their encounter. Once he'd appreciated that she was no cunning temptress he had sent her flowers and an apology. He'd been amazed when she'd ignored those olive branches and failed to make use of the phone number he had included.

His mood darkening at the length of time his thoughts had stayed focused on the Ryman woman, Atreus suddenly wondered if he should offer her compensation to surrender her tenancy on his estate. Out of sight would be out of mind, and that might well be the best cure for what afflicted him. He had no doubt that he was too intelligent and logical to succumb to the attraction of a woman who was so outrageously unsuitable for him in every way…

'You dumped Sarah?' Lindy repeated, turning to glance at Ben.

'She was getting serious. Why do women always do that?' Ben enquired, with the pained expression of a male continually tortured by besotted females.

Look in the mirror, Lindy almost told him. She could

still recall when she had fallen under the enchantment of Ben's floppy blond hair, light green eyes and rangy frame. That had been way back when they'd first met at university, and he had put her firmly in the pigeon-hole marked 'Friends'. There had been no jumping ship. Some of the best days of her life had been wasted while she'd wished that she was tiny, cute and giggly instead of shy, sensible and quiet. Since then Lindy had got over him, and grown accustomed to watching him cut a destructive swathe through a long line of beauties. Ben didn't want commitment, it seemed, just a good time. A City of London trader, he had a successful career and all the worldly trappings that ranged from a flash car to smart suits and the membership of the right gym. Yet Ben never really seemed happy with his lot, Lindy acknowledged ruefully.

'If you weren't as keen as she was, I suppose you were better breaking up with her,' Lindy retorted evenly. Her soft heart went out to Sarah, who had sounded like a pretty nice person and who was probably grieving now over the loss of him—as Lindy had once grieved without even the excuse of ever having had him.

'You are the most fabulous cook.' Ben sighed, taking another bite of her crumbly iced carrot cake and savouring the taste.

Lindy compressed her lips, too well aware that no such proficiency would ever increase her appeal to the opposite sex. She was convinced that her real problem was that there was too much of her. Ever since she had been likened to a fertility statue at school, and bullied unmercifully on that basis, she had despised her full-breasted, generous-hipped body. Diets and exercise seemed to have little impact, and although she carried no surplus weight anywhere else she was embarrassed by her healthy appetite. Ben always dated small, skinny girls who made Lindy feel enormous and clumsy.

Lindy had dropped out of university when her mother fell ill. An only child from a poor home, she had had to give up studying for a law degree to nurse her mother through a long and sadly terminal decline. On the brink of returning to university Lindy had come down with a nasty bout of glandular fever. By the time she had recovered her own health she had lost interest in studying and had gone for an office job instead. Her flat-sharing days in London with her friends Elinor and Alissa had been fun, but since then both women had married, moved abroad and had families, so their meetings now were few and far between. Even so, it had been during a summer visit to Elinor and her husband Jasim's English country home that Lindy had first fallen blissfully in love with the countryside. As soon as she had found a rural property at a rent she could afford—The Lodge, a small gatehouse at the edge of a grand estate—she had taken the plunge and jumped off the hamster's wheel of urban working altogether.

Since then Lindy had devoted herself to making a living through pursuits she enjoyed. She grew lavender and roses, and made pot-pourri and candles which sold well via the internet. She took occasional part-time jobs when her bank account needed plumping up, but devoted most of her free time to helping out at the local animal sanctuary. She had acquired two rescue dogs:

Samson and Sausage. Her friends might insinuate that she was throwing her youth away, but Lindy was content with her home, her small income and her simple life.

Of course every Eden had to have a serpent, she conceded ruefully. Hers was Atreus Dionides, the new, fabulously wealthy owner of Chantry House, a wonderful Georgian jewel of a mansion surrounded by a beautiful estate. Thanks to him, she was no longer free to roam where she liked through hundreds of acres of parkland and wood. Worst of all, her single unforgettable meeting with the wretched man had humiliated and distressed her so much that she had actually considered moving.

'Are you quite sure that you don't mind looking after Pip?' Ben checked again, on his way out of the front door.

'He'll be fine here.' An essential streak of honesty made Lindy sidestep the question, for if truth be told Pip was far from being her favourite house-guest.

The Chihuahua belonged to Ben's mother, who expected her son to look after her pet whenever she went on holiday. Unhappily, Pip was a very cross little animal. Had he been larger he would have had to wear a muzzle. As it was, the tiny canine continually growled, snapped and barked, and even Lindy's love of dogs was taxed by Pip's bad temper and tendency to bite.

Lindy walked Ben out to his car. 'You shouldn't have parked on the drive. I don't have a parking space here. The estate manager did ask me to ensure that my visitors parked outside the gates,' she reminded him awkwardly.

'The new owner is really making life difficult for you. If he keeps it up, I bet it could constitute harassment,' Ben replied, climbing into the driver's seat and opening the window on the passenger side to continue the conversation.

Lindy tensed and then froze when she saw a long dark limousine gliding through the tall black gates. In a trice, she had dropped down into a crouch by the passenger door, so that she was hidden from view by Ben's sports car.

'What on earth are you doing?' Ben demanded with raised brows.

'Just don't drive off until the limo has gone past!' Lindy hissed, staying down, her face as red as a beetroot and as hot as fire.

The limousine continued down the drive at a stately pace and disappeared round a corner. Lindy slowly rose up to her medium height, glossy dark brown hair rippling round her shoulders, her violet-blue eyes strained and uneasy.

'What were you doing?' Ben asked in a tone of wonderment.

'Never mind.' Lindy shrugged rather unconvincingly. She told Ben she would see him the following Friday, when he came back to pick up Pip, and hurried into her cottage as fast as her legs would carry her, where she found the Chihuahua snarling viciously at poor Sausage, who had taken refuge beneath a chair.

Six weeks had passed since Lindy had met Atreus Dionides, in circumstances that still brought her out in a cold stricken sweat of reluctant remembrance when she strived to adjust to the reality that the Greek shipping tycoon had seen her stark naked. As he was the very first male who had ever seen her in that state, and he had utterly humiliated her, she was still struggling to get over the experience. Had she had the slightest suspicion that anyone might see her she would not have removed so much as a sock in public. After all, she was self-conscious even in a swimsuit, and skinny-dipping wasn't something she had ever done before...or would ever do again in this lifetime.

In fact every time she thought about that afternoon she cringed and cursed her stupidity. On what had turned out to be the hottest day of the year she had spent the morning helping to unload a delivery of hay at the animal sanctuary. Riding home on her bike, her clothes sticking to her overheated skin, she had thought longingly of the river, where the rocks formed a safe natural pool. The previous summer she had paddled there on several occasions.

Of course back then the estate had been deserted, for it had still belonged to an old man who'd spent most of his time abroad and who had placed no restrictions on his tenants' movements. Atreus Dionides, on the other hand, surrounded himself with high-tech security and knew to the letter of the law what rights he had and what rights his tenants had. The estate office had wasted no time in sending out a letter laying out the new ground rules and stressing the new owner's desire for total seclusion and privacy within his extensive grounds.

But on that hot day six weeks ago Lindy had only intended to cool her bare feet for a few minutes. It was a quiet part of the river, where she had never seen another living soul before and where the trees and shrubs on the banks provided dense cover. Aware that Atreus Dionides usually only used the house at weekends, and that it was midweek, Lindy had succumbed to temptation and impulse and had done something totally out of character. Stripping down to her birthday suit and leaving her clothes in a pile, she had sunk slowly into the pool with a heady sigh of pleasure, revelling in the clean, cold refreshment of the water on her hot damp skin.

'What are you doing here?' an authoritative male voice had demanded, only minutes after her immersion, and she'd very nearly jumped out of her skin in fright.

Whirling round wide-eyed, Lindy had focused on the male poised on the bank and hastily dropped lower in the water to conceal her breasts. Sporting a sophisticated urban black business suit, teamed with a white shirt and silk tie, Atreus had looked bizarre against the backdrop of the natural woodland and all the more unreal. She had known who he was immediately as she had seen his photo when the local newspaper had published an excited article about the new owner of the Chantry estate. Even in black and white newsprint he was a very handsome man, if a little cold and grim in his chilly perfection of features. In person, however, Atreus Dionides was a glowing vision of bronzed masculinity and dark Mediterranean good-looks that would have stopped any woman dead in her tracks.

'This is private property.'

Lindy had crossed her arms in front of her lest the water was not providing sufficient concealment. 'Er… I'm sorry. It won't ever happen again. If you go away I'll get out and get dressed.'

'I'm not moving anywhere,' Atreus had delivered loftily. 'You still haven't told me what you're doing here.'

'It's a hot day. I fancied a swim to cool off,' she'd explained uneasily, while wondering why on earth he felt the need to ask when the answer should have been obvious.

'Stripped, ready and waiting for my first appearance?' the Greek tycoon had retorted with sizzling derision. 'I don't go for naked ladies in the woods, or for brief outdoor encounters. You're wasting your time.'

As it had dawned on Lindy that he actually suspected that she might have whipped off her clothes and got in the water purely in an effort to lure him into some sleazy sexual encounter, she's been so aghast that she'd simply gaped at him in amazement.

'Which of my staff told you I was coming out here?' Atreus Dionides had shot at her.

'Are you always this paranoid?' Lindy had questioned in disbelief. 'Look I'm getting really cold. Move away and I'll get out and be off your land before you know it.'

It had been immediately evident that her reference to paranoia had gone down like a brick thrown through his front window, since he'd pushed back his big wide shoulders and, his aggressive jawline clenched, fixed his dark-as-treacle eyes on her. 'Who tipped you off about my presence here today?'

Her very blue eyes had widened. 'Nobody, I swear. I'm just an ordinary trespasser in the woods—one of your tenants, actually—and I would like to get out of the river and go home now.'

'You're a tenant?' Atreus had queried harshly. 'So,

you're trespassing in spite of the estate office's request that you respect my privacy?'

'I live at The Lodge. If I'd known you were at home I'd never have dared,' she'd admitted truthfully, trying and failing to suppress a shiver, because she had only been able to bear the cold water while she was free to move around and jump up and down to keep warm. 'Now, please be a gentleman and return to your…er… walk.'

'The creed of the gentleman is long dead.' He'd produced a mobile phone. 'I'm calling Security to deal with you.'

And that was when Lindy had really lost her head with him. 'How much of a bastard do you have to be? I've said sorry. What more can I do or say? I'm a woman standing naked in freezing water and you're threatening to muster more men to see me like this?' she'd shouted at him in horror. 'I'm very cold, and I want my clothes!'

Hard, dark and unrepentant eyes had rested on her hot, angry face. 'I'm not preventing you from retrieving them.'

And she hadn't been able to wait any longer. By that stage her feet had been so cold she'd been in pain, and she hadn't been able to bear to stand there at his mercy any more. Utterly mortified, and inflamed by his intransigence, she'd waded out without looking anywhere near him. He'd not turned his back as any half-decent man would have done either. He'd stayed where he was and he hadn't apologised. The very fact that no man had ever seen her naked before had made the ordeal that much more painful for her. Unbearably conscious of her bare breasts, and the all too great expanse of the rest of her, almost sick with embarrassment, she'd had to struggle with the difficulty of dragging her jeans and T-shirt over her wet skin. Naturally she hadn't extended the time of her exposure by trying either to dry herself or put on her bra and knickers first.

She'd run all the way back to The Lodge, where she'd sat shell-shocked and tearful over the indignity of the ordeal he had put her through. Forty-eight hours later Atreus Dionides had sent her a superb bouquet of expensive flowers with a card that had contained an apology and the suggestion that she call him to arrange a dinner date. She had not been able to credit his nerve. His insolent invitation had simply sent her into paroxysms of frustrated rage.

Lindy was, after all, quite friendly with his housekeeper, Phoebe Carstairs, and as such was already reasonably well acquainted with his reputation as a womaniser. Phoebe had yet to see her wealthy employer with the same woman twice. According to Phoebe, Atreus liked dainty blondes in very high heels, and they all fawned over him like groupies and slept with him the first night they arrived. Lindy had read between the lines: Atreus was accustomed to a diet of flattery, awe and easy sex, with women capable of amusing him only for a single weekend.

Lindy was not and never would be that kind of a woman. Furthermore, how dared he even suggest that she would want to lay eyes on him again after the brutal, callous way he had treated her? He had shown the true colours of his character by the river. On the surface he might well be everything the newspaper had suggested—

a phenomenally brilliant businessman who had taken a failing family company and transformed it into a contemporary Goliath which dominated the world shipping markets. And he was breathtakingly handsome and extraordinarily rich and privileged. But below that lustrous, classically beautiful surface he was a hatefully cold and unfeeling guy, with no manners and a considerable contempt for women. If Lindy had to wait a lifetime to see Atreus Dionides again it would be too soon.

But in fact she was to see Atreus again much sooner than she expected—and in circumstances that would prevent her from expressing her antipathy in the manner she would have liked.

Her bedroom was the only room in her compact gate-house which provided her with a view of Chantry House. All she could actually see was the west wing of the extensive property, and at present that was not a pretty view because for many weeks that part of the building had been shrouded in unsightly scaffolding while it was being converted into staff accommodation. It was a clear night, without clouds, and when Lindy was closing the curtains shortly before midnight she immediately noticed a puff of smoke issuing from the roof. A frown line dividing her brow, she stared until she saw another, floating up slowly into the night sky. There was no chimney, and nobody living there yet either. She snatched in a dismayed breath, her fingers biting into the curtain as she peered out at the house. She was striving to crush back the bone-deep terror of fire that was already bringing her out in a cold sweat. Could it really be a fire? A suspicion of an orange glow behind a formerly blank window unfroze her from her position. She immediately reached for the phone to call the emergency services.

Then, in a frantic rush, she raced downstairs and snatched up her mobile phone to ring Phoebe Carstairs, who lived in the village and was the sister of Emma, who ran the animal sanctuary.

Phoebe ran out into her garden to take a look at Chantry House from across the fields.

'Oh, my goodness, I can see the smoke from here! We'll have to try and get the house cleared—it's full of priceless furniture and paintings!' Phoebe exclaimed in consternation.

'Phoebe…' Lindy interrupted as the other woman outlined her plan to call in the neighbours to help. 'Is there anyone staying in the house at present?'

'Mr Dionides arrived this afternoon… Oh, yes, and the cat—Dolly. I borrowed her from Emma to catch mice. I'm trying to call Mr Dionides…on the landline right now…but he's not answering. Oh, no, maybe he's been overcome by smoke! Look, you're much closer than I am. You'd better go and knock him up before he gets incinerated in his bed!'

Wincing in reaction at that unfortunate turn of phrase, and suppressing the panic and reluctance awakened by Phoebe's instruction, Lindy fled outside and jumped on her bike. She knew she had no choice but to get involved, and she was determined not to let her fear of fire prevent her from doing what she had to do. She pedalled frantically down the drive. There were no lights on. The mansion looked dead. Letting the bike fall to the gravel, she took the steps to the front door two at a time and hammered as noisily as she could on the giant knocker. Breathless and fiercely concerned, she kept on thumping the knocker until her arm ached and she had to change hands. By the time the big door finally opened, she could hear cars coming up the drive.

'What the hell—? It's after midnight.' Atreus Dionides stared out at her with a frown of incomprehension. He was still fully dressed in an elegant pinstriped suit. With his luxuriant black hair dishevelled and a blue-black shadow of stubble roughening his strong jawline, he was no longer immaculate in appearance, but he looked startlingly masculine and…sexy, Lindy conceded—in some shock at this awareness occurring to her. Her tummy flipped, and perspiration dampened her short upper lip. She was embarrassed for herself.

'The west wing is on fire!' she gasped.

Atreus dealt her a look of frank incredulity. 'What are you talking about?'

'Look, your house is on fire…don't be pig-headed!' Lindy yelled at him, sensing that being obstinate and independent of thought ran through his every fibre, like a name stamped indelibly into a stick of seaside rock.

Atreus strode down the steps. 'On…fire?'

'West wing. Top floor!'

His long, powerful legs cut the distance to the corner of the house at a rate she could not keep up with. Once there, he stilled at the sight of the glow lighting the darkness, while Lindy's tummy gave a sickening lurch and cold fear chilled her to the marrow. A biting phrase of guttural Greek escaped him before he was galvanised into action.

Several powerfully built men had already jumped out of a big four-wheel-drive to race across the gravel towards him. Lindy recognised the musclebound males who seemed to travel everywhere with him as his body-guards. He rapped out instructions to them and they walked straight into the house.

'Is it safe to let them go inside?' Lindy queried worriedly.

'If it were not I would not send them. The seat of the fire is a considerable distance from the library,' Atreus responded loftily, his irritation at that suggestion of censure unconcealed. 'My laptop and sensitive papers must be retrieved.'

Lindy could not credit that he could still be concentrating solely on business when the superb paintings she could see decorating the hall walls were under threat. Didn't he appreciate how terrifyingly fast a fire could move through a building? A terrifying shiver of remembrance that was a powerful hangover from her childhood experiences ran through her. Clenching her hands into fists of restraint, she turned away to approach Phoebe, who was surrounded by a cluster of locals. All of them were frozen into inactivity in the weird fascination of spectators watching a potential disaster develop.

'There's no time to waste. Let's get the artworks out,' Lindy urged.

A chain of willing helpers formed, and the first paintings were removed and passed out through the windows from hand to hand. Lindy, always a talented organiser, co-ordinated the effort, and once the Dionides bodyguards and estate workers joined them the salvage operation began to function with greater speed and efficiency. Two fire engines arrived and Atreus went into immediate consultation with the senior officer in charge. Ladders went up and hoses began to cover the ground. Chantry House sat on a hill, and water would have to be pumped up from the lake if the flames got a firm hold.

The task of clearing valuables from the vast mansion was eased by the fortunate fact that many of the rooms were awaiting redecoration and still empty. As the pressure on the salvage operation lessened Lindy watched in fierce trepidation as jets of water were directed into the burning building and billowing clouds of black smoke poured into the night sky. Even the smell of the smoke in the air made her feel queasy.

'The fire's travelling through the roof void,' Atreus ground out.

'Did the cat get out okay?' Lindy asked, belatedly recalling Dolly, the animal the housekeeper had mentioned.

Atreus urged her back onto the lawn as the orange glare behind a sash window loudly cracked the glass. 'What cat? I don't have animals in the house.'

Lindy dealt him a look of consternation and raced over to Phoebe. A storage lorry was reversing in readiness to load the paintings stacked on the tarpaulins that had been spread on the grass.

'Did Dolly get out?' Lindy asked frantically.

'Oh! I forgot about her!' the older woman admitted guiltily. 'I closed her in the kitchen for the night. I didn't want to risk her getting out and wandering round the house.'

The fire team in the hallway told her she couldn't enter the building. Tears of frustration in her eyes, Lindy pelted round to the back of the house. Would she really have the courage to go inside? she asked herself fiercely, doubting her strength of will in the face of such a challenge? The back door lay open. Her legs felt weak and woolly. She thought about the cat and, sucking in a deep jagged breath, conquered her paralysis and stumbled forward to race into the house. She sped down the flagged corridor and past innumerable closed doors. For a split second she froze in fear, for the smell of the smoke was rousing ever more frightening memories. But commonsense intervened and she snatched up a towel in the laundry room and held it to her face because the acrid smoke was catching horribly at her nose and her throat. Long before she reached the kitchen door, it had become a struggle to breathe.

She could hear a dull roaring sound behind the kitchen door and her courage almost failed to her, but she was powered by an image of Dolly's terror and the sick memory of herself as a child, trapped in a burning house. Using the towel to turn the door handle, in case it was hot, she opened the door just as a man shouted at her from behind.

'Don't open the door...*no!*' he roared, but she was on an adrenalin rush and she did not even turn her head.

She was shaken by the discovery that the ceiling was on fire. Although there was a scattering of small burning pieces of debris on the floor, the kitchen was still eerily intact within that unnatural orange glow of impending destruction. The heat, however, was intense. Dolly had taken shelter under the table. An elderly black and white cat, with big green eyes, she was clearly not her usual placid self. A smouldering piece of wood lay nearby and Dolly was snarling at it, with her hackles lifted and her fur standing on end.

Lindy surged forward and snatched up Dolly just as the most dreadful rending noise sounded from above her. Inadvertently she paused and obeyed a foolish compulsion to look up. Someone lifted her bodily off her feet and hauled her backwards. A burning beam fell on the table and rolled off again, showering sparks and choking dust only feet away from her. She had been right in its path, and the fear of what might have been hit her hard and left her limp.

Atreus carried Lindy and the struggling cat to safety and withstood a volley of reproof from the fireman who had followed his rescue bid. She was coughing and spluttering as Atreus lowered her to the cobbled yard outside, and she breathed in the clean air with feverish relief.

'How could you be so stupid?' Atreus yelled at her, full volume. 'Why didn't you stop when I shouted at you?'

'I didn't hear you shout!'

'You risked my life and your own for an animal!' Atreus launched at her in condemnation.

That verbal attack shocked her, and at the same moment she feverishly fought disturbing recollections of the household fire that had many years earlier taken her father's life. The combination made her eyes prickle and overflow and she flung him a speaking glance of reproach. 'I couldn't just leave Dolly to die in there!'

The cat was now curled up in Lindy's arms, with her furry head tucked well out of view. She was paying not the smallest heed to the crackling flames leaping through the roof of the west wing, or to the noise and activity of the human beings rushing around. Dolly had had enough excitement for one day and recognised a safe haven when she was offered one.

'You could have been killed or at the very least seriously injured,' Atreus admonished fiercely.

'You were a hero,' Lindy pronounced through clenched teeth of ingratitude. 'Thank you very much for saving my life.'

Fighting to contain his anger with her, Atreus gazed down at her defiant oval face. She wasn't beautiful but there was something about her, a heady *je ne sais quoi* that made him blatantly aware of her femininity. Was it those clear bright eyes? The luxuriant mane of long dark hair? Or the voluptuous figure that had infiltrated his dreams and caused him more disturbed nights that he cared to remember? She was full of emotion, a far cry from the reserved and controlled women he was used to dealing with. Her tear-filled eyes were as bright as amethysts, her lush, vulnerable mouth as ripe as a peach, and she continued to tremble as if the fire was still overhead. Anger lurched inexplicably into more complex responses that tensed his big powerful frame with surprise and electric sexuality. Hunger for her hit him as hard as a punch in the gut.

'I know I don't sound grateful,' Lindy added gruffly,

staring up at him, striving not to notice how beautifully his thick black lashes enhanced his stunning dark golden eyes. 'But I am really. Dolly was so frightened—didn't you see her?'

'*Nasi pari o Diavelos,*' Atreus swore raggedly under his breath. 'I saw only you.'

His intensity slashed through her strained attempt to behave normally. Her mouth running dry in the tension-filled atmosphere, she collided with his smouldering gaze and her ability to breathe seized up. He swooped like the predator she sensed he was at heart. He did not ask, he simply took, and his wide sensual mouth engulfed hers with a hot, driving energy that sizzled through her unprepared body like flame consuming tinder-dry wood. She moaned at the penetration of his tongue between her lips and the slow, sensual glide of it against hers, because her body was going haywire.

Sultry heat was tingling through her nerve-endings in a seductive wave. She tried to make herself pull back from him but could not find sufficient will-power to contrive that feat of mind over matter. Her nipples were lengthening into pointed pulsing buds constrained by the lace cups of her bra, and there was a treacherous yearning burn and an embarrassing dampness between her thighs. Together those sensations were winding her up as tight as a clock spring. As he pressed her against him, even through the barrier of their clothes, she was hopelessly aware of the hard, thrusting evidence of his arousal.

'Full marks for surprising me,' Atreus said huskily, surveying her with bold appreciation as he tilted back his handsome head. 'You are hotter than that fire in there, *mali mou.*'

Lindy, who had never seen herself as being hot in any capacity, sucked oxygen into her depleted lungs and accidentally, in her eagerness to avoid Atreus's scrutiny, caught the eye of the woman who had taken up a hesitant stance several feet away. It was Phoebe Carstairs.

'I'm sorry for interrupting, Mr Dionides,' the older woman said awkwardly. 'But I thought I could take care of the cat for you.'

On wobbly lower limbs, Lindy detached herself from Atreus and moved away to hand over the cat, who had tolerated being crushed between their straining bodies without complaint. She could not meet Phoebe's eyes; she was in shock…

CHAPTER TWO

'WE CAN make tea, coffee and sandwiches at The Lodge,' Lindy told Phoebe only minutes later, whipping herself straight back into her sensible self and suppressing all memory of that temporary slide into a persona and behaviour alien to her. 'Everyone will need a break and my house is the most convenient. I have to get my bike. If you have nothing more pressing to do, follow me down in your car.'

But even back within the cosy confines of her safe home Lindy discovered that she couldn't stop her hands shaking. She might have mastered her thoughts, but her body was still caught up in shock. She leant up against the sink, breathing in and out in steadying streams. She had gone into the house and got Dolly. That was all that mattered. She hadn't let her terror of fire paralyse her as it had threatened to do, she reminded herself soothingly. She was not the hysterical type. She was not. She would leave the past where it belonged and stay calm. There would be no crying or silly fussing. The deed was done and nobody had got hurt.

Slowly her hands began to steady and she felt in control again. That reminded her that for a timeless instant in the circle of the Greek tycoon's arms she had felt frighteningly out of control. Of course the fire had roused distressing fragments of memory which had knocked her very much off balance. How silly she had been, clinging to him like that! But these days what was in a kiss? she asked herself in exasperation. In the press, kisses had become almost meaningless in the face of far more intimate embraces, and in the literal heat of the moment were men not more prone to such physical reactions?

It hadn't meant anything—of course it hadn't. It was just that they were both shaken up and rejoicing in being alive and unharmed. Goodness, she wasn't Atreus Dionides's type at all! She wasn't small, blonde and beautiful, or even wellgroomed. Lindy glanced down at the corduroy skirt and V-necked sweater she wore and a rueful peal of laughter parted her lips. The kiss had just been one of those crazy inexplicable things and she would soon forget about it….

But she would not forget how he had made her feel. No, indeed. It would take total amnesia to wipe out the memory of that jaggedly sweet pleasure—jagged because it hurt to feel anything that strong and sweet, because it had melted every bone in her body and dissolved her self-discipline. No other guy had ever managed a feat like that. In fact, never until now had Lindy realised what all the fuss was about when it came to sex. She might not yet have met a man she wanted to sleep with, but she had certainly kissed plenty of frogs in her time. By no stretch of the imagination was Atreus a frog, but that had no bearing on the fact that he was as out of her reach as an astronaut on the moon.

Phoebe finally arrived with a laundry basket packed with provisions. The owner of the village shop had opened up specially to sell her bread and cooked meats, and had donated a pile of paper cups. The two women set about making trays of sandwiches.

'Lindy?' Phoebe said tautly, breaking the companionable silence. 'Please don't be offended, but I feel I should warn you to be careful with Mr Dionides. I have every respect for him as my employer, but I can't help having noticed that he's a very smooth operator with women. I don't think he takes any of them seriously.'

'The kiss was a flash in the pan—one of those daft things that just happens in the heat of the moment,' Lindy responded in a dismissive tone of faked amusement. 'I don't know what came over either of us, but it won't be happening again.'

'I would hate to see you getting led down the garden path,' the housekeeper confided in a more relaxed tone.

'I'm very resilient and not given to flights of fancy,' Lindy countered.

And she reminded herself of those facts when Atreus himself put in an appearance an hour later. She saw him across the crush in her small packed living room where, to find a space, people stood or sat on the arms of chairs, or even lounged back against the walls. Atreus was unmissable because he towered over everyone else, his dark well-shaped head instantly visible. He was talking on a mobile phone, the shadow of stubble outlining his

masculine jaw line heavier than before. He had fabulous
bone structure, from the defined width of his proud
cheekbones divided by his arrogant blade of his nose
to the unsettling fullness of his wide, sensual mouth.

She had to drag her attention from his hard, handsome face to notice that there was a long rip in the
sleeve of his jacket, and the cuffs and front of his shirt
were smoke-stained. She wondered with a stab of
concern if he had got hurt. She glimpsed the glimmering gold of his stunning eyes as he frowned, ebony
brows pleating, and she ducked back into the kitchen
before he could see her. Even after that brief exposure
her heart was already hammering as fast as if she'd run
a marathon. He was gorgeous—there was no other word
to better describe him. Instant exhilaration and renewed
energy leapt and bounded through her, banishing her
weariness, overpowering any sensible train of thought.

'More tea?' Phoebe prompted.

'No. I think the rush is over.' As the kitchen door
opened Lindy swivelled, and when she saw who it was
she felt ridiculously like a schoolgirl being confronted
by a grown-up who knew she had a huge crush on him.

'So this is where you are,' Atreus drawled. 'Come
into the other room.'

'I'm really busy—'

'You're a hive of industry, a very capable woman. I'm
impressed, but it's time you relaxed,' he intoned, closing
a dominant hand over hers and tugging her willy-nilly
back to the door where he stood.

Never comfortable in receipt of praise, Lindy frowned.
'I didn't do anything that other people didn't do.'

'You organised them all. I saw you in action. You're a remarkably bossy little thing,' Atreus remarked with unhidden amusement.

Nobody had ever described Lindy as 'little'. But then he was very tall, and in comparison to him she supposed that she could be considered small. Her fingers trembled in the hold of his. After those unexpected compliments she could hardly catch her breath, never mind speak. They were on the threshold of the living room. Heads turned in their direction and stayed turned at the sight of them poised there together. Her creamy skin flamed. She saw the speculative looks they were attracting and averted her gaze.

'It doesn't take much to encourage gossip round here,' she warned him ruefully.

'Does that bother you? Conventional women don't strip and jump into rivers in broad daylight,' Atreus countered.

Lindy froze. 'I still haven't forgiven you for the way you behaved that day.'

Atreus was not accustomed either to seeking forgiveness or indeed absolution. Women invariably made life easy for him by affecting not to notice his mistakes or omissions. Last-minute cancellations and his appearances in the company of other women were always ignored to ensure that he called again. He had learned that when it came to her sex he could get away with just about anything.

'You were a real seven-letter-word that day at the river!' Lindy proclaimed without hesitation, when he made no comment.

Atreus tried to recall when he had last heard anyone utilise such care to avoid a swear-word and he was amused.

'You were rude, thoroughly unpleasant and unreasonable, and you humiliated me!' Lindy spelt out in a fiery rush to get her point across.

'I apologised to you,' Atreus reminded her, with more than a touch of impatience. 'I rarely apologise.'

It was true that he had apologised, Lindy acknowledged ruefully, wondering if she was being unfair in still holding spite. After all, the man had saved her from serious injury when she'd rescued Dolly. He had also proved that in a crisis he was cool, courageous and protective, all sterling qualities of character which she very much admired. So why couldn't she escape the suspicion that treating a woman well didn't come naturally to Atreus Dionides?

'I don't know why you're flirting with me,' she told him flatly.

'Don't you?'

The doubt in his tone provoked her into looking up, and she met smouldering golden eyes below the black sweep of his lashes. Excitement hurtled through her like a wild wake-up call. Thought and breath were suspended. Without any warning at all she wanted his mouth so badly on hers that being denied it hurt. In shock, she tore her gaze from his and retreated into the kitchen.

A split second later all the lights in the house went out. A buzz of dismayed comment was accompanied by the sound of switches being put on and off without success. The kitchen door opened.

'Your electricity supply must be connected to that of Chantry House, which has been disconnected for safety.' Atreus's accented drawl came out of the darkness. 'It'll take some time to reorganise that, and it's unlikely to be today.'

'Oh, great,' Lindy muttered ruefully, leaning back against the kitchen cupboards and pushing her dark hair off her damp brow. The shower she had been dreaming about was out of reach now.

The locals began to leave with a chorus of thank-yous for her hospitality.

'You go as well, Phoebe,' Lindy urged the Chantry housekeeper, who was hovering at her elbow. 'It's been a long night and there's no need for you to stay on. Most of the cleaning up has already been done.'

'If you're sure?' Phoebe said uncertainly.

'Of course I am.'

'Why don't you come home with me?' the older woman asked. 'At least we have electricity.'

'We're not that far away from dawn. I'll be okay,' Lindy pointed out, reckoning that her companion, who had five children and a husband packed into her tiny terraced house, had quite enough people to contend with when she got home. She groped below the sink to locate her torch, and lit Phoebe's departure through the back door, locking up in the older woman's wake.

'Lindy?'

Lindy flinched in surprise at the sound of the Greek tycoon's distinctive accented drawl, travelling from the room next door. 'I thought you'd already gone,' she admitted, able to distinguish now between different shades of light and dark and picking out his tall, dark silhouette by the living room window.

'Some thanks that would be for the assistance you

gave tonight—abandoning you here without either power or heating,' Atreus derided. 'I have a suite booked at Headby Hall and I'd like you to come with me.'

'I couldn't possibly,' Lindy breathed, taken aback by that casual invitation to the leading country house hotel for miles around.

'Don't be impractical. You must be as eager for a shower and a break as I am,' he pointed out. 'In little more than four hours I have to be back at the house to meet the insurance assessors and the conservation team being put together as we speak.'

'I'll be fine here,' she asserted.

'You would genuinely prefer to sit here unwashed and cold rather than accompany me to a more civilised and comfortable location?'

Her small white teeth set together hard, because he was making her sound peculiar while at the same time his tone somehow contrived to suggest that such standoffish behaviour was only what he had expected from her all along. 'Give me a couple of minutes to pack a bag,' she told him, her voice as abrupt as the decision she had reached.

By the light of the torch she flung pyjamas and a change of clothes into an overnight bag. The dogs had food, water and cosy kennels, and although they were accustomed to sleeping indoors with her they would be all right until the morning. Even so, she was belatedly stunned that she could have agreed to go to a hotel with Atreus Dionides, for such bold behaviour didn't come naturally to her.

Lindy eased into the back of the limousine with as

much cool as she could muster. In the act of regretting her agreement, she turned to address Atreus—but his phone was already ringing again and his attention was elsewhere. She listened to him talking in what she assumed to be Greek and asked herself why she should feel so apprehensive. After all, he was only being kind in offering her an escape from a cold, dark house without hot water.

Headby Hall was the ultimate in luxury hotels, and Lindy had never crossed its threshold before. She was horribly conscious of her humble clothing and severely tried by Atreus's efforts to get her to walk through the foyer ahead of him when what she most wanted was to reach the lift without being noticed by a single living soul.

'Aren't you tired?' she asked him in wonderment when he completed yet another phone call.

'I'm still operating on adrenaline.'

'I'm sorry about the house. I know that the work you were having done was almost complete.'

'I have other houses,' he asserted.

Without thinking, Lindy rested a light hand on his arm. 'I noticed the rip in your jacket. Did you get hurt?' she asked anxiously.

Atreus looked down into her warm, sympathetic gaze and wondered when a woman had last looked at him as if she was restraining a powerful need to offer him comfort and a hug. Never, he acknowledged wryly, not even when he had been a child. In his experience women were usually more gifted at taking, and there was a hefty price ticket attached to anything on offer with any greater depth.

'It's only a scratch.'

Meeting his brilliant dark golden eyes, she felt her mouth run dry and her tummy lurched. The lift doors opened and she stiffened and tore her gaze from his. They walked down a private corridor to a door that was already being opened by a member of his staff. Tense with unease, Lindy entered a splendid, sumptuously furnished reception room adorned with fresh flowers. Designer luggage was being carried into one bedroom while her ancient holdall was already comfortingly visible through the doors of a second.

'I've ordered some food for us. You didn't eat anything while I was around,' Atreus remarked.

'I'll get changed,' Lindy muttered, heading for the second bedroom with alacrity.

In the *en suite* bathroom, she stripped where she stood and used the hotel toiletries to wash her hair and freshen up in the shower. It was wonderful to rinse away the smell of smoke that seemed to have impregnated her skin and everything she wore. Clean again, she dried her hair with the dryer provided, using her fingers and then fetched her clothes from the holdall. She donned a long green skirt and a cream T-shirt, and left her legs and feet bare because she couldn't face struggling into tights or shoes. She grimaced at her reflection in the mirror, for her glossy dark brown hair had fallen into the natural waves she disliked and she was convinced that her face was as pink as a freshly scrubbed lobster.

A trolley of food now stood beside the table and chairs in the reception room next door. Atreus was waiting for her and, like her, he had opted for informality. His black hair was damp and swept back from his lean, darkly handsome features. He was wearing black designer jeans and an open-necked shirt. As she appeared he studied her for a long moment and then slowly smiled.

And that smile on his wide, sensual mouth lit Lindy up inside like the blazing fire that had devoured a good third of Chantry House. It left little room for anything but instant reaction on all fronts. Her face was hot, and she sat down because she felt dizzy. Eyes screened by her lashes, she surveyed him, from his straight brows and dark deepset eyes to his newly shaven jawline, no longer defined by a blue-black shadow of stubble. There was something about the exact arrangement of his arrestingly beautiful features that drew her more than mere good-looks, she acknowledged in a daze. He magnetised her, exuding an irresistible pull of energy that overwhelmed her usual common sense. Sexual attraction had never hit her so hard.

Lindy accepted a couple of snacks and nibbled at them without much appetite while Atreus talked about the meetings he already had lined up for the morning. Even the sound of his voice set up a responsive vibration in her backbone. When she met his eyes she felt as if the ground had vanished and she was in mid-air, in the act of falling from a great height. It was terrifying and exhilarating and, because such excessive sensations were previously unknown to her, she decided that feeling that way around him was wrong and dangerous.

Indeed, as soon as an opportunity offered itself Lindy rose to her feet and smoothed damp palms down over her skirt. 'I'm very tired. I think I'll turn in now. Thanks for supper…and the shower was very welcome,' she added with a warm smile.

And just like that she was gone.

Atreus studied the closed door of her bedroom in amazement and wondered when he had last run into a brick wall put up by a woman flatly refusing to acknowledge or respond to his signals. Never. He was torn between amusement and frustration.

Lindy leant briefly up against the back of the door and tried to be proud of her self-restraint. She had resisted him, the most beautiful sexually compelling male she had ever met. She was still stunned that he had found her attractive. Or had it simply been a matter of her being the only woman available for a little dalliance after a stressful day? Was that her putting herself down again? Whatever, she had no doubt that he had had every intention of their ending what remained of the night in the same bed.

That would have been a very foolish move on her part, she told herself ruefully. The idea of a one-night stand with a man she hardly knew filled her with distaste. On the other hand, a little voice she didn't recognise murmured inside her head, he might well have been a once-in-a-lifetime experience. Or was that wishful thinking? She was ashamed of the way her mind was working. She had never planned to be a virgin at her age; it was just something that had happened when a serious relationship failed to transpire. Atreus was pretty much the first man to seriously attract her since those first heady days in Ben's radius. Of course she was curious about sex, but that was not an excuse to conduct an experiment. If she had been embarrassed when he'd seen her naked in the river, how would she feel meeting him in future if she had shared a bed with him?

With a shudder of reaction at that mortifying thought, Lindy embraced her cautious, sensible self and climbed into bed naked, enjoying the cool feel of the sheets against her bare skin. She had never been so tired in her life, but she still felt very jumpy and found it hard to relax—even though her limbs felt like lead weights on the comfortable mattress. She set her mobile phone alarm to rouse her at eight and mentally counted sheep. Within minutes she was sliding into a deep sleep. Her dreams, however, were very far from being soothing. Too many disturbing memories had been unleashed by the fire, and all her rigorous attempts to suppress those upsetting images while she was still awake had failed to lay them to rest.

'Lindy...wake up!' She fought through the barriers of sleep and realised that her shoulder was being shaken.

She sat up with a start, her eyes flying open not on the scary scene which had been unfolding behind her lowered eyelids but on a lamplit and momentarily unfamiliar room. Bewildered, and very distressed by what she had recalled, she only then processed the reality that she was shaking and sobbing.

'You were dreaming. You're awake now,' Atreus asserted, sitting down on the edge of the bed. Barechested, he had clearly only paused to pull on his jeans before coming in.

As Atreus entered her field of vision Lindy belatedly

acknowledged his presence and stiffened in alarm. 'Did I wake you up?'

'You were screaming at the top of your voice. That must have been some bad dream,' Atreus responded, his attention roaming to the ripe swell of her full breasts which were only just covered by the sheet and resolutely shifting upward again.

A violent shudder rippled through Lindy. 'Because it wasn't a dream,' she shared, on the back of another heaving sob. 'When I was f-four years old, I was in a house fire.'

Atreus tensed, frowning while he watched the tears drip off her chin and listening to her sniff. She was really crying, and not in a cute way either, for her nose had turned pink and her eyelids were swollen. But there was something extraordinarily touching about her genuine distress, and he closed an arm round her in an abrupt and almost clumsy movement.

It was one of those very rare occasions in life when Atreus felt out of his depth. Being supportive didn't come naturally to him. He had grown up in a family famed for its reserve and formality. He had been taught to avoid emotion like the plague and he had no close ties with his surviving relatives. He had never had a serious relationship with a woman, and had always walked away when an affair threatened to become complicated.

The warmth of his arm was comforting. Lindy struggled to control the sobs and the tempest of emotion still rising inside her. 'Afterwards, my mum told me that my dad must've fallen asleep with a cigarette in his hand and the sofa caught fire. He'd been drinking—my mum was in hospital. I woke up and there was smoke coming under the door and a funny smell,' she related shakily.

Atreus swore half under his breath in Greek. 'And yet you went into a burning house to save a cat tonight?' he breathed, in wrathful incredulity.

Lindy's mind was still firmly lodged in past events. 'I tried to go downstairs but I could see something was in flames at the foot. I was terrified, so I started screaming for Dad.' Her voice cut off, and she twisted and buried her face in the warm living flesh of Atreus's bronzed shoulder. 'For a moment I saw him, but until tonight I didn't remember that I had actually seen him. He was trying to come to me but the fire got him!' she sobbed brokenly.

Atreus was appalled. A dark frown stamping his features, he wrapped his other arm round her shuddering body and held her close. He was thinking about the selfless way she had rushed to the fire at Chantry House and helped out in every way she could. Not by a word or even a gesture had she hinted at what that intervention must have cost her emotionally. 'You're a very brave woman, *mali mou.*'

'I'm just ordinary.' Lindy snatched in a sustaining breath and choked back another sob, fighting with all her might to get a grip on her flailing emotions. 'I don't know why I'm crying now about something that happened so long ago.'

'The fire at Chantry last night brought it all to the surface again. How did you escape when you were a child?'

'I believe a fireman rescued me, but I don't remember

it. I was incredibly lucky to survive.' Her voice petered
out in shock as she finally registered that the sheet
between them had slipped. Her bare breasts were
crushed against his hair-roughened masculine torso.
'I'm so sorry I woke you up.'

'You didn't. I couldn't sleep,' Atreus admitted, long
lean fingers lacing into the tousled tumble of her dark
hair to turn her face up.

Smouldering dark golden-brown eyes assailed hers,
and then he brought his handsome mouth down and
captured her lips with a piercingly sweet eroticism that
cut through her defences like a knife. Breathing in little
fractured bursts, Lindy drowned in those hungry, drugging kisses, her body quickening and heating in
response. There was a frantic driving edge to every sensation: the stingingly tight sensitivity of her nipples,
the tugging pull of dissatisfaction at the heart of her.

Atreus closed his hands round the creamy magnifi-
cence of her jutting breasts and moulded them with a
husky masculine sound of satisfaction. He used his
thumbs to chafe the quivering pink tips until, in pursuit
of closer contact, he pressed her back against the pillows
and put his mouth to her breast instead.

A gasp was dragged from Lindy, who was reeling in
sensual shock from the impact of his lovemaking. The
tug of his lips and his teeth, and the brush of his tongue
on her tormentingly sensitive nipples, made her squirm
while desire flared ever higher and stronger inside her.
That she had to struggle even to think straight, however,
scared her.

'We hardly know each other!' she protested.

'This is the very best way to get to know me, *glikia mou*,' Atreus intoned with conviction

'But I didn't want to get to know you!' Lindy objected, guiltily studying the clinging fingers she had knotted into the springy depths of his black hair.

'You want me and I want you. Why should that be a problem?'

'Because it is... I don't do stuff like this.'

'You don't have to do anything,' Atreus declared with single-minded purpose.

'You're not my type,' she told him in desperation.

'Why didn't you say so sooner?' Atreus levered back from her to gaze down at her with shimmering golden eyes full of enquiry.

Lindy crossed concealing arms over her breasts.

'I love looking at you,' Atreus confided, stroking an appreciative hand down to the point where her surprisingly small waist segued into the violin curve of her hip. 'You have the most spectacular shape.'

The intensity of his appraisal convinced her of his sincere approbation and lessened her discomfiture. Without being aware of any prompting to do so, Lindy slowly, shyly parted her arms again, because she was discovering that she really loved the idea of him looking at her and admiring her. Not a single compliment on that score had ever come Lindy's way. Until that moment her voluptuous curves had been a physical flaw and an embarrassment which she hid to the best of her ability. But, transfixed by the glow of bold appreciation in Atreus's gaze, she felt like a goddess come to earth to mesmerise mortal man.

'You looked at the riverbank,' Lindy accused him.

'*Ise omorfi*... you are beautiful...of course I did. The glory of you took my breath away, *mali mou*.'

He had barely finished speaking before Lindy stretched up and sought his wide, sensual mouth for herself again. She savoured the taste of him like a precious wine, parting her lips eagerly for the erotic plunge of his tongue while she quivered at the clenching tightness of response low in her pelvis. He had ignited a hunger in her that she could not resist.

'Is this a yes?'

'Yes...'Lindy whispered, feeling madly daring and sexy for the first time in her life while she defied the voice of restraint and reproach striving to be heard in the back of her head.

The pressure of his mouth on hers was an enticement of no mean order. Her head fell back against the pillows, her neck extending in a soundless sigh as he touched her where she had never been touched before. Little tremors of fierce response assailed her while he teased the honeyed folds of flesh between her thighs. The pleasure was exquisite, but as her excitement grew the pleasure came closer to sensual torture. The more he touched her, the more she wanted, and the less she wanted to wait. He suckled the distended peaks of her breasts and her spine arched, and she cried out as he probed the narrow passage at the swollen heart of her.

She was dimly aware of him removing his jeans and a moment of panic claimed her. 'Don't get me pregnant...' she warned him. 'I'm not using anything.'

'That's not a risk I would ever take,' Atreus imparted, donning protection and hauling her back to him with impatient hands. 'I want you so much it hurts.'

'Will it hurt?' Lindy pressed awkwardly.

A look of bemusement clouded his smouldering gaze. 'Why should it hurt?'

'I haven't done this before...I just wondered.'

Atreus studied her with frowning intensity. 'I will be the first?'

Her body tingling, her face burning, Lindy nodded.

Atreus groaned out loud, recognising the anxiety in her violet-blue eyes, acknowledging that she continually managed to surprise him. 'I'll be very gentle, *glikia mou,*' he swore—he a man who had never tried to be gentle before.

And he was: coaxing and teasing her responsive body until she was on fire with wanting him. She waited in an agony of anticipation and desire for the moment when he eased his rock-hard shaft into the velvet-soft sheath of her womanhood. She saw pleasure score his lean, hard features and marvelled at the extraordinary sense of intimacy a split second before a sharp pain provoked her into venting a cry of dismay.

He stopped, talked to her in husky Greek, kissed her until she relaxed again. And then it went on, the slow, deep penetration that made her gasp and moan with increasing fervour and excitement while he arched her up to receive him and plunged back into her again. Suddenly she was riding a high of erotic sensation, out of control and abandoned to the wild need he had incited. The orgasm, when it came, took her by surprise and stunned her, before the irresistible waves of shuddering physical satisfaction took over.

'You were amazing,' Atreus told her with a blazing smile of approbation.

'So were you,' Lindy whispered, feverishly trying to suppress the screaming fit of self-doubt, shame and incredulity ready to pounce on her. She wrapped her arms around him and kissed him, fighting the lingering shards of doubt and regret as hard as she could. She found him amazingly attractive and had acted on it, she told herself staunchly. There was no point beating herself up about what could not be changed.

Taken aback though he was by that affectionate kiss, and what has undeniably been a hug, Atreus still tugged her back to him when she attempted to back away. 'I can't wait until the next time, *mali mou*.'

Her eyes widened.

'I don't do one-night-stands,' he told her in reproof.

'Don't you?' Discomfiture was beginning to claim her, for she was feeling very much out of her depth.

A slashing grin curved his beautiful mouth. 'And neither do you…'

CHAPTER THREE

SAMSON and Sausage gave Lindy a rapturous welcome when she returned home, while Pip picked at his food and snarled whenever the other dogs came within yards of his feeding bowl. Awesomely conscious of Atreus waiting impatiently indoors for her, Lindy ignored her usual tasks and went straight back inside with her pets in tow.

Samson, a Jack Russell terrier with perky ears and a cheerful propensity to treat everyone like a long-lost best friend, went straight over to greet Atreus. Sausage hung back, while Pip put on a burst of speed and, barking furiously, raced straight over to the interloper and sank his teeth into his trouser leg. Samson started to bark as well and, aghast, Lindy waded in, urging peace on all parties while she strove to detach Pip from his glowering victim.

'I'm so sorry. He's a very bad-tempered dog. Thank you for not kicking him away.' Lindy removed a snarling Pip and then gasped, 'Oh, my goodness he's lost one of his teeth!'

'Is it embedded in my leg?' Atreus asked.

'No, it's lying here on the carpet,' Lindy answered, deaf to his tone of irony. She peered into the cross little Chihuahua's mouth and was shocked by the sight of his swollen gums. 'I never realised he had such bad teeth. He must be in a lot of pain. Poor little thing.'

While Lindy soothed and quieted the canine attacker with copious sympathy, Atreus fumed in silence. He had never had anything to do with dogs, and now he had been bitten by one in circumstances guaranteed to bolster his repugnance. 'Are you coming up to the house with me?'

Lindy froze, violet eyes locking to his lean, darkly handsome face. 'I would rather not draw attention to our...er...new...er...'

As her voice trailed off without her finding an appropriate word, Atreus stepped in. 'Intimacy?'

The word struck Lindy like a brick and she paled, guilt looming large, for the word seemed richly redolent of beds and tumbled sheets—imagery that assailed her conscience like a panic attack. 'Yes. I don't want anyone to know.'

That was not a request Atreus had ever received before. Women usually wanted to show off their association with him, not hide it. But he had always had a high regard for discretion and prudence. The Dionides family were, after all, famous for their dislike of publicity. Birth, marriage and death, and occasional references in the business press, were unavoidable exceptions for so very rich a family. But beyond that level Atreus and his relatives shunned public notice and abhorred the brash, extravagant lifestyle of the celebrity world.

'I'll be very discreet,' he assured her. 'We'll see each other at weekends, when I come down here.'

Lindy studied him with perplexed eyes, for she could not yet accept that they could be a couple in any way, never mind a couple with an ongoing relationship.

'We've got nothing in common,' she pointed out.

'Differences are stimulating,' Atreus traded smoothly, averting his attention from the little rat-like dog baring its crooked teeth at him from the shelter of her arms before she put it through to the kitchen. The Jack Russell had dropped a rubber bone expectantly at his feet, while the short hairy one was fussing beside a chair and for some reason regarding him with equal anticipation. Atreus decided to spell out his feelings: 'I'm not into pets—particularly indoors.'

'I suppose you didn't have any when you were a child,' Lindy responded, giving him a huge look of sympathy and not one whit perturbed by his loaded statement. 'That's such a shame. But you'll soon get used to my pets.'

She was trying to imagine seeing him at weekends, slotting him into her ordinary activities and failing abysmally to rise to the challenge. Even the idea of him becoming a part of her life struck her as astonishing. 'I don't know why you want to see me again.'

Atreus was bewildered by a response which had never come his way before. A faint stab of guilt assailed him because her lack of vanity and pure likeability shone from her. She was not at all like his usual lovers, he acknowledged wryly. She didn't know the rules he played by and she would probably get hurt. He recalled the total lack of cool and control she displayed when she hugged him and he almost winced. But she would eventually learn, he reasoned steadily, squaring his broad shoulders.

She would have to learn—because he would not contemplate not seeing her again. The bottom line was that he wanted her in his life. Obviously he was ready for a change, for something different, and she would be a breath of fresh air. She was strong, discreet and honest, qualities which he valued highly and which were hard to find in her sex. He would relax with her at weekends, stepping back from the long, stressful hours he worked and the boring social occasions. He met her bewildered violet-blue eyes and realised that if anything he wanted her even more powerfully than he had some hours earlier. The strength of his desire made him uneasy, but it also propelled him forward to ease her into his arms.

Always more comfortable with the physical than the emotional, Atreus lowered his arrogant dark head and brought his mouth down on hers with passionate urgency. That kiss was like an electric shock, first stunning Lindy and then spreading tingling waves of reaction through her. The pressure of his lips and the plunging penetration of his tongue jolted her and made very fibre of her body sing with sexual awareness. Her nipples tightened, her tummy flipped, and looking up into his smouldering dark golden eyes left her dizzy.

'I want to take you back to bed,' he admitted in a raw undertone of frustration, both hands splayed on her hips to hold her close enough to feel the hard male heat of his arousal. 'Once was very far from being enough.'

Lindy reddened, struggling with the notion of herself as some sort of temptress but loving it—and the proof of it in his physical reaction to her too.

'Unfortunately I have a meeting up at the house,' he reminded her.

'Several,' she told him with a smile.

'Either come with me or go back to the hotel. You can do nothing here without electricity.'

'I may not be able to make candles, but I can cut lavender and make pot pourri,' she contradicted.

'But you don't have to do any of that right now.'

The bell at the front door buzzed.

Lindy peered out of the window and saw her friend's car. 'It's Ben,' she said.

'Ben?' Atreus queried, moving to the window to note the BMW parked on the drive.

'A good friend of mine. He's here to collect Pip, the little dog that nipped you. Pip belongs to his mother,' she explained.

Ben strode straight into the hall. 'I'm on a day off so I thought I'd come down early. It interferes less with my social life,' he confided, with a speaking roll of his eyes.

Lindy launched right into telling him about Pip's swollen gums. She urged him to take the little animal to his mother's vet for a check-up. 'Painful teeth could explain why he's so cross. He needs treatment urgently,' she stressed. 'I'll go and get him for you.'

'Aren't you inviting me in?' But Ben was talking to thin air, because Lindy had already hurried off to slot Pip into his travelling basket.

'Where did the limo outside come from?' Ben called in her wake.

A split second after Lindy returned with the basket

Atreus appeared on the threshold of the sitting room.
'It's mine—'

Lindy introduced the two men with a pronounced
casualness that brought a gleam to Atreus's dark watch-
ful gaze. Ben recognised the name at once, and immediately adopted a more businesslike manner.

'Chantry House almost burnt down last night. A
crowd of us helped to clear up,' Lindy explained.

'But Lindy offered the most valuable assistance,'
Atreus imparted.

Lindy stiffened in surprise when Atreus curved a
light arm to her spine. Ben noticed, and sent her a
frowning questioning glance. Her cheeks burned.

'I'd like to take you out for lunch as thanks for
putting up with Pip,' Ben announced.

'Unfortunately Lindy is already booked,' Atreus
breathed silkily.

'Sorry,' Lindy muttered, wondering why on earth
Ben should have suddenly invited her out for a meal
and then understanding as she picked up on the bristling attitude between the two men: Ben was curious.
She felt like a bone between two dogs, and was thoroughly irritated, both by Ben's unprecedented invitation and Atreus's arrogant assumption that his last-
minute invitation would take priority with her. But it
did take priority, she conceded ruefully, even if she
disliked his methods.

'I'll call you later,' Ben told her stiffly.

'No, you can't leave yet. I'll make coffee for us.'

His stunning dark eyes cool as ice water, Atreus
opened the front door. 'I'll pick you up at twelve.'

'What the blazes are you playing at with that guy?' Ben demanded within seconds of the door shutting in the Greek tycoon's wake.

Lindy was tempted to tell Ben to mind his own business, and had to remind herself that close friends were entitled to ask awkward questions.

'He's been flirting with me…that's all,' she replied lightly, finding it quite impossible to even consider telling Ben the truth.

'Of course that's all,' Ben agreed with wounding conviction. 'I would very much doubt that you have what it takes to tempt Atreus Dionides into anything more. He's a billionaire shipping tycoon and he only dates stunningly beautiful women.'

'Coffee,' Lindy pronounced through clenched teeth, resisting the humiliating urge to tell Ben that while he might not find her attractive Atreus certainly did.

Ben didn't stay long, because Lindy wanted time to get dressed for lunch. He was not as relaxed with her as he usually was, and she wondered if it was insane of her to suspect that the suggestion that another man might be interested in her had thoroughly irritated her platonic friend.

Lindy put on the smartest outfit in her wardrobe— an elegant black trouser suit. Atreus had let his body-guard come to the door for her, and when she got into the limousine he treated her to a thirty-second apprai-sal before saying, 'I prefer skirts on women.'

'Do you?' Lindy bridled at that untimely comment. 'Am I supposed to write that down in a little black book and never wear trousers again?'

'Where does Ben fit in?' Atreus enquired, neatly sidestepping her tart response.

Lindy gave him a puzzled frown and then laughed. 'I thought he was the love of my life when I was a student of eighteen, but unfortunately, he didn't see me in the same light. I got over him, we became friends, and we've been friends ever since.'

Atreus lowered lush black lashes over his shimmering dark golden gaze. He had not taken to Ben, and the admission that she had once been in love with the other man simply underlined his reservations. But Atreus was proud of the fact that he had never experienced the urge to be possessive with his lovers. He met her strained violet-blue gaze and suddenly smiled, because he could read her like a book. She was pleased that he had invited her to lunch, but still nervous of being seen out in his company.

'We'll eat in the hotel suite,' Atreus murmured, closing a hand over hers to urge her across the depth of seat separating them.

'Atreus…' she gasped, in the aftermath of a long, drugging kiss that left her feeling intoxicated. 'Throughout the history of the world there couldn't be two people less suited than us.'

'You have such old-fashioned ideas, but I like them,' Atreus growled, his mouth following a line down her neck to her throat that made her shiver violently, every nerve-ending screaming on high alert. 'Just as you like this—don't you?'

'Well…er…'

'Tell the truth,' he prompted lethally.

'It just feels indecent, and that's not who I am or what I'm like!' Lindy protested with the shattered incomprehension of a woman suddenly finding herself flat on the backseat of a limo in broad daylight.

'But the bottom line is that you like it, *glikia mou*,' Atreus replied with irrefutable logic. 'As for you not being like this, what would you know about who you really are when you waited so long to take a lover? Educating you promises to be a very exciting exercise.'

A lean hand sketched a provocative line along the tautness of her inner thigh below her trousers and she honestly thought she might spontaneously combust from the level of heat and longing centred at the heart of her. Her lashes slid down. What had come over her? Where had all her common sense and caution gone? Into twenty-six years of clean living, low self-esteem and loneliness, a little voice answered. Not a bad life, but undeniably a life without any breathtaking highs.

'Do we have to eat first?' Atreus said huskily in an erotic growl.

Lindy tried and failed to swallow. Excitement was clawing at her, and no matter how hard she fought it she could already see how much influence he had over her and how much she was changing. If that was the effect he could have in twenty-four hours… But it wouldn't, couldn't, last long between them. It was a kind of madness, an attraction of opposites: sudden, startling and sexy, but surely destined to burn out fast. And when it was over she would be miserable….

Lindy looked up into his lean, dark beautiful face and

decided that she could live with the prospect of that misery if it meant that she had him all to herself for a little while.

Four months later, Lindy and Atreus were still together almost every weekend.

By now Lindy was madly in love, and so happy she wakened with a smile on her face. But her mood was punctured suddenly one day by the sight of a photo in a gossip column. Atreus with another woman. It had been taken at a charity ball and the beautiful brunette was curved round Atreus like a second skin. Lindy felt quite sick looking at the photo, but she told herself that she would make no mention of the matter. She did not want to act possessively. The very idea of it hurt her pride, and she knew he would have a low tolerance threshold for such behaviour.

But after a couple of nights of disturbed sleep she realised she could not keep silent. They were lovers, and she needed the assurance that she was the only one in his life. When she dined with Atreus at Chantry House that weekend, Lindy planned to use subtlety to introduce the delicate subject of what he did when he was away from her during the week.

The graceful Georgian mansion had been restored to its former splendour in record time by builders and decorators working round the clock in shifts. Standing on the sidelines, Lindy had found that efficient restoration project highly educational. Atreus had not lowered his standards of excellence by so much as an inch, and the feat had been completed in a timeframe which most people had deemed impossible.

When no useful opening to the controversial topic occurred during their meal Lindy became increasingly restless and distracted.

'What's the matter with you?' Atreus asked as they vacated the dining table.

Feeling like a total coward for having failed to raise the subject, Lindy glanced at him uneasily. 'What do you mean?'

'You're very quiet, *mali mou*. It's not like you.'

'There was a photo of you with another woman in a gossip column this week.' In spite of her intention to make a light, non-accusatory enquiry when it came to the point, Lindy simply blurted out the facts and then cringed at her lack of skill.

Even though he knew exactly who, when and where, and even which newspaper, Atreus was too practised at keeping his own counsel with women to admit the fact. 'Was there?'

'You attended a charity ball with her.' Taut with tension and anxiety now, Lindy spun round in the drawing room, where drinks were being served and stared at him with strained eyes. 'Who was she?'

'A friend... I have many,' Atreus responded smoothly.

Painful colour lit Lindy's cheeks. 'You don't think I have any right to ask, do you? But I don't expect to be one of a crowd when I'm sleeping with you,' she shared, in an awkward rush of words.

The conscience that rarely troubled Atreus stung him in the face of that honest admission. Although he had found it safest and easiest never to define the boundaries of relationships, or make promises he might not wish to keep, her naive candour on the issue and her obvious concern pierced his emotional armour.

'Lindy—'

'Just tell me the truth. I have to know. To be honest, I've hardly slept a wink since I saw that photo,' she confessed unevenly.

Atreus reached for her hand and used it to propel her under his arm, ignoring her taut, stiff posture. 'I thought you would be more sensible,' he reproved. 'I only ever have one lover at a time, but I have many female acquaintances who act as my companions at various charitable and stuffy social engagements.'

Her heart still beating very fast with the apprehension that had built up in her since first seeing that photo, Lindy breathed easily again. She felt quite light-headed with relief. *I only ever have one lover at a time.* That was the one thing she had needed to hear. It shook her to appreciate that she had set no parameters at all in their relationship. Then she had fallen into it and then fallen crazily in love so fast she had never thought about rules. In any case Atreus, she recognised ruefully, was the sort of guy who would probably want to break a rule as soon as anyone was foolish enough to try and impose one on him.

In the early hours, she lay awake while he slept. Her body was heavy with tiredness, languor and sensual satisfaction. Her heart was light with love and contentment. But her mind was still racing over the conversation they had had after dinner. Although his response had given her peace of mind, she was convinced she had lost

stature in his eyes by betraying her desperate need for
reassurance. She could not escape the suspicion that
she had ended up looking weak and insecure, which was
not an impression that she wanted to give for Atreus was
much more intrigued by strong, confident women. And
that was what she was now, Lindy consoled herself.
Strong and confident and not in need of reassurance. It
was not a slip she would make a second time.

Over a year after Lindy reached that decision, Ben
Halliwell made one of his increasingly frequent unan-
nounced visits to The Lodge. Having abandoned the pot
pourri she had been bagging in the cellar, Lindy invited
him in for coffee. He polished off two homemade cheese
scones before coming to the point.

'If you really want to know where you stand with
Atreus Dionides, you need to look at this.' Ben settled
a page torn from a magazine down on the table in
front of Lindy.

Caught unawares, Lindy stared and saw an image
that shot the equivalent of a flaming arrow of pain right
through her heart. Her skin broke out in perspiration and
nausea made her tummy lurch. Once again it was a photograph of Atreus with another woman on his arm: a
very beautiful blonde with jewels at her throat and a
fancy evening gown. With a clumsy hand Lindy thrust
the picture back at Ben in rejection, a look of reproof
in her steady gaze. After all, it was not the first time she
had seen such a photo, and she reckoned that it would
not be the last. But she was annoyed with Ben, who

never missed an opportunity to criticise Atreus or to try and show him in a bad light.

'Atreus was attending a charity benefit for a children's hospice on Monday night,' Lindy explained. 'That woman is probably one of the organisers.'

'Stop telling yourself whoppers and making excuses for him!' Ben's exasperation was unconcealed. 'Carrie Hetherington is a wealthy, well-connected socialite, and he's obviously not ashamed to be seen out in public with her—'

'Atreus is not ashamed of me, either,' Lindy argued vehemently. 'You're not being fair to him. I was the one who asked him to be discreet about our relationship, not the other way round. I didn't want to be seen out and about with him…I didn't want people gossiping about us, and I would die if my photo appeared in the newspapers!'

Ben groaned out loud. 'How can you still be so naive? He's not being discreet, Lindy. He's made you a dirty little secret in his life.'

Lindy rammed her hands down on the table surface and plunged upright. 'That's a horrible thing to say!'

Momentarily, Lindy saw stars as a bout of dizziness engulfed her. Assuming she had stood up too quickly, she breathed in slow and deep until the feeling of being light-headed receded.

'Whether you like it or not, it's the truth,' Ben continued, without even noticing how pale she had become. 'You're his mistress, not his girlfriend, and he only ever sees you at weekends, when he's down here. He never takes you out.'

'I'm not his mistress!' Lindy hissed back at Ben in passionate rejection of that label.

'But you're not a size zero hottie from his world, either. So exactly where do you fit in?'

Wounded by Ben's cutting reference, Lindy studied him with pained eyes. 'Why are we even having this conversation? Why are you always attacking Atreus?'

'We've been friends for years and Atreus has spent the last eighteen months messing you around. It's a dead-end affair. The way he treats you he might as well be a married man, and you might as well be his bit on the side.'

'Atreus treats me very well!' Lindy argued, dropping back down into her chair.

'He's a billionaire. He can afford to be generous.'

'I'm not talking about money,' she said with distaste. 'You don't understand what we have.'

'I think you're the one who doesn't understand. You fell in love with him and started living in a cosy little dream world. You seem to have suspended every critical faculty you ever had. I'm only trying to wake you up. You're wasting your time with Dionides. He's not going to give you what you want,' Ben completed with ringing conviction.

'You don't know what I want.'

'Don't I?' Ben gave her an ironic look. 'This life is all wrong for you. You want marriage and security, but you've settled for an affair that you persist in viewing as the height of romance. Answer me one question. If you're so happy with Atreus, why have you still not got around to introducing him to Elinor and Alissa?'

'Elinor and Alissa aren't in the UK very often,' Lindy

said defensively. One of whom lived in the Middle East and the other also spent a fair amount of time abroad.

'Do they even know that Dionides exists?'

Lindy reddened, because he had come closer to the truth than she was prepared to admit with that question. Only a few weeks had passed since she had finally phoned Elinor and Alissa to tell them about Atreus. 'Yes, of course they do, but I don't want to talk about this any more. I get very annoyed when you criticise Atreus, and I can't possibly discuss my relationship with him with you.'

'Just think over what I've said,' Ben urged. 'Or ask Dionides where your relationship is going. I guarantee that you won't like the response he gives you.'

To change the subject, Lindy asked him about his recent advancement at work. No topic could have been closer to Ben's heart. Her tension began to evaporate, but a leaden, hollow feeling still sat in her stomach.

'I have my boss's wedding to attend two weeks from now,' Ben informed her when he was on the brink of leaving. 'I thought of you immediately because it's being held at Headby Hall, which is only a few miles from here. I know it's short notice, but will you come with me as my partner?'

Lindy looked at him in surprise. 'I don't know. I—'

'Please,' Ben sighed. 'I would look sad, turning up on my own.'

Lindy laughed at the image of Ben looking sad, while dimly wondering why his once busy love-life had slowed down so much of late. He no longer had a new woman in his life every few weeks and, with more time on his hands, she had seen a great deal more of him in recent months. 'All right, give me the date and I'll mark it on my calendar.'

'Will it cause trouble between you and Atreus?' Ben asked with a hint of mockery.

'Of course it won't cause trouble.' Her chin tilted. 'Atreus doesn't question what I do.'

Brave words, Lindy acknowledged after Ben's departure. In truth she rarely did anything at weekends that would disrupt her time with Atreus, and he and Ben had not hit it off at their one and only meeting. Her mood had been buoyant before Ben's arrival, because it was a Friday and she would be with Atreus again in just a few hours. But Ben's comments had hit home hard. He had spoilt her day by making her question her relationship with Atreus.

As a rule Lindy lived from weekend to weekend, and nothing in between really mattered. It was just time to be got through before she saw Atreus again. Until Ben had cruelly thrust that wretched photo beneath her nose she had managed to pretty much ignore the reality that Atreus inhabited another world entirely when he was away from her. Was that because she had stopped buying newspapers and magazines after seeing Atreus in print with another female companion?

That was a tough question, and one that Lindy couldn't answer. Atreus had long since explained the reality that those acquaintances were of a social rather than intimate nature. The more she got to know Atreus the more she had grown to trust him, and the affair that she had once assumed would swiftly burn out had lasted and deepened.

In fact Lindy had lived on a high of happiness for almost eighteen months. Atreus phoned her almost every day. And he genuinely cared about her. He did. He might not show it in an emotional manner, for he was not a man given to issuing constant compliments or verbal reassurances, but he certainly demonstrated his concern in other ways. Hadn't he flown back from Greece when he'd learned that she was in hospital because she'd been knocked off her bike by a car? Hadn't she wakened to find him seated by her bed in the middle of the night? Hadn't she come home to find a brand-new hatchback car waiting to glide into the parking space being cut out of the lawn that bounded the drive for her benefit?

They had had their first real argument over that car. She had refused to accept it, and he had ranted about how dangerous the bike was, until the dissension between them had reached such a peak that she'd given way out of a genuine fear of losing him. The only other bone of contention between them was his ongoing refusal to accept rent from her as one of his tenants.

'How do you expect me to accept your money?' Atreus had demanded angrily. 'You work long hours to make a living. Do you think I don't know that? Why should you pay rent to me when I have more money than I could spend in one lifetime?'

That debate was still continuing in the background, for while Lindy doggedly continued to ensure that the rent was paid every month, Atreus continued to have the money returned to her bank account. When she stopped to wonder what the estate manager must think of the whole stupid business, she just cringed. All too many people were well aware of her involvement with the owner of the Chantry estate. It had been naive of her to imagine it could be otherwise. She had even run into the vicar of her church one afternoon at Chantry House. Atreus had innumerable staff as well. People knew, but minded their own business; it had taken Ben to confront her head-on. But what right had he to talk? Ben who, as far as she knew, had never once had a serious relationship with a woman.

Around six that evening Lindy came down the stairs with her weekend bag and her dogs. She was wearing a well-cut grey pencil skirt with a fine purple sweater, and black patent shoes with high heels. Since she had met Atreus she had gradually transformed her wardrobe and her appearance. Newly found confidence in her body had persuaded her to experiment with more figure-flattering garments. Her old shapeless skirts and loose sweaters had gone to the church jumble sale. Her hair had been styled from a haphazard mop into a sleek bouncy mane that framed her face, and she had rediscovered make-up.

But if Atreus had noticed a single change while she polished up her image he hadn't mentioned it, Lindy acknowledged wryly. Nor had her improved looks given him the urge to take her out and show her off. Why was she so contrary, though? In spite of her having once told him that she didn't want to be seen out in public with him, she now craved such an invitation. But she was not about to ask Atreus any stupid questions about the future. She was secure and happy as she was...

Twenty minutes later the limo drew up outside and Lindy, with her dogs at her heels, climbed in. The luxury vehicle whisked them up to the big house. The chauffeur opened the door and sidestepped the dogs to greet her. Phoebe Carstairs only worked weekdays. Every weekend a French chef and several Greek menservants came down in advance of Atreus's arrival and took charge of the household to ensure the assiduous level of service and attention to detail that the tycoon expected from his staff. There was lightness in Lindy's step and a bubbling anticipation inside her. Following the path of Dmitri's helpful hand, she headed straight for the library, which Atreus used as an office...

CHAPTER FOUR

A STUNNING vision of masculine style in a charcoal-grey business suit flawlessly tailored to his tall, well-built frame, Atreus was poised by the library's elegant windows while he talked on the phone. For a split second Lindy paused to refresh her eyes with the sight of him and revel in the pleasure of seeing him again. He swung round, his lean, breathtakingly handsome features briefly shedding their often sombre aspect with a sudden flashing smile. Samson and Sausage squeezed past Lindy to race across the room and hurl themselves at him. Knowing that that energetic welcome would go down like a lead balloon while he was on the phone, Lindy threw herself in the dogs' path and acted as a barrier between her lover and her pets.

Atreus closed a steadying arm round her as the impact of the animals against the back of her legs almost unbalanced her. The glow of warmth in her eyes captivated him. He liked the way she never hid anything from him, never tried to play it cool. He found her as straightforward as he found others of her sex artificial.

As the evocative scent of her hair and her skin made his nostrils flare, he was instantly aware of the erotic pulse at his groin. He lowered his head to press his skilful mouth hotly to a tender spot just below her ear, a move he had long since learned drove her wild. With a sensual moan of surrender, Lindy quivered with the delicious awakening that was hurtling like liquid fire to her every pulse-point and nerve-ending. Atreus said something rather abrupt into his phone, set it down, and hauled her to him with impatient hands to kiss her breathless.

'A weekend isn't enough for me when it's followed by five days of celibacy,' he growled when he finally let her breathe again.

Lindy was thrilled by that admission. 'I suppose I could come up to London occasionally,' she began, eager to gain an entrance into that other part of his world which had so far been closed to her.

His jawline clenched. 'I like things the way they are. I'm free to concentrate on business during the week. We both have plenty of space.'

Her eyes dimmed. She didn't want that space, had never wanted that space, and only put up with his frequent unavailability in silence because it seemed to be what he expected from her. That belated admission shook her. Just when had she started fitting in with his wishes and ignoring her own? But what woman wanted her lover to see her as clingy? she asked herself defensively. Atreus might be her only source of experience, but she knew that a needy, demanding woman could make a man feel trapped.

Cursing the insecurity that Ben's outspoken criticism had roused in her, Lindy blanked out her anxious thoughts and rested back in the seemingly secure circle of Atreus's arms.

She loved him so much, and she had a whole weekend to luxuriate in. Was she about to let her lack of confidence spoil what they shared? She hadn't intended to fall for him—had thought intelligence would help her to hold back and protect herself from getting too attached to a man who was unlikely to stay with her. But there had been no protection from his innate charisma and high-voltage sexuality, or the clever brain that consistently intrigued and entertained her. She sank deeper and deeper into love every time she saw him. By the end of the first three months of their affair she had been a totally lost cause.

Atreus was suspicious of her sudden suggestion that she see him in London during the week. Where had that unfortunate idea come from? Had the one-time love of her life been muckraking again? Atreus wondered grimly, for he was already aware that Lindy's alleged friend had visited her that afternoon. Ben Halliwell was a thorn in Atreus's side, playing a waiting game and always ready to make trouble. Lindy was so impressionable, Atreus reflected ruefully, keeping her close while he smoothed a soothing hand down over her taut spine, recognising her mood of disquiet with growing annoyance. Perhaps it was time that he had a word with Halliwell and warned him off. Lindy, who thought the best of everyone and the least of herself, would never do it for him. Evidently it had not yet occurred to her that her old friend now wanted what he had so carelessly rejected at university, and Atreus was in no hurry to point out Ben's change of heart.

'I missed you,' she confided, only to regret the revealing admission as soon as the words left her lips.

His arms tightened round her. 'The week went very slowly,' he conceded, letting his mouth graze over hers and then return to part her lips with a sudden hungry urgency that sent the blood hurtling in a mad race through her veins. Her knees went weak, the tug of craving in her pelvis almost more than she could bear in silence. It had not taken him long to teach her that desire could be a cruel taskmaster, for while her brain teemed with troubled thoughts and fears, her body was only capable of craving the urgency of his. Lindy closed her eyes tight in frustration, fighting to restrain the intensity of her longing, hating the knowledge that she only ever felt really secure in bed with him. That was when she felt most needed and valued, and what did that say about their relationship?

'What's wrong?' Atreus murmured.

Lindy cursed his sixth sense where she was concerned, his unexpected ability to pick up on what she was feeling. 'Nothing.'

Although he was unimpressed by that obvious falsehood, Atreus was too hot for her to hold back. He lifted her up to him and plundered her mouth with a need and intensity that made her head spin and her arms wrap round his neck. 'Dinner will be late tonight,' he told her thickly.

It took only a clipped word from Atreus to restrain the dogs from following them upstairs. Her heart was pounding when he lowered her down in the bedroom.

Unzipped, her skirt shimmied down over her hips. Her sweater was tossed aside. With an earthy, masculine sound of satisfaction, Atreus appraised the succulent swell of her creamy breasts within her bra and lifted her onto the bed, pulling off her shoes in the process.

'By Friday lunchtime you are all I can think about,' he said huskily, long fingers briefly framing her face as he claimed another kiss and unclipped the bra to gain full access to her luscious curves.

'I thought we were going to talk,' Lindy framed breathlessly, fighting the erotic languor overcoming her and the paralysis of intelligent thought.

Having already shed his jacket and tie, and unbuttoned his shirt, Atreus sank down on the bed beside her with a groan of reluctant amusement. 'The state you've got me in, I'm not fit to talk, *mali mou*.'

Her fingers splaying across the bronzed hair-roughened contours of his superb torso, Lindy could not even think about what it was that she had believed she'd wanted to talk about as other, more basic promptings took charge of her. The burning and dampness gathering between her thighs ignited an almost unbearable yearning. His lips closed round a distended pink nipple while he skimmed off her panties. The very first touch of his mouth on her torturously tender flesh made her spine swoop off the mattress in a responsive arch. Her heart thundered and her legs trembled when he teased the sensitive bud below her mound. Very quickly she reached a saturation point of arousal, when waiting became an intolerable torment, and a pleading moan of protest parted her lips.

'You couldn't possibly want me yet as much as I want you, *glikia mou*,' Atreus countered with fierce conviction, strong hands anchoring to her hips to pull her under him.

But as her body braced for his possession he fell back from her with a stifled curse and reached for the protection he had almost forgotten 'We don't want any mistakes in the contraception department,' he told her, with a grim edge to his rich dark drawl. 'That would wreck everything.'

Even as he drove into her wildly receptive body that edge in his voice lingered in her memory and chilled her. She suppressed her disquiet and told herself he was only being sensible. He sank his hands below her hips and plunged deeper into her. The delirious pleasure his love-making always gave her had taken on an unfamiliar driven urgency. Excitement was cascading through her in a dazzling storm of white-hot sparks. He ground into her and she gasped, what remained of her control melted by the flames of excitement. His wildness thrilled her and the ecstatic climax she reached took her body's capacity for enjoyment to new heights. Even as the exquisite waves of erotic bliss consumed her, she was conscious that she was crying—and shocked by the fact.

'I must have been good, *glikia mou*,' Atreus breathed with irrepressible satisfaction, holding her locked in his arms and kissing her before falling still to stare down into her wide shaken eyes. 'We share the most unbelievable chemistry. No other woman has ever given me so much pleasure in bed.'

Lindy cherished the rare compliment that made her feel more important than any of her more glamorous predecessors, but her mind was still working back over what he had said only minutes earlier.

'Why did you say a mistake with contraception would wreck everything?'

Atreus tensed. 'Because it's the truth. I don't want a child with you.'

Inside herself, where he couldn't see, Lindy, who loved children and who had dreamt in whimsical moments of having his baby, recoiled from that cruel candour. Her dreams were suffering an axe attack. 'Don't you like children?' she asked.

An alarm bell was by now ringing in Atreus's handsome dark head, and his ebony brows drew together in a frown. She had never admitted it, but he knew how much she liked babies. Her friends sent her photos of their children and she gushed over them. Months ago he had reached the conclusion that the homeless dogs and cats she doted on were most probably substitutes for the babies she would one day have.

'A couple of paternity battles took the edge off any desire I might have to reproduce,' Atreus confided, opting for the truth.

'Paternity battles?' Lindy parroted in dismay. 'Are you saying that you already have a child?'

'None that I know of—a reality that some women have in the past chosen to regard as a challenge.'

Lindy collided with hard dark eyes and recognised that this reality still had the power to rouse his anger. 'In what way...a challenge?'

'A rich man is a lucrative target in the paternity stakes,' he extended with rich cynicism. 'Thankfully,

DNA tests proved that I was not the father of either child. But if I hadn't been able to prove that I would have been made financially responsible for those women and their offspring for many years to come.'

'Naturally you wouldn't want a child in those circumstances,' Lindy remarked with understanding.

'I will only want a child when I'm married.'

That declaration hung there like a second slap in the face; having already told her that he didn't want a child with her, or until he was married, he was effectively letting her know that she was not in the running as a potential wife. Had she thought she might be? Lindy eased away from him with the stealth of a mouse hoping to escape a cat ready to pounce. All of a sudden, lying in Atreus's arms no longer felt like a safe and proper harbour.

'And what sort of woman are you planning to marry?' she heard herself enquire. Having gone so far, she thought she might as well fully satisfy her curiosity.

Atreus skimmed a glance at her pale, pinched profile. 'I don't think we should stray any deeper into this conversation.'

'Atreus, it's clear that you've already thought in depth about your future and planned it all out,' Lindy pointed out in a tight, stretched tone he had never heard from her lips before. 'I think it's a reasonable question for me to ask after the length of time we've been together.'

Annoyed with her for opening the subject in the first place, and disregarding his every attempt to head her off at the pass, Atreus rested simmering golden eyes on her. 'I'll marry a wealthy woman from a background similar to my own.'

Until that deeply wounding moment Lindy had not appreciated just how far her dreams had gone. Nor had she grasped how painful it might be to realise that she had never had and could never have a chance of becoming a contender in the bridal stakes. She had neither wealth nor background to impress him with, and as such could never be anything other than a casual lover on his terms. In an abrupt movement, she snaked out of bed and began to get dressed in haste.

Ben's confident assurance that she wouldn't like the answer she got from Atreus was already reverberating like a death knell in her ears. Atreus didn't love her. Feeling as he did, how could he possibly care for her in any way? He didn't even see her as being in any way special. That she was poor, industrious and the child of working class uneducated parents would always hang on her like a badge of shame in his eyes.

'Lindy…what's going on here?' Atreus demanded in growing exasperation.

'Nothing's going on,' she fielded flatly. 'But I do I think that you should have been more frank with me months ago. I didn't realise that I was in a dead-end affair.'

'What's dead-end about it?' Atreus raked back at her with splintering impatience. 'It's not as though I'm planning to get married any time soon!'

'You're such a snob, too!' Lindy delivered her judgement with scorn. 'I haven't got money or a fancy family tree, so you've never taken me seriously…'

Atreus was a vibrant male presence as he lounged back against the tossed pillows, his wide shoulders and bronzed torso providing a startling contrast with the plain white bedlinen. 'Why would I take you seriously?' he cut in lethally. 'We've had a good time together. Snobbery didn't come into it. In fact, it's more likely that the differences between us made our relationship more entertaining…'

'Well, I'm not finding it entertaining at this moment!' Lindy launched back at him, her lush mouth biting off that last word as she forced her lips shut again. She didn't trust herself. She could not be sure what words might come out of her mouth next, and she was fighting to retain a little dignity. Even so, she was devastated. The man she loved was talking down to her in the shallowest and most patronising way, telling her that they'd simply had a good time together when her feelings for him ran so much deeper and stronger. She had entertained him because her differences had provided him with a welcome diversion.

Atreus was stunned by Lindy's behaviour. From the outset of their affair he had enjoyed the fact that she didn't throw tantrums or suffer from petulant moods. She was calm, laid-back in temperament and sensible, not given to making unreasonable demands or staging arguments. She only revealed her passion between the sheets, where he found her eagerness for him insanely, brilliantly sexy.

He sprang out of bed, crossed the floor and lifted her off her feet without further ado.

'What the heck do you think you're doing?' Lindy demanded furiously.

'I'm taking you back to bed in the hope that you regain your senses, *glikia mou*,' Atreus imparted in an aggrieved tone.

'I'm not getting back into bed with you!' Lindy hissed, swatting away his hands and sliding straight back off the bed again. 'We're finished!'

CHAPTER FIVE

WITH a groan of disbelief, Atreus lay back against the tumbled pillows and studied Lindy's flushed and resolute face. 'I don't expect this kind of silly melodrama from you. You find out that we're not heading to the altar and that's it? It's all over? Doesn't that strike you as more than a little unreasonable?'

'No. Every word you've said makes it clear that you don't respect me or take me seriously in any way!' Lindy argued vehemently. 'I'm just someone you sleep with at weekends and never take out in public, and that's not enough for me.'

Atreus sat up in a sudden movement, anger stamped into every angular line of his hard, handsome face. 'It's been more than enough to keep you happy all this time—and do I have to remind you that you're the one who did not want to be seen out with me in public?'

'I'm your mistress!' Lindy condemned with a shudder of disgust. 'Aren't I?'

'That's an old-fashioned label and I'm not an old-fashioned guy,' Atreus fired back at her, seeing just how welcome candour would be at that precise instant.

'Can't you even admit that that's what I am?' Lindy shouted, her hands coiling into tight fists as she fought to get a grip on her self-control again.

Atreus lodged scorching golden eyes full of censure on her. 'Okay, you're my mistress.'

Eyes welling with stinging tears of shame and hatred, Lindy stared at him. She wanted to throw things and scream. She had wanted him to deny that she was his mistress, because that title struck her as the final humiliation.

'But that doesn't mean that you're not an important part of my life,' Atreus delivered with measured cool. 'You are important to me.'

'For sex, amusement…a woman to spice up your country weekends who doesn't cause you any hassle,' she completed bitterly, her heart beating so fast and so loudly in her ears that she feared she might be on the edge of a panic attack, even though she had never had one before. But then she had never been in such pain. Pain that flailed her with self-loathing and anger and the most appalling sense of loss, for Atreus was so much a part of her life that she could barely muster the courage to even imagine a future without him.

His mistress—that was all she had ever been. All these months she had deceived herself with wishful thinking, imagining a deeper connection and assuming an equality that had never existed between them. A mistress: a woman who gave discreet sexual pleasure, stayed in the background of her lover's life and looked for nothing more than his approbation and financial support. No wonder he had been so determined to make her accept the car he had bought her, and no wonder he had refused her rent payments! After all, a mistress was supposed to be rewarded and even supported by her lover. That was the deal. Awkward questions such as she had just asked were not part of that deal.

'I do value you,' Atreus breathed in a raw undertone. 'I've never stayed with one woman as long as I have stayed with you.'

But Lindy had another angle entirely on the surprising longevity of their affair. Without challenging him with words of love, she had adored him, admired him and lived to please him. She had asked for nothing. Why would he have walked away from so convenient an arrangement? He said he valued her. But even when telling her that she was important to him he was careful to employ dispassionate words which promised nothing deep or lasting. The caution with which he spoke also warned her that Atreus Dionides had never had any doubts about her exact status and place in his life. A mistress was all she had ever been, and that she could ever have believed she might mean more to him now struck her as pathetic and laughable.

As the door thudded shut on her silent departure, Atreus ground out a roughened curse. What had got into Lindy? He would have sworn that he knew her inside out, but she was behaving like a stranger. Where had that temper come from? Where had those damnable questions come from? Out of the blue? Or was it Ben Halliwell he should be thanking for this denouement?

Atreus raked lean fingers through his tousled black hair, enraged by what had happened. He had been taken by surprise and he wasn't accustomed to that. How could she be so foolish? They were perfect together as they were. What was wrong with being his mistress? Hundreds of women would have killed to occupy her position. Labels and silly discussions about where they were going had never been necessary between them. She had never tried to subject him to such a conversation before. Why should she have done? He knew he made her happy and prided himself on that fact.

It cut both ways: she pleased him as well. When he needed to work she never voiced a word of objection; she would just go off to the animal sanctuary and put in a few hours there. Often he would end up looking for her. She was easy to be with, stubbornly independent, and well able to manage without him around. She had slotted into his schedule as though she had been tailor-made for the purpose.

But that did not empower her to make ridiculous demands and throw his generosity back in his teeth, and nor would he necessarily forgive her for those errors of judgement. Had she truly thought he might consider marrying her and having a family with her? Just as though he was some Joe Nobody instead of one of the richest men in the world, with a social pedigree in his Greek homeland that could be traced back several hundred years?

Was he so much a snob? When it came to matrimony, surely his family were entitled to have certain expectations of him? Hadn't his father's divorce, remarriage and subsequent loose lifestyle caused the Dionides family incessant grief and mortification? The family had had to pick up the pieces in the end: not his deluded father and his feckless mother, but his aunt and uncle, who had ultimately been landed with the task of raising him to adulthood. A responsible man did not marry out of his own order.

Atreus was as outraged with Lindy as he was frustrated by her departure. Just as quickly, however, he recalled his awareness at the outset of their arrangement that she had no idea of the rules he played by and was likely to be hurt. The logic was irrefutable: he should let her go now, close the book on their association.

Lindy had never known she had it in her to be as emotional as she was that night. Eyes dry, head held high, she had stalked back to the lodge on foot with her dogs, fury washing over her in heady bursts. But her anger with Atreus was no greater than her anger towards herself. Why on earth had she got involved with him? She couldn't sleep, she tossed and turned, fell into a doze a couple of times and then, wakening, instinctively looked for him and went through the whole ghastly drowning sense of loss all over again. Samson and Sausage got up on the bed and lay beside her, pushing their heads under her hand, nudging her with their warm bodies in an effort to respond to her misery.

Atreus would never have let the dogs into the bedroom, never mind onto the bed, she reflected numbly, seeking some reason to celebrate their break-up. But still more tears leaked from her sore eyes. It had happened so fast that she had had no time to prepare, and now her whole world seemed empty and without structure. She was used to going horse riding first thing on Saturday mornings. Atreus had taught her to ride and had tipped her out of bed soon after dawn every Saturday without fail. When he wasn't involved in business he was relentlessly active, with buckets of surplus energy that required a physical outlet. Her face burned as she recalled how available she had always been—as hot for him as he was for her. Shifting uneasily in her bed, she frowned as a bout of nausea made her tummy lurch, and a moment later she flung herself out of bed and raced full tilt for the bathroom.

Lindy was almost never sick, and she wondered if her emotional distress had somehow affected her digestive system. As she freshened up she accidentally brushed her breast with her arm and winced at the painful tenderness of her flesh. She knew that some women experienced sore breasts during the latter half of their menstrual cycle but she'd had a light period only a few days ago. Her momentary tension faded. Obviously her hormones were out of sync and her body was going haywire, doing things it had never done before. But at least she had no grounds to suspect that she might have fallen pregnant, she told herself in urgent consolation.

Early on in her relationship with Atreus Lindy had begun taking contraceptive pills, but side effects had forced her to come off them again and give responsibility for protection back to Atreus. He had never taken the smallest risk with her which, bearing in mind his feelings on that issue, she reckoned painfully was fortunate. He would surely give an ex-mistress who had become pregnant with his child short shrift. It was not hard to assume that, put in such a situation, he would prefer a termination to an actual birth—an approach which would ensure that there was no permanent damage inflicted on his precious aristocratic family tree. She was very, very thankful that she was not being faced with that particular challenge.

That weekend Atreus returned to his London life early, and he did not visit the following week. Whenever he thought of his country home, he thought of Lindy, a fact which infuriated him since he had never considered himself to be remotely sensitive or even imaginative. Regardless, his memory threw up images of Chantry in which she always featured, and the merest hint of the scent of lavender made him grit his teeth.

He remembered the melting taste of her ginger fudge shortcake and wondered if he was entering his second childhood. He remembered how terrified she had been when he'd put her on a horse, although nothing would have made her admit the fact. He remembered that she never said a bad word about anyone, and that when he was late or curt she said nothing but simply looked disappointed in him, which somehow made him more punctual and more polite. He woke in the night, his body aching for her, and reached for her to find she wasn't there.

He had never had a problem with anger. He had never regretted breaking up with a woman. After all there was always another dozen queuing to fill the space in his bed. Every woman was replaceable; this was a mantra he had believed in from an early age. But even though he plunged straight back into socialising, he discovered that his tastes had changed. He liked a woman to appreciate the value of a comfortable silence, one who ate without caring about calories, one who went out without fussing about her appearance, one who listened and responded with intelligence when he talked. And the less easy he found his search for a substitute the angrier and more frustrated he became.

The following Friday he was about to cancel his trip to Chantry again when it dawned on him that there was a solution to what ailed him.

He called his estate manager and freely admitted that he would like the tenant in The Lodge to relocate. He suggested that a substantial cash inducement be offered to bring about that desirable result. He travelled down to Chantry that afternoon.

He would not have looked in the direction of The Lodge at all, had he not noticed that Ben Halliwell's BMW was parked there. He frowned, still galled by the idea that this *agent provocateur* had contrived to escape unscathed from the trouble he had caused. Atreus opened the door of Chantry with a glum expression to discover the Georgian house horrendously quiet. There were no dogs to greet him with lolling pink tongues, shrill barks and frantic wagging tails…. Setting his even white teeth together, and reminding himself that he had never liked animals indoors, Atreus sat down to dine on the very best his French chef could offer. But the selection didn't include any ginger fudge shortcake.

* * *

That same afternoon, Lindy was grateful for the diversion of the evening wedding party she was to attend with Ben, although she was fairly sure that she wouldn't be eating anything at the supper. The stomach upset she had first suffered a couple of weeks earlier had since come back to haunt her on several occasions. Evidently she had caught a virus, and her body was finding it hard to shake it off. As such illnesses always ran their course, she saw no point in consulting her doctor. She'd put fresh linen on her own bed for Ben, having decided that it would be cruel to put someone as tall as him on a sofa for the night. She had had her hair done and had bought a misty-blue dress for the occasion. Ben was good company and she would enjoy herself.

Lindy was determined to cast off the awful sense of abandonment she had suffered in recent weeks. It was as if she and Atreus had never been together at all. No man had ever been more easily got rid of; he had not even tried to change her mind, which suggested that she had never been the slightest bit important to him. In time she would stop missing him, thinking about him all the time, crying herself to sleep. Some day, she told herself fiercely, she would be capable of saying, *Atreus…who?* and meaning it.

Ben could not conceal his satisfaction at having been right about Atreus when Lindy told him that the affair was over. Assuring her that time healed everything, and that she was far better off without her Greek lover, Ben promptly forgot the matter again while he got on with the important matter of socialising with the well-connected guests present at the wedding supper. Lindy

longed for the solace of her female friends, Elinor and
Alissa, believing that only another woman would understand what she was going through. She planned to phone
them and tell them what was happening very soon.

Resolute in his goal of getting through the weekend in
much the same way as he had always done, Atreus went
out riding the following morning. From a distance of a
hundred yards as he rode back across the park he saw
Ben Halliwell's car, still parked in the exact same
position as it had been the evening before. Halliwell had
spent the night. With Lindy.

A thunderbolt of primeval rage roared through
Atreus's powerful frame like a sudden all-encompassing storm. It was so potent that as he dug his knees into
the stallion to head for The Lodge he was not conscious
of any thought at all. Every atom of his anger and frustration had found a fitting focus at last.

Lindy had slept badly on the lumpy sofa. When the
doorbell sounded the dogs went bonkers, barking. She
rolled off the sofa, ignoring her feeling of nausea, and
was putting on her cotton wrap when Ben shouted
downstairs. 'Who the heck is that at this hour?'

'Haven't a clue,' she called back.

'It might be for me. Geoffrey Stillwood did say
something about inviting me out for a day's hunting,'
Ben reminded her. 'Not something I've tried before,
but I should show willing if the invite is issued by my
boss's father-in-law!'

Lindy's nose wrinkled at the thought of deer being
killed for sport. It had been a challenge for her to keep

her views to herself while she'd listened to that conversation the night before. Tightening the sash of her wrap, she opened the front door. Her eyes opened very wide at the sight of Dino, Atreus's black stallion, cropping the lawn. Atreus, sheathed in tight jodhpurs, polished boots and a black jerkin, was on her doorstep, and even his worst enemy would have been forced to admit that he looked drop-dead gorgeous in that get-up.

As Samson and Sausage charged out and careered round Atreus's feet in rapturous doggy welcome, stunning dark golden eyes lanced into her. 'It didn't take you very long to take another man into your bed,' Atreus condemned with seething scorn.

'I'll take care of this,' Ben announced from behind Lindy, pushing her to one side to gain the space to step out. Unshaven, and in jeans, boots and a sweater, it was obvious he had got up in a hurry.

'Do you think you can?' Atreus sent him a contemptuous look of challenge. 'I'm not in the habit of fighting over loose women.'

'There's not going to be any fighting,' Lindy assured him indignantly, only to fall silent, her jaw dropping and her lips framing a silent 'oh' of shock and horror when Ben took a swing at Atreus and struck him on the chin.

'Don't talk about Lindy like that!' Ben slung at the tall Greek, full blast.

'How unexpected—a City trader who can put his money where his mouth is!' With that sardonic quip, Atreus punched Ben so hard that the blond man hit the ground like a fallen tree.

Thirty seconds later, as a groaning Ben began clambering shakily upright for another bout, Lindy stepped between the two men and voiced outraged words of reproof. 'No! Stop it right now!'

'Stay out of this,' Atreus urged, powerful arms closing round Lindy from behind to lift her bodily out of his path and set her out of harm's way.

'Don't you dare tell me to stay out of it!' Lindy raked back furiously at him, just as the sound of a perky mobile phone ring-tone cut through the tense atmosphere.

Atreus strode back to attack just as Ben dug out his phone and answered it, raising a hand palm first to Atreus in a ludicrous gesture that urged his Greek opponent to give him a moment's breathing space.

'Geoff? Hello, Geoff… No, of course it's not too early for me,' Ben was saying in a smarmy tone while checking his watch. 'I would love to… When? Right, I'll be there as soon as I can.'

Wearing a newly purposeful expression, Ben swung round to Lindy in haste. 'Where's the nearest country clothing shop?'

Somewhat taken aback by that sudden request, Lindy obliged with the information. Ben then raced back indoors to collect his stuff, all desire to continue his fight with Atreus in her defence evidently forgotten in his excitement at being invited out on a shoot by a member of the local gentry.

Atreus interpreted the expression of blank disbelief on Lindy's face. 'Financial traders have a reputation for being cold-blooded,' he remarked. 'No Greek male would ever stop to take a phone call in the middle of a fight.'

'If that's the best you can say for yourself it's not a

lot!' Lindy fired back, unimpressed. 'How dare you come here and suggest that I sleep around?'

Atreus lifted a broad shoulder in a slow mocking shrug, an ebony brow lifting. 'I'm not cold-blooded. I didn't think you'd get over me so quickly.'

Taken aback by the cruel comment that went too close to the bone for comfort, Lindy reddened but stayed silent on the score that she no longer owed him any explanations. She watched him take the lead rope hanging from the iron ring at the corner of the house and approach the black stallion. 'What on earth are you doing?' she asked.

'What do you think?'

Lindy didn't know what to say, because sensitivity made her shrink from mentioning past intimacies. On several occasions when they had been out riding they had tied up the horses outside The Lodge and fallen laughing and breathless into her bed below the eaves, hungry to sate the desire that rarely left them. She did not want to recall those painfully sweet memories which had evidently meant so much more to her than to him.

Ben brushed by her with a muffled apology and a hasty promise to ring during the following week. It was as if his angry conflict with Atreus had never happened. She wondered if Atreus could really believe that she had slept with Ben. Did that mean that he had never trusted her friendship with the other man? Or was Atreus simply being insulting because she had dumped him?

When Atreus was sure that he had tethered Dino securely, he strolled back to Lindy, six foot three inches of devastatingly handsome masculinity. Involuntarily, she found herself staring, helplessly feasting her starved eyes on him. Clad in riding gear, Atreus was every woman's fantasy. In close-fitting breeches and boots, he possessed a male beauty and sleek grace of movement that knocked her sideways. Desire infiltrated Lindy in a heady surge, and her mouth ran dry and her knees went wobbly.

'Why are you tying up Dino?'

Hot golden eyes slammed into hers and she felt the burn of that sexual smoulder low in her pelvis. He meshed one hand into her tumbled brown mane, tipping her head back so that his mouth could come down hard on hers. As he backed her indoors her senses swam and her heartbeat raced. Shock and satisfaction tore her composure apart. 'We can't…'

Atreus kicked the front door shut behind him and pressed her back against the panelled wall of the hall. 'Tell me no,' he challenged.

But the sensual taste of him was on her lips again, and like a shameful addict she could not resist her craving. Just one kiss, she told herself, bargaining with her conscience. Just one more kiss, she thought a split second later, while he crushed her against the wall and acquainted her with every muscular line of his lean, powerful body. He plundered her soft mouth, nibbling, stroking and delving into the sensitive interior until he had sent her temperature rocketing to a crazy height. She rejoiced in the hard muscular heat of him, all logic overpowered by his passionate urgency and the rigid swell of his erection against her.

Lean hands glided upward, pushing her wrap and nightdress out of his path even while she tensed and trembled. A tight knot of desire had formed inside her and she tried to fight it—even when a little voice in her head dared to whisper that Atreus had seemed to be jealous of Ben. Could he have missed her so much that he was now trying to get her back? In the state she was in, giving credence to such thoughts was fatal.

Atreus nudged her legs apart to probe the slick honeyed folds between her thighs. Beneath his ministrations she moaned and leant back against the wall for support. Once he had centred his attentions on the tender swollen bud below the soft curls on her mound tingling ripples of seductive delight controlled her, and no thought, no word or warning could have returned her to solid earth again. She stretched up on tiptoes to savour the driving hunger of his sensual mouth again.

Atreus closed both arms round her and swept her off her feet. Sexual need had never driven him with such ferocity. He felt like a runaway train, hurtling down a mountain, and it was an amazingly exhilarating experience. He carried her up the stairs into the bedroom and tumbled her down on the rumpled bedding, pushing up the wrap and the nightdress so that he could savour her voluptuous curves to the full.

A soundless sigh of appreciation escaped him as his lustful gaze locked to the glorious bounty of her breasts. He came down on the bed to suckle the tantalisingly distended pink nipples and mould the soft creamy fullness of her flesh with deep satisfaction. Preoccupied as he was with those distractions, it took effort for him to free a hand and withdraw a condom from his pocket, to unsnap his jodhpurs, wrenching down the zip with unhidden impatience.

Lindy was on a high of trembling expectation. Two of the things she most loved about Atreus were his unpredictability and his unashamed passion for her body. She saw his urgency as a compliment which only matched her own for him. Before he could don protection she pushed herself up and pleasured his straining sex with her tongue.

'No,' he ground out in a voice of aching gratification. 'You'll make me come, *mali mou*.'

Empowered by the realisation that he was trembling with eagerness, Lindy fell back again. He gripped her hips and arched her back, sinking with a driven groan into her lush opening in a long, deep thrust. A frenzy of excitement gripped her as he lifted her up to receive his every stroke. The surge and ebb of his body into hers was primal and pagan, and she writhed in abandonment beneath that fierce onslaught of pleasure and possession. Nothing had ever been wilder or more satisfying, and the end came for them both in an intense climax that made his magnificent length shudder over her.

Frantic confusion assailed Lindy in the aftermath of their lovemaking, for she had no script to follow and no idea what she had been thinking of when she'd allowed things to go so far. Her overwhelming hunger for him had been satisfied but at what cost? she wondered in painful mortification.

Atreus emerged from the same experience shell-shocked. He was unnerved by the acknowledgement that he had been out of control for the first time in his life. His mood was not improved when his attention fell on the man's black bow tie lying on the carpet by the bed. Halliwell's tie…obviously. Distaste filled Atreus, and his reaction was instantaneous. He pulled away from Lindy and sprang off the bed to stride into the bathroom next door.

In the silence, Lindy tugged down her disarranged clothing and shuddered at what she had allowed to happen. He had neither held her nor kissed her afterwards; everything had changed between them; everything was different. She slid off the bed on nerveless legs, her body still quivering from the rampant impact of his and the excruciatingly tender state of it in the aftermath of his devouring passion. Like a woman running from the scene of a crime, she sped downstairs.

Atreus splashed his face and dried it. He was seething with anger and a daunting sense of bewilderment. He had not wanted sex since he'd left her. But he never, ever went back to a woman. When it was over, it was over. He had always walked away from relationships before they could reach the messy stage, but what had just occurred had been messy to say the very least. Brilliant, fantastic sex, he conceded bitterly, but inappropriate— particularly when she had wasted no time in inviting another man into her bed.

He had wanted Lindy again only because she was familiar, he decided grimly. But since when had he found the familiar so appealing? So sexually irresistible? Had he grown past the age where he wanted a constant parade of variety in the bedroom? Was he now ready for a more settled lifestyle? Perhaps it was time for him to begin looking out for a wife rather than another lover. That bold step forward in thought, away from Lindy and on to a more traditional horizon, pleased Atreus and steadied his resolve.

'I'm sorry,' Atreus breathed coldly, when he found Lindy waiting for him in the living room.

'I'm not sure I understand what you're apologising for,' Lindy admitted stiltedly, frantically avoiding direct eye contact. She sensed his detachment and it chilled her that he could switch off again so easily.

'What we had is over and done with,' Atreus declared without hesitation. 'I shouldn't be here when I don't want you back.'

Lindy marvelled that she managed to continue breathing through the savage sense of rejection that that blunt declaration had dealt her. He had dragged her off to bed and made passionate love to her but it had meant absolutely nothing to him. Indeed, his hostile attitude made it clear that he very much regretted their renewed intimacy.

'You know…' Lindy began hesitantly, despising herself in advance for the plea of innocence she was about to make without any encouragement from him. 'I didn't sleep with Ben. I slept down here on the sofa.'

Against his own volition Atreus directed grim dark eyes at the sofa and the bedding still lying on it in an untidy heap. He looked away again, refusing to dwell on what she had said, refusing the suggestion that the information could have any power to influence him. 'It doesn't matter. You're not my business any more,' he said drily. 'I crossed boundaries I had no right to cross today. It won't happen again.'

Watching Atreus leave, Lindy felt as if someone was squeezing her heart dry of blood. She couldn't breathe for the pain of it. She watched him ride off from the window and then drew back to cover her tear-wet face with trembling hands. She felt sick again, and she wanted to bang her head against the wall to hurt herself—because she felt that she deserved to be punished for the way she had let herself down. How could she have been so foolish as to go to bed with him again? Particularly after he had suggested she was a loose woman? Where was her self-respect? She and Atreus had never been on a level playing field. It seemed that his convenient affair had been her heartbreak…

CHAPTER SIX

FORTY-EIGHT hours later, Lindy was doggedly engaged in packing orders for her customers, in preparation for heading off to the post office, when the doorbell rang. She had to sign for the envelope the postman gave her, and she tore it open with a frown.

It was a notice to quit The Lodge for non-payment of rent, and it requested that she move out within two months. Lindy's eyes were wide with disbelief. In recent months she had received a couple of letters pointing out that she owed the Chantry estate rent arrears. When the second letter had arrived she had gone to the estate office in person, to point out that she had paid the rent but that it had been continually repaid into her account. The estate manager had apologised, explained that it was a computer-generated letter and said that she should just ignore it. He had turned down her offer to write a cheque to cover the rent arrears then and there, and had said something about that not being Mr Dionides's wish. Advising her to ignore any similar letters that she received, he had shown her to the door. When she'd mentioned the matter to Atreus, it had been evident he already knew about it. He had told her not to worry about an oversight made by a new member of staff and that the problem would not arise again.

Now those recollections could only send a shiver down Lindy's tense spine. She thought it very probable that Atreus would prefer her to vacate The Lodge now that their affair was over. Had he sunk low enough to use those supposed rent arrears as an excuse to evict her?

Truly taken aback by that suspicion, Lindy sat down to reread the letter, which was written in clear language and even gave the final date by which she was to vacate the premises. It also said that if she was prepared to leave ahead of that date her rent arrears would be reduced accordingly. It was that last point which confirmed Lindy's sinking suspicion that Atreus simply wanted her off his country estate as soon as possible, and that realisation was just another kick in the teeth.

Indeed, Lindy felt utterly overwhelmed by that final blow, which struck at the very base of her security. She knew that she ought to consult a solicitor, but she also knew just how pricey legal assistance could be. If she was going to be forced to move out she would need every penny she had to secure new accommodation and relocate. And if Atreus was so determined to get rid of her, did she really want to fight to stay? Or to run the risk of having her affair with Atreus alluded to within the public arena of the County Court? After all, her relationship with Atreus and his double-dealing with her rental payments would be central to any defence she attempted to mount. She shuddered at the prospect, but the concept of staying on at The Lodge when her presence there was evidently so very unwelcome was no more appealing.

She loved her compact home, and it provided a perfect base for her business. She had enough land to grow lavender and roses, and the cellar was ideal for the equipment required for pot pourri preparation and candle-making, as well as for the storage and packing of her products. Where else would she find such a base at an affordable rent? It would also be a rare rental property that allowed both the running of a business and the keeping of pets. She fondled Sausage's fluffy ears while the tears trickled down her cheeks. As if that frightening letter were not enough, she also felt sick once more. What a louse Atreus was, and what a rotten, selfish, ruthless rat he was proving to be! No, he had not been joking all those months ago when he had warned her that the creed of the gentleman was long dead. Now that he had decided he no longer wanted her around, Atreus wanted to throw her off his country estate like so much rubbish!

It was in that wretched mood that Lindy phoned her friend Elinor. This time Lindy was too upset to hold anything back, and the whole story came tumbling out, laced with tears and regrets and disbelief that anyone she loved could be treating her so badly. Elinor, who was now the epitome of a very sedate royal princess, residing in Quaram, her husband's country, said some very blunt and unprincesslike things about Atreus, while adding that Lindy was to stop worrying because she already had the perfect solution in mind. Lindy came off the phone feeling reassured and less fearful, although she could not really have said why since she could not see what Elinor could realistically do to help from thousands of miles away.

But that same evening, her other close friend Alissa phoned, and explained that Elinor had consulted her. Alissa immediately offered Lindy the use of a vacant cottage on the country estate which her husband, Sergei Antonovich, had recently bought as a home for his family in the UK.

'I can't let you do that,' Lindy told Alissa ruefully.

'Of course you can. It would be wonderful to be able to see you more often. Did I mention that it's much closer to London as well? And much nearer Elinor's place too. Sergei says that good tenants are really hard to find these days and you'd be very welcome, dogs included. Say yes, Lindy, please,' Alissa pleaded. 'I'm pregnant again, and I would love the company when Sergei's away on business.'

Lindy's eyes stung with tears at the warmth of that request. Her hormones seemed to be operating on a supercharged level, for her emotions were seesawing all over the place and tears flowed more readily to her eyes than they ever had before. It was that acknowledgement which made her decide that possibly she ought to consult the doctor, in case there was something more serious wrong with her than the persistent tummy bug that had not stopped troubling her.

In bed that night she burned with so much anger against Atreus that she could not sleep. He might be about to get his wish to see her move off his exclusive turf, but she wanted him to know what she thought of his despicable methods for achieving his own ends. In the darkness she sat up and put on the light to reset her alarm clock. Tomorrow, she decided, she would catch the train to London in order to see Atreus one more time, before she wiped him out of her mind and her heart for ever!

Atreus frowned when he learned that Lindy was waiting outside his office.

What was her game? What could have persuaded her to come all the way to London to see him? He did not want a scene caused at his place of work. Dionides Shipping was a conservative environment, and Atreus had always kept his private life rigidly separate from his working day. His even white teeth clenching, he caught a glimpse of the wary way his PA was regarding him—an unwelcome reminder that for the past few weeks Atreus had been struggling to control a disturbing tendency to explode into anger in a way that was far from being the norm for him.

Lush black lashes screened Atreus's brilliant dark eyes and concealed his bewilderment at his own behaviour. When, he wondered in frustration, could he expect to return to feeling like himself again? Whatever, he had no choice but to see Lindy and draw a line under that unfortunate affair. He was already seeing how an unconventional relationship with someone who did not belong to his world could have unexpected and destructive repercussions. It was a lesson his foolish father had never learned, and Atreus had no intention of following in his late parent's footsteps.

Lindy was trembling when she walked into Atreus's big, imposing office. She had got out of bed at dawn to ensure she was well groomed, because there could be no satisfaction in suspecting that he might be looking at her and marvelling at how he had ever got involved with her in the first place. With her hair tamed into a blade-straight fall and a light application of make-up, wearing a burgundy blouse teamed with a pencil skirt and a smart knitted jacket, she felt strong enough to confront him.

Atreus sprang upright, his tall, powerful physique sheathed in a perfectly tailored black pinstripe business suit. He studied her, immediately aware of the impact of her soft pink-glossed mouth, the even more tempting swell of her full breasts below her shirt and the violin curve of her hips. His reaction to her appeal was instant and earthy, and it infuriated him to have so little control over his libido. There was a decided touch of sarcasm in his tone when he asked coolly, 'How may I help you?'

And, that fast, Lindy wanted to hit him. There he stood, looking absolutely gorgeous the way he always did, and how dared he address her as if she was an importunate stranger? How dared he look down on her from his intimidating height with that hateful aloof expression when it was only days since they had made love? That, it seemed, was an injudicious recollection, for her eyes stung hotly when she finally acknowledged that they had not made love. It took two people to make love. Atreus had only been having sex: casual, uncommitted, very physical sex.

Lindy walked right to the edge of his desk and

slapped the Notice to Quit she had received the day before down in front of him. 'I wanted to hand this back to you personally,' she informed him with gutsy calm, her dark brown hair flipping back like heavy silk from her flushed face, her blue eyes very bright. 'I did nothing to deserve this kind of treatment. If I'd known eighteen months ago what I know about you now, we would never have had a relationship. You're a man without conscience and a horrible bully!'

Astonished by that censorious attack, Atreus was studying the document she had received. 'I did not authorise this!' he proclaimed in angry rebuttal.

'Didn't you? But you do want me off your estate, don't you?' Lindy noted the faint hint of colour that accentuated his wonderful cheekbones. 'What gives you the right to disrupt my whole life? Where did you think I was going to move to on my income, with two dogs and a business to house as well as myself?' A scornful laugh fell from her lips. 'Of course—the point is that you didn't care.'

'I have no intention of evicting you for non-payment of rent,' Atreus ground out in an accented drawl that was roughened with scantily controlled rage. 'In the circumstances that is a ridiculous charge—and someone will lose their job over this...'

'Your estate manager, who has four kids and another on the way?' Lindy fired back at him in unconcealed disgust. 'Atreus, you made this situation. Don't make someone else pay the price for it going wrong. He's an employee who is clearly aware that you want me to leave the estate.'

Atreus sent her a fierce appraisal. 'I was willing to offer you generous financial compensation for simply considering the prospect of moving.'

'So your estate manager probably thought he would win brownie points with you by getting rid of me on the cheap.' Lindy shrugged, the generous curve of her lips compressing to a thin line. 'That doesn't free you of the responsibility for the distress and inconvenience that I have been caused.'

Irate at finding himself in the position of being reproved for his behaviour, Atreus held up two hands to still the flood of condemnation flowing from her. 'You're not listening to me. I deeply regret any distress that has been caused, but this was not a mistake of my making.'

Lindy shook her head unimpressed. 'You don't think so? You're a ruthless bastard, Atreus. You have a God-given belief in your right to put your wishes above everyone else's, no matter how selfish or wrong you are in principle. Oh, yes, that's one more thing you lack—principles…'

Atreus stared back at her with chilling intensity. 'You are here to strike back at me because I walked out on you at the weekend?'

It was Lindy's turn to get mad. 'No, I am not!' she protested, her eyes brightening with fury. 'I just wanted you to know what I think of you, because I won't agree to see you or speak to you again if you get down on your knees and beg!'

'Message received, but the scenario you suggest is highly unlikely to happen,' Atreus derided, soft as silk. 'However, you may disregard this foolish document and make your own decision about where you live and do business without any fear of interference from me or from any of my employees.'

'It's too late for that. Ironically, you're going to get what you want—I'm moving out just as soon as it can be arranged,' Lindy admitted tightly. 'I'm lucky that I have some real friends, who don't feel the need to use the power of their wealth and position to persecute people who dare to annoy them!'

His lean, darkly handsome features set hard, Atreus strode round his desk. 'What a drama queen you can be!' he condemned. 'How can you possibly accuse me of persecuting you?'

Lindy was recalling his pronounced air of detachment when she had first entered his office, and the turmoil of her teeming thoughts suddenly fixed on the recognition of one deeply unsettling and wounding fact. 'I can see now that you were never comfortable with being involved with me. I didn't fit, I didn't match your high expectations, and I was never good enough in your eyes to be anything other than a mistress. I will never forgive you for the way you have treated me.'

An ebony brow quirked. 'I'd like to get back to work now…if you're finished?'

And all the way back home on the train his unemotional parting words haunted Lindy. How could she still be so in love with a man like that? And how could he be so horribly, hatefully indifferent to her? But she had no regrets about having paid him a visit. This time he knew how she felt, and she could only hope that something of what she had said stayed with him.

The following day Lindy went to see her doctor. She was sent to the nurse for tests and sat around afterwards in the waiting room, feeling dreadfully tired and nauseous again even though she had been sick earlier that morning.

When she was called back in the doctor had a shock in store for her.

'You're pregnant,' she was told.

Her response to the doctor was that it was totally impossible! The doctor looked weary, as though he had heard that claim before, and asked to examine her while making enquiries as to her menstrual cycle. It was true that she'd felt her system was a little out of kilter, she acknowledged, but she argued that no risks at all had been taken. The doctor cheerfully pointed out that certain unmistakable changes were already taking place in her body, and informed her that it was possible to have an unusually light period in the early stages of conception, before the pregnancy hormones fully kicked in. By the time he had told her that condoms could have up to a twelve percent failure rate in the first year of use, she was beginning to sink into the shock of acceptance.

She drove home with care, struggling to adapt to the reality that she and Atreus had quarrelled bitterly and broken up while all the time a tiny new life was growing inside her womb. Her sense of wonder and warmth towards that little being was soon disrupted by less pleasant feelings. Atreus didn't want her and he would certainly not want her baby. The knowledge chilled her, but Atreus had been brutally frank on the subject of children. He would only consider having a family when he was married—to a suitably rich Greek woman.

Alissa rang to chat at length about her plans for Lindy's move, and midway through the conversation Lindy blurted out that she too was expecting a child.

'My goodness! Have you told Atreus?'

Lindy explained in some detail why nothing would persuade her to organise such a ghastly confrontation. 'I couldn't face it—not knowing that he doesn't want the baby or me.'

'The sooner you move the better,' her friend commented soothingly. 'Don't worry about it. You don't need Atreus Dionides any more.'

Lying in her bed that night, Lindy tried to convince herself of the same fact, drumming up a recollection of Atreus's every masculine flaw and telling herself that she would be a much happier person without him. Unfortunately she could only remember how happy she had been while she was with him, even if that happiness had been built on shaky foundations. But she knew she was a survivor and that Atreus had been a bad choice, different as he was in every way from her.

That acknowledgement made and accepted, Lindy splayed her fingers protectively over her slightly rounded tummy and allowed herself to think of how comforting it would be to see Elinor and Alissa on a more regular basis. She wanted her baby. She wanted her baby very much, even though she was worried sick about how she would manage to raise a child alone, without a father's support.

CHAPTER SEVEN

'YOU'RE selling a country fantasy along with your products,' Alissa pointed out, rearranging the skirt of Lindy's floral sundress on the summer swing seat on which she was reclining, with a pretty basket of freshly cut lavender by her side. 'Your customers want to believe you are living that fantasy.'

Before the hovering photographer could zoom in to take another photo of her Lindy pushed herself up heavily on her elbows, gasping at the effort it took to rise from a supine position since she had lost the ability to bend in the middle. The baby bump had taken over, and even a pretty dress and professional make-up couldn't make her feel attractive when the solid mound of her pregnant tummy reminded her of a Himalayan peak.

It had never occurred to her that her accidental pregnancy might coincide with one of the hardest working periods of her life. But that was how it had turned out in the four months that had passed since she had left the Chantry estate. Having taken up residence in an idyllic and recently renovated thatched cottage, complete with a couple of acres of ground, Lindy had begun to calculate how she could make her business more lucrative and therefore more secure for her child's sake. Idle conversations on that score with Atreus had long ago ensured that she knew exactly where she was going wrong in her pursuit of profit. Atreus had told her she needed an upmarket catalogue and fancier packaging, and she had now followed through on that useful advice. Alissa's husband, Sergei, had insisted that even the smallest business required publicity to sell its products, hence the interview she had given earlier that day, and the photographer now snapping fluffy shots of her, the dogs and the beautiful garden.

There was no fantasy in her world now, Lindy conceded ruefully. It had taken a lot of concealer to hide the big dark shadows below her eyes from sleepless nights. In the months since they had parted Atreus had been seen out and about with an ever-changing collection of women, and rarely with the same one twice. Recently, however, that had changed. Just weeks back Atreus had been photographed dining out with an extremely eligible Greek heiress, who…yes…naturally was tiny and very beautiful. The gossip columnists had got very excited and had wasted little time in forecasting wedding bells for so well-matched a pair.

Lindy had honestly believed she was fully recovered from Atreus until Alissa had passed her a glossy magazine containing an article that made it very clear, to Lindy at least that, Atreus was indeed thinking of marrying Krista Perris. Lindy had been very brave about the news while she had an audience, but had wept buckets once she was alone. It had hurt so much to see Krista and Atreus pictured together in a full colour spread in that magazine. Krista, heiress to another shipping fortune, was so patently perfect for him in every way. Elinor's husband, Prince Jasim, had urged Lindy to waste no more time in getting in touch with Atreus and telling him that she was pregnant, and Sergei had even offered to tell Atreus personally—an offer Lindy had hastily declined, reckoning that the Russian billionaire would pull few punches at such a meeting.

In a move that had convinced Lindy that Atreus was serious about Krista, Atreus had taken Krista home to meet his family. The picture of Atreus and his beautiful petite heiress heading into a party being thrown by his relatives had hurt Lindy the most. After all, it was an honour that he had never considered Lindy worthy of receiving. There was no way that Lindy wanted to pop up right now, with a big pregnant tummy, to break news that would scandalise the Dionides and the Perris families, appal Atreus and devastate his bride-to-be.

Lindy was far too proud and independent to stage such a tasteless denouement. She was getting by fine without Atreus and would continue to do so. To be happy at the same time was expecting too much of herself. As far as possible she was concentrating on her business and the child she carried, and she never, ever consciously allowed herself to think about Atreus Dionides. With the single exception of the baby, Atreus had been a mistake—the biggest mistake she had ever made.

* * *

Woken from her sleep at an unusually early hour for a Sunday morning, Lindy sat staring aghast at the double-page spread in the tabloid newspaper. It was luridly entitled 'Tycoon's Secret Mistress and Child'.

'This is my worst nightmare!' she gasped, stricken, while she studied the photo of her that appeared in the catalogue which innocently advertised her business. 'How on earth did they get hold of this stuff?'

Alissa, who had seated herself at the foot of the bed, groaned. 'It looks like someone who knew you when you were living on the Chantry House estate put two and two together and decided to talk to the press—probably for a pay-off.'

Even before she'd read the accompanying text Lindy had broken out in a cold sweat. But when she digested an account of her relationship with Atreus in which she was described as a 'weekend mistress', and their sudden split was mentioned, together with hints that rumours of her pregnancy had circulated even before her departure from Chantry, her blood boiled with angry mortification. It was even more humiliating to see herself depicted side by side with a gorgeous picture of the ultimate size-zero hottie and heiress Krista Perris.

Her mobile phone started buzzing like an angry wasp on the bedside table, and after a moment of hesitation she snatched it up. Shock paralysed her when she heard Atreus's rich, dark accented drawl.

'Have you seen the article in the *Sunday Voice*?' Atreus enquired with freezing bite.

'Er…yes.'

'I'm flying down to see you to deal with this. I'll be with you in just over an hour.'

'I don't want you to come here—to my home—I really don't want to talk to you, either!' Lindy argued vehemently.

'I didn't offer you a choice,' Atreus asserted, and the phone line went dead as he hung up on her.

Alissa frowned when Lindy informed her of Atreus's plans. 'It may not be what you want, but you do need to sort things out with him, Lindy.'

'Why?' Lindy manoeuvred her heavy body out of her comfortable bed and turned angry blue eyes full of enquiry on her friend. 'After the way he behaved, I don't owe him anything. And you and Elinor agreed with me!'

'In the heat of the moment. I hate to admit it, but it was Jasim who made me stop and think. He's always so level-headed. Even if you don't feel you have a claim on Atreus Dionides, your baby does, and it's much wiser to get this out into the open now, rather than try to keep it a secret. On the face of it, the press have done that for you.'

Trembling with alarm, and a shameful sense of anti-cipation at the prospect of seeing Atreus again, Lindy breathed in deeply to steady herself. It had not yet occurred to her to think of her unborn child as an indi-vidual, with the right to seek an independent relation-ship with Atreus at some point in the future. Alissa's reminder had sobered Lindy, however, and forced her to acknowledge how complicated the issue of her child's paternity would become if she did not deal honestly with it in the present.

'There are reporters waiting out on the main road,'

Alissa told her. 'If you want to go out, I'd advise using the farm lane.'

'Thanks for the warning. I need a shower.' Lindy sighed, and headed in the direction of the bathroom.

'I'll stay a minute and pick out something for you to wear.'

'Where are the children?' Lindy was belatedly noticing the absence of Alissa and Sergei's lively toddler, Evelina, and their six-week-old baby boy, Alek.

'I left them with Sergei.'

Having witnessed Sergei in the role of childcarer when Alissa was recovering from giving birth to their son and their nanny had fallen ill, Lindy was surprised. Before Lindy had taken charge Sergei had tried to hand his newborn son a bottle, and had given Evelina a packet of biscuits instead of a meal.

'He has to learn how to handle them some time, and he assured me he would manage fine,' Alissa quipped, with the smile of a woman who liked to see her husband occasionally faced with the challenges of childcare.

Lindy ignored the pretty feminine outfit which Alissa had selected for her to wear and went for an embroidered black skirt and a black camisole top, both of which she was convinced minimised the size of her stomach. By the time she heard the noisy clatter of a helicopter approaching she was extremely tense. She let the dogs out, not wanting the fuss of their greeting Atreus indoors.

The helicopter bore a large scarlet Dionides logo, and it landed in the paddock next to her cottage. From upstairs, her heart beating very fast, she watched

Atreus's bodyguards emerge first and check the surrounding area before their employer appeared. The dogs circumvented the efforts of the bodyguards to head them off and hurled themselves at Atreus with joyful jumping abandon. No doubt he would be a little less immaculate than he usually was when he finally fought free and reached her doorstep, Lindy reflected, without even a small stab of conscience. She hated him, she totally and absolutely hated the man she had once loved because of the power he still had to hurt her.

In the act of brushing his suit free of dog hairs and muddy pawprints, Atreus saw Lindy in the doorway, blue eyes violet-bright and the summer sunlight picking up the sheen of her chestnut-coloured hair, which had grown in length since he'd last seen her and now fell well past her shoulders. Bitter icy-cold anger engulfed him, because he had always trusted her and had never dreamt that she might pull such a stunt on him.

'If we had to see each other I would rather it hadn't been here. This is my home,' Lindy told him with quiet dignity. 'And you're spoiling my Sunday. You're going to make me late for church.'

Atreus was distracted by her concluding comment, snatched back to the weekends when he had regarded keeping her in bed with him rather than rushing off to church as the ultimate challenge.

'Who sold the story to the *Sunday Voice*?' he queried, before he had even entered the cottage.

His lean bronzed features were cool and grim, but he could not conceal the hot angry gold of his arrogant gaze. He was still the most beautiful man she had ever seen, and the admission annoyed her—for she felt that a truly intelligent woman would by now be indifferent to his vibrant dark good-looks.

'How would I know?' Lindy riposted. 'Lots of people knew about us in the village, even though they said nothing to my face. Everybody on the estate knew as well. We weren't exactly the world's biggest secret.'

'So, you're saying that *you* didn't sell it?' Atreus caught a sideways glimpse of her altered shape and stared at the fecund swell of her stomach with frowning force. There was certainly no doubt that she was pregnant.

Shifting uncomfortably beneath that stare, Lindy shot him a furious glance. 'No, indeed I did not. I'm not short of money, and I wouldn't sell details of my private life even if I was!'

Atreus was treating the elegant modern fittings of the living room to a curious appraisal. 'This seems to be a comfortable house.'

'It is. Alissa oversaw the renovation project for all the buildings on the estate, and she never does anything by halves,' she advanced. 'If you've come all the way here to accuse me of giving the press that story, I can assure you that you're barking up the wrong tree. I had nothing to gain and everything to lose from that article appearing in print because I value my privacy.'

Razor-sharp dark golden eyes scanned her angry resentful expression. 'I didn't come here to argue with you.'

'No?' Elevating a brow and standing her ground, Lindy looked unimpressed by that claim.

'No,' Atreus framed flatly. 'But I am very angry that

such an outrageous account of our relationship has been published and I intend to sue.'

'Good for you,' Lindy pronounced, tongue in cheek. 'No doubt you'll win, and six months from now, when everyone has long since forgotten the original article, the newspaper will print a retraction low down on some boring page where virtually no one will even notice it or read it. Is it really worth all that hassle?'

Her mockery made his black brows draw together. 'It's not quite that simple. My family in Greece will be very much shocked by that item…' He cloaked his stunning eyes with dense black lashes. 'You may not be aware of it, but I have been thinking of getting engaged…'

Lindy wrinkled her nose. 'Too much information, Atreus,' she said, very drily.

Atreus threw back his wide powerful shoulders as if he was bracing himself to continue. 'What I intended to say, if you had not interrupted me, is that this story is a source of embarrassment for Krista, the woman I'm currently seeing, and to her family and friends as well. We are not the only people affected by what appeared in the newspaper today.'

Lindy was feeling sick with tension, and listening to Atreus talk about the effect of that article on Krista only made her feel worse than ever. Had he ever cared about her that way? For even a moment? Had he even thought of how performing this knight on a white horse act on Krista's behalf might make Lindy feel? But then why should he think or even care now? His indifference was like a knife twisting inside her, and she was defenceless against the pain of it.

She shook her head, the shiny strands of rich brown hair rippling across her slim shoulders. 'I really don't know what you're doing here.'

'I want you to agree to make a statement that the child you are carrying is not mine. Just to set the record straight for us all,' Atreus completed, smooth as silk. 'I have brought one of my company lawyers here with me. He's waiting in the helicopter and will advise you on the correct wording.'

Astonished by his request, Lindy stared back into level dark golden eyes and felt her heart breaking inside her. All of a sudden she was wondering if everyone had been right when they'd advised her to set aside her own feelings and tell Atreus that she was pregnant as soon as possible. She had waited, kept silent, and now an awful lot of water had passed under the proverbial bridge. His life had moved on to a fresh chapter that had no place for her in any capacity.

'You're so organised,' Lindy remarked stiffly, moving away from him to stare out of the window. Far from impervious to her tension, the dogs nudged against her legs and Sausage released an anxious whine. 'It's all right,' she told the elderly dog, reaching down somewhat awkwardly to pat his shaggy head. 'I'm fine.'

'Lindy…' Atreus let her name trail off. 'The rumours set off by that article will be repeated again in the future if action isn't taken against them now.'

Colour flaring over her cheekbones, Lindy spun back— or at least she tried. But she had moved too fast, and her sense of balance was no longer reliable. As her head swam she clutched at the back of the chair next to her, to steady legs that felt as safe and dependable as bendy twigs.

It came as a complete shock when Atreus strode forward to close a supportive arm round her. 'Are you all right?'

'No,' she said a little shrilly, in growing distress at the situation in which she found herself. 'Anything but.'

The disturbingly familiar scent of his skin, his hair and his cologne was washing over her and arousing agonisingly acute slivers of intimate memory. She remembered him too well, and she stiffened in consternation when her body reacted accordingly. Her breasts swelled and tightened inside her bra, while a sliding sensation of warm awareness stirred between her thighs. She drove out that humiliating sexual awareness with an image of Krista Perris, with her long blonde hair, tiny designer-clad body and cute smile: the woman he was thinking of marrying. The effort of it almost broke her in two. Pulling away from him in an abrupt movement, she slid a seeking hand down to the arm of the chair and sank heavily down into it.

'You've wasted your time coming down here with your lawyer in tow,' she murmured between compressed lips. 'I can't help you.'

'You mean, you won't help me?' Atreus gritted, his exasperation unhidden.

Lindy lifted her head. 'Just whose baby do you think this is?'

Atreus shrugged. 'That's none of my business. I merely want a statement from you to tidy this up, so that neither I nor my family will be haunted by unsavoury rumours of an illegitimate child for years into the future,' he completed impatiently.

Lindy threaded slim fingers unsteadily through the hair tumbling over her warm brow. A little more stable in body now that she was seated, she was fumbling for the right words but already regretting the fact that she had remained silent about her pregnancy for so many months. Her secrecy had left him horribly unprepared for the announcement she now had to make.

'I can't agree to make that statement for you because I would be telling a lie,' Lindy explained with care. 'I know you don't want to hear this right now, Atreus...but this is your baby.'

His eyes narrowed, his lean strong face tightening, his jawline taking on an aggressive slant. 'That's not possible.'

'There's no such thing as one hundred per cent reliable birth control,' Lindy countered. 'Somehow it went wrong for us.'

'I don't believe this. You staged this vulgar press exposure to try and con me into believing that this is my child?'

Lindy's hands closed tight on the chair-arms so that she could lever herself upright again. 'That's the end of our little talk, Atreus. I want you to leave now.' She walked briskly to the front door and yanked it open with the suggestion of suppressed violence.

'This is ridiculous. You can't throw a bombshell like that at me and then demand that I leave without explaining yourself,' Atreus ground out, dark golden eyes censorious and hot as molten metal.

'The first point I would like to make is that I don't

have anything to explain. The second is that I will not tolerate being accused of trying to con you or anyone else. You got me pregnant—deal with it!' Lindy slung back at him in furious challenge.

Brilliant dark eyes fringed by inky lashes fiercely focused on her, Atreus closed his hands over hers. 'I don't want to set my lawyers on you, Lindy—I only want to know why you're doing this…'

Lindy forcefully wrenched her fingers free of his hold. 'How dare you? You hounded me out of my home, you disrupted my whole life, and you got me pregnant! Now you're threatening me with your lawyers?'

'Nobody's going to threaten you,' another voice cut in, with rasping bite.

Atreus and Lindy swung round. Sergei Antonovich was poised several feet away. 'Alissa has been worried about you and it seems she had good cause.'

When he saw the other man, Atreus became so tense he might have been chipped out of solid granite. 'Sergei,' he acknowledged grittily. 'I appreciate your concern, but we don't need an audience right now.'

The Russian tycoon sent Lindy a questioning glance. 'If legal advice is required, you will have full access to any assistance you need.'

'Thank you,' Lindy breathed, tears prickling behind her eyes, because Sergei and Alissa had been so very kind and supportive when she was at her lowest ebb, and she really appreciated that. 'But you don't need to stay.'

Lindy stepped back indoors and wished she had controlled her temper enough to have stayed there in the first instance. Fighting with Atreus or letting other people get involved in what was a hugely private issue would only exacerbate the tensions between them. Leaving Atreus to follow her, Lindy moved back into the living room and resisted a provocative urge to ask him if Krista Perris knew where he was. 'Would you like coffee?'

'Yes. Exactly when did you get so friendly with Antonovich?'

'He owns this place. My friendship is with his wife, Alissa. I have mentioned her to you several times. Alissa and I shared a flat a few years ago.'

'I didn't make the correct connection.'

Atreus watched her switch on the kettle in the light-filled kitchen. He breathed in slow and deep, studying her taut profile and the unfamiliar shape of her pregnant body. His baby? The thought struck him hard. Accidents happened. He knew that—of course he did. But how could any man know whose baby it was inside a woman? And, having been burned more than once by allegations, he was more suspicious and cynical than other men.

'Is it my baby?' he prompted, in a driven undertone.

'Yes. It's your baby,' Lindy confirmed heavily. 'And you don't have any excuse that I know of to even ask me that question.'

'Halliwell's bow-tie was lying on your bedroom floor the last time we slept together,' Atreus shared flatly.

Taken aback, Lindy studied him. 'That was the night Ben and I went to a wedding party at Headby Hall. I let him have the bed and I slept on the sofa,' she explained slowly. 'You never mentioned the bow-tie at the time…'

His lean dark features hardened. 'I didn't see the point.'

'I'm carrying your child. I expect you to trust me when I tell you something.'

'That's a tall order for me,' Atreus admitted.

'You expected me to trust you when you were photographed in the company of other women in London during our relationship,' Lindy reminded him darkly.

Challenged, Atreus shrugged a magnificent shoulder and sipped his black coffee. 'I've never lied to you.'

'DNA tests can be dangerous during pregnancy.' Lindy spoke in a curt, harried tone. 'I won't risk a miscarriage just to satisfy your lack of faith in my word.'

Atreus set his even white teeth together and said nothing.

In the uneasy silence Lindy began talking quickly and quietly. 'I was ten weeks pregnant before I found out. We'd already broken up. Right from the start I knew I wanted this baby, but that you wouldn't.'

'You had no right to make such assumptions.'

'Assumptions based on fact. You had already told me that you didn't want a baby with me, and that you would only want one when you were married,' Lindy pointed out doggedly. 'So, based on those comments, I naturally made the assumption that you would want me to either have a termination or hand over my child for adoption.'

'*Never*!' Atreus bit out rawly. 'Never would I have suggested such a solution!'

'Well, I wasn't drawn to those options either, and couldn't see any point in lowering myself to tell you that I had conceived,' she admitted tautly.

His dark golden eyes were bleak. 'In what way would you have been lowering yourself?'

Lindy recalled how she had felt when they broke up, and how much worse she had felt after that final time when they had shared the same bed. She swallowed hard. 'You hurt me a lot. That Notice to Quit I received was the last straw. I just couldn't face having anything more to do with you.'

Incensed with her version of womanly logic, Atreus swore in Greek under his breath. 'Even though you knew I wasn't behind that debacle over you staying on at The Lodge?'

'No, but you wanted me gone—out of sight, out of mind. I saw that in you,' Lindy condemned quietly. 'I didn't feel that I could afford to depend on you.'

Atreus almost groaned aloud. She saw all that was worst in him and concentrated on that. He knew he was not perfect. He knew he was not a saint. But he would never have walked away had he known that she needed him, and he was insulted that she could have thought otherwise. Suddenly he felt confined in the small room. He had a deep craving for the energising light and burn of a hotter sun on his body, for the timeless beat of the Aegean waves on the shore on his private island of Thrazos, where he could be himself.

'You weren't fair to me,' he told her boldly. 'You didn't give me a chance.'

'Well, it doesn't matter now. Life has moved on for both of us.' Lindy forced a determined smile onto her strained face. 'Look, all this has been a shock to you. Why don't you leave so that you can work out how you feel about the situation? Then we can talk.'

'Some things I already know. If your baby is mine,

I cannot possibly consider marrying another woman.'
Pale and taut beneath his bronzed complexion, Atreus
settled glittering dark, steady eyes on Lindy's startled
expression. 'What sort of a man do you think I am? I
could not turn my back on you or my child. In those circumstances both of you would have first claim on my
loyalty and support.'

Rocked by his confirmation of the fact that he had
been thinking of marrying Krista Perris, Lindy folded
her arms in a defensive movement. 'I don't want any
sort of a claim on you. I don't want to mess up anyone
else's life—yours or your girlfriend's.'

His lean strong face had a stern aspect. 'There's
nothing you can do. Things are already messed up and
we can't change that, but we can do what has to be done
for the child's sake.'

'My life is fine just the way it is at the minute,'
Lindy protested. 'I have a business, a healthy income,
and somewhere secure to live. I don't need anything
else. I don't need your loyalty or your support—it's too
late for all that.'

'It's not too late for the baby.'

'You don't even want the baby!' Lindy hurled at him
in bewilderment. 'For goodness' sake, you've already
admitted that you're on the brink of asking another
woman to marry you!'

Atreus gave her a grim look. 'But I want my baby to
have everything I didn't have. A normal home, loving
parents, a solid knowledge of who he or she is, and
security. If I marry another woman the child won't have

those essentials, and I owe my own flesh and blood more than that.'

Oxygen feathered in Lindy's dry throat as she finally appreciated that he no longer doubted her. 'So you accept that I'm telling the truth and that this is your baby?'

His rare charismatic smile momentarily lightened the hard set of his wide sensual mouth. 'When did you ever lie to me?'

It was a small confirmation of the trust they had once shared, and it almost brought tears to her eyes. It was a relief that he did not still doubt her claim that he had fathered her child. She twisted her head away and dropped it to stare at her linked hands. It was news to her that Atreus had not benefited from a secure home with loving parents. He never mentioned his childhood, but she was aware that both his father and mother had been dead for a good number of years.

'So you really want to play a role in this child's life?' Lindy prompted uncertainly.

His lean strong face clenched. 'I want more than that. But we can discuss that some other time, when you look less tired.'

Lindy did not appreciate his assurance that she looked tired. Unfortunately emotional stress and tension always exhausted her, and although the nausea she had suffered no longer bothered her, she was still waiting to enjoy the reputed 'glow' of pregnancy. 'I don't want us to be enemies.'

'You don't need to worry about that. This pregnancy

may be an unforeseen development,' Atreus drawled softly, 'but, as you'll discover, I can roll with the punches.'

'Not perhaps the most tactful euphemism you could have used to reassure me,' Lindy quipped wryly, looking up at him and noting how the sunshine gleamed over his black hair, warming his bronzed skin and accentuating the stunning gold of his eyes. For a split second, before she got her control back in place, she craved his touch with every fibre of her being.

'I'm in shock,' Atreus confided ruefully. 'I'll get over it, though. This baby will change everything.'

Lindy appreciated his honesty, but it hurt. She didn't know what she expected from him any more. In his swift acceptance of her condition and his paternity he had exceeded her expectations, but nothing could stop her reflecting that her revelation was already threatening to turn his life upside down. He insisted that he wanted a role in their child's life. He had said that he couldn't marry Krista now…

Was that because he knew his gorgeous girlfriend would not accept a husband who came with the baggage of an acknowledged illegitimate child? How did he really feel inside? Was he in love with Krista? And would their relationship continue even though they didn't marry? Recognising that she wanted answers to questions that were really no longer any of her business, Lindy suppressed her teeming thoughts. One problem that she did fully acknowledge was that she was still too vulnerable to Atreus. She needed to guard against that weakness and learn how to keep her distance—mentally and physically.

CHAPTER EIGHT

FORTY-EIGHT hours later, Atreus was shown out of Krista's apartment by her maid. His lean, darkly handsome face was grim with suppressed emotion. He was angry with everything and everyone, himself included. He thought he was very probably angry with the whole world, and it was not a mood he wanted to inflict on Lindy. Drawing out his mobile phone, he re-arranged their meeting for the following morning.

'Are you all right?' Lindy heard herself ask, catching an odd note in his deep voice that disturbed her.

'Why wouldn't I be?' Atreus suppressed a groan at that query and compressed his handsome mouth hard. 'I'm sorry for the last-minute change of plan.'

Grimacing at her slip in asking such a personal question, and with her cheeks burning, Lindy hastened to say as casually as she could, 'It's not a problem.'

At her end of the phone she glanced in the hall mirror and winced. Hair tamed within an inch of its life: check. Full make-up: check. New outfit calcu-lated to make the most of what shape she retained:

check. Did she never learn? Why was she doing this to herself?

She walked back into the living room, where the remnants of a light lunch remained on the dining table and exchanged a rueful smile with her guest. 'Atreus just cancelled,' she shared.

'Oh, dear…' Princess Elinor of Quaram, a willowy redhead who had been on the brink of leaving, sat down again and occupied herself by brushing her younger son's hair off his brow. Tarif, a cute-as-a-button toddler with his father's black hair and his mother's light eyes, returned to the toys he had been playing with. 'That's unfortunate.'

'It's not like him. Something must have come up,' Lindy declared, watching her friend's older boy, Sami, and her daughter, Mariyah, flying a kite in the paddock with the help of their tall, athletic father. 'But I'm not bothered. I'm being sensible now, and I'm over Atreus.'

Her companion gave her a doubtful appraisal.

'No, seriously—I am over him,' Lindy emphasised.

'If you say so,' Elinor said mildly. 'But I think you've had a traumatic time over the last few months. Don't rush into making any big decisions.'

Lindy struggled to stay calm while she waited for Atreus's arrival the next morning. He was the father of her baby and otherwise no big deal, she told herself earnestly. All right, so he was gorgeous, but he was with another woman now, and her only remaining connection with him was an inconvenient pregnancy. She watched him pull up outside in a gleaming black Bugatti

Veyron and she made herself hang back and count slowly to ten before she went to open the front door.

Atreus thrust a bouquet of roses into her arms. Startled by that almost awkward gesture from a man who had never given her flowers even when they were lovers, Lindy muttered her thanks. Flustered, she abandoned him to go off and put the flowers in water.

Curiously untroubled by the scent of lavender in the cottage, Atreus paced the wood floor, impatient for her return.

In full polite hostess mode, Lindy reappeared with a tray of coffee and biscuits for him, and homemade lemonade for herself. 'My business is doing very well at present,' she told him proudly.

Atreus tensed. 'There's a lot of physical labour involved in your business. I'd like to hire someone to take care of that side of your work.'

'I don't need any help. I'm not sick or delicate, just pregnant.'

'I talked to a friend who's a doctor. He said that heavy work is not a good idea at this point in your pregnancy.'

Her teeth closed together with a snap. 'I think that's my affair.'

Brilliant dark eyes clashed with hers head-on. 'Not when you're carrying my baby.'

The speed with which he voiced that direct challenge for supremacy shook Lindy, who had contrived to forget just how interfering and bossy Atreus could be. She breathed in deep to hang onto her temper, telling herself that it was good that he should take an interest in her health. 'I wouldn't do anything stupid.'

'You might. You don't like accepting help,' Atreus pointed out with infuriating accuracy. 'So recruit an assistant and I'll cover the expense until you're fully fit again.'

Lindy could not breathe in deeply enough to douse the fire of temper he had ignited inside her. 'I appreciate your anxiety, but how I live and how I choose to manage my business is my concern.'

'But you are my concern,' Atreus purred, like a prowling jungle cat.

'Since when?' Lindy challenged.

His dark golden gaze narrowed. 'Since you conceived. If you had told me the day you found that out, we would still be together.'

Lindy veiled her gaze. 'So you say—but then we can all be wise after the event. Five months ago you made it very clear than an unplanned pregnancy would destroy our relationship.'

'After my experiences with women in that field it was second nature for me to talk in that vein. It's what I do now that it's happened that speaks best for me,' Atreus informed her with firm conviction. 'And I'm here today to ask you to be my wife.'

In the act of pouring lemonade into a glass, Lindy switched her attention to him, her violet-blue eyes wide with disbelief. Frozen as she was by shock, she went on pouring the lemonade until the glass overflowed onto the tray beneath. The deluge only stopped when Atreus strode forward and lifted the jug from her paralysed grasp.

'I don't believe you just said that,' Lindy admitted unevenly.

'You're expecting my child. What could be more natural?'

Lindy dealt him a transfixed appraisal. 'I can't think of anything more *un*natural! We broke up because you spelt out the fact that you would never consider marrying someone like me. What about Krista?'

His strong jaw line hardened. 'That's over and done with.'

'But you were planning to marry her!' Lindy protested.

'Was I?' Atreus treated her to an impassive look that revealed nothing.

'You took her home to meet your family, which for you was quite a statement,' Lindy pronounced, her pride still smarting over the reality that even after eighteen months she had never met a single member of the reclusive Dionides family.

Determined to prevent her from muddying the water with pointless references to Krista, Atreus lifted and dropped a wide shoulder. 'There's little point in discussing what might have been now.'

Sensitive as she was on the issue of Krista Perris, Lindy turned her head away sharply, as if he had slapped her.

'I want to talk about us.'

Lindy almost laughed out loud. 'There is no us. The fact I'm pregnant doesn't wipe out the last few months, or the reasons we split up.'

Atreus breathed in deep. The silence was laden with tension.

'And I'm not interested in playing a role in a shotgun marriage. I suppose I should say thank you for asking,' Lindy replied in a doubtful tone, 'but you thought I was totally unsuitable as a wife when we broke up, and you weren't shy about telling me that. I don't see what's changed.'

Atreus could no longer restrain his ire. 'Look in the mirror. Our baby needs both of us—and in my family we get married when a woman is pregnant.'

'Whatever turns you on.' Lindy grimaced, and closed both hands round her glass of lemonade. 'But I'm afraid it's not something that I could agree to, and I think I'm doing both of us a favour in being the sensible one.'

Atreus regarded her with fulminating eyes. 'What's sensible about it? You will be denying my child my name.'

'That doesn't have to be an issue. If necessary, names can be changed by deed poll,' Lindy informed him.

'Only if we're married can I be a proper father to our child!' Atreus lanced back at her, far from mollified by her prosaic assurance that names could be legally changed outside the bonds of matrimony.

'I think we're both adult enough to know that that's not true. I will be happy for you to take an interest in our child, but we don't need to get our lives tangled up on any other level,' Lindy stated, tilting her chin. 'Let's be honest, Atreus. You moved on from me pretty quickly, and neither one of us wants to go back.'

Scorching golden eyes clashed with hers. 'Don't tell me what I want. You don't know what I want.'

Lindy thought that getting married to Atreus would be wonderful—but only for a little while. Once the novelty of having a child wore off for him she would be left with an empty marriage and a husband who didn't love her, who had once let her go even though she loved him. The pain of losing Atreus a second time would be more than she could bear, so why put herself through such an ordeal? Just for the short-lived joy of being able to call herself his wife?

'As separate individuals sharing a child we can enjoy a mutually respectful relationship. But if we marry we will just end up getting divorced, because I'm not and will never be the wife you really want,' Lindy told him starkly.

'And how do you make that out?' Atreus demanded rawly, astonished by the barrage of arguments she was employing against him.

'Because you picked Krista Perris, who is everything I am not. She's Greek and she's rich and she's doll-sized. I can't compete and I don't intend to even try.' Strong pride made Lindy lift her head high, for she meant every word that she was saying. She didn't want to be hurt again. She didn't want to be a second-best wife, tolerated for the sake of her child. She knew her vulnerability, and was determined to protect herself from further pain and disillusionment.

'I'm not asking or expecting you to compete with her!' Atreus slammed back at her. 'But I am expecting you to think of what is best for the baby you are carrying. Being a parent is about making sacrifices. It is not about what we want but about what our child needs to thrive.'

Unhappily aware from his words that he was not even able to pretend that she might have gifts equal to Krista's in other fields, Lindy nodded stonily. 'Lecture over? I know all about sacrifices. I spent the first four months of my pregnancy being sick at least once a day.

I've lost my figure. My clothes don't fit any more. I get so tired I'm in bed by ten most nights. I can't do physical things I used to take for granted.'

Atreus reached down and closed his hands over hers to tug her upright. 'I get the picture—I was insensitive,' he conceded in a raw, driven undertone. 'But I assumed that you would want to marry me. Was that so arrogant?'

The tears that came so easily to her eyes since she had fallen pregnant almost overflowed. The appeal in his hot golden gaze went straight to her heart. Angrily blinking back the moisture in her eyes, she lifted a hand and smoothed the stubborn angle of his jaw in a soothing gesture. 'No. If I hadn't been pregnant, if you had asked me six months ago, I would have been ecstatic. But that time has gone, and we can't get it back because everything has changed. A divorce would be much more traumatic for our child.'

'I just might make a bloody good husband!' Atreus bit out in furious reproof.

'With the right woman, yes. But that woman,' Lindy framed unsteadily, 'isn't me. I wouldn't fit in. I couldn't be what you want and you'd end up hating me.'

Strong arms banding round her, Atreus stared down into her earnest blue eyes and kissed her with all the unstudied intensity of a man fed-up with talking. Utterly unprepared for that radical change of approach, Lindy quivered in feverish shock from the moist dart and dance of his tongue, her breath catching in her throat as an earthquake of response flooded her all too willing body. He slid a hand below her top, flipped loose her bra and closed his fingers round a firm breast with a growling sound of satisfaction that reverberated through his deep chest. With the fingers of one hand she clung to his shoulder, leaning on him while he stroked her throbbing nipples. Excitement was running amok through her sensation-starved body until her imagination jumped ahead a few minutes, to the moment when she would have to surrender her clothing. The thought of lying on her bed like a beached whale while Atreus became much too closely acquainted with her new barrel-like measurements was sufficient to make Lindy pull hurriedly away from him.

She vanished into the cloakroom at speed, to set her clothing to rights and to tell herself off for acting like a wanton hussy. Was it any wonder that he couldn't recognise the meaning of the word no when she threw it at him?

Dragging herself back out of cover to face him again was a huge challenge, but, pink with embarrassment, Lindy returned to the living room.

Atreus dealt her a slow, sensually assessing look from smouldering dark golden eyes. 'We could finish this dialogue in bed...'

Lindy froze.

'I can't think why you look so shocked. That was where we were heading until you took fright.'

Lindy recognised the tough edge of assurance in his measuring scrutiny and knew that her response had weakened her position. 'I didn't take fright... I just realised that what we were doing was absolutely wrong.'

'How?' Atreus incised aggressively.

'If we're not getting married but we hope to raise a child together we need to forge a new relationship—as friends,' Lindy informed him squarely.

'When I want to drag you off to bed I'm not capable of being your friend, *glikia mou*.'

Outraged by his attitude, when she saw her own as being by far the more reasonable, Lindy snapped, 'Of course you could. You've managed without me for months. You've been out with at least a dozen other women!'

Atreus released his breath in a sharp hiss. 'So that's what I'm paying for?'

Lindy squeezed her hands into fists and prayed for self-control. 'You're not paying for anything, Atreus. I'm not that kind of woman. I'm not trying to settle some stupid score.'

Atreus sent her a glittering glance, fierce pride etched in the sombre set of his handsome features. 'I asked you to marry me. Shouldn't that be enough to clear the decks between us?'

Lindy paled. 'I want what's best for both of us.'

'And you also want me,' he stated with insolent certainty. 'Desire is a healthy basis for marriage but a seriously bad basis for friendship.'

Agonised colour washed to the very roots of Lindy's hair. 'Then we'll have to settle on something in between and learn as we go,' she argued shakily. 'Because if you're serious about wanting to be part of our child's life I'm more than willing to accept you in that role... but not as my husband.'

'When do you next go for a medical check-up?' Atreus shot at her without warning, his dissatisfaction with her unhidden.

'Next week,' she answered tautly.

'Let me know the time and the place now and I'll be

there. Without flowers or a proposal,' he added with
silken derision.

Lindy lost colour. He was offended. His pride had
been hurt. She didn't blame him for feeling as he did.
He was a very rich man who had probably been raised
from no age at all to see himself as one hell of a marital
prize. All his adult life women had been trying to get
him to the altar without success. Yet he had offered up
his freedom as a sacrifice for the sake of their unborn
child and she had dared to reject him. But wasn't that
wiser than letting him plunge into a marriage to her in
which she was convinced he would end up feeling
trapped and hating her? It would have been so easy to
say yes, she acknowledged painfully, so easy to simply
take him at his word, bury her head in the sand and
accept him.

Having arranged their next meeting, Atreus sprang
back into his Bugatti. It was a dangerously fast vehicle
that she would have nagged him for driving had she
been his wife. Of course he would just have given her
one of his dark stubborn looks and gone ahead and
driven it anyway, she reflected ruefully. Atreus would
never be tamed or obedient, and she wasn't sure she
would ever find it possible to stop wanting him.

Ben dropped in for a visit the following evening and told
her she was crazy to have turned down Atreus's
marriage proposal. 'What the hell were you thinking
of?' he demanded in apparent disbelief. 'Now you're
going to be saddled with a child, it was the best offer
you're ever likely to get!'

Since the day Lindy had told Ben that she was pregnant she had seen a great deal less of him. The possessive attitude he had appeared to develop towards her during her affair with Atreus had vanished. Ben seemed to think that a woman with a child had zero attraction for other men and little chance of meeting a permanent partner. That attitude, added to his aversion to anything to do with pregnancy, had not endeared him to Lindy, who found herself trying pointlessly to suck in her stomach when he was around. It was finally beginning to dawn on her that Ben was very immature.

The weeks that followed marked a new departure in Lindy's relationship with Atreus. He was more distant with her, but much more involved in her life than she had ever dreamt he would be. As he had suggested she took on an assistant to help with the business, and her stress level eased while she worked shorter hours and found it easier to take time off.

Atreus accompanied her to all her medical appointments, and when she was sent for a scan at the nearest hospital he met her there. He was endearingly fascinated by the images of the baby on the monitor, and quite stunned by the news that she was expecting a boy.

Afterwards, he insisted that she dine at his London apartment and that she stayed there for the night. Exhausted by the day she'd had, and in no mood to face the journey home by herself, Lindy agreed and called her assistant, Wendy, to ask her to feed the dogs. Never having visited Atreus's home before, she was very curious, but the huge, airy penthouse apartment with its

designer furniture and wide open spaces had an anonymous, impersonal quality that left her cold.

During the meal, Atreus excused himself to take a
phone call, and when he returned, he found Lindy fast
asleep in her dining chair.

Lindy wakened in the early hours because she was
too warm. Although she could only feel a sheet over
her, there was good reason for her high temperature.
Instead of putting her in one of his guestrooms Atreus
had put her in his bed, with him, and she was clamped
to his lean and powerful heat-exuding physique like a
second skin.

'Go back to sleep, *mali mou*.' Atreus urged huskily.

A single exploratory shift of position had left Lindy
wildly aware of the feel of his aroused body against her
own. 'You shouldn't have put me in the same bed as
you,' she censured.

'When did you turn into such a prude?'

Avoiding any form of intimacy was her protection,
she admitted inwardly. In her mind she was already fan-
tasising about what he might do next, and the burn of
long abstinence from such pleasures sat like a hollow
ache at the heart of her.

'Stop teasing me,' she urged stiffly.

'Relax, you're safe,' Atreus asserted.

Cut to the bone by that assurance, Lindy sucked in a
sustaining breath. Of course she was safe. Why on earth
had she thought she might be otherwise? Simple proximity to a female body had caused his arousal. After all,
he could hardly find her swollen form sexually appealing. She was amazed he had had an arm round her, and

wondered if she had burrowed into him while she slept. After all, he never touched her now in that way when she was awake. There had been no more unexpected kisses, not so much as a flirtatious word out of place.

'No sex outside marriage,' Atreus breathed silkily.

Lindy pushed herself up on one elbow. 'What did you say?'

'Sex is out of the question unless you're prepared to marry me.'

In the dim light creeping round the edges of the curtains he was a dark silhouette against the sheets. Lindy glowered furiously down at him. 'I don't want sex!'

Atreus just laughed.

'I mean it, I…don't…want…sex!' Lindy launched, even louder, her face burning in the darkness.

'Liar,' Atreus murmured softly.

Her teeth gritted. 'I'm not staying in this bed with you!' she announced loftily, lunging at the lamp by the bed to switch it on.

'I know it's very frustrating to be able to look but not touch. And, yes, I do notice how you look at me,' Atreus informed her.

'There are times when I really hate you!' Lindy hissed.

Atreus slid out of bed with fluid grace, reached for the robe lying by the bed and extended it for her use. Lindy clambered out of bed a great deal more slowly than he had. Although she was ready to hate him she had planned to stay in the bed, but his move called her bluff. She was awesomely conscious of her proportions in the sensible bra and panties he had mercifully left her clad in, and almost in tears of mortification at having to expose herself to that extent. Naturally the robe would not close across her stomach.

He showed her into the guestroom next door.

In silence, Lindy cried herself back to sleep in a cold bed. She didn't like his sense of humour. Of course he didn't still want to marry her! But she was cringing at the knowledge that he seemed to have the ability to see through her pretences of being simply pleasant and friendly around him. She felt fat and horrible and deeply unsexy, and she wished she had kept quiet when she'd awoken, so that she could have continued to enjoy lying that close to him again.

There would be no opportunities for such togetherness after the baby was born. Their dealings would become much more detached once their son was in existence. Atreus had a very strong sense of responsibility and he had proved that he was extremely reliable. As soon as he'd realised she was pregnant he had become thoughtful of her comfort and very supportive in every way. But she was already worrying about how they would share their newborn child, and whether it would mean that she had to adjust to being regularly parted from her baby.

Later that morning she was woken up with breakfast on a tray. When Atreus strode in she was happily reflecting that there was a lot to be said for being spoiled, and even more to be said for a man who took the trouble to spoil you.

'I know the baby is due in only a couple of weeks, but I think I should introduce you to my family before our son is born,' he imparted, poised at the foot of the bed, looking impossibly sleek and groomed and gorgeous in a business suit.

Lindy avoided looking at him now for longer than two seconds, because she knew that it was not safe to do so. He could spot lusty admiration at fifty paces and she needed to be more careful. But his invitation to meet his family shook her, and she shrank from the challenge of following heavily in tiny Krista's light and delicate footsteps.

'I don't think I'd be allowed to fly at this stage…'

'Private jet,' he pointed out gently.

Lindy could not think of a ready excuse that he would not shoot down in flames. When Atreus got an idea in his head he was unstoppable. 'Suppose…just suppose I went into labour,' she urged, trying to scare him away from the idea.

'We've got plenty of doctors in Athens,' Atreus responded cheerfully, already resolving to ensure that there was a contingency plan for any emergency…

CHAPTER NINE

DURING the flight Lindy asked Atreus about his family.

'Since my grandfather died my Uncle Patras and Aunt Irinia have become the most important people to me. When I was seven years old, they took me into their home,' Atreus advanced with studied casualness.

'I didn't realise that your parents died while you were still a child.'

'They didn't. My mother was a heroin addict and my father couldn't cope with her and a child. When the social services got involved because I was rarely at school my father's family intervened. Patras and Irinia agreed to bring me up. Their own children were already adults, so it was a considerable sacrifice for them to take on a seven-year-old.'

'A heroin addict?' Lindy repeated, settling shocked and concerned eyes on his lean strong face, for it had never occurred to her that he might not always have enjoyed a happy, privileged and secure background.

'She was an artists' model, famed for her wild bohemian lifestyle. Before he met her my father was an exemplary husband and businessman who never put a foot wrong. But he walked out on his marriage for her and even turned his back on his responsibilities at Dionides Shipping. He never worked again. He lived on his trust fund,' Atreus shared with biting contempt. 'He did marry my mother, but they were too different for it to work.' His handsome mouth twisted. 'I barely remember them, but I do remember the violent arguments and the fact that the house was always full of noisy strangers coming and going at all times of the day and night.'

'It must have taken a lot of guts for your father to stand by your mother. I suppose he had given up so much to be with her that he felt he had to make the best of things,' Lindy mused.

'That's not the family point of view,' Atreus said drily

Lindy didn't say that she already knew the family point of view just by watching him and listening to what he had to say and how he said it.

'My father let everyone who ever depended on him down—his first wife, his family, his child, even our employees at Dionides Shipping.'

'Is he dead now?'

'He died in a car crash ten years after my mother died of an overdose. He was a weak, self-indulgent man. He lived abroad and he never made a single attempt to see me again.'

Lindy was heartbroken on his behalf. She could see how deep that final omission and hurt had gone. Indeed it was obvious to her that Atreus had been taught to be deeply ashamed of both his parents, and she thought that was a cruel burden to give a child to carry into adolescence and beyond. She now understood why Atreus had once confidently assured her that he would only marry a woman from a similar background to his own. But this awareness only made her marvel at the reality that, in spite of the undoubted conditioning he had undergone, he had still asked her to marry him. What she had just discovered gave her a whole new view of him and of his marriage proposal.

When he escorted her into the Dionides family home, a handsome country mansion outside Athens, Lindy was elegantly clad in a terracotta linen dress and matching light jacket.

'Before we join my relatives, I should warn you that they are very much shocked by the fact that we are not even engaged, not to mention married. I told them that they needed to move with the times, but I doubt if they took my advice on board,' Atreus drawled wryly.

Lindy groaned. 'You have a great sense of timing. I wouldn't have got off the jet if you'd told me that any sooner.'

'I'm the head of the family and they have excellent manners. No one will be rude,' he told her with some amusement.

But, even though he spoke the truth on that score, Lindy hated every moment of the meeting that followed. The interior of the house had a formal funereal gloom, and an echoing silence that seemed a fitting backdrop for the very reserved group of people waiting to greet them. There were about fifteen people in a big room shaded by lowered blinds. The atmosphere, for all the heat outside, was distinctly chilly and unwelcoming, and Patras and Irinia Dionides were the chilliest of the lot. Eyes were swiftly averted from her pregnant stomach, and the fact that a baby was on the way was never once mentioned.

For that reason when Lindy felt a disturbing tightening sensation in her abdomen she did not dare refer to it. As she sat there, trying not to shift position too often, the tightening gradually reached the level of pain. She began to breathe with care, while making frantic calculations and wondering whether she was having a scare or if it was the real thing. When her nerves couldn't stand the suspense any more, and a gasp escaped her at the strength of a particularly strong contraction, Atreus turned to her with a frown of enquiry.

'I think I might be going into labour,' she whispered as discreetly as she could.

Well, there was nothing discreet about Atreus's reaction to that. In the middle of a conversation he leapt upright, yanked out his phone, stabbed out a number and began speaking in an urgent flood of Greek. Consternation spread like a tidal wave, engulfing the room, and while concentrating on keeping calm Lindy tried to console herself with the reflection that going into labour in front of her hosts would presumably linger longer in family memory than whatever favourable impression Krista Perris had left behind her.

'It is just as well that I reserved a room at a maternity clinic in case we needed it,' Atreus informed her with decided satisfaction, bending down to lift her off her feet and carry her out of the house to the waiting limo ousine. 'There's also an excellent obstetrician standing by in readiness for our arrival, *agapi mou.*'

Lindy was impressed, and some of her anxiety ebbed away. 'You really do shine in a crisis, Atreus.'

But little else relating to the birth of their son went as they expected. Lindy was in labour for hours, and she was becoming increasingly tired when the foetal heart monitor revealed that the baby was in distress. She was then whisked off for an emergency Caesarean. But her son was the most beautiful baby she had ever seen, with a shock of black hair and a cry as effective as a fire alarm.

Afterwards, Lindy drifted in and out of an exhausted sleep, still suffering from the effects of the anaesthetic she had had. At one point she opened her eyes and saw Atreus staring down into the crib with one long finger caught in his son's grasp. Caught in the act of appreciating his newborn son, Atreus looked happier than she had ever expected to see him.

'Do you like him?' Lindy whispered with a hint of teasing.

'If you can forgive him for what he's put you through, I certainly can,' Atreus declared, brilliant dark eyes shimmering with strong emotion. 'He's so perfect. Have you seen the size of his fingernails yet? They're tiny—he's like a doll. Do you think he's healthy?'

'He was ten pounds! He's a big baby and of course he's healthy.' Lindy was touched by his concern and enthusiasm but she had to force her eyes to swerve away from him again. Just looking at Atreus could make her heart pound, and she wondered when, if ever, her fascination with him would fade. In comparison to him she was a mess, with her tousled hair and unadorned face. Atreus, on the other hand, looked astonishingly vibrant for a male who had missed a night's sleep. Even with his lean, dark and devastating features adorned by a dark shadow of stubble, his tie missing and his suit crumpled, he looked utterly gorgeous.

Atreus straightened from the crib and spread his arms wide in an emphatic gesture. 'I know already that I want to be able to see him every day. I want to be there when he smiles, takes his first step, says his first word,' he told her, in a tone of urgency that locked her troubled gaze back on him. 'I want to pick him up when he falls over, to hold him, be there for him. All those things are hugely important to me. But if you don't marry me I'm unlikely to ever be that close to my son.'

And, watching Atreus stroke an infinitely tender fingertip down over their baby's little face, Lindy was suddenly powerfully aware that she was no longer the primary focus of his interest.

It was clear that Atreus had fallen passionately in love with his first child. She knew in her bones that he would make a terrific father, driven to give his own child what his father had not given him in terms of time, interest and affection. Surely no one else would ever love their child so much as his own father? How could she deny Atreus and her son the closest possible relationship available to them?

And she was still in love with Atreus, wasn't she? Brooding over the truth that she had tried to avoid, Lindy almost stared a hole in the blank space of wall.

When Atreus was in her life she was much happier.
Even seeing Atreus on a platonic basis, as she had been
for the weeks before the birth, had lifted her spirits a
great deal, and his support from the instant she went into
labour had been invaluable. Feeling as she did about
him, didn't marrying him make sense? And even if their
marriage didn't last, at least she would have the consolation that she had tried to make it work.

'All right,' Lindy mumbled sleepily, finally breaking
the taut, tension-filled silence.

Atreus closed a lean brown hand over hers. 'All
right...what?'

'I'll marry you. But be sure and tell your family that
it was all your idea,' she urged, squirming at the mere
concept of meeting his relatives again after her undig-
nified exit from their home the previous afternoon.

His ebony brows drew together as he frowned. 'What
made you change your mind?'

'I think our son should have two parents,' Lindy
mumbled drowsily. 'You and I both grew up without a
father.'

Atreus released her hand. 'Get some sleep, *glikia mou.*'

Her feathery lashes dipped, and then suddenly her
eyes flew wide again. 'You'll have to wait until I can get
into a decent wedding dress!' she warned him.

They decided to call their son Theodor, which was one
of the few names that they both liked, and in a matter
of days Theodor had become known as Theo.

Atreus's relatives visited them in the clinic. They
were surprisingly animated, and a great deal more

likeable after being introduced to the youngest and
newest member of the Dionides clan.

As soon as Lindy was fit to travel she and Atreus flew
back to London. After a week in Atreus's penthouse
apartment, with a nanny to help out, Lindy regained her
mobility sufficiently to head back home to her cottage
and her dogs. While she was occupying one of the guestrooms in Atreus's apartment she had not felt at home.

Alissa and Elinor had insisted on organising the
wedding, and Lindy was glad of their assistance and
their company. Atreus, after all, was working very long
hours, and within a fortnight of returning to the UK went
off on a two-week business trip to Asia. When he visited
in between times, he focused all his attention on Theo,
but was otherwise cool and distant. Lindy waited in
vain for his attitude to warm up. She had naively
believed that once she'd agreed to marry him everything
would go straight back to the way it had been between
them, but it was soon clear that she was very much mistaken in that hope.

As their wedding day drew closer, Lindy became
more and more apprehensive. She'd found a beautiful
dress, and was relieved that she had regained her figure.
Of course she had been fairly active during her pregnancy and had not put on a great deal of weight. She was
offered interviews by several celebrity magazines which
she turned down. She knew that Atreus loathed that
kind of publicity, and saw no reason why she should surrender her privacy purely because she was about to
become the wife of a very rich man.

The night before her wedding, Lindy stayed in Alissa

and Sergei's fabulous town house. She lay in bed, castigating herself for not having had the courage to tackle Atreus and persuade him to talk to her about feelings he had never once acknowledged he even had. Was he actually suffering from a case of cold feet? Did he regret proposing to her in the first instance? Was he ever going to touch her again? Was he even planning on a normal marriage? Or was he only marrying her to give Theo his name and gain better access to his son?

Those were the fears tormenting Lindy on the day of her wedding, as it dawned on her that her love might well not be enough to oil the wheels of her marriage. Her mood was not improved by the acknowledgement that she was too much of a coward to force those issues with him lest it provoke the cancellation of the wedding.

Elinor, who was acting as her Matron of Honour, loaned her a fabulous tiara to wear with her veil, while Alissa, her bridesmaid, gave her a gorgeous pair of designer shoes. A sapphire and diamond necklace arrived from Atreus, and it was obvious that Alissa had known in advance about that. It was a magnificent gift, and Lindy put it on and spent some time admiring the glittering jewels in the mirror.

'You're the quietest bride I've ever come across,' Elinor complained. 'Is there something wrong?'

'No, of course there isn't,' Lindy disclaimed hastily.

'It's okay to have doubts and be scared,' Alissa declared cheerfully, giving Lindy's shoulder a gentle squeeze. 'Everyone feels like that. Marriage is such a big step, and you've seen so little of Atreus since you came back from Greece.'

'I didn't realise he would be working so much,' Lindy confided ruefully.

'Sergei and Jasim were exactly the same, but when you're living together you'll find more time for each other.'

'You've had a bumpy courtship,' Elinor pointed out. 'You need to talk about what you both want and expect from your marriage.'

Lindy felt it was easy for Elinor, not knowing all that had happened before, to give advice of that nature when Jasim was so obviously deeply in love with her, his wife, and knew no greater happiness than to make her happy. If Lindy had had the confidence of knowing that Atreus was in love with *her*, she wouldn't have had a single worry in her head. But she strongly suspected that if she asked Atreus to sit down and talk about their mutual wants and expectations within marriage he would run for the hills…and never come back.

When she walked down the aisle at the church, her heart hammering so loudly in her ears that she felt light-headed, Atreus turned to watch her progress. He treated her to a keen head-to-toe appraisal, taking in the off-the-shoulder wedding gown which faithfully followed her womanly curves and complemented them with its simple, understated design. His stunning eyes gleamed like molten gold, and her mouth ran dry because she knew that look, recognising that irrefutably sexual smoulder in his gaze with a leap of answering response and profound relief.

'You look ravishing,' Atreus told her in a roughened undertone when she drew level with him.

It was the most personal thing he had said to her in

weeks, and her bosom swelled with pride. He held her hand, his thumb gently caressing the soft inner skin of her wrist, and while little quivers of growing awareness rippled through her body, her brain tossed out the doom-laden thoughts that had been tormenting her.

The ring on her wedding finger, Lindy accompanied Atreus back down the aisle, a buoyant sense of contentment powering her. They would be great together, she promised herself, and she would work so hard at their marriage. She would be a brilliant wife in every way possible.

Those uplifting ambitions shrieked to a sudden forced halt outside when Lindy, watching as the Dionides security team went toe-to-toe with the paparazzi, noticed an unexpected face in the crush. Eyes widening, she stared at Krista Perris, sheathed in a body-hugging bright scarlet dress and with a tiny feathered fascinator on her blonde head that was the last word in cute frivolity. She looked dazzling, and all the men in her vicinity were sucking in their stomachs and straightening their shoulders in the hope of attracting her attention.

As Lindy slid into the wedding limo, she wasted no time in venting her annoyance. 'What's Krista Perris doing here?' she demanded.

Atreus frowned. 'Why shouldn't she be here? My family and hers have been friendly for many years.'

'I didn't realise that,' Lindy admitted gruffly, already regretting her revealing outburst.

'It would have been unthinkable to remove her name from the guest list, but I'm surprised she decided to attend,' Atreus commented, turning his handsome dark head to take another look at the diminutive blonde, his bold bronzed profile clenching taut. 'She looks very well.'

That was all Atreus had to say to put Lindy's nose out of joint, and Lindy was unable to suppress the thought that it was *her* wedding, *her* day, and that Krista Perris had probably had the joy of being eye-catching, beautiful and the centre of attention every day of her entire life. Although resenting Krista's presence made Lindy feel like a mean, jealous cat, she couldn't help feeling insecure and threatened. She reckoned that Atreus was to blame for her feelings by not being more frank with her—until it occurred to her that she would have felt a great deal worse had he told her that he was in love with Krista. His honesty, she conceded heavily, would only be welcome if he was able to tell her exactly what she wanted to hear. And that comforting conclusion seemed unlikely when she recognised his tension at the slightest reminder of the other woman.

At the reception, held at an exclusive hotel, Lindy caught hold of her little flower girl, Alissa and Sergei's daughter Evelina, before she could run in front of a waiter laden with a tray of glasses. She then paused to check her hair in a huge gilt wall mirror.

'You look pretty,' Evelina piped.

'Thank you,' Lindy was saying with a smile when, without warning, another face joined hers in the reflection and made her stiffen in sharp disconcertion.

It was Krista Perris, flamboyant as a flame in her red dress and fascinator, a silken swathe of blonde hair framing her intent face as she stared back at Lindy with malicious eyes. 'You're the wrong bride,' she pronounced softly. 'And Atreus and everyone here knows it. He'll never stay with you.'

A split second later Krista had moved on, leaving Lindy temporarily unsure that her cool and derisive indictment had actually been said out loud. But the proof was in the hair which had risen at the nape of her neck and the gooseflesh on her bare arms.

The wrong bride. It was a label that hit Lindy hard. Even so, she hadn't been able to prevent the same thought from occurring to her when she first laid eyes on Krista, whose smooth sophistication and social assurance acted as a perfect mirror for Atreus's own.

Of course Krista hated her, Lindy reasoned, while the speeches were being made and her mind was free to drift. Guilt was biting deeply into Lindy. Krista and Atreus had been seeing each other and, whether she liked it or not, their relationship had become serious enough for Atreus to consider marriage. Then out of the blue had come the revelation that Atreus had an ex-mistress, pregnant with his child, and Krista's romance had crashed in flames. Naturally Krista was bitter. She must have been hurt, Lindy reflected uneasily, her conscience stinging at the knowledge that her decision not to tell Atreus about her pregnancy was responsible for his breaking up with Krista. How must Krista feel, witnessing Atreus's marriage to another woman when only a couple of months ago Atreus had been Krista's lover?

Lindy had tried not to think about that fact since Theo's birth. Atreus had made it very clear that he had no wish to talk about Krista, and Lindy had felt obligated to respect that embargo. It was not so easy to stay silent now, at her wedding, where she could see that the Dionides family and the Perris family were close friends and that a marriage between Atreus and Krista would have been hugely popular.

Be grateful for what you have, not what you don't have, Lindy scolded herself while Atreus whirled her round the floor in the opening dance. But she could not forget the fact that when Atreus had had a free choice he had relegated her to the background of his life and kept her a secret. He had never pictured her in the starring role of bride, or as the mother of his son. In the end fate had refused him that freedom of choice.

Later, Lindy watched while Atreus took Krista onto the dance floor. She noticed heads turning in the direction of that spectacle, and heard a buzz of comment spread round the room. She was watching them too, her heart in her mouth while she struggled to repress a dangerous mixture of curiosity, jealousy and insecurity. Atreus and Krista talked easily, Krista smiling up at him, laughing and flirting with every look and every flick of her long, glossy hair.

'Stop it,' Elinor whispered, leaning closer to Lindy to admonish her friend. 'I can see you torturing yourself and it's silly. If he had genuinely cared about Krista he would never have married you.'

'I don't think I can make that assumption. Atreus was so determined to do the very best he could for his child. Even before he was born Theo made the scales weigh heavily in my favour,' Lindy shared ruefully. 'Did you see how Atreus's family greeted Krista? Like she was a long-lost daughter.'

'I also saw the women of the family hanging admiringly over Theo when his nanny appeared with him. He's the next generation, and I'd say he's done a very successful job of breaking the ice.'

The ice-breaker was cradled in her arms, black lashes down, like silk fans on his little sleeping face, and Lindy dropped a kiss on her son's satin-smooth brow. When she returned to watching her husband she noticed that the smiles Atreus and Krista had worn had ebbed, and that an intent and serious conversation now appeared to be taking place between them. She quickly looked away again and told herself off very firmly. She was letting nerves and insecurity spoil her wedding day.

Lindy would not let herself mention Krista again. She had not been unaware of Atreus's air of reproof when she had mentioned the heiress earlier that day. After all, she was the wife. Krista was a former girlfriend, and the decent, mature thing to do would be to overlook Krista's nasty comment and be generous. Any desires in that direction, however, were slaughtered by the taunting glance of satisfaction that Krista sent Lindy after she persuaded Atreus to stay with her for a second dance.

Late that night Atreus and Lindy flew by private jet to Greece, with Sausage and Samson travelling with them on pet passports. Lindy was exhausted and slept for much of the flight, wakening more refreshed for the final stage of their journey. They were heading for Thrazos, the private island which Atreus freely admitted was his favourite place in the world. She had not been fit enough to make the trip after Theo's birth, so Atreus had suggested that they spend their honeymoon there.

When they reached the house on Thrazos Lindy could see very little in the darkness. Somewhere down the hill she could see the sea glimmering in the moonlight as they walked from the helipad onto the terrace surrounding the well-lit villa. Atreus handed Theo to his nanny, and a housekeeper took charge to show them into the nursery.

'Oh, this is lovely,' Lindy commented, having strolled into a big room with natural stone walls and a relaxing décor of chunky wood furniture and pale draperies. Deep windows overlooked the grounds.

'Barring emergencies, we should be able to stay here for about six weeks, *mali mou,*' Atreus informed her, a brilliant smile curving his mouth as she spun round in surprise. 'Yes, that's why I worked day after day after day last month—so that we could enjoy the longest possible break here on the island.'

'I wish I'd known that. You just seemed so busy…'

'Well, I'm not busy now, *glikia mou,*' her bridegroom said huskily, pushing her hair back off her cheekbones with gentle fingers.

'Have you brought a lot of women here?' The question just leapt off Lindy's tongue.

Atreus dealt her a wry look. 'No.'

'Krista?' Lindy prompted, unable to control her need to know just how deeply enmeshed the Greek woman had been within Atreus's life.

His eyes narrowed. 'Yes, she's been here.'

Even as a chill spread inside Lindy at that confirmation she wished she had not asked that stupid question. She shrugged a shoulder. 'I don't know why I asked.'

'The only woman I want here with me now is my wife,' Atreus intoned, lowering his handsome dark head to taste the pouting pink curve of her full mouth.

The hot, urgent taste of him was as intoxicating as the finest wine, while the pure sexual charge he emanated sent her senses leaping and dancing with eager energy. He scooped her up into his arms and strode down the corridor with her into a large airy bedroom with doors out onto the terrace. He set her down with great care on the edge of the massive bed and crouched down to remove her shoes.

And Lindy thought, though she did not want to think it, *I wonder, did he sleep here with Krista?* He tipped up her reddened lips and took them again with the driving hunger that never failed to set her on fire. After all, it had been so long since he had touched her. There had not been a single kiss or caress, and he had shown no sign of wanting her again until he'd looked at her in the church today. She knew that restraint had been necessary in the first weeks after Theo had been born, but they could have shared other intimacies, could at least have shared a bed occasionally. Yet Atreus, who had a remarkably healthy libido, had kept her at a distance. Why was that? What had lain behind all that uncharacteristic restraint and indifference to her womanly wiles? And as he unzipped her dress she wondered if desire for the other woman had held him back from her. Her heart sank, and the warmth and liquid heat within her faded away as shame washed over her. Was he only making love to her now because he knew she was expecting him to? Would he make comparisons? Wish that…?

In a sudden movement of frantic repudiation Lindy thrust Atreus back from her and sprang to her feet, reaching behind her to zip her dress up. 'I'm sorry, I can't do this…I just can't!' she gasped in stricken recoil.

His darkly handsome features clenching hard, Atreus froze. For an instant he studied her with sombre dark eyes, and then he took a pointed step back from her. Her face flamed. 'That's your prerogative. *Kalinichta*,' he murmured without any expression at all.

Reeling in shock from what she had done, Lindy watched him stride out. Tears welled up with stinging effect and rolled down her cheeks. Why did she have to be so horribly insecure? What madness had possessed her? It was their wedding night and she didn't want to spend it alone. What sort of a start was this to their marriage?

CHAPTER TEN

'I SCREWED up,' Lindy told Theo frankly.

There was a magnificent view from the deep terrace that ran the length of the villa on the seaward side. A glorious roll of orchards and lush green land ran down to the sea, which washed the white sand of the cove far below. Lindy, however, was not rejoicing in the scenery, or the beauty of the day. All her attention was pinned to her son, who was reclining in his baby seat. The little boy was kicking his feet with visibly dwindling energy. In his little blue cotton playsuit he looked extremely cute, and she smiled down at him even though she didn't feel remotely happy just at that moment. The stupidity of her own behaviour had come home to roost; she had stuck a spoke in the wheels of her new marriage and she didn't know what to do about it.

Three weeks had passed since their wedding night, when she had crashed and burned in jealousy, and Atreus was still sleeping in one of his own guestrooms. The only time they actually touched was when they passed Theo between them, or when Atreus believed she might be in danger of falling. The rest of the time she was as untouchable as the carrier of some noxious plague. Rejection, she had learned, didn't motivate Atreus to try harder; it made him keep his distance.

That fact apart, the honeymoon was ironically proving an outstanding success in every other way. Atreus might be treating her like a maiden aunt who required physical support on steep paths or when boarding a boat, but he had spared no effort when it came to entertaining her. The island of Thrazos was hilly and green and ringed by beautiful deserted beaches, and Atreus had willingly shown her over every part of it. There was a fishing village at one end, with a picturesque harbour, and almost every day they set sail there on Atreus's yacht and went off exploring.

Golden day had followed golden day, under a sky that stayed resolutely blue and unclouded. Sometimes Lindy found it stiflingly hot, and she hogged every bit of shade available, but that same heat seemed to energise Atreus. Out at sea there were breezes to cool her over-heated skin, and she thoroughly enjoyed the refreshing swim stops and picnics at secluded sandy coves, so that before long her enthusiasm for sailing almost equalled his own. It infuriated her that even when so much was wrong between them Atreus betrayed not the smallest sense of awkwardness. He was polite, calm, and brilliant company, and she dreaded the evenings when she was most often alone. After dinner, when Theo was tucked up for the night, Atreus often retired to his office to work, and Lindy invariably went to bed first.

She loved the more relaxed lifestyle on the island and

lived in casual clothes, only putting on a dress when the sun went down. She had dined royally on local dishes at the taverna down by the harbour. She had sat there below the plane tree on one memorable evening, watching Atreus dance a ceremonial dance with the other men in celebration of a saint's day. The only freedom he had known growing up had been on Thrazos. His over-protective guardians had been happy to see him spend his free time here on the island. It was on Thrazos that Atreus had learned to sail, and he knew everyone in the town by name, pausing to greet people in the narrow streets and ask knowledgeably after their families.

On the yacht they also sailed to more sophisticated haunts on the island of Rhodes. Atreus had purchased a beautiful set of modern designer jewellery for Lindy in Rhodes Town, and she had shopped in the designer outlets to add to a holiday wardrobe that had turned out to be inadequate for her needs as the days passed. Theo travelled almost everywhere with them. At the end of their first week he had been baptised in a simple but moving ceremony held in the island's church, Ag Roumeli. He was a pack-up-and-parcel baby, happy to sleep or eat anywhere and at any time without complaint, and she found him a pure joy to look after.

Lindy gazed down into her son's big dark eyes. 'I screwed up,' she said again, thinking wretchedly about the wedding night which she had wrecked. 'But your father is very slow on the uptake,' she complained, thinking of all the loaded hints she had dropped since, not one of which had been taken up and acted on.

In an effort to redress the damage she had made

several first moves: reaching for his hand, dressing in her most inviting outfits, looking, smiling, striving to flirt...all to no avail. In despair she had even steeled herself to sunbathe topless on the yacht, only to be warned, as she lay there in self-conscious embarrassment, that she was asking to get burned. Either she no longer had what it took to attract Atreus, or only a grovelling apology was going to break the ice.

That evening, when Atreus had gone off to work in his office and Lindy had filled as much time as she could saying goodnight to Theo, who was usually asleep before she was even out of the nursery, she decided that it was time to be more aggressive in her tactics.

Atreus glanced up with level dark eyes full of enquiry when she appeared in the open doorway. 'Something up?'

Lindy could feel colour burrowing up below her skin in a sunburst of heat. She brushed her damp palms shakily down over the skirt of her elegant white sundress and breathed, 'I'm sorry about the way I behaved on our wedding night.'

Arrogant dark head lifting at an angle, Atreus lounged back in his chair and studied her with stunning golden eyes. 'Is that a fact? If that's true, why has it taken this long for you to do something about it?' he countered drily.

Having had to push herself to the brink to make her approach and apology, Lindy wanted to scream in frustration. Atreus was always so contrary. He never managed to do what she expected or wanted him to do. Here she was, trying to bridge the chasm between them, while he chose to take a more hostile stance at the most inopportune moment. 'You didn't say anything, either,' she pointed out helplessly.

'It wasn't my place or my problem. It was for you to speak to me. Something you seem to find very intimidating,' Atreus derided. 'Of course, you did do the exact same thing when you realised you were carrying my child.'

Dismay filled Lindy and she gave him a reproachful glance. 'Don't drag that in as well—that's over and done with!'

'No, it's not. Not when you're still hiding things from me. I find it hard to believe that I used to think you were so open and honest.'

'I was very stupid on our wedding night.' Lindy knotted her hands together as she fumbled for the right words. 'I don't know how to explain it you.'

'You're going to have to find a way, because until you have explained it to my satisfaction I'm not sharing a bed with you again.' Atreus spelt out that assurance without hesitation.

In receipt of that thrown gauntlet, Lindy gritted her teeth. 'You're being horribly unreasonable.'

Atreus sprang upright and strode forward. 'Not at all, I've been generous beyond all expectation,' he returned in hard contradiction. 'Some men might have walked out on you and the marriage on the same night. I stayed and gave you time to work it out. If this is the result after three weeks, I'm not impressed.'

Temper was jumping up and down inside Lindy like hot steam trying to escape. 'Obviously I shouldn't have bothered trying to apologise!'

'It was done with such little grace that it was a waste

of your breath,' Atreus conceded, in a far from conciliatory way.

Provoked even more by his cold-blooded calm and scrupulous civility, Lindy was so wound up she was trembling with temper. 'There are times when you can really make me hate you, Atreus, and this is one of them. I was jealous of Krista—there I've told you. Are you happy now?' she demanded fiercely, resenting him for dragging that demeaning truth out of her. 'When you admitted you'd been with her here in this house, and presumably in that same bed, I was scared you'd be comparing us, that you really wanted her and not me... I freaked out, all right?'

Atreus viewed her with steady narrowed eyes and a strong air of frowning disbelief. 'You pushed me away because you were jealous of Krista?' he pressed.

'Of course I was jealous of her!' Lindy slammed back, blue eyes very bright as she lifted and dropped her arms in speaking emphasis of the point. 'How could I not have been jealous? You took her straight to visit your family. I was with you eighteen months and you never took me anywhere near them. Your family love her. She's everything I'm not. You said you wanted a rich wife from the same background as you, and who fits that description more perfectly than Krista Perris?'

'Only on paper.' Atreus was still staring fixedly at her, and in a sudden movement he closed the space between them and pulled her to him, hugging her close to his lean, powerful body in an embrace that left her breathless. He pushed her hair back off her brow in an almost clumsy movement. 'You crazy, crazy woman,' he censured. 'You had no need to be jealous.'

'She's really beautiful,' Lindy reasoned, pain rather than resentment tugging at her uneven voice.

'But it's you I want, *agapi mou*,' he whispered raggedly, brilliant eyes of hot liquid gold scanning her upturned face. 'It's always been you.'

Lindy leant into his strong supportive frame, wanting to believe what he was telling her yet not daring to do so. 'That's so hard to believe.'

Atreus hauled her up against him and tasted her mouth with a burning, driving hunger that left her shivering in delicious quivering surprise. 'Day by day, hour by hour, you've been killing me with your happy smiles and cheerful conversation. I thought you didn't care if we were no longer lovers,' he ground out. 'How was I supposed to work out that you were jealous of Krista?'

'At the wedding Krista told me that I was the wrong bride and that you'd never stay with me,' Lindy shared in a shamed undertone, for even repeating that melodramatic warning mortified her.

Atreus frowned, and swore long and low in Greek. 'You never tell me anything,' he condemned afresh, throwing the ball back in her court.

'I didn't want to run to you and tell tales about Krista…that's so juvenile,' she groaned.

'But if you're juvenile enough to believe that kind of silly nonsense,' Atreus reasoned, with an incredulity he couldn't hide, 'telling me would have been more sensible.'

'For goodness' sake,' Lindy interrupted vehemently. 'I felt guilty about Krista so I didn't want to make a fuss. After all, if I hadn't fallen pregnant you'd still be with her!'

His lean, strong face clenched. 'No, I wouldn't be.'

Silencing her with that unexpected contradiction, Atreus lifted her up into his arms and carried her down to the master bedroom at the end of the corridor.

'Sometimes you drive me insane,' he admitted quietly. 'I didn't know why you behaved that way on our wedding night but I was reluctant to force the issue. I was aware that your main reason for marrying me was Theo. You made that very clear. And I understood. Our marriage was the best solution to his birth—but what about us?'

What about us? It was a question that neither one of them had tackled in advance of their marriage, although they had examined what it would mean for their unborn child from every possible angle. Somehow Lindy had been guilty of just blindly assuming that everything would come right without any specific input from her.

As Atreus settled her down on the wide divan bed, Lindy compressed lips still tingling pleasurably from the pressure of his. 'It's your fault I felt so insecure. You kept me at arm's length before the wedding.'

'You turned me down when I asked you to marry me. How was I supposed to behave?' Atreus framed grimly. 'I didn't know where I stood with you, and the bond we had left felt too fragile to risk for the sake of sex.'

Engaged in kicking off her shoes, Lindy gave him a troubled look at that explanation. 'I had no idea you felt like that. There's only one reason I turned you down— I thought you were only asking me to marry you because you felt it was your duty to do so because I was pregnant. And I didn't want any man on those terms.'

'That's not how I felt, *agapi mou.* But then I didn't really understand what I was feeling until after that point,' Atreus conceded heavily. 'So it's hardly surprising that you had no idea either.'

Lindy stood up and, emboldened by that kiss, slid her arms round his neck. 'I don't like sleeping alone…'

Atreus locked her to his big powerful frame. 'Do you honestly think I do?'

'That night after I had the scan, when you took me to bed with you in your apartment, you wanted me then—'

'And I knew you wanted me. But I wanted something more lasting for us than occasional sex when you were in the mood,' Atreus breathed, unzipping her dress and peeling it down her helpfully extended arms.

Lindy had turned hot pink. 'I'm not that shameless!'

'No?' Atreus nibbled her full lower lip while he dispensed with her bra and moulded her creamy curves.

'All right, I can be. You taught me bad habits,' she muttered, feverishly unbuttoning his shirt and yanking it off him with more haste than cool. 'But occasional wouldn't be enough for me.'

Atreus gazed down at her with sudden unholy amusement, and laughed out loud as he tugged her down on the bed with him. 'I didn't want to end up in some undefined messy relationship with you and my child.'

'So, it was marriage or nothing?' Lindy completed, spreading her fingers over his muscular hair-roughened torso in a wondering caress of reacquaintance. As she let her hands slide wantonly lower, she felt his shudder of response with deep loving satisfaction.

Stripping off the remainder of his clothing, Atreus caught her to him and kissed her with a force of hunger and urgency that told her how much he needed her.

'You made it clear that you were only marrying me for Theo's sake,' he reminded her.

'When did I do that?' she queried, her eyes pools of enquiry as she flopped back breathlessly against the pillows and gloried in the feel of his long, lean body settling over hers.

'After Theo's birth.'

Lindy blinked. 'I forgot about that. You asked me why I'd changed my mind... Theo wasn't the only reason. I was saving face.'

'I didn't know that. I was too much aware of how much I'd hurt you in letting you go in the first place,' Atreus admitted in a taut undertone.

'Probably only because I told you. You're not exactly on the ball when it comes to other people's emotions.'

The wry hint of a smile momentarily stole the gravity from his face. 'Or even my own.'

Something in the troubled expression of those black-lashed eyes yanked painfully at Lindy's heartstrings and she stretched up to kiss him. That kiss deepened and strengthened with a passion more powerful than any they had yet experienced together. Conversation was forgotten as more primitive needs drove them. At the instant he entered her wildly responsive body her excitement surged to a burning peak and the explosive heat inside her overflowed, sending ripples of quivering pleasure that left her sobbing his name with delight.

'Now you feel like you're mine again, *yineka mou*,' Atreus said huskily, bestowing a tender kiss on her lush mouth and holding her until the wild pounding of her heart and her thrumming pulses had subsided to a bearable level

Lindy lay in the blissful togetherness that followed feeling happier and more at peace than she had felt for many, many months. Luxuriating in his proximity, she knew that being close to Atreus again felt like coming home. *It's you I want...it's always been you.* That was all he had had to say to win her back, heart and soul, and of course she wanted to believe every word of that assurance—even though she felt that it would be the ultimate vanity not to accept that he had to be exaggerating.

Stunning golden eyes scanned her preoccupied face. 'What are you thinking about?'

Lindy smiled. She had the perfect answer to that unfamiliar question from his quarter. 'You. Happy now?'

'I'm amazingly in love with you,' Atreus confessed with a ragged edge to his delivery. 'It's the first time I've been in love. It hit me in the face, but I still didn't recognise what it was. I was miserable without you. Nothing felt right any more.'

'You love me?' Lindy repeated in astonishment. 'Since when?'

'Probably the first month we met,' Atreus admitted. 'I wasn't brought up to pay heed to emotions. I was raised to respect a code of head over heart, and it worked like a charm until I met you. I'd fallen in lust, but never in love. I never really cared about a woman until I met you.'

Lindy treated him to a blissful smile. *I was miserable without you.* It was all she needed to hear to forgive the memory of those wretched months without him. 'How miserable were you?' she prompted, wanting every gory detail.

'I didn't like Chantry House without you in it. The

place felt flat and empty. I couldn't concentrate at work, and I was so bad-tempered two of my PAs asked for transfers. I missed you so much, and I was totally unprepared for feeling like that. When I let you go, I decided that it was probably time for me to look for a wife rather than another lover.'

'Why?'

'I'd been so comfortable, so settled with you. Did it never occur to you that we lived together like a married couple on our shared weekends? It was the most stable relationship I'd ever had,' he volunteered. 'But, no matter how many women I met, I couldn't replace you.'

'You found Krista,' she reminded him a shade tartly.

'I didn't need to find Krista. I've known her all my life. I turned to her because she seemed to match that blueprint in my head of the woman I should marry to have the best hope of a successful relationship,' he admitted, tugging Lindy out of bed and into the *en suite* bathroom, where he switched on the shower in the wetroom.

Lindy looked up at him, noting the dark reflective look in his eyes, realising that it was a struggle for him to tell her so much. 'Why did you say she was only perfect on paper?'

His lean, strong face shadowed. 'It was the truth. From the start she courted publicity, which I hated. That's why we visited my family so quickly—because she had ensured they knew we were seeing each other from the first week.'

That information told Lindy that he had not been with Krista anything like as long as she had believed.

She stepped beneath the water with him. 'And of course your family was ecstatic.'

'If they'd known as much as I now know about her, they would have been considerably less keen. Krista and I have nothing in common but our backgrounds. She's never worked a day in her life, and doesn't even understand the need for it.'

'That must have been a crash course in compromise for a workaholic like you,' Lindy guessed, slippery with shower gel as he subjected her to a slow, thorough wash. 'But you still brought her here to the island.'

'That was light years back, when we were teenagers. She was only one in a whole crowd of friends who came out here for a party.'

'Oh...I assumed it was much more recent than that,' Lindy faltered as he spun her under the water to rinse her.

'You must be joking. Krista doesn't like a quiet life, or the outdoors. She can't live without shops and clubs, and she thinks sailing is very ageing for the skin,' he completed with suppressed scorn.

Lindy laughed at that news. 'No, I suppose you're right. She definitely wasn't the perfect woman for you.'

'*You* are the perfect woman for me, but I was so stupid I didn't recognise the fact until it was almost too late,' Atreus groaned, wrapping her with care in a big fleecy towel. 'I should have walked away from Krista sooner than I did, but I kept on thinking that eventually I would see something more in her. I didn't sleep with her.'

Anchoring her towel more securely, Lindy stared up at him in bewilderment. 'You...didn't?'

'No. I knew that once I did her expectations would

be roused, and I backed off because I wasn't sure about her. When I saw that newspaper and realised you were pregnant, it hit me very hard…'

'So hard that you flew in with a lawyer to help me make a statement denying that it was your child!' Lindy tossed back.

'I was angry, and jealous that you were carrying what I believed to be another man's baby. It never crossed my mind that the child might be mine. We had been apart almost five months at that point,' Atreus reminded her, linking a towel round his lean hips as he uncorked a bottle of wine from a cabinet in the bedroom and filled two glasses with pale liquid.

'I'm sorry I didn't come and tell you that you were going to be a father when I found out myself.' Lindy sighed guiltily. 'I can see how much it complicated everything. You had to tell Krista and break up with her—'

'That's not how it happened,' Atreus cut in, pressing a button that made the glass doors slide back, enabling them to walk out onto the sun-drenched patio beyond that overlooked the grounds.

Lindy sipped her wine. 'How did it happen?'

'I went to see Krista to end the relationship and tell her about you,' he admitted levelly. 'The maid assumed I was expected and let me into Krista's apartment, where I found her and a selection of her friends enjoying a cocaine party.'

Lindy froze, and stared at him in consternation.

'I'd often found her very moody, and I was blind not to suspect that drugs were involved. I'm fiercely anti them,' Atreus breathed grimly. 'That was the moment that it hit me in the face—I had let the love of my life walk away and had then wasted my time trying to idealise a woman who couldn't hold a candle to you. I was ashamed I could be so out of touch with my own feelings that I hadn't even appreciated that what I felt you was love and respect and friendship, and all the other things that a successful marriage needs to thrive. I had it all and threw it away!'

Shocked as much by what he had told her about Krista as by being told that he loved her, Lindy set her glass down and wrapped her arms round him. 'No, you didn't. I started asking questions and you just weren't ready for that. It all blew up in our faces.'

Atreus dealt her a rueful appraisal and gripped her hands hard in his. 'Don't be kind to make me feel better. I don't deserve to feel better on that score. You had to leave for me to appreciate you, and if I'd lost you for ever I would only have had myself to blame for it.'

'Do Krista's family know about the drugs?' Lindy asked awkwardly.

'When I saw her at the wedding she promised to tell them, because she needs to go into rehab.'

'Was that what you were talking about when you both looked so serious?'

'I know that once she tells her family she'll get the support she needs. If she doesn't, I'll do it for her. Now, can we talk about us instead of Krista?'

Her eyes softened. 'Of course.'

'Thankfully,' Atreus murmured, dark golden eyes clinging to her animated face with warm appreciation, 'I got a second chance with you through Theo being conceived. And second time around I'd learned what I needed to know. I knew exactly what I wanted and what I was fighting for—your love.'

A rueful laugh fell from Lindy's lips. 'You never lost my love. There were weeks when I thought a lot of bad, unforgiving thoughts about you, but I still loved you underneath.'

Atreus sank down on the sofa on the patio and scooped her onto his lap. 'And…now?' he queried tautly.

Lindy helped herself to his wine, because her own glass was out of reach, and kissed him with joyous abandon. 'Can't you tell how I feel? I'm crazy about you.'

'Crazy enough to apologise…'

'You wanted to make me grovel!' she condemned.

'It was the fate you deserved,' Atreus told her. 'I was devastated when you pushed me away on our wedding night, *agapi mou*.'

Her eyes stung with sudden ready tears of remorse, for she could tell by his voice that he had indeed been knocked back hard by her rejection. She kissed him again, more than willing to make up for that mistake. They became entangled on the sofa, and as things heated up they headed back indoors to the comfort of their bed, where they made love, exchanged lovers' promises and jokes, and lay together feeling very blessed to have found each other…

Almost three years later, Atreus and Lindy hosted a weekend party on Thrazos, to celebrate their third wedding anniversary.

Sergei and Alissa had sailed in on their latest yacht, *Platinum II*, and Atreus and Lindy, Jasim and Elinor had

been given the full tour of the fabulous brand-new craft.
The men had stayed onboard longer than the women and
children, while Atreus had manfully withstood Sergei's
teasing about his own small craft, saying that he had to be
the only Greek shipping tycoon alive without a huge yacht.

'I hope Atreus doesn't go off and buy a bigger yacht
now. You wouldn't believe how competitive men are
about them,' Alissa lamented. 'I bet you anything that
if Atreus does buy one it'll be larger than *Platinum II*.'

'I don't think so. Atreus likes to sail a yacht single-
handed. If he bought anything bigger than what he has
now, he would need to take a crew out with him. He also
likes speed, and sometimes races her.'

'I can see Sergei liking that,' Alissa quipped with a
grin. 'I might like it too—more exciting than football.'

Well aware that Alissa was not over-enamoured of
her husband's favourite sport, or his ownership of a
football club, Lindy laughed. 'But it's much more dangerous,' she warned.

Children were chasing round the villa, hotly pursued
by their nannies and Samson, Sausage and Alissa's dog,
scruffy little Mattie. Lindy bustled about, checking that
everyone had what they needed to be comfortable, but
she did not have much to do because their housekeeper
was so very efficient.

Soon they took the children outside, to let them burn
off their energy. Elinor's three kids, Sami, Mariyah and
little Tarif, were inseparable from Alissa's two, Evelina
and Alek, and Theo fitted right in. Tall for his age, like
Alek, and also a daredevil, he raced about on sturdy
legs. Prince Sami, the eldest and now the direct heir to

the throne of Quaram, was undeniably the leader of the group. Mature for his years, he was already demonstrating the social skills he had begun learning from the moment his father, Jasim, became King of Quaram, when his grandfather, Akil, had passed away.

'They're such great company for each other,' Elinor pronounced with satisfaction. 'If the children are fully occupied we get to spend more time together.'

'You're pale, Lindy,' Alissa remarked anxiously as their hostess supervised the arrival of a tray of cool drinks. 'Let me take care of that. You've been very busy today and you should sit down.'

'I'm fine…it's the heat.' Lindy settled heavily into an armchair, stretched out her legs and tried to relax. She was six months pregnant with twins, and as far as she knew both were girls. Theo couldn't wait for them to be born, and Lindy was already looking forward to the prospect of doing girlie things with her daughters and choosing pretty clothes.

They dined in state that evening on *Platinum II.* It was a wonderful meal, blessed by a lot of laughter and solid friendship, but by late evening Lindy was glad to walk back into the peace and comfort of their own bedroom.

Atreus eased her down on the bed and thoughtfully flipped off her high heels for her.

'Happy anniversary, *agapi mou*,' he murmured, sliding a jewellery box into her hand.

'It's not until tomorrow,' Lindy reminded him.

'But tomorrow we will have company, and tonight we're alone.' Atreus flicked open the box for her and removed a gold bracelet hung with charms.

Her interest quickened as she realised that the dainty charms had been selected to have relevance to her life. There was a little boy with a football, a big dog and a little dog, a racing yacht, a tiny island, and a cat—which revealed that Atreus had noticed the scrawny feral moggy she had smuggled into the house after all. But most precious of all was the diamond heart charm etched with her husband's name.

'My heart in your hands,' Atreus told her, his eyes brilliant with emotion as he framed her smiling face with caressing fingers. 'I want to thank you for the gift of three wonderful years and a child I adore…not to mention the two on the way…'

'Yes, we've done very well on the family front,' Lindy whispered, all her attention locked to his lean, dark, devastatingly handsome profile as he clasped the bracelet on her wrist. 'But the most important thing is that you make me feel incredibly happy and valued. That's why I love you so much.'

'The longer you're with me, the more I love you, *agapi mou*,' Atreus intoned, bending his dark head to steal a passionate kiss that shimmied through her nerve-endings like a delicious wake-up call. 'And I'm never going to stop loving you.'

Her trust complete, she locked her arms round him as best she could with her tummy in the way. With a sound of amusement low in his throat, he rearranged her on the bed for greater comfort, and smoothed a loving hand over the swell of her stomach. 'You're beautiful,' he told her softly.

And she knew that in his eyes she was. Her happiness knew no bounds. 'We're together for ever,' she told him lovingly.

With his next kiss he sealed the deal.

* * * * *

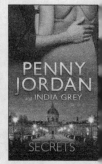
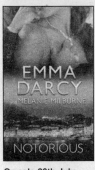
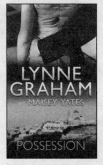